£3·00

Also by the same author:

THE RAGGED CLIFFS TRILOGY . . .

Ragged Cliffs

Inheritance Lost

An Equal Judge

The Bent Brief

The Silver Songsters

Julian Ruck

DINEFWR
PUBLISHERS

Published in 2014
in the United Kingdom by
Dinefwr Publishers
Rawlings Road, Llandybie
Carmarthenshire, SA18 3YD

The author would like to stress that
this is a work of fiction and no resemblance
to any actual individual or institution
is intended or implied.

A catalogue record for this book
is available from The British Library.

ISBN 978-1-904323-30-3

Printed in the UK

For my father-in-law, Illtyd John Loveluck,
'Britain's Greatest Boy Soprano' 1938,
without whom this novel could not
have been written.

AUTHOR'S NOTE

Arturo Steffani's famous 'Silver Songsters' choir topped many a theatre billboard during the years 1934-1948. The choir and soloists made 18 records for Decca, Panachord, Rex and Regal Zonophone labels.

They also sang live for BBC Radio.

The novel is based on true events but the main characters and storyline are entirely fictional.

INTRODUCTION

London

The old man sat down at the Steinway piano and allowed his hands to hover above the white ivory keys. His tired, water-filled eyes objected to the brightness that leapt up from the keys as stubbornness and determination gripped his fingers. He couldn't help it, but in spite of all he knew they still trembled with memory and a certain fear.

It had been such a long time.

Brittle blue veins on the backs of his hands throbbed and seemed to bully his mind into action. He held back, fought even. Would his fingers still be able to answer the call? Would they still bend, move and delight with a subtlety that could inspire complete silence and sometimes uncalled-for tears?

His mind travelled back to a song he had first heard as a fourteen-year-old boy coloratura soprano, one that even his eighty-five years of living had been unable to diminish or erase. At last, his own particular courage moved into the worn-out fingers and ordered them to play. The people around him stopped and listened. They felt his journey and knew that they must join him.

The old man went back in time.

He remembered.

The 21 Silver Songsters sang again through his fingertips.

PART 1

CHAPTER 1

Berlin. February 1936

Issy Kaddar stood before the *bima*, a tall desk in front of the Ark, a secret and hallowed depository for the sacred scrolls of his ancient religion. Some of these scrolls lay on top of the desk, intent it seemed on intimidating his ability to memorise and recite. The synagogue was quiet as faces watched and expected.

It was his *bar mitzvah*. He had become a man, an adult in the eyes of his Jewish faith. His father was no longer responsible. He stood proud and erect, all fourteen years of him, facing the audience beyond the *bima*. Issy was tall for his age but well proportioned. His muscles were developing in all the right places; he had been spared the misdirected, gangly limbs of pubescent revenge. His face, untried and untested, enjoyed a handsome bone structure as jet black hair curled and danced without restraint, like his father's in more youthful times.

Issy pulled his deep blue eyes away from the fearsome scrolls of antiquity and looked at his father standing at the front of the synagogue. He saw an expression of pride shine from the man's face, and yet his mother, standing alongside, seemed to shed a tear or two from her resigned eyes. This contradiction confused him for a few moments, but his uncomplicated youth prevailed as he took one last look at the extracts from the Book of David that lay in front of him. The Rabbi's words came back to him: 'Learn that you might see, boy. Learn!' And Issy had learnt. Becoming a man now depended on it.

He took a deep breath and began his recitation.

The beauty in his voice soothed the struggle and tragedy in his history and calmed the fear of slavery and rejection. In it, resonated the misery and victory of his past. All in the synagogue were forced to release their minds and bodies to a sound that seemed to sing and fly from every darkened corner of their Holy place. None could resist its comforting arms as it murmured gently and healed.

The silence and awe from those who listened and felt was complete.

CHAPTER 2

"Professor, I am sorry but this demand has come from a greater power than my humble self. There is nothing I can do."

Issy's father looked at his superior and heard the man's embarrassment. He didn't blame him, he understood. "First my office," he said quietly, "and now my telephone. Neither am I allowed to use the university library. How am I to work, Doctor? How am I to teach without books? How will my students learn?"

"I am sorry Ezra, I really am. Please believe me. Now . . . er . . . I have another appointment, so if you will excuse me . . ."

Ezra looked distracted for a moment, his life without a library uncertain, "Yes, yes of course, Doctor. I understand. I think I'll go home now, there doesn't seem much for me to do for the rest of the day. Perhaps I'll take a walk, the sun is shining and as you know we historians spend far too much time away from the sunlight." Ezra Kaddar made a brave effort to ease the Doctor's discomfort. He had heard the sincere words, the contrition and had believed none of it. The new charismatic Chancellor, Herr Hitler, was tightening his grip, and democracy was not about to be his only victim.

Later that afternoon Professor Ezra Kaddar sat alone in his study. His fingers played with an old fountain pen. It had been his father's, and as he kept pulling the top on and off fond memories clashed with fear and trepidation. He placed the pen back down on his desk and allowed his long, refined fingers to tinker with the grey, goatee beard that covered his chin. He stroked and twirled with concentration, the fingertips moving from moustache to beard. History books covered every wall of his study and tried to tempt him with knowledge from the past. His fine intellect recognised that there were infinite swathes of knowledge and wisdom that he knew nothing at all about, but even so over the years his eyes and his mind had absorbed some of the lessons contained in his books, and he despaired at the waste of such wisdom.

Although the Jewish population in Germany was less than 1 per cent, even so Ezra could not help but hear the seething whispers and toxic undertones of accusation. There were many of his countrymen who still felt the sting of humiliation resulting from the armistice of 1918. The lies continued to inflame and misinform: it was the Jews who were to blame for Germany's defeat in the First World War. They had sold out the country to a Jewish-led international conspiracy, they had poisoned and destroyed the blood of the German *Volk*, and they had become the focal point for extreme politics and a ruthless capitalism that sought to benefit only themselves.

It was all total nonsense of course, but Ezra knew that the German people were starting to believe it because they wanted to believe it. It was their only hope. Hitler was their saviour, a terrible Messiah, a man who could give them back their self-respect. Their wealth. A man whose strong hands would guide them out of social chaos and anarchy. A ruthless dictator was better than a weak and powerless democracy after all.

Already thousands were in 'protective custody' in an attempt to cleanse and sanitise. Ezra could feel the wanton persecution coming. Jew hating, the blight of his ancestors, his people, was in the air again despite the fact that most German Jews gave only lip service to their traditions and religion. Some of them were even more Gentile than the Gentiles! He knew that mass hatred lay not far from his own doorstep. A scholar of history, he knew too about empires. He knew their temperaments, their capricious natures. They rose and they fell. The Reich would be no different. He knew where his country was going and his hands shook.

Whilst his father feared for the family's future, Issy knew that he had to fight. He didn't have to win, he just had to put up a fight. If he could do this then he would be left alone. He knew it. The schoolyard had become an ancient arena as boys lusted after violence. They had become the bloodthirsty spectators of more primitive times as they waited and watched, their eyes raw with anticipation. The taunting insults excited as the spectators circled and waited.

"Filthy little Jew! Smelly little Jew boy! You're not allowed to play here! Go home, dirty Jew boy! Go home!" The bigger boy shouting the abuse despised, even though he didn't quite know why. He lunged at Issy. Fists swiped and tried to kill. Issy took the punch and fell to the ground. He had to put up a fight. He had to. He recovered quickly, leapt up and managed to throw a decent punch back; he was lucky, his fist connected and his assailant howled. Blood poured from the other boy's nose, but it didn't stop him as rage urged him on. Issy was knocked to the ground again. This time he was unable to get up. He curled up his body and waited for the kicks that he knew must surely come. Nothing happened. He looked up and saw his attacker hesitate; this was his chance, his only chance, to try again even though he was dazed and hurt. He managed to stand up, fists clenched and ready. The other boy looked at him, no one moved. The boy's hand wiped away the blood pouring from his nose. "Go home, Jew boy," he said quietly, "go back to where you belong." With that, the boy turned around and walked away.

Issy had put up a fight and been left alone.

CHAPTER 3

"There is no other way, Rachel." Ezra, a tall man, stood before his wife, who was not much shorter than himself.

"But our friends, our family, Ezra!" His wife was refusing to see again.

"If they have any sense at all, they too will get out. For God's sake, Rachel, can't you see how dangerous it is for us to remain in Germany?!"

"You are exaggerating, Ezra. What danger?!" Rachel persisted. "It's just the times. So what if a few of your precious privileges at the university have been taken away from you. So what?! Everyone is short of money, everyone is struggling, even the places of learning. You are fretting too much, Ezra."

Ezra knew that his reasoning would get him nowhere. His wife was a strong-willed woman and this had always been one of her main attractions, but every so often it infuriated. She would fight him at every turn, it was her way. Rachel pushed aside her long, brunette hair, a sure sign of frustration and annoyance. Her deep brown eyes flashed and challenged. She was the practical one, Ezra the romantic intellectual. Brilliant, yet sometimes fooled by his own learning. Ezra looked at his wife's magnificent anger and tried not to smile. God, the woman was still beautiful, even in middle age! Her dark olive skin and petulant passion still fired his imagination and ardour. His wife would have said that he still attracted her in the same way, but never to his face as that really would have been asking too much.

"I will not move Ezra," Rachel announced, "and that's final!" A sigh of resignation from Ezra declared a peace treaty. Anything for peace.

"Very well, my love," Ezra soothed. "Have it your way."

Ezra knew how to deal with his wilful wife and her rebellious nature. Out and out war rarely achieved anything. Her stubbornness was renowned.

Later that same night Issy felt his bedclothes being tugged. Sheyna. "Wake up will you, Issy? I want to talk." His sister was already sitting down on his bed and judging by the tone in her voice was not about to take 'No' for an answer.

Issy sat up. "What is it, Sheyna? Do you know what time it is?"

"It's late, does it matter? Stop being so nasty – I'm worried." Issy looked at his sister. She was thirteen years of age, her long black hair falling over a nightie that was being stretched and pulled in directions that were hitherto unheard of. She was turning into a real beauty, and even her own brother sometimes felt hopelessly disarmed when confronted by her determined demands. Like everyone else when impaled by her deep blue eyes, he felt obliged to give in. He couldn't see her eyes now as it was too dark, but he knew they were there, searching and pleading. Breaking him down. He sat up.

"So, what's the matter, Sheyna? Can't it wait?"

"No it can't. Now be quiet and listen. . . . I'm worried Issy. What's going on in our country? We're Jews, Issy. I don't like what I'm hearing at school. The other girls are being horrible, girls who I thought were my friends are no longer talking to me. They don't call at the house anymore either. What's happening Issy? I can't sleep I'm so frightened." Issy could hear the anxiety in his sister's voice, the fear. For once he listened. He loved his sister. They were always quarrelling, but the love was always there. He would protect her to the death. He knew what she was talking about as he was experiencing the same problems, but at least he could fight back. Sheyna could not fight back though, since girls didn't fight, did they? He leaned forward and put his arms around her. He always knew when his sister required his affection.

"Don't worry Sheyna. It's just the times. Things will pass. I'm here, mother and father are here. No one is going to let anything happen to you." He gave her a hug. "Now go back to bed. You have to be strong. We all have to be strong . . . "

Suddenly the noise of smashed glass disturbed the secure silence of the house. He heard his father shouting and leapt out of bed to see what was wrong. The family lived in a wealthy district of Berlin that was peaceful and law abiding. Whatever could have caused the noise?

Before he reached his bedroom door his mother rushed past him and went straight to her daughter. "Issy, go to your father, now!" she ordered. He did as he was told and ran down the stairs to see what was happening. Smoke was pouring into the hallway as he saw his father running towards the kitchen.

"Quick, boy!" his father shouted. "Help me to get some more water! Don't dawdle now!" Issy knew serious trouble when he saw it and dashed after his father. "They have smashed the front windows and poured petrol onto the drawing room floor! They're trying to burn us all to death, Issy! Now quick! As much water as you can carry! Use anything you can lay your hands on! Quick as you can! . . . Rachel! Come on, where are those buckets?! Hurry up, woman! Hurry!"

An hour or so later the family were sitting down in the kitchen. All the windows had been opened. The smell of fire trembled from wall to wall as cold air tried to dissipate the last remnants of stubborn smoke. No one spoke for a while. No one dared. Fear and shock kept tongues still and silent. Why? Who? For years they had always lived among friends, people who cared.

At last Ezra spoke, "We were lucky. Extremely lucky. Most of the petrol had fallen outside the window ledge. Where were the fire services? I rang them twice and still no one has come." He looked at his wife, his children, his precious daughter curled up in his wife's lap. The beauty, the innocence. "No more, Rachel. Start packing first thing in the morning. I will make all the other necessary arrangements."

There were some occasions in their marriage when even Rachel knew that her husband's word was final. This was one of them. There would be no reprieve, no negotiation, no compromise. Compliance was the only option. She leaned across the kitchen table and took her husband's hand, "Very well, Ezra. I will start first thing in the morning."

CHAPTER 4

South Wales

Two months after the Kaddars had decided to make their escape from Nazi Germany a young boy was being shouted at in Llantwit Major, South Wales.

"Up and down the scales, you no-good boyo, John Rees!" Pryce the Piano bellowed. "Up and down the scales! Practise! Practise! Practise!"

John Rees might have been the most annoying menace in the school, the music master thought, but by Christ the boy could sing! He sang better than the bloody angels on a good day and that's a fact. Even he was in heaven listening to the little sod – which was probably as close as he was ever likely to get to the damned place! The missus would make bloody certain of that, the nagging old trout. The boy was supposed to be having piano lessons; he was good, no question, but his voice was always too much, it always misled.

John tried harder as he looked at Pryce's hands running along the piano keys. Well, 'trying' was probably putting it a bit too strongly. He didn't have to try at all. His voice just came out with the notes of their own accord, he had never known how. He didn't sing to hurt himself after all – who did?

Illtyd John Rees – everyone called him John, it was easier to shout – had been named after St. Illtyd, a venerated papist from the 5th to 6th century AD whose claim to fame was that he had managed to miraculously attach Illtyd's home town of Llantwit Major (then an island apparently) to the mainland. The Saint had also managed to establish a church and monastery in Llandaff which was to become a centre of learning for the great and the good, not least amongst the devout acolytes who had flocked there were Saints Gildas, Samson and Maglorious.

Some in the town did indeed believe that John's voice had been bestowed by the good Saint himself, but other wiser souls knew better. John may have had a voice that could make even a Catholic after Confession weep (he apparently enjoyed a Catholic's conscience too – brittle and fragile, so the vicar maintained anyway) but the boy also had an irritating dose of Hell in his character. Not of the malevolent sort most would have agreed, but he was full of Hell nevertheless and drove his long- suffering parents to distraction. He was the local copper's worse dream come true and his music teacher's inspiration. This was Illtyd John Rees.

Impertinent good looks were already starting to shake themselves loose from the leftovers of puppy fat as a mop of floppy red hair tinged with gold bounced around his forehead, and the sparkling green eyes – although sometimes they could be brown, one could never actually tell – that were always trying to anticipate where the next thump was coming from. When John smiled, his white teeth could have undone even one of the Pope's storm troopers, not that there was a Jesuit within one hundred miles of Llantwit Major – at least none that the locals knew about.

At last the music teacher finished his bullying. "Right, John Rees, that's enough for now. Piano lessons have gone to Hell on a handcart again, never mind. Don't tell your mother. Make sure you attend choir practise tonight or God help you. I'll be round your house with all the Llantwit police force if you don't turn up. Got it? Seven sharp, right boyo?"

All of 'em? John thought. There was only one copper in Llantwit, but he kept quiet; it didn't do to rile Pryce the Piano, particularly if Mrs Pryce was playing up.

"Right, Sir."

"Good. Now bugger off home, your mam will be wondering where you are. She'll play hell with me if you're late again."

John couldn't get away fast enough, and there was still choir practise to go. As he slammed the door shut – he always did this just to annoy the music teacher – he wondered how his pet toads were doing. They should be nice and warm at the bottom of his bed; he just hoped his mam hadn't spotted them. If she had there would be another of many thick ears.

John made his way through the old area of Llantwit Major. There was a newer part now, since at least a few more houses were being built on the other side of town. He headed for the ancient church and a short cut that ran through the cemetery. Although it was getting dark, in spite of April trying to drag out the nights, he felt no fear. His twin brother and all the other relatives who were six foot under kept an eye out for him.

He stopped now and again to enjoy a good dawdle and to look at the mossed-up epitaphs of relatives he had never known. A sinking sun allowed him to stare at second cousins, aunties, uncles and even the occasional grandparent. He often wondered what they had been like: tall, short, dark or fair, kind or nasty? What had they died of? He knew something about death, but not as much as his mam and pa. They seemed to spend days talking and shouting about it. For John, death was all about hymns, angels, heaven and beautiful pictures. His twin had gone to the best playground in the world and that's all that mattered. Death didn't really mean anything to him, why should it? Sam's death was far too frightful for him to understand. He still looked at the photograph of his brother that stood on his bedroom windowsill from time to time. Sometimes he would turn Sam around to look at the sunlight and trees. Other times he would stare at his brother's eyes and wish. The small legs and hands would make him cry if he stared long enough, but he didn't know why.

He stopped at his brother's grave and allowed a memory or two to sharpen the dusk. Sam had died seven years ago. He had been the runt, the sick one. John had never quite understood why God had decided to make them twins, and yet at the same time make Sam so weak. So different. Neither of them even looked alike. Sam was small and black haired. John was the opposite. Weren't twins supposed to be copycats? He remembered the schoolyard fights, his bleeding knuckles. He had always protected Sam, fought his battles for him and had lost a few of them too. His brother had tried to fight back, but his lungs had always struggled and heaved, had always given in. John smiled for a moment, felt the loss that he could not comprehend and walked on. His young mind had yet to recognise the unforgiving permanence of death, his youth having made him peculiarly immune.

At fourteen John was an independent individual, in spite of his mother's constant fussing. His mam worried and tried to avoid her son's future. She knew he would leave many a broken heart in his wake. All women loved a scoundrel and loveable, handsome scoundrels more so – she knew, she was married to one even if he could quote the World War I poets until the birds stopped singing!

The Rees house stood at the end of a narrow lane. It had once been a vicarage, a dreary, grey-bricked place that on many occasions John and his brother had managed to brighten up with childish pranks and never-ending laughter. Their parents had laughed then too. Thick walls kept the cold out – or at least tried to. Draughty windows didn't help, but his mother always kept coal fires burning in all the downstairs rooms. Bedtime was still the highlight of the day, even if Sam was no longer there to tease and love; starched white sheets and huge brass bed warmers with long wooden handles coaxed sleep into eyes that really wanted to stay awake forever. Forbidding and stern the house may have been, but it was a comfortable home, one crammed with bent pine dressers, solid oak chairs that grumbled with age and thick kitchen tables. Sparkling brass horseshoes hung around fireplaces waiting to pounce and faded antimacassars were placed on huge armchairs that did their best to oblige any visitor seeking hospitality and warmth. There was no 'parlour' as such.

The Rees's were part of a new and growing 'middle class'. Owen Rees, John's father, was a teacher, a pillar, a veritable Welsh Parthenon like the local doctor, Dr Murphy. The wages were small but respectable, and certainly enough to keep his wife, Gwyneth, at home and food on the table. Gwyneth had inherited some money from her own parents which also helped the domestic finances. They owned their house too, courtesy of Owen's dead father, so there was no working-class rent to pay.

The now deceased Mr Rees senior had bought the house from a vicar who was too holy and too drunk to worry about whether or not he had the legal title to sell it. A legal debacle had ensued when the Church as usual conveniently forgot such things as love for one's fellow man and Christian charity. Eventually not only had the Church lost the legal war but also all the purchase monies from the 'sale' to Owen's father – the Holy vendor, i.e. the vicar, having pissed all the sale monies down his local pub's toilet. "Divine retribution," Owen Rees was often heard to comment.

One of the four bedrooms was always kept warm no matter what. It had been Sam's room. His red dressing gown still hung behind the door looking at a pair of battered red slippers neatly tucked under a chair waiting for something to happen. Gwyneth kept the eiderdown turned back, while a few precious toys sat on the pillow and waited along with the slippers. Now and again a scruffy brown teddy bear fell onto the clean sheets, but was always put back where he belonged. Like Gwyneth, the toys and the slippers, he remained patient and still, not wanting to disturb the peace. None of them knew exactly what they were waiting for, but they waited all the same.

The back garden sloped, meandered and ran amongst trees and shrubs that hid, revealed, complained and giggled, depending on the wind. John had his own private zoo in the garden. There was Wilf the hedgehog, Percy the rat, Cyril the dormouse and of course Othello the otter. Othello would only appear now and again if the river not far away started to play up, but he had always managed to avoid one of John's boxes. Not that John ever kept one of the creatures in a box for long, they had other things to do after all. Besides you didn't treat friends like that.

"And where have you been, John! You're late again as usual. What about your homework? And there's still choir practise."

"Not me, mam! Pryce again. Honest. He loves my voice."

John's eyes darted from one corner of the kitchen to the other seeking a way out while Gwyneth Rees stood before him, hands on slim hips and ready to do battle. She was a petite woman with a powerful right hand. Or so she liked to think. Her intelligent hazel brown eyes rarely missed anything apart from the overindulged misdemeanours of her mischievous son.

"Before you go skulking off John Rees, I want to know what two toads were doing at the bottom of your bed, you disgusting child!" Gwyneth Rees was in one of her scowling moods, a bad sign. It was such a pity too, his mam always looked so lovely. Checkered apron filled in all the right places, mounds of auburn hair flowing everywhere that never quite dismantled her spanking prettiness, and hands that at this very moment were twitching in readiness.

"Ah – well now, mam . . ." John replied, "it was like this you see—" He didn't get any further. *Whack*! "Ow! What you do that for, mam?! I was only keeping them warm! It's cold out there!" John's left hand went straight to the ear that had been the immediate victim of his mother's angst while his right hand shot up to protect the other one. He knew his mam, there was never any messing about and she rarely stopped at one swipe. Mind you she had to be fast to get the second blow in, not that any of them ever hurt anyway, his mam could never hurt anyone.

"John Rees! You'll be the death of me I swear! Too much like your father. Spitting image too. God help me!" Watch out, his mam was calling the name of the Lord in vain, she must have had 'Words' with his father again. Where was he anyway? He was normally at home by this time. Down the boozer trying to drown his sorrows again no doubt. All the men in the village went there to drown their sorrows. Must be a hell of a sad place, John thought.

When his mother had calmed down – she hadn't tried to give his other ear a bashing so she must be upset, pa again probably – he asked, "Mam, you haven't killed Tom and Harry have you? I mean they weren't doing any harm to anyone after all?"

Gwyneth Rees looked at her only son. She had lost one, and as always her heart reached out to this one, annoying little devil that he was. The hair that shone like a polished gold sovereign and penetrating green eyes always left her feeling utterly hopeless where her anger was concerned. The boy was impossible, irresistible. So much like her, so much like his father. Her voice softened.

"Of course not, John. I put them out in the garden. Somewhere damp. Toads don't like being at the bottom of warm beds you know, they wouldn't have lasted long, believe me. They are lucky I found them. Now go and get washed and ready for choir practise. I'll have some supper ready for you when you get back. Go on now or you'll be late again."

Gwyneth Rees watched her son leave the kitchen and as always her heart nearly broke. There should have been two boys, two suppers. Two maddening tormentors. Samuel had been so young, so perfect. She had never shortened his name, not that this inclination had anything to do with the Bible. What good had the Bible been anyway? It hadn't stopped the damp Welsh climate and tuberculosis killing her precious child, had it? There were times when she loathed and hated Wales, its murderous valleys and soaking wet air. The land had taken so many lives, its precious soil demanding body after body as its green beauty sang a bitter song of death and disease. Coal pits and industry never took prisoners, and never put women and children first either. Any slight cough or chesty murmur from John and he was straight up the doctor's, no argument.

Dr Murphy always sat in front of his rolltop desk and listened, his ashtray full of Capstan Full Strength dog-ends and his face exploding with livid, alcohol-inflamed thread veins. He didn't care much about his own liver and lungs, but other people's were another matter. After all he had taken the Hippocratic Oath, hadn't he? The doctor, a patient man, prodded and explored Gwyneth's surviving offspring with a caring eye and without complaint. He understood. His stethoscope would hover over pristine flesh, his fingers would tap a favourite tune and the diagnosis was always the same. "Go home Gwyneth, you will never get over your loss, but one day you will learn to live with it. Go home."

Gwyneth shook herself and turned back to the kitchen sink. Owen, her husband, had gone to the pub instead of coming straight home from the school. She knew why. Last night she had refused his advances again. Her dead son had returned. He always returned at night, the time when darkness resurrected tragedy and loss. She had tried, God she had tried. She remembered the early days of unconditional passion. The sunny fields, the yellow, comfortable hay. The kisses that never stopped while secret fingers tempted and excited. The love. Her husband had been a young, dedicated English teacher then. He would woo her with poetry and smile at the words that made her love so much. Her husband was a good man and deserved better. She picked up a plate as a tear fell down her pretty cheek. "Oh God, Dr Murphy!" she cried. "When will I ever learn to live with it? How can I live with it? When will I ever be normal again? When?! When?!"

27

CHAPTER 5

The church choir was composed of twenty-two boys and twelve men. Fourteen of these provided the canon fodder, most of them sounding like water gurgling down a drainpipe. The most prominent artistes were the first and second tenors and the sixteen boy sopranos.

Evan Evans, the choirmaster, stood in front of the assembled choir. He raised his hands and the choir stopped chattering; singing was a serious business, as was his sixteen-piece dance band with which he toured the country. All in the choir knew not to play up when Evan Evans was around; choirmaster he might be, but pious churchman he was certainly not – indeed his nickname around the public houses of South Wales was 'Evans the Blessed Fornicator'.

Evan Evans never joked about music. All the boys knew that when he thumped his hands on the piano and yelled, "*Duw* (God), you daft buggers! Can't you hear you're singing flat?!" They were singing flat. No one knew how he managed it. Some of the boys believed he had a magic wand instead of a baton stuffed into his arse pocket, but manage it he did. Evan Evans just had a wonderful ear for music, and magic didn't come into it.

Tonight the choirmaster was smiling. It might have had something to do with the new brown soft felt hat that sat on the chair behind him. A bowler hat had always been his calling card, but Evans was a man renowned for his sartorial attention to the latest fashionable detail, and bowler hats were rapidly being replaced by the more raffish and tilted felt hat. The film stars at the local picture house were in the vanguard of thirties fashion and Evans was never far behind them. The narrow pinstripe suit with its padded shoulders, long jacket and wide straight trousers could only mean one thing – a woman. Evans was always smartly dressed, but tonight he had obviously taken extra care with his appearance. The stench of French cologne fighting with the devoted mustiness of the church couldn't be missed either. Evans continued to beam, but the boys were never too sure what one of his smiles meant as he had a habit of smiling before clipping one of them around the ear hole.

"Gentlemen!" Evans enjoyed the choir's full attention. He always did. "I am pleased to announce that we have a new member joining our choir. He will replace young Dafydd ap Griffiths, who will shortly be going back to North Wales, so his mam tells me anyway."

Evans sneered at the skinny streak of vocal cords in the choir stalls. The boy was one of the better sopranos and the choirmaster didn't like having his choir disrupted. A new voice could bugger up all his work, not to mention the perfection he demanded. Not quite finished with the offence committed upon his precious choir he added, "No sense of humour, you North Walians. Mind you your mam had you, young Dafydd, so that's one redeeming quality I suppose! No decent voices up there either, boyo, your mam will be sorry. *Arglwydd mawr!* (Good Lord!)"

His demolition job on both Dafydd and North Wales completed, Evans turned towards the back of the church, a place darker than Hell itself, and waved his arm. "Come on, boyo. Don't be shy now, come and meet the choir." For the briefest of moments the boys thought they saw a genuine trace of kindness in Evans's smile. None of them could be too sure though, you could never tell with Evan Evans. There was a shuffling of young feet and a head of curly black hair appeared out of the darkness. "Now then, gentlemen, I want you to welcome Issy Kaddar, our new boy soprano. He's from Berlin – Germany, in case some of you unschooled spivs don't know where that is. I want you to show him some of our famous Welsh hospitality

29

. . . and that includes you young Dafydd, even if you are one of those humourless buggers from North Wales, God help us."

"Yes, sir," came the choir's response. Where Evan Evans was concerned no other response came to mind. The older members did seem a little reserved though, more restrained, as if they knew something the boys didn't.

"John Rees, *Duw mun*, I see you are lurking at the back again. Take Issy under your nefarious wing and look after him. He's the same age as you, a few months older anyway. You'll teach him how to misbehave if nothing else. Show him the ropes – and none of your wicked ways! Understood, Rees?" Evans didn't wait for a reply, he never did. He knew he was taking a chance with John, but he also knew that the boy was a kind soul and wouldn't be deterred by the creeping anti-Semitism that had already appeared on some of the faces of the older choir members. The new boy's name didn't need much imagination to work out that he was from Jewish stock.

John had no idea why he had been chosen for this honour, but it was fine by him; someone different to talk to and from another country too. That was even better. Evans pushed the newcomer in John's direction. Issy felt nervous and reserved since he was still getting used to the lilts, tilts and breakneck speed of the Welsh accent. As for the Welsh language itself, well that really was beyond him. He hadn't been able to make any sense of it at all. His English was fluent though, his mother had seen to that. She had been born and bred in London and had met his father while working as a secretary at the university there.

John came down from the back of the choir stalls to meet his new friend. "Come on, er . . . Issy, up the back with me," John whispered, "away from the eyes of Evan Evans. He's a mean bugger – most of the time anyway." He took Issy's arm and led him back to a place of safety.

Before any more words of welcome could be said Evan Evans howled and the choir burst forth with 'God Shall Wipe

Away All Tears'. Evans had chosen this hymn to warm up the choir. Personally he had no interest in God, who was worse than all the bloody priests, ministers and reverends put together, sanctimonious devils the lot of 'em! He loved His music though with a passion that would have made Him proud. He also loved the women He created, lovely creatures all of them. One such beauty would be waiting for him by the church gates after choir practise. Thighs like legs of succulent Welsh lamb and breasts like two glorious steaming suet puddings! Hallelujah!

When Evan Evans had finally finished tormenting his young charges they were allowed to go home. As John and Issy walked through the churchyard John grumbled about the paltry four pennies he had just been paid for his troubles.

"Fourpence, Issy! Fourpence! What a cheek! The top boys get sixpence and we're both better sopranos than they are." John looked at his new friend and smiled, "Well, you're nearly as good as me anyway. See what I mean! That Evan Evans is a mean bugger I'm telling you, gets his pound of flesh too."

"Never mind, John," Issy replied. "I've heard that most choirboys don't get paid anything. We should be grateful." John looked at Issy for a moment. The boy was definitely quieter than himself, less cheeky anyway. There was a calmness about Issy too that was unmistakeable.

"Ye-e-s . . . I suppose you're right," John had to agree grudgingly. "Do you have to go straight home, er . . . Issy? Funny name that. Where did you get it from?"

"It's from the Old Testament. Issy is short for Israel."

"Oh, there you are then. Look – Issy . . . it's Friday night, and 'Johnson's Fish and Chips' cart is just round the corner. Don't worry if you haven't got any money; I've got enough for the two of us." It was Issy's turn to look at this strange-talking boy who had taken him under his wing. It had been a long time since he had spoken with anyone his own age.

"Well, my mother is expecting me home," Issy replied as a smirk appeared on his face, "but – well, never mind that too."

So there was a mischievous streak in the boy after all. This Issy from Berlin was going to make a fine friend John decided.

"Grand! Come on then, my mam will play hell with me too so we can both end up in the *cachi* (shit). Best bit about Johnson's Fish and Chips is the side bit that he scrapes all the leftover batter bits into. Lovely a bag of that is, only costs a halfpenny too, as long as you don't mind the bits of burnt black fat. Mind you, you can have his fish and chips too Issy, I'm not mean, not like Evan Evans anyway. As long as I've got a half-penny left over for some aniseed balls I'm happy. Do you like aniseed balls?"

"I've never heard of them."

"They're sweets. I'll give you a few the next time I see you. Don't have them in Germany do you? Never mind. How did you manage to end up here anyway? Berlin is a long way away." The openness and directness of youth did not offend.

"I'm Jewish, John, and right now we Jews are not liked in Germany. My father has explained, but I don't really understand. Perhaps I will when I'm older. Now come on, let's try these fish and chips that you've told me about. I think I can already smell them!"

They walked around the corner of a side street and there was Johnson's horse and cart. The cart was more like one of those gypsy caravans that sometimes wandered into this part of Wales. Bright yellows and greens ran up the sides of the 'caravan' to compete with a rusty funnel that poured out smoke into a sky that was as black as Johnson's temper. The fish and chip man rarely smiled, but his fat gut and flowing jowls suggested that at least he never went hungry.

Johnson always scratched his greasy beard first and then his fat arse before dishing out fish and chips wrapped in news-paper. The portions were never as generous as his arse, but the grub tasted good all the same. The black print added to the taste too. As the two boys neared the cart their stomachs forgot all about parental ill humour. John ordered while Johnson peered, scratched and scowled. Eventually John passed one package to Issy and kept the other one for himself. Hunks of brilliant white cod, freshly caught from the Irish Sea, played with batter that had been made for the Gods. Chips the size of small potatoes crunched and steamed with dripping. The fat and soggy newspaper added the final touch to the best fish and chips in South Wales. The two boys licked and slurped on their fingers, unaware of the cold night air and the anger of their mothers who would surely find out when both boys were unable to eat the suppers that waited for them at home. When they had finished and belched with satisfaction John asked, "Where do you live anyway, Issy?"

"Not far. A house just up the road. On the corner."

"I know, is it the white one? Sits on its own. Big front garden. Oak tree in the middle of it."

"That's the one."

"Big place. Your pa must have plenty of money."

"No. Not at all. We lost a lot in Germany. We lived in a much bigger house there." There was no boasting in Issy's voice, no attempt to impress, he was just stating a fact.

"What's your pa do then?" John persisted with the usual Welsh curiosity. This was a new friendship after all and he liked this Jewish boy from Berlin. There had been an immediate warmth between them, an ease that promised more than a fleeting friendship.

"He used to teach at the university in Berlin," Issy replied. "He's a professor. History." Issy was not the least bit put out by John's questioning. He liked the boy's innocent frankness. His boldness. It made a change from the whispers of recent times.

"Teacher, eh? Like my pa. He teaches English though. Teaches me lots too, and it's not just English either! Come to think of it, maybe he could give you a lesson or two. You need it what with that funny accent of yours, but your English isn't that bad mind I have to say, considering you've lived in Germany all your life. Where did you learn to speak it so well?"

33

"*My* English?" Issy replied, slightly annoyed. "*Your* English isn't too wonderful, John, if you don't mind! Your accent is terrible to understand! Anyway, my mother is English. Born in London. At home my mother would speak only English to my sister and I. German was spoken when we were all together as a family."

John ignored the rebuke, and besides there was a smile on Issy's face. He had meant no offence and John enjoyed a bit of banter.

"Where does your pa teach then? Not at my school that's for certain. Does he wear one of those funny hats then, you know like Shylock in *The Merchant of Venice*?"

Issy laughed. "No, he doesn't. Oh, and before you ask, my father teaches at the university in Cardiff. He doesn't wear a yamulka on his head or have a long grey beard either!"

"Yamulka?"

"Kippa, then," Issy tried to explain.

"What? Kipper?! You Jews don't wear kippers on your heads, do you? Jesu, they must make your hair stink! No, you're having a joke. You must be." John was not so sure though. Issy was a foreigner after all, even if he could speak good English.

Issy laughed again. "Oh, skull cap then. Now do you know what I mean? You must do, you know all about Shylock."

"Oh right, I see." John still wasn't so sure though. Odd lot these Jews, wearing kippers on their heads.

"My family is not very orthodox, John," Issy explained. "We're not Hasidic or anything. My father doesn't wear a long black coat or tall black hat. He doesn't have dreadlocks either."

"Orthodox? Dreadlocks? Speak English will you, Issy? What are 'orthodox' and 'dreadlocks' when they're at home then?"

"Well, 'Orthodox' means . . . er . . . 'piety' . . . I think. Or 'Hasidut'. . . um . . . very obedient . . ." Issy looked at the perplexed look on his new friend's face. "As for dreadlocks . . . well . . . Oh never mind John, Judaism is a complicated religion, so let's leave it at that."

"I know what 'pious' means. My pa is always going on about the 'pious bastards' at church. Oh and 'hypocritical bible thumpers'. He goes on about the cat being a pious, murdering bugger too. He doesn't go to church himself, but my mam makes me go. Never understood why. Every time the vicar calls round my mam goes into a right fret, particularly if she's got a bottle of Guinness and a fag on the go! I don't mind the choir though. I love singing." This was a good chance for John to change the subject. Religion had not been a happy subject at home since the death of Sam.

"Me too," Issy replied, content to follow John's lead. After all, religion or at least its name, had brought only violence and upheaval into his young life.

"Praise be to that then!" John exclaimed. "At least we have something in common!" The two boys laughed. "Come to think of it Issy, what school do you go to? There's only one for our age in Llantwit and I haven't seen you." Issy couldn't help but smile again. This John Rees certainly didn't allow good manners to get in the way of curiosity.

"I start on Monday. We've only been in Llantwit a couple of weeks. There, now does that answer all your questions, John? You'll be asking me next when I go to the toilet!"

"Oh, I'm sorry. Being a bit nosey am I? Just tell me to shut up. I won't mind, honestly." John played with his hands for a few moments, this time obviously embarrassed by another supposed rebuke.

"Don't be silly, John. You're entitled to be nosey. You've just bought me fish and chips haven't you? Come on, here's my last penny toward the meal, and a fine meal it was too. My turn next Friday – but I will want my penny back. We Jews are a thrifty lot, you know." Issy laughed, and in that moment the two boys knew that they would be friends for life. No matter what. It wasn't something their young minds could touch or even explain.

They just knew.

CHAPTER 6

The following Monday morning John was ill with an alarming bout of schoolitis. He hadn't forgotten about Issy's first day at school, but a fourteen-year-old's consideration tended to be like the household cat – it came and went according to its mood and its belly. Issy would be fine with or without him. Besides, there was a particularly inconvenient arithmetic test to think about and John didn't like arithmetic; he recalled momentarily how Sam had loved it and was always happy to give him the answers. Geometry and algebra were fine but arithmetic . . . that was another matter. The only things he knew how to count were the coppers in his trouser pocket.

"I'm ill mam! I'm telling you. My stomach is hurting . . . oh . . . oh . . . I'm going to be sick!" John ran off to the toilet, retching as he did so. When he returned to the kitchen his mother seemed to have swallowed the bait.

"Right then, back to bed, John. I'll call Dr Murphy. He'll be round later on to see you I expect, so you'd better not be trying to pull the wool over my eyes. Now go on, up to bed." John did as he was told, relieved that the puking drama had worked. Dr Murphy wouldn't be a problem – he had fooled him before.

A couple of hours later Dr Murphy was sitting on John's bed. "Right then, boyo, what's the matter with you then?" he said, pulling back the sheets and prodding John's stomach. "Bad stomach, eh? Your mam tells me you've been sick, is that right?"

"Yes, Dr Murphy," John whimpered. The doctor's hands were like shovels and hellish cold. The man towered above him, big and bear-like. His Scottish tweeds stank of tobacco and old whisky. No one had yet managed to work out whether he was

Irish or Welsh. His name was Irish, but he spoke with a Welsh accent. Apparently he had been a major in the medical corps during the last war. His huge fingers were always twirling his handlebar moustache one minute, then digging around his waistcoat pockets the next. He never seemed to keep still. Some of his patients reckoned it had something to do with the constant dodging of Hun bullets out on a mud-soaked battlefield. No one was really sure though. His fidgeting, like his name, remained an enduring mystery. The doctor ran a hand through his thick wad of grey hair. He was only forty-five, but violent death and ravaged bodies had aged him prematurely.

"Mmmmmm." He pursed his lips. "Have you been out much lately, John?"

"Er – no more than usual, doctor," John replied cautiously. He was wondering where this was going. Dr Murphy was not as daft as his mam.

"Well, I think you need a good dose of fresh air, boyo. I have to go to Porthcawl to see a patient, so you can come with me. Some fresh air will be just the ticket. You do feel up to it now, John? We don't want to make your condition worse now do we?" Condition? What 'condition'? There was nothing wrong with him. John started to get worried. Was there really something wrong with him? Oh shit, his plan was backfiring and his stomach really was starting to play up now.

"Er . . . well, if you think it will do me good, Dr Murphy."

"I do. Now get dressed while I go and have a quiet word with your mam." A quiet word. What 'quiet word'? What the hell was wrong with him? When he eventually arrived downstairs, his mother was waiting for him with a scarf, an overcoat, a balaclava and woollen gloves. Spring had arrived, so it wasn't that cold. What was his mother fussing about? Still he had better go along with it, otherwise he would be rumbled – bad stomach or not.

"You must wrap up warm now, John. We don't want you catching another virus now, do we?" Virus? First 'condition',

37

now 'virus'. He was dying, that's why the doctor and his mother were being so nice to him. As his mother fussed and clecked Dr Murphy remarked, "Your boy has a voice like an angel I'm told, Gwyneth, is that right? The little shit – excuse my language, Gwyneth – should be singing with the angels, that's for certain. I should know, I delivered the rascal. His birth was a fluke, touch and go that one!" So much for the doctor being 'nice' to him! With that Dr Murphy walked out to the car and John obediently followed him.

The doctor's bright red Morris Cowley saloon sat in the road and tempted. There weren't many cars around Llantwit, and John had often dreamed about sitting in the luxurious leather passenger seat. The roof was down and images of Rudolph Valentino and Greta Garbo swayed around John's imagination as he followed the doctor out to the car. He couldn't believe his luck. One look at the car had cured his 'bad' stomach, but he made certain that his face remained pained and humble. John could shame both Valentino and Garbo put together when he put his mind to it. The doctor started up the car and off they went to Porthcawl.

After the doctor had seen his patient he drove to the sea front and parked the car. "Right, now John Rees, breathe in all that lovely sea air. You'll be feeling grand before you know it." After a few minutes of silence interrupted only by the occasional swoop and ugly scream of an unkempt seagull the doctor asked, "Fancy an ice cream, John?"

"Well, I don't know doctor. My stomach is still bad."

"All right then. I'll just buy one for myself then." Before opening the car door the doctor said again,"Sure now? Lovely ice cream down here. Will make you weep it will!"

"Well I . . . if it won't make me feel ill doctor. I mean I don't know . . ."

"Who is the doctor round here, John? Of course it won't make you ill. Wait here, I won't be long." When the doctor had gone John smiled to himself. Porthcawl, ice cream, a car fit for

Valentino, and all because he hadn't felt like going to school! Bugger, he should do this more often!

Doctor Murphy returned but instead of getting into the car he walked around to John's side. "Roll down the window boyo, will you?" he ordered. John couldn't wait. The doctor was carrying two huge cornets covered in nuts and chocolate. The colour quickly returned to John's sickly cheeks. He wound down the window and almost grabbed the ice cream from the doctor's hand. His face was partially stuck out of the car window frame in anticipation.

"Here we are then John," the doctor said, "here's that ice cream I promised you." With that the doctor shoved the ice cream right into John's face. Not content with the initial impact the doctor moved the cornet from ear to ear, chin to forehead and back again. "There now, John Rees. That's what happens to lying little sod's who try to mitch off school! Bad stomach, my arse! There's damn all wrong with you, boyo! Hadn't done your homework or something, no doubt. Worrying your mam like that! Don't you ever try this again. Do you hear me?!" John heard, but not before trying to retrieve some of the ice cream with his tongue. It was bloody lovely too. Next minute the doctor was back behind the steering well. "Here we are," he said, "here's a proper ice cream." As he handed John the other cornet he added, "Here's a handkerchief too, to wipe your chops." John did as he was told. He usually did, in the end.

As they drove back to Llantwit Dr Murphy suddenly asked, "Who is your father, John?"

"Why – Owen Rees of course, doctor."

"No, he isn't boyo. Where'd you get that from? Dr Ghosh is your father."

"Doctor Ghosh, doctor Murphy?"

"Yes, Dr Ghosh, you stupid boy."

"But Dr Ghosh is . . . is a tarbrush, Dr Murphy."

"That doesn't mean a thing, boyo. Trust me. Dr Ghosh is your father and don't you forget it. He's not black anyway, just a bit brown."

"If you say so, doctor," but John couldn't remove the puzzled look on his face. Still, if Dr Murphy said Dr Ghosh was his father then Dr Ghosh *was* his father, and who was he to argue?

John's mother was waiting for them in the kitchen as Dr Murphy and her son arrived home unannounced. The doctor, never one to wait for invitations, just barged his way around Llantwit trying to keep death at bay. No one challenged him; he gave life and sometimes took it away. His hands were more powerful than God's, and that's all there was to it. They also warmed the damp Welsh climate, which was a damn sight more than the good Lord had ever managed to do. The man was revered and respected, his hands miraculous, his word law.

"Here we are, Gwyneth, I've returned the Prodigal Son."

"Has he been behaving himself, doctor?"

"Oh yes, Gwyneth. He's had an ice cream too – in more ways than one. The bad stomach didn't seem to object, did it John?" John edged closer and closer toward the kitchen door. He didn't like where this was going. Was Dr Murphy up to one of his tricks again?

"No Dr Murphy, it's fine now, thank you."

"How gratifying, John. Now, before you try to escape to your bedroom tell your mother who your father is."

"Well, Dr Murphy" – John did not want to get on the wrong side of the doctor again, anything to please – "why, Dr Ghosh is of course."

Gwyneth Rees exploded. "Dr Ghosh? Dr Ghosh?! Heaven forbid! Dr Ghosh?! Where did you get that from? You wicked, wicked boy!" With that Gwyneth caught John by the ear and gave his other ear a right royal lamping. "So your father's a tarbrush is he? A sambo? How dare you! How dare you! Up to your room now and you stay there until I tell you to come down! There's no supper for you tonight either!" John managed to avoid the clout that was supposed to send him on his way, but not before hearing Dr Murphy say, "See what I mean, boyo, that's what happens to liars and boys who mitch off school."

That evening his supper was put outside his door. His mam couldn't starve him if she tried.

Later that night, while John enjoyed the deep sleep of mischievous innocence, his father Owen returned home. Gwyneth heard the usual fanfare of toppled milk bottles and obscene threats of retribution. She stayed in bed and waited. Would her husband be in a state of loving drunkenness or would his inebriation be one of tired belligerence and spite? She could never tell. As usual she just hoped that he would fall into bed and forget she was there.

She drew the bedclothes up to her chin – a protective reaction – although she wasn't quite sure why she always did it just before Owen came to bed. He had never been violent, physically anyway. The same couldn't be said however where his talent with the use of the English language was concerned. His tongue could rip and shred without conscience or mercy. It could also love so much.

For a moment Gwyneth remembered again the unspoilt days of bards and poets, her husband's gentle touch, the poetic smile that flew across his face and demanded kisses that she could never stop. What had happened? She knew the answer, but still tried to remember the country walks, the love. Sometimes it was all she had, the memory of how they had once loved. How they had once kissed.

Owen stumbled up the stairs and paused on the landing. He opened his son's door and peered through his beer-soaked eyes. The darkness confused him for a moment before he walked into the room and finally found his offspring. He looked down at his flesh and blood and touched John's cheek as if he wanted to make certain the boy was still his. He stayed where he was for a few minutes and somehow managed to wish. The drink never seemed to stop the impossible wishes no matter how hard he tried. Briefly he blamed his son. Felt anger toward him. Why had he been spared? Why? John had been the most difficult of his two boys, the most awkward. Sam? He had been so placid, so clever. Why? He touched John's cheek again. The love was still there, but sometimes it was tainted by a selfish grief, a grief that wanted to hurt and reject. Owen hated these feelings toward his only child, but drink fed and ignored, revisited and sometimes stayed. He turned away from his conscience and left the room. One day he would try and make it up to the boy. One day.

Owen felt the warmth of his wife's body as his hand gripped one of her buttocks. For years he had always gone to sleep gripping his wife's rump. She had a wonderful rump too, like two warm loaves of doughy bread just pulled out of the oven. Even Shakespeare would have wept trying to describe it. The delicate mounds of flesh were better than roast beef, Yorkshire pudding and ten pints of bitter any day. His fingers moved from cheek to cheek and then sank into the more intimate folds of flesh that hid between her legs. At one time Gwyneth would have moaned with acceptance and opened herself to him. Day or night. Kitchen sink or bed. Now, there was nothing. He didn't give up, but her dryness cooled his hopeful ardour.

"Go to sleep, Owen. Go to sleep," Gwyneth ordered with a hint of regret. She missed her husband's body, but was unable to do anything about it. Samuel again. A few moments of silence went by then the alcohol exploded.

"Christ, woman! A man has his rights you know!" Owen shouted. The beer and whisky hadn't finished their work yet. There was no loving emotion in her husband's voice, no words from the poets now. "Why are you doing this, Gwyneth?! Why?! Sam is never coming back! We have to carry on! We have to!" Owen moved on top of his wife and tried pushing himself into her. There was no romance, no secret touch, this had all gone the day Sam had died. Gwyneth resisted as she tried to gently push Owen away and ignore the threat.

"Leave me alone, Owen," Gwyneth said quietly. "Please leave me alone for God's sake. And stop shouting, John will hear you."

"Leave you alone, woman? Leave you alone? The hell I will! I'm a man for God's sake! A man! Although you seem to have forgotten the fact!" He pushed himself up and hit Gwyneth across the face. He had never touched her before in a violent way. For a moment there was total silence. Owen stared at his wife in the darkness, his knees resting either side of her. The beautiful face he adored looked back at him without anger. Without accusation. His heart wept with frustration and hurt as he mumbled, "I'm sorry," and left the bed.

Gwyneth allowed the tears to fall as her gentle fingers touched her cheek. Where had her love gone? Owen hadn't really hurt her, but she had felt his rage. She understood and shed more tears.

John had heard the shouting. There were some things that children were never able to sleep through, but all he had been able to do was beg God to make his parents love each other again.

CHAPTER 7

John and Issy stood in front of four other boys. They were all dressed in the same clothes. Grey knitted Fair Isle jumpers, grey short trousers and long grey woollen socks that had given up trying to reach scruffy knee caps a long time ago. Black leather shoes in varying states of ruthless wear and tear dug into the ground and kicked up clods of earth as eyes tried to avoid the inevitable scrap to come.

"You were offside, I'm telling you!" John shouted at one of the boys who had thrown the ball to the floor and was squaring up to him. John's red hair was about to ignite.

"No we bloody well weren't, Rees!" the boy shouted back. "So why don't you just bugger off! That was a goal fair and square!" John Rees was renowned for his temperamental antics on the football field. "That was a goal!" insisted the boy, who was much bigger than John. "So fuck off!"

John sized up his opponent, a bit taller and bigger across the shoulders, but so what? "Now look here, Squint, that was no bloody goal I'm telling you! You're cheating, and my friend here knows it too!" Issy moved closer to his new friend. Four to two, he had known worse. "That's the trouble with you, Squint, you four-eyed sod. You can't see bugger all with those saucers on your eyes, so why don't you just fuck off instead!" Before John could raise a fist there was another shout from behind a hedge adjoining the field.

"John! Get over here! Now!"

"Oh shit," John muttered as he looked at Issy and instinctively moved away from the boy he was about to punch. "That's my pa, Issy. Look out! Oh shit, shit, *SHIT*!!" He left the four boys snarling at Issy, who was starting to calm things down, and walked towards the spot from where his father's voice had come. Unable to see him, he tried to push his head through a small hole in the hedge. Before he was halfway in a huge hand grabbed him by the hair and hauled him through the hedge, arms, legs, torso the lot.

"Aaaaaagh!" John yelped, only to see his father's furious face staring at him. Owen was standing above him, there was no escape.

"I ever hear you use that four letter word again, John, God help you! Do you hear me?"

"Yes, pa!" With that his father walloped him across the ear. It hurt too, not like his mother at all. "Now, get back to the house and stay in your room until I say you can come out. Is that clear?!"

"Yes – yes, pa. I'm . . . er . . . sorry. Won't say that bad word again I promise."

"Good, then you won't mind the end of my boot to help you along the way will you?" With that John nearly took off with the impact. "Next time it will be my belt, John Rees! Now get home with you!"

John didn't wait around. He knew his pa. He rarely hit him, but when he did he meant business. John did as he was told and began the walk home. As his scuffed shoes struck the ground with a firm step – he didn't like being clobbered for all that – confused thoughts struck his mind too. These days there was a difference in his father's hands. John didn't know whether they were punishing his mischievous antics or punishing him for just being alive. He tried hard to ignore these fears and consoled himself with the fact that parents always loved their children; anything else would have been stupid. Mind you, Abraham had come close to killing his son, hadn't he? Maybe his father had remembered the last time John had helped him up to the front door of the house. He had been ordered by his mother to go and get his father from the pub, and what a job that had been! As he was supporting his father up the path the temptation had just been too much, John had used one hand to keep his father's body upright and the other to purloin as much short change out his father's pockets as he could. Owen Rees had never said anything – but who knows, he was a teacher after all and even blind drunk he had one hell of a memory! Mind you, his eyesight wasn't too good when the ale was in.

John remembered the time he had come home with quite a respectable school report for once. His father had just returned from the boozer and slumped down in his favourite armchair. As Owen read the report he slurred, "Very good, John, very good indeed. I'm very proud of you." John had looked on in despair and moaned, "Oh, pa! You're reading it upside down!'

It didn't take long for these thoughts to be quickly pushed from his mind. His father loved him he was sure, it was just that Sam sometimes got in the way. He often saw his brother's rattling chest in his father's eyes, so it wasn't hard to forgive his pa. What else could he do anyway? Pa's were pa's and that's all there was to it.

Owen watched John walking away. The boy had not lowered his head in shame or supplication; such pride was both disarming and troublesome. Owen knew that his son would feel no anger at his punishment and he wished he himself could be so brave. For a moment the memory of the night before seemed to strangle Owen's heart: for the first time in his life he had hit a woman – and his wife at that, a woman whom he loved beyond any pretty words of the poets. His cowardice both repelled and revolted him. How could he have done such a thing? The beer-drenched memory dug into him and destroyed as his mind attacked the questions he didn't want to answer. Had the violence perpetrated upon his son been an act of self-flagellation or even revenge instead of punishment for having a foul mouth? Had he made John a victim yet again of his own grief and rejection? There were times when doubt, resentment and anger over-whelmed him and times when he wanted to cast his son away for stealing all his wife's affection and love. If the boy sniffed,

Gwyneth would be beside herself; if Owen sniffed, he could just get on with it. John came first in all things, from the doctor to the food on the table. He remembered his drunken wishes and despaired at the conflict that would not go away. Love and hate continued to fight with his paternal instinct. As his son turned a corner and moved out of sight, Owen loathed the man he had become. He also loathed both the son he had and the son he had lost. But neither the other Owen nor Sassoon could relieve his own self-inflicted turmoil. Neither could they save him from the terrible love of a father and husband.

As Owen walked after his son he pleaded with himself that John had not noticed his grieving confusion. His viciousness. The fingers on both his hands reached up to his forehead and tried to sooth away the fearsome love that bombarded his anxious conflict.

It all had to stop. It had to.

Gwyneth was waiting for Owen in the kitchen when he returned home not long after his son. She saw the disturbed expression on her husband's face. He had been out walking again. Walking and thinking, she knew the signs. They hadn't spoken since the row last night, not that it needed a row to put communication on the back burner. Intimacy both in bed and speech had been neglected a long time ago.

Owen sat down at the kitchen table and looked at her. He was a handsome man, a man built for books. There was no silent crudity attached to his limbs, no awkwardness. His body was wiry and firm. Exact. The lines on his face were delicate and yet intense. Creases of learning and a passionate love of poetry had given him an elegant and refined demeanour. He was thirty-seven years of age – two years older than his wife – but grief and intellect were beginning to deepen the years that jumped out of his face. The grey wool suit, crisp white shirt with its severe detachable collar and dull brown necktie left few in doubt that he was a man of learning. The privilege of university was a gift granted to few, of whom Owen had been one. As he continued to look at his wife, his green eyes below his shining black hair challenged Gwyneth not to love him.

"You're being a bit quick with your hands these days, Owen," Gwyneth said, her voice devoid of anger or recrimination, "me last night, John this afternoon."

"I'm deeply sorry for hitting you, Gwyneth," Owen replied quietly. "Did I hurt you? God knows I didn't mean to." The contrition in his voice was sincere. Gwyneth could see that her husband was suffering. For a moment she wanted to go to him, to put her arms around him and love him in a way that only she knew. Something stopped her again, the 'something' that was tearing her family apart. She sat down on a chair opposite her husband. She had known for some time that they could not go on the way they were. Last night had been the last straw. Even so she was still unable to feel anger or disgust. How could she?

"I've been thinking Owen . . ."

"Yes?" Owen's eyes wanted and pleaded.

"Well . . . maybe – maybe another child . . . would – well . . ."

"Another child, Gwyneth?" replied Owen, utterly stupified. "How are we supposed to manage that then? You won't let me come near you."

"I know Owen and I'm sorry, I really am. I don't know what's happened to me, I really don't. Since Samuel's death I know things haven't been right. It's not good for John either. Sometimes I feel your resentment toward the boy too. It shouldn't be like that, it really shouldn't. Perhaps I do fuss over him too much, but I can't help it, Owen. John is so precious, you must understand. I also know that sometimes you resent me – like last night. But I don't blame you, Owen. Seeing you hurt doesn't give me any pleasure. I don't mean to do it."

Owen sighed. "Gwyneth, ever since Sam died – and it was nobody's fault for God's sake, in spite of you constantly blaming yourself – we have forgotten our marriage vows, it seems to me anyway. We should be sticking by each other not fighting.

Do you believe you are the only one who knows grief, pain, the death of our child? Do you think you are the only one who cries in the morning and again at night? Whose veins ache with every heartbeat? I may not shed tears Gwyneth, that's a man's way, but inside there isn't a day that goes by without my heart sobbing at the loss of Sam. I miss the boy too, just as much as you do, I just happen to show it in a different way, that's all. I have feelings, Gwyneth. Deep feelings. There are times when I despise myself for feeling the way I sometimes do toward John. Why was Sam taken and not John? Why do you exercise favouritism toward John instead of me? I know these thoughts are wrong, of course they are. I also know that I love John so very deeply, certainly as much as you do. Even so, I am your husband and should come first in all things. You are certainly first where I am concerned. Like you, sometimes I just can't help feeling angry, rejected – bitter even. You know how much I love you, Gwyneth. Don't push me away. It hurts too much. And I don't believe I deserve that." He paused, shook his head and then leant forwards. "Have you really stopped loving me, Gwyneth? Have you? I must know, because if you have how would another child make any difference?" Gwyneth looked at her husband, and for a brief moment the memory of their first kiss returned.

"No, Owen. No . . ." – she struggled to find the right words – "I haven't stopped loving you . . . I've just . . . I've just forgotten how to show it." She looked at the face she had cherished for so long and knew that she could never turn away as she felt her husband's anguish and struggled with his trial. "Oh, Owen, I still feel I could have done more, should have done more for Samuel. I just don't seem to be able to forgive myself . . .

"I do love you, Owen. I have never stopped loving you. I hate myself for the way I sometimes treat you; it's almost as if I am blaming you which I know is so very wrong. I can't help it. I don't seem to be able to do anything about it, no matter how hard I try. Doctor Murphy has told me that one day I will learn to live with it, but there are times when this seems to be so impossible. So difficult . . .

"Another child, Owen? I know another child can never replace Samuel, but it may help to bring some renewed love into our marriage – a new beginning perhaps. I don't want us to continue like this. We are destroying one another, and it can't go on." Tears started to fall down her cheeks as she reached across the table and took Owen's hand. "Forgive me, Owen. Please forgive me. I will try. I promise I will try." Owen looked at his wife, the sadness in her love. The tragedy. His heart cried out, his eyes struggled.

"Gwyneth, Sam is gone," he said gently as he put his other hand over hers, "there is nothing we can do about it. We are still here, still here to love one another and John. I have been wrong too. So very wrong. I should never have struck you. Never. Too much beer, too much me. Let's both try as hard as we can. It will take time I know, but there is plenty of love still between us. I know there is." He looked at his wife and stood up. He held out his arms. "Come here, my Gwyneth. Come and hold me. Please." Gwyneth stood up, unable to deny the depth of emotion in her husband's eyes. She went to him. Perhaps the particular love of earlier days could return.

It had to.

CHAPTER 8

"*Veni, vidi, vici*!!" the Latin and English master shouted. His terrifying black gown defied ignorance as it engulfed and intimidated the young boys who sat and looked on, their eyes not daring to look elsewhere. The master's waves of white hair flew into every corner of the classroom as his fingers pointed and accused, "I came, I saw, I conquered! The mighty Caesar would have had difficulty teaching you pathetic specimens, but I am more formidable and ferocious than even Caesar – and don't you forget it! I will conquer your reluctance to learn, by God, I *will* conquer . . .! Now, Jones! I hold you with my glittering eye and *you will* sit still! Do you hear me, boy? *Do you*?!

The boy Jones sat still and cowered.

"And which master of verse am I quoting Jones, you spineless specimen? What? What? Speak up boy!"

"Er – er, Wordsworth, sir," the boy Jones just about managed to whimper.

"Wordsworth? *Wordsworth*! Oh . . . oh . . . I am undone! God help me . . ." The Latin Master, Horace Horace (his actual name was Ianto Morgan but his propensity for always bellowing passages from the Roman lyric poet Horace, not to mention the English Romantics, had earned him the nickname 'Horace Horace') immediately gripped the side of his desk as his legs started to buckle. His hands went to his chest as he moaned in pain. "Oh! Oh! See what you are . . . are doing to me, boy! You are giving me heart failure! Heart failure God help me! Such ignorance! Such . . . such, nay *homo extra est corpus suum cum irascitur*.* Now then you useless spivs, you barbarian hoard, turn to page forty-nine of your Latin grammar books.

* An angry man is beside himself.

"Look lively now! And by the way Jones, you can write out the *Ancient Mariner* three times, on my desk first thing. Wordsworth . . . you spiv!" The 'heart failure' had vanished as quickly as it had arrived. Horace Horace was up to his usual antics, so nothing to worry about.

Compasses stopped mutilating ancient oak and disfigured desktop lids remained firmly closed, cutting off boredom's only means of escape. Now there was nowhere for it to hide. All eyes looked down as there was a rustle of deliberate page turning and a silence that would have made even Caesar pause for thought before his triumphant crossing of the Rubicon.

Horace Horace's face glared and spat at the intellectual chaos that abused every minute of his noble vocation, and yet every now and again the Gods on Mount Olympus would deliver a fanfare of youthful enthusiasm and raw intelligence. This new boy Issy Kaddar was a bright spark he was sure, someone who merited extra attention particularly where that loathsome, indolent urchin John Rees was concerned. Rees sat at the back of the class, as usual. Kaddar sat next to him. The two had obviously become companions which meant that Kaddar was on a road to certain and ignominious perfidy. The Latin master would be his salvation or so he hoped. Damn that John Illtyd Rees! Clever when he wanted to be and certainly conniving, but he was a nefarious insult to the Gods nevertheless!

"Now, pay attention you bunch of unholy buffoons! And you John Rees, down to the front of the class where I can see you, you evil, misbegotten ruffian you!" Horace Horace had not forgotten the drawing pins on his chair or the black ink. The rod that twitched next to his desk would cross a few backsides today, and John Rees would soon be sitting directly in its sights. Horace Horace forgot Ceasar for a moment as the swish and thwack of willow against podgy young buttocks tickled his sadistic fantasies.

John struggled to keep his eyes open as the Latin master's fingers drew chalky lines of unintelligible nonsense on the blackboard. Knowing that falling asleep would result in a sound thrashing, he tried to think of something to prevent this certainty taking place. He looked around the classroom at the other boys while his hand reached into his pocket. Pity, Dai Dubbler was too far away but . . . perhaps with the right angle it might be worth a try. Dai was a twin too, just as his name suggested (his father hadn't been having a joke apparently), but he was always sobbing and howling about something or other and you only had to look at him to set him off. Mummy's boys, he and his brother. Their shoes were always polished and their clothes clean, crisp and ironed with a firm hand. Not real boys at all.

John slowly withdrew a catapult from his pocket. His hand then dug around in the same pocket and found the ammunition. An aniseed ball. A big one. He managed to catch the eyes of two boys who were in his line of fire. They knew what to do. The weeping Dubblers were always fair game, so were their lugholes that stuck out like flags on St David's Day. Horace Horace carried on scribbling in his own world while John's two fellow assassins ducked behind their desk lids pretending to look for something. John took aim as he bent down to do up a shoelace that didn't need doing up at all. His aim came, he saw the target and then he conquered. It was a perfect shot, followed by a howl of pain, a deluge of tears and another sound thrashing. Only this time it was Dubbler's arse that got the rod for disturbing a tyrannical disciple of Socrates and his philosophical musings.

When the bell called the end of learning for that day John and Issy began the walk home. They were still laughing about Dubbler's misfortune and the size of his ear. Let his mam sort that one out with her iron! As they were walking out of the school gates four of the senior boys stood in their way. John knew two of them, in fact he had gone fishing with them a few times. They had always been friendly enough, but now there was something threatening in their manner. He couldn't understand it. There were no smiles or harmless banter.

"What are you doing with the Jewboy, John?" one of the boys asked, a boy whom he had thought was a friend. "He's not one of us."

"He's my friend. What's it got to do with you?" John replied with a note of defiance.

"Watch it, Rees," one of the other boys warned.

"Get out of our way, will you?" John ordered as he barged past one of the boys, a tall skinny specimen. Before he managed to go any further he was grabbed either side by two of the boys while the other two attacked Issy.

"We don't like Jews around here!" one of the boys shouted. "My dad has told me all about you lot! Money grabbing bastards the lot of you. Killed Jesus too!" The boy's fist landed firmly on Issy's chin sending him straight to the ground. The two boys then started kicking Issy who was still senseless from the punch and unable to defend himself. John could not look on and watch his friend being beaten. In a split second his cheeks started to glow with temper and blend with his red hair. A few seconds later and they were redder than his hair. Size and numbers had never bothered John before and they were not about to bother him now.

With a loud shout he yelled, "You buggers! Leave my friend alone! He's done nothing to you!" He managed to twist away from one of the boys holding him while at the same time punching him right between the legs. There was a shriek of agony as John did the same thing to the other boy who was holding him. John knew that he and Issy would be beaten to a pulp if brute force were allowed to prevail. Their assailants were older and stronger. John's performance had managed to distract the other two boys trying to kick Issy back to Germany. In those few moments Issy managed to come to his senses and fight back. He jumped on the back of one the boys who had been attacking him and sent him flying to the floor at the same time lashing out with his foot at the other boy. Like John, instinct had told him to kick where it hurt most and to do it as fast as possible. Surprise and shock were the only two weapons he and John had. Two of their attackers were now writhing around on the ground grappling with their pristine manhood while a third vomited his guts into the gutter. The boy who had been thrown to the floor took in the scene and quickly decided that his testicles were far too precious to be mauled by two little shits who still believed that their cocks were meant for stirring tea. He jumped up and ran off, shouting "We'll get you John Rees, you and your little Jewboy friend. Don't you worry, we'll get you!"

"Aahh, bugger off Jenkins!" John shouted back. "Mind I don't catch you first!" He turned around to face Issy and couldn't help smiling. "Come on, Issy," he said through labouring breath, "let's get out of here before those daft sods come to their senses. There won't be a second chance."

"Good idea, John," Issy smiled back, even though his jaw still ached. "And thank you for helping me. I won't forget it."

"That's all right, I know you'd do the same for me. Now come on before those buggers get a whole bloody army after us!"

As they walked away memories of other fights and battles made Issy clench his fists at no-one in particular. Will it never end, he thought sadly? Will his father's 'diaspora' never find a place to live?

Later that afternoon the two boys were standing in front of a sturdy Victorian villa. A massive oak tree stood in the front garden, its huge branches stretching upwards in an attempt to grasp heaven by the neck and make it its own.

"You haven't met my family yet, John. Come on in, my mother's lemonade was famous in Berlin."

"You haven't met mine either come to think of it," John replied. "You can come round for supper one evening – I know my mam won't mind."

"I'll look forward to that. Now come on in and stop talking. You Welsh are always yapping. You're worse than my sister!"

A sister? Issy hadn't mentioned any sister before. "I am a bit thirsty, now you come to mention it," John replied. "Scrapping is hard work. All right, but I can't stay too long though as my mam will have supper ready and she's already cross enough with me at the moment, what with trying to mitch off school, making out my pa was a tarbrush and using foul language on the football pitch. Oh, and not to mention toads in the bed!"

"All the usual things then, John," Issy commented with a smile. His own mother never stopped nagging him about something or other. The mess in his bedroom, teasing his sister, there was always something.

They walked into a kitchen that was tough, efficient, business-like and German. Formidable thick slabs of pine insulted flat pieces of delicate marble. Knives of all shapes and sizes stuck out of wooden blocks and stabbed the air while polished copper pans hung from the ceiling reflecting every movement that went on below. A row of brass bells trailing across one of the walls whispered among themselves while they waited for something to happen.

"What are those bells for, Issy?" John asked, "I've never seen bells in a kitchen before."

"Well, if you are in one of the other rooms and you want the butler, you press a button in the wall, a bell rings in here and along he comes."

"Butler! You have a butler? Like 'Jeeves'? I've read all about him. Great fun. Servants? Your pa must be rich despite what you say."

Issy laughed at his friend's enthusiasm.

"No, John. I'm only teasing you. We don't have a butler. We don't have servants either. Unless you call the lady that comes in to help my mother out a few times a week a 'servant'. As I told you John, my father lost a lot of money in Germany. We can't afford servants and butlers. We didn't have them in Germany either – well, the butler anyway. Now then, let me find some of that lemonade I promised you."

As Issy hunted around the kitchen a young girl walked in.

"Issy, where have you been?" Sheyna Kaddar demanded. "And who are you?" she said as she turned towards the strange boy with golden, red hair. Her white teeth seemed to smile with her lips, although John couldn't be too sure. Taken slightly aback by such girlish boldness John answered, "Er . . . I'm, er . . . John, a friend of your brother's."

"Oh, are you? Well, where has he been then? He never answers me. He hasn't answered me now, see what I mean?"

"Oh Sheyna, what do you want? Where's mother?" Issy finally replied after emerging from behind a cupboard door.

"Out in the garden, Issy. Is that lemonade?"

"Yes it is. You can have some if you promise to go away somewhere. Go and play with your toys or something."

"Toys! Toys! You're just showing off now Issy, so stop being so stupid. And who are you to decide who has lemonade or not! Idiot! At least your friend isn't so rude!"

John had never had a sister. The closest he had come to girls was the Sunday School outing to Barry Island and that had been enough. Soppy things, girls – and bossy too. This one seemed just like all the others, although he had to admit she was extremely pretty, for a girl anyway. And cheeky as well, even if she had paid him a compliment.

"John and I have things to talk about," Issy said with growing impatience. "Boys' things. You're too young, so go away."

"I'm not too young! You're only a year older than me, although you act like a five-year-old. Now hand over some of that lemonade – please?" For a moment Issy nearly weakened, his sister's big blue eyes were almost too much. He understood why his father could never say 'No'.

"Well, being as you are so grown up Sheyna, the next time the ghosties come to get you, you can stay in your own bedroom. Now for the last time, go away!"

"Oh, like that is it? Right, well, I'm sure mother will be most interested in your smoking habits. Now, hand over the lemonade or else!" There was stalemate for a few seconds, but Issy knew when he was beaten. Besides, he never quite knew what his little sister was capable of when she put her mind to it. He handed over the jug of lemonade.

"Now, will you go away?"

"Certainly . . ." Sheyna mocked as she poured herself a glass of lemonade. "You boys talk such rubbish anyway." With that she turned around and walked out of the kitchen, but not before giving John a smile that was pure destruction, thirteen or not.

"She's a real nuisance that sister of mine!" Issy groaned. "Come on John, I'll show you the summerhouse. No one ever uses it apart from me. It's my own private place. Even Sheyna doesn't bother to go there. Too dirty for her delicate little skin. Girls eh, who needs them?"

"You can say that again, Issy," John confirmed as he followed his friend through the kitchen door.

When Sheyna was on her own she thought about her brother's friend. She had heard Issy talking about him, but that was all. Issy could be so spiteful sometimes, and secretive. His friend hadn't said a word during their argument, yet she could tell that he was on her side. There had been something in his eyes when he had looked at her.

The summerhouse sat in a secluded spot at the bottom of the garden. It was an ideal place for furtive mischief and juvenile plotting. Overgrown tress and clumps of untendered bushes hid it from adult gaze and sibling treason. Issy pushed open a door that creaked and moaned at the sudden intrusion. The summerhouse didn't like having its peace and quiet disturbed.

"Do you smoke, John?" Issy asked.

"Now and again, when my parents aren't around," John answered, straightening his back as he did so. Did he smoke? Of course he did. He was a teenager now, a grown up!

"Same for me. It's all right for them to smoke – but not us, eh? Sit down for a minute while I get my hidden supply." Issy walked over to an old cupboard that sat behind a wilted cane chair. The summerhouse was an ideal place for a quiet, grown-up smoke. He opened a drawer and pulled out a mangy packet of tobacco, cigarette papers and a box of matches. "Sorry, they're not Sobranies; my father smokes them sometimes, but he keeps them hidden away. Pipe tobacco is all I'm able to pinch without him noticing. Bit strong, but never mind. Can you roll?"

"Of course Issy, I've been smoking for years!" John didn't want to feel a novice when it came to blowing his lungs apart. Issy handed him some dry tobacco and a cigarette paper. He watched John as he tried to make a respectable cigarette. His efforts were a disaster. He couldn't roll the paper properly, let alone make it stick, so the tobacco fell all over the floor.

"Oh, give it to me John. You're hopeless!"

"Sorry. You see I'm only used to Player's Navy Cut. My pa is usually too aled up to notice when I swipe a few."

Issy saved the day by expertly rolling two perfect cigarettes, despite the tobacco being as dry as one of John's toads. He handed one to John and struck a match. When both cigarettes were lit they sat down on some wicker chairs and started to draw on them like two old soldiers waiting for the next call-up. After a couple of puffs John started to choke, cough, splutter and go green. "Oh Jesu! . . . Issy, what is this stuff? Oh shit, it's strong!"

Issy started to laugh. "Thought you smoked, John. Strong, isn't it? Germany's best." Before the two boys could puff any further there was a shout of "Issy!" from the garden. "Oh no! It's my mother!" Issy exclaimed as he leapt up.

"Quick, put the fags out!" He ran to the door and nearly bumped into her as she was just about to enter the summer-house.

"What's going on, Issy?" Rachel Kaddar asked with a wary look in her eyes. "I've been looking all over for you. Your sister said you came down here with a friend. Up to no good I expect. Your supper is ready, and where's this friend of yours? Maybe he would like to join us." Issy was trying to block his mother from entering the summerhouse, facing her as he pulled the door closed behind him.

"Er – no, mother. John is just off home," he said, then turned back towards the door. "John!" he shouted as he pushed it open, "come and meet my mother." John stumbled up to the door and stood behind Issy. Dizzy and drunk from the smoke he managed to mumble.

"Um . . . er, um . . . yes, hello Mrs Kaddar."

"And whom might you be, young man?"

"Er . . . John – John Rees."

Rachel Kaddar eyed the two boys up and down. Her intense brown eyes missed nothing.

"Do you know any other words apart from 'Um' young man, or do you just have a speech impediment?" Rachel demanded as she sniffed the air. "Aahh . . . can I smell tobacco smoke, Issy? Your father's tobacco smoke if I'm not mistaken."

"What? No, mother. It must be the smoke from the fire we've been trying to make. Thought we'd burn some of the dead leaves. You know how father is always moaning about having to clear them all up."

"Oh, really. I can't see any fire." Mrs Kaddar cast her evil eye upon the miscreant John Rees. "Is this true young man?" This woman was a frightening spectacle. Tall, stern and with that look of 'Don't damn well argue with me' in her eyes. Not like his mam at all. There would be no fooling around with this one.

"Oh yes, Mrs Kaddar. Couldn't really get it going on account of the damp weather we've been having lately."

"Really? . . . The dampness doesn't seem to have affected the combustibility of your trousers."

"The what –? Comb – er– what?" The next thing John saw was smoke coming up from his trouser pocket. It wasn't long before he felt the heat.

"Ahhhhh – I'm on fire!" Before he could say another word, Mrs Kaddar had picked up a bucket of rainwater and thrown it over him.

60

"There now, John. That should cool down your ardour for tobacco. Next time you want to put a cigarette out use an ashtray instead of your pocket. Now, in the house the pair of you! We need to dry you out, young man. What will your mother think if she sees you in that mess?"

The two boys did as they were told and started to walk up to the house. John seemed none the worse for wear, although the top of his leg was a bit hot. No actual burning though, that brute Mrs Kaddar had seen to that. Ice cream missiles, being dragged through hedges, buckets of water, what next?

As Rachel watched the two boys walking towards the house her indulgent smile was replaced by a sadness that seemed to overwhelm her. Her son was growing up so quickly and there was nothing she could do about it. A sudden chill ran through her as her husband's words of imminent war rang in her ears.

CHAPTER 9

"I've never seen anything like it, John," Issy enthused as he and John trod on a pathway made of smashed wine bottles. "That Earl or whoever he was must have done a lot of drinking – champagne too by the look of it."

"Evan Evans is probably hoping we will fall down on our arses and cut ourselves to shreds if I know him. Where's the rest of the choir anyway? We're each doing a solo so Evans tells us. Mind you, you never know with him."

It was early July and summer was starting to seriously announce itself. The two boys had settled into an easy friendship and neither really bothered with anyone else. A unique trust had grown between them, together with a loyalty that never needed to be spoken about. And although too young to understand the depth of their friendship both knew it was there, even if they couldn't exactly explain it.

"It's a huge house, John," Issy remarked, almost overwhelmed by the grandness of what faced them. It reminded Issy of fairy-tale castles with turrets that imprisoned dreams and drawbridges that kept a cruel world out. There were no drawbridges in front of them of course, but for Issy they were there in his mind, protecting those inside and allowing them to be what they were without fear of violence and persecution.

"Mansion more like, Issy. Given to the miners, so my ma tells me. A place for them to convalesce. You know, dusted-out lungs. Not many of them ever come out. You won't get me down the mines, that's for certain. That's why we're here. Singing for them. Don't know whether a few songs will make much difference though."

"No, it must be a terrible job. We're lucky our parents are well off enough to give us an education . . . By the way, John, do you know where you're going?"

"Of course I do. There's the main entrance . . . I think. Come on. Yes, it must be, there's Evans ordering everybody about. I'm still trying to work out how he got us here. We're not singing in the Penyfai Male Voice Choir after all. I tell you what: my mam will agree to anything as long as it's singing. Never seems too bothered about the piano. Strange woman, my mam."

They were met by Evan Evans, all wide-brimmed Panama hat, Irish linen and polka-dot silk scarf. As usual he stank like a pox doctor's clerk. His two-tone brown and cream brogues completed his usual attention to sartorial perfection. At first he didn't notice the two approaching boys as he was too busy peering at all the pretty nurses that seemed to flurry around everywhere.

"Ah, there you are. 'Bout time too, boyos. Where the hell have you been? We're about to start. Inside. Quick! You know what you have to sing?"

"We do," the boys answered together.

"Right, well you can sit quietly until it's your turn. You won't be singing until the very end so in the meantime behave yourselves. Oh and John, let's have that peashooter of yours – and the peas please! You think I don't know it's you causing all the annoyance with the older members of the choir. Not a bad shot though I have to admit. Don't think the vicar is too pleased with your antics though, you caught his ear good and proper last Sunday. Mind you, that will teach the old sod to rant and rave against the evils of the flesh. Sanctimonious old sod! Anyway, with a wife like that it's no wonder he's a woman hater!" Evans laughed at his own joke while the two boys sniggered. The vicar was a sour old devil they had to agree. His wife was even worse; she was from North Wales too to add insult to injury, according to Evans anyway, but then in his book anyone from North Wales needed a barrel of ale just to make them smile, let alone laugh. His dislike of those up North was a bit of a mystery; something to do with a broken heart so the gossip went, but no one knew for certain.

The two boys followed Evans into what had once been a grand ballroom. The room was quiet apart from the occasional phlegm-choked cough, heave of worked-out lung and squelch of an imprisoned fart struggling for blessed release. Sticks and wheelchairs occasionally tapped and squeaked along with the clattering of false teeth, while demolished eyes, and forgotten hopes of easy breathing sank into hearts that had given up long ago. Wrecked coalfaced bodies sat waiting patiently for the calloused and last deathly grip of the shovel – only this time it would carry earth instead of coal.

The Penyfai Male Voice Choir sang a medley of songs that brought a sparkle or two, if not the odd tear, to some of the grey and barren eyes that had lost even a hint of life. The rows of sympathetic male voices concluded with 'Men of Harlech' and best of all Verdi's 'Let us drink'. The last song brought back memories of fifteen-pint Saturday nights and crude fumblings with starched white nightgowns. The blue coaldust scars on some of the ancient faces stretched and jumped with a misty past, but only for a few moments. Coal, the assassin of Hope, had done its work, but still lurked in every corner and in every mind that tried to enjoy the singing.

It was Issy's turn to sing. He stood up and faced the audience. Gounod's 'Ave Maria' challenged the Grim Reaper as Issy's voice defied his harvest and his intent. Where the choir had been noble and manly, Issy soothed and touched. His words reached into the souls waiting to take flight and urged them to postpone their journey at least for a moment. When he had finished, demolished hearts started to revive and eyes truly opened for the first time in months.

It was John's turn next. He sang Rudolf Friml's 'Smilin' Through', a livelier and more distracting song. As his voice sang and moved around the ballroom, eyes no longer saw only useless epitaphs and faded marble and ears no longer heard funeral marches and those embarrassed specks of conversation that whirled around the nonsense of a jam sandwich and bottle of stout wake. The two boy sopranos gave life and a moment of joy to those who had simply forgotten both. Their singing held and lifted, gripped and never let go. For the first time that day decaying hands managed to lift up and clap; there was life after the mines after all. One young man standing at the side of the proceedings had heard it all, but for some unknown reason his hands refused to join in. There was nothing sinister about his lack of enthusiasm; he had other things on his mind. Important things.

When it was all over Issy and John followed the choir to a room where tea had been set out. Tea weaker than knat's piss, a few stale rock cakes and some curled-up ham sandwiches about to give up the ghost like everyone else in the place, was all that was on offer. The Home relied largely on charity, so fancy food was a limited luxury. As they were making the most of the cake and sandwiches, stale or not – they had to be quick, the older singers didn't give a shit for the young stars or their sissy voices – the man who had refrained from clapping approached them.

"Hello, lads." The man smiled. "My name is Rampley Rimpole. I run the home here. And what are your names?"

'Rampley Rimpole'! John nearly spat out his bit of cake – 'Rampley Rimpole'! Jesu, his mam must have really, really hated him giving him a name like that!

Rimpole eyed the two boys up and down as they gave their names. Curiosity tinged with admiration stared down at them. Rimpole was a tall, thin man who had obviously experienced trouble finding a decent tailor – the bottoms of his trousers flew at half mast, so every time he took a few steps they beat the living daylights out of his ankles. The jacket he wore dropped and drooped in all directions giving the impression of a man who never knew where he was going. "Your singing was splendid," Rimpole beamed, "truly splendid." Before the boys could make some kind of polite response, Rimpole asked, "Have either of you ever heard of Dan Burrows?"

"Er . . . no, can't say that we have," John replied, looking at Issy with a bewildered expression.

"No? Never mind. Well, Dan is a highly respected business-man in Cardiff and a good friend of mine. He also has a keen interest in people with special talents. Especially singers. He sometimes promotes new talent for stage and variety, you see. I have a feeling he may be interested in you both. Could you do an audition for him?" 'Audition'? What was that the two boys wondered? Rimpole noted the boys' confusion. "Sing some-thing for him so that he too can appreciate your talents."

"Well . . . er . . . we'll have to ask our mams . . . er . . . Mr Rimpole," John replied.

"Of course – naturally your parents' permission will be needed. Are they on the telephone?"

"Yes, but don't ask me the number. What about you, Issy, can you remember yours?" For the first time Issy spoke. He was as mystified as his friend with all this.

"Of course I can, John." He then rattled off the number.

"Hold on a minute, hold on," Rimpole ordered, having trouble hiding his excitement. "Let me get somthing to write with." He reached into a pocket for a pen and a notebook and wrote down Issy's telephone number. Definitely *not* working class, Rimpole's thoughts confirmed. Speech, clothes and now the telephone. There was money in the background. Not wealthy, but enough. Neither the boys nor their families needed money for the singing, which could have been a problem.

"That's grand, boys. Grand." Rimpole was almost blushing with enthusiasm now, as Dan would see him right if these two boys came up to expectations. They had been given a unique gift, both of them. They were special, no doubt about it.

CHAPTER 10

Two months passed before anything more was heard from Rampley Rimpole. John and his parents were sitting down having supper, a shoulder of Welsh lamb and mint sauce, his favourite, although there was always a fight between him and his father over who should have the biggest portion of the crispy bits.

Lately John had noticed a definite warmth between his mother and father, even love. For years suppertime had always seemed strained somehow, his parents rarely talking apart from the occasional grunt. These days they actually smiled at each other, even touched hands when passing plates or cutlery to one another. Rum lot parents, he thought, maybe it had something to do with his father giving up the ale; either that or Dr Murphy had finally found some miracle pill for his ma. She didn't seem so down in the dumps these days and she had stopped fussing about his health. His father had changed in other ways too; at least he spent more time with him and seemed more affectionate. Mind you, he would always love his pa, aled up or not.

It was as if a great truce had been achieved in the Rees household. A knock at the front door disturbed this sudden change in domestic well-being. Owen left the table to see who it was. John heard his father say, "Come in young Issy, we're just finishing supper. No doubt you are calling for that reprobate son of mine." John heard a mumbled response. Issy was always a little quiet when adults were around – quiet, but nevertheless extremely polite. In this respect the two boys were decidedly different. John was never quiet and there were times when he could be downright defiant and objectionable, not to mention the odd tantrum when he couldn't get his own way.

His reddish hair had something to do with it, so his mam believed anyway.

Issy was the exact opposite to his friend. Reserved and thoughtful, he would think things through where John would jump in regardless of the consequences. Issy was the more calculating of the two, although his 'calculations' were usually based more on a perceptive wisdom beyond his years than deviousness. In this respect he was more mature than John.

When the two boys were together it was difficult to tell which one led and which one followed. Issy's inherent shyness was due more to modesty than weakness, and Issy was always more nervous about his singing than John. His Welsh friend on the other hand was a natural actor who loved having an audience, playing to the gallery and showing off. For Issy an audience sometimes intimidated and made him uncomfortable, not that he would ever let on. That wouldn't do at all, not with John around anyway.

Issy shuffled into the dining room. He had been to the house on numerous occasions, so John's parents had come to know him quite well.

"Er . . . hello, Mrs Rees. My mother has had a telephone call from a Mr Dan Burrows. She was wondering if you would give her a call. It's about an audition. I couldn't remember your telephone number." Not that the two boys ever communicated by telephone.

"Audition?" Owen asked as he looked at John. "What's this about an audition?" John had forgotten all about Rampley Rimpole and Dan Burrows.

He explained to his father what had happened with the Penyfai Male Voice Choir. Before his father could answer Gwyneth Rees said enthusiastically, "Why that's wonderful! John on the stage!" She had heard all about Dan Burrows and his connections with the stage. "Who'd ever have thought it?" The thought that John might have to go away didn't enter her head.

"Steady now, Gwyneth," Owen immediately cautioned. "Don't jump to conclusions. It's only an audition and we don't know yet what it's for, although I must confess our son here does have a fine voice. And you, Issy; you have a fine voice as well." Owen had heard of Dan Burrows too. There were not many people in their part of Wales who hadn't. "Well done both of you!"

Owen looked at his son and smiled, with genuine emotion and pride in his eyes. If he had reservations he kept them to himself for the time being. Theatre and variety didn't enjoy the best of reputations, but he wasn't prepared to spoil the moment – for now anyway.

"Here's my mother's telephone number," Issy said. "She's expecting your call." Gwyneth took the proffered piece of paper and went into the hallway to use the telephone, a black heavy affair John was not allowed to touch. Before picking up the receiver she turned to Issy who was standing in the doorway.

"Oh for heaven's sake what's the matter with me?" Gwyneth said. "I've forgotten your surname, Issy?"

"Kaddar, Mrs Rees."

"Right. Well, you two boys go and make yourselves useful while I talk with Mrs Kaddar. You can start with the dishes. Go on now, and I don't want you trying to eavesdrop either!" The kitchen door was closed firmly behind them as their imaginations began to run riot. Neither of the boys had taken Rimpole seriously, but all of a sudden things had changed. 'The stage' – now this really was an adventure to write home about, wasn't it just!

CHAPTER 11

A week later the two boys were carted off by their mothers on a train to Cardiff. Rachel and Gwyneth were dressed for a day out. It was August now and the sun was just itching to be exploited – in a modest way of course. Long cotton dresses plastered with all the colours of the rainbow floated just below their knees, while wide-brimmed hats tilted over their eyes and made it difficult for them to walk through narrow doorways. Both wore silk scarves to finish off the colourful spectacle: a deep blue one for Gwyneth's pale shoulders, a bright red one for Rachel's olive complexion. They made an eye-catching pair, especially as both women had allowed their hair to fall freely around their shoulders. Auburn and brunette, no man could miss them.

Neither Issy nor John noticed the beauty walking beside them – since when were mothers beautiful anyway? – but they did notice the maternal intrusion on their young manhood. After all, they were quite capable of going to Cardiff on their own! Both mothers still ruled, however, no matter how much they complained. Whose day out was it anyway, they moaned?

When they first arrived in Cardiff they were dragged around numerous shops and arcades while their mothers retched torrents of verbal nonsense, before being taken to a music shop filled with sheets of paper covered in quavers, semi-quavers and wrong notes, instruments, and scurrying musicians. Black-lacquered ebony grand pianos shone and gaped at pieces of brass standing to attention as strings, taut and nervous, twanged at expectant shop assistants. The place was an emporium of cacophonous chaos. Out of this mess walked a short, fat little man with grey curly hair: Dan Burrows, a man who owned much more than a music shop.

"Ah, how do you do, ladies!" Burrows boomed. "I am Dan Burrows, the gentleman you have come to see. Welcome to my modest musical emporium." Then he turned theatrically to John and Issy. "So these are the two young sopranos that I've heard so much about. Wonderful!"

After a quick thrashing of the two women with a leer that would have done a Tiger Bay tart proud he kissed the backs of their hands, almost dribbling in the process. Seeming reluctant to take his piggy eyes away from the two beauties standing before him he examined Issy and John from head to toe. Handsome boys the pair of them, a good start.

The clothes that Burrows wore left no one in any doubt that summer had arrived. He was dressed in baggy white trousers, a yellow and green striped woollen blazer, a navy blue cravat with white stripes and a shirt whose collar spread out across his lapels. His clothes were as loud as his voice which managed to curb and subdue every instrument in the place. A big fat cigar stuck out of a pair of podgy lips as he introduced himself. Not waiting for an answer from his guests Burrows said, "Now then, let's see what you two boys are made of. George! George! Come over here and seat that lazy rump of yours at one of the pianos. The Steinway I think."

A bearded man with fingers as thin and as light as newspaper appeared from nowhere. Burrows grunted, pointed and led the way.

As the boys followed, mothers in tow, John was immediately reminded of his hedgehog and a fattened-up badger, since that's exactly what this Burrows man looked like, or at the very least a cross between the two. The man's eyes never left Gwyneth or Rachel, leading the two boys to conclude that they had just met another Evan Evans. The buggers were everywhere, but this one was much older than Evan Evans, the dirty old sod. Their own mothers too! Not that either of them knew much about the wanton ways of men and women, they just had an idea and nothing more.

"Let's have you first – Issy isn't it?" Burrows ordered, "Sing what you like." Issy stood alongside the pianist and whispered something. The pianist nodded, tapped some keys and off they went. Issy sang 'Love's Old Sweet Song', a composition he had picked up from his mother who constantly sang it around the house. When he had finished he went and sat down next to his mother, unaware of the attention the two boys were beginning to receive.

It was John's turn next. He had already decided to sing Friml's 'Smilin' Through' again. It was one of his best, and as usual he wanted to impress. Having spoken quietly in the pianist's ear, he cleared his throat and nodded.

Fingers browsing through music sheets paused as musicians looking for the right note stopped their searching and instruments stopped playing. Even the air stood still and listened. Soon, normally tone-deaf passers-by were drawn into the shop as John's voice urged and demanded. More followed, unable to resist. Everything came to a standstill as pure musical magic calmed and inspired. The boy's voice gave beauty itself a lesson or two. There were no limits, no bounderies to the wonder of his notes as he sang and forced bodies to tingle from shoe to shoulder.

When John finally finished singing there was a breathless hiatus in the shop, a sudden mystery that all who had been listening wanted to unravel and understand.

Nothing moved.

Then a crash of applause erupted, followed by an excited burst of chattering. As Gwyneth Rees looked at her son and felt an enormous pride, she also had a vision of Samuel standing next to him, his dark intensity contrasting with John's brash self-awareness. If only there had been two of them.

Dan Burrows had heard all he needed to hear. He looked at the two mothers and said, "Can your two boys go to the Kemble Theatre in Hereford next Saturday? Expenses paid naturally." Rachel and Gwyneth looked at each other. Rachel was the first to speak.

"What for?" she asked.

"Madam, there is a fellow and some other boy sopranos I want them to meet: Steffani and his '21 Silver Songsters'."

"And whom might they be, Mr Burrows?" Rachel was already on her guard, the man's clothes and face having seen to that.

"A choir, madam. And may I say one of the best in the land. Twenty-one boy sopranos all singing together. Have you not heard of them? Why, they are famous. They are the only act of their kind. Their singing is sublime – absolutely sublime. Why, your boys here could be famous too. Their voices could take them to the top of the bill at the *London Palladium*! I exaggerate not, I assure you!"

John and Issy just looked at each other. London? Famous? All they did was sing a bit for goodness sake! Their mothers looked at each other too seemingly lost for words, for a moment anyway. Gwyneth was the next to speak, now confronting the prospect of John being away both from home and her loving bosom.

"If this Steffani man wants our boys to sing in his . . . er, Silver Songsters you say . . . that would mean them going away, wouldn't it? Who would look after them? What about their education? Where will they stay? And how long will they be away?"

"Now, now Mrs Rees. You have nothing to worry about. Of course the boys will be required to travel all over the country. Their voices will be heard far and wide, but we employ a gentleman, a Mr Bertram Sideway, to take care of all their needs – all the things you are rightfully concerned about. Mr Sideway is a kindly, educated man, charming and eloquent, and your boys will not want for anything I assure you. While on tour they will be properly looked after. They will receive lessons during the day, have no fear, and their lodgings will be of the highest quality. So will the food. Anything else would be a crime; why, if the boys are not properly looked after how will they sing? How will they entrance an audience? As for their time in the Songsters . . . well, nature will see to that. Er . . . a boy soprano is not a boy soprano for long, if you see what I mean, although it is not unknown for a boy to keep his soprano voice until he is eighteen. Unusual, but as I say, not unknown. Oh, the boys are well paid too—"

"Yes, that's all very well, Mr Burrows," Gwyneth interrupted, at the same time looking at Rachel, "but we will need to discuss all this with our husbands before we go any further." The thought of John leaving her made her stomach turn. John was her little boy after all, her only little boy.

"But of course, Mrs Rees. You can also meet Steffani himself and the other boys should you so wish, and of course the veritable Mr Sideway."

"We will," Gwyneth confirmed.

"In the meantime can the two boys still do another audition for Steffani himself on Saturday?" Burrows asked. "A mere formality I assure you. You see I provide the financial support for the Songsters. I back them, if you like."

"I suppose so," Gwyneth replied, although none too sure how Owen would react. Rachel was not too sure how her own husband would react either. The *kinema* and thespian endeavour both wallowed in tales of ill repute. Still if the boys were properly looked after . . . it would be such an adventure for them. The chance of a lifetime. Gwyneth was thinking similar thoughts, but letting John go would be a struggle. She had lost one child, but then could she deprive her only son of such a wonderful opportunity? The London Palladium no less!

74

CHAPTER 12

The following Saturday Rachel and Gwyneth had finally given in to their sons' demands that they should be allowed to go to Hereford on their own. The boys didn't want their 'mummies' sticking their noses into their own 'private affairs'. More than anything else they didn't want to look like a couple of sissies. There was nothing more embarrassing than being seen with your mam, particularly if she was all scrubbed up as women were wont to do whenever there was a shop in sight. More to the point, mams were embarrassing if girls were in the immediate vicinity, and John believed there would be girls at the Kemble Theatre. There had to be. The stage was all about glamour, girls and songs after all.

The Kemble Theatre was bound to be better and posher than the boys' local picture house, or 'Bug House' as it was called in local parlance on account of the flees that always seemed to be so ravenous on a Saturday morning. Apart from anything else the theatre was also far more alive! Actual people did the talking and singing!

As the two boys settled down on the train the business of 'girls' entered the conversation. John had been impressed by Issy's pretty sister, but hadn't said anything only because he hadn't quite known what to say. That was the trouble with 'girls'; they were an unknown quantity. More recently and for some unknown reason they hadn't seemed quite so silly and stupid. John wondered if Issy felt the same way. He looked across the compartment at his friend who was staring out of the window. There were times when Issy seemed to be in some other place that John knew he could never reach.

"Your sister is very pretty, Issy," John finally managed to blurt out, not really knowing why he felt compelled to make such an observation. Issy continued to look out of the window, seeming to be more interested in the steam that wafted past on its journey to nowhere and lazy green fields that vanished in less than a moment.

"Is she?" Issy at last managed to reply, still hypnotised by dancing steam and the occasional surly cow. "Can't say I've ever really noticed. That's all she does is annoy me – well, most of the time anyway." John looked at his friend. He waited, but nothing else came out of Issy's mouth. Frustrated with the lack of response John being John intruded into Issy's world again.

"Have you ever kissed a girl, Issy?" He wanted an answer. This was serious.

Issy continued to look at the passing countryside, absorbed again. Issy was always absorbed in something or other, a bit like Sam in some ways. At last he turned his eyes onto John, "No, John. Can't say that I have. Seems a sloppy business to me. There was a girl, when I was about six or seven. Can't remember now. Think we promised to marry each other or something."

"Don't be daft now, Issy." John persisted. "I'm talking about a proper kiss. You know, a French kiss." He had no idea exactly what a 'French kiss' was, but that wasn't the point. Everyone else at school knew it must be the normal way of kissing – a bit like his mam's before he went to bed, but more hugging and slobbering, like they did at the pictures.

Issy was more honest than John when he said, "Not sure I know what a 'French kiss' is. I thought only adults did that type of thing."

"Jesu, Issy!" John was almost tearing his hair out now." Don't you ever see a girl and want to kiss her?!"

"Well er . . . yes, of course I do! What are you getting so worked up about? Can't say I've met one yet that I would really like to kiss though. Like I say, seems a sloppy business to me."

"That's something then; I was beginning to wonder if you were a queer or something!"

"Queer? *Queer*?" Issy was cross now, "Heavens! Say that again John and I'll knock your bloody teeth out!" Issy didn't really know what a 'queer' was either. He just knew that at school fists would fly if any boy was called it. John was starting to laugh, even though he too had no idea what a 'queer' was. He had never seen Issy so angry; normally he was always so placid and in control.

"All right, all right, Issy, don't get so worked up. I was only joking . . . must have hit a sore point though . . ." John couldn't resist baiting his friend, it was so funny. He continued to laugh which didn't help matters.

"John! I'm warning you—!"

"Calm down Issy, calm down," John managed to say at last. "I'm only joking." He rarely heard Issy swear, as he was usually the one with a foul mouth. Before long Issy started to see the funny side of things too and began to laugh with his friend.

"Anyway, what's all this about Sheyna?" It was Issy's turn to tease. "Want to kiss her do you? I'll see what I can arrange."

"What! What! Don't you dare, Issy! I mean it!"

"Well now, I'll have to think about that," Issy smirked. "Could of course tell her you're a queer, couldn't I?"

"What? Jesu! Don't you dare! Never mind about my teeth, Issy! Look after your own, I'm telling you!" Now it was Issy's turn to laugh, and before long both boys were chuckling together. They were rarely angry with each other for long. When they eventually stopped teasing one another they started to talk about more serious things, like who was this Steffani chap, what was he like? What were the boys in the Silver Songsters like? Were they really about to be famous? It was all so exciting.

When the train arrived in Hereford the two boys made their way to the Kemble Theatre. Their audition was for eleven o'clock.

Finding the theatre wasn't difficult, finding Steffani was. The theatre appeared to be all closed up so the boys had to hunt around for a door that was open. Eventually they found one down a back alleyway. They walked in, shouted 'Hello' but no one answered. They could hear some singing and drums beating from the ceiling above them so they decided to follow the noise. As it was still quite early the boys assumed that the singing was a result of rehearsals or something. There were definitely people around somewhere, so they went up some stairs, opened another door and arrived in the orchestra pit.

A man was standing next to an upright piano watching about fifteen boys march up and down the stage to the beat of six drums all hammering out the 'Parade of the Tin Soldiers'. All the boys were singing in unison to the drums and did not miss a note, a beat, or for that matter a step. John and Issy watched with amazement as the boys not only sang, but also marched with the precision of trained soldiers trooping the colours. The boys had to be Steffani's 21 Silver Songsters.

The man standing by the piano and issuing occasional instructions ignored John and Issy; at least he seemed to be unaware of their presence. John coughed loudly, although his cough was more or less drowned out by the drums. He coughed again, only this time followed it up with a shouted, "Excuse me, please!" The man finally turned around raising his hands as he did so. The Songsters and the drums stopped.

"And who are you?" the man asked.

"Dan Burrows sent us," John replied.

"Ah, yes. Dan told me to expect you. Issy Kaddar and John Rees if I'm not mistaken. I am Steffani; you can call me Steff if you find it easier, I don't mind. Most of my boys call me Steff anyway." He smiled at the two boys.

He was above average height and in his late thirties. A cigarette dangled from his lips as if trying to find somewhere to hide. He was dressed in grey flannels, brown tweed sports jacket, starched white shirt and bright yellow cravat, sufficiently ruffled to camouflage an over-indulged Adam's Apple. Wisps of oiled black hair tried to hide a balding scalp without much success. A long nose capable of sniffing out the slightest hint of incorrect note or key stood out from a face that could only be described as modestly handsome. Although his name immediately implied someone of Italian origin, there was no olive skin and certainly no Italian accent. In fact as the boys were to find out later on his real name was Frederick William Wiskers from Beccles in Suffolk. He came from German stock and had never been anywhere near Italy. None of this however detracted from his love of music and the piano, or his indifference to whether or not someone was a Jew – particularly if they had money. He normally accompanied the choir with the piano and was even known to sing himself on occasions.

Steffani's voice was deep and commanding as he said, "Go and stand at the side of the stage for a while and learn something, boys. Once the rehearsal is over you can both sing the same songs you sang for Dan, is that all right? He speaks very highly of you both, but I'd like to hear you myself before considering you for the Songsters. I'll accompany you on the piano. Now off you go." The two boys did as they were told, wondering at the same time who the boss actually was: Dan Burrows or Steffani?

An hour or so later Steffani clapped his hands and shouted, "That's enough for now!" to the boys on the stage. He then shouted at John and Issy to come back down to the orchestra pit and do their audition. Issy's stomach jumped with nerves just as it always did, whereas John remained calm and seemed to take everything in his stride. For once Issy was jealous of his friend, and for once he was the one losing control.

Some ten minutes later when Issy and John had finished stretching their vocal chords Steffani remained seated at the piano. He seemed to be deep in thought.

The voices of two of his Songsters were starting to break; they could still harmonise, but that was all. He needed replacements – fast. He was also getting short of money. Some new blood might just do the trick. Steffani sighed to himself as he lit another cigarette. He was always short of money somehow, no matter how many bookings he had. This John lad though might be the answer to his financial troubles. There was something extra in his voice, something special. His friend was good, certainly good enough for the Songsters, but this John boy, well, with a little extra tuition, who knows?

"I'll want you both here for tomorrow night's performance," Steffani ordered. "You won't be doing any solos until I know what you are both made of. That will take some time – and practise, lots of practise." He dug into his trouser pockets and withdrew some coins, "Now, here's some money for your train fare and something to eat on your way home. I'll speak with your parents later this evening. Now off you go, and be here midday tomorrow for rehearsals. Twelve sharp, got it?" John and Issy nodded, took the coins and walked out of the theatre. Neither of them said a word until they had reached the station. Issy was the first to speak. "Well, John, do you think we are going to be famous then?"

"I don't know Issy, but I do know that there weren't any girls anywhere to be seen in the theatre."

Later that same evening and after numerous telephone conversations Rachel Kaddar confronted her husband.

"I beg your pardon, Rachel. Did I hear you correctly?" Ezra Kaddar demanded. "Our son singing on the stage? Variety? Good God! Touring the country with some oily Italian? Have you taken leave of your senses, woman?"

"Now dear. Don't get all upset, you know how it affects your work. And the man is English not Italian."

"'Don't get upset!' And how long has this conspiracy been going on for? Issy wouldn't just be made this offer out of nowhere. Do you think I'm stupid! A 'Silver Songster' indeed!" Rachel had decided to keep quiet about the whole business until all the auditions were over and the necessary assurances given where the boys' welfare was concerned. Assurances or not, she had a feeling that her husband would be virulently opposed. She wasn't far wrong either, but then she knew how to handle her husband and besides, where the children were concerned, her husband rarely interfered.

"My dear Ezra, will you please listen? Both Mrs Rees and I have discussed matters at length. We have also been assured by both Mr Burrows – a respected businessman with a fine reputation for fair dealing I hasten to add – and Mr Steffani himself said that the boys will be well looked after. And before you say anything, Issy's education will not suffer. A gentleman named Bertram Sideway sees to board, lodging and also their daily lessons. Both Mrs Rees and I have spoken with him and we were both impressed. He is a man of letters, no doubt about it. He studied at Cambridge and this has been confirmed by the other gentleman. Due to the fact that Issy and John are required tomorrow night we have been unable to actually meet Mr Steffani or Mr Sideway as we had hoped, but having spoken with both gentlemen on the telephone both Mrs Rees and I are satisfied that the boys will be properly looked after. We can still meet these gentlemen at any time should we so wish. Ezra, we must not be selfish. We *must* not!" Rachel stamped her right foot on the floor of his study, just to add emphasis to her determination to have her way.

Ezra was wondering how long it would take before Rachel started the foot-stamping, one of her more endearing habits. Add a raised voice, a hand on hip and the rest was as certain as Hitler's eventual destruction. She had made up her mind and Hell on earth wasn't about to change it.

"But Rachel, do you not think the boy has been moved around enough?" Ezra tried to say gently. "Is it not time he had some permanence in his life? Some stability? We haven't long been in this country after all, and consider why we arrived here in the first place."

"I know all that, but can you not see that Issy now has a chance to put all that behind him? He also has a chance to see so much, to experience so much. Can any school teach him those things? He's not going away for good after all. It will only be for a year or two. How long do you think he can be a boy soprano for heaven's sake? He's fifteen next month. It's an opportunity of a lifetime, Ezra, and I will not deprive our son. I will not! Dear God, boys his age have fought in wars and there are plenty in Wales who are down the coal pits before they are hardly out of their nappies! He sings so beautifully, and it is only right that others should enjoy his talent. He is going to be a Silver Songster and that's all there is to it! No more argument, Ezra!"

Ezra Kaddar looked at his wife. There were times when he won the war and times when she did. This was one of those occasions when she won. He stood up from his desk and sighed. "Very well, be it on your head. But if Issy turns out to be a Nancy boy, to use common parlance, then don't blame me!" With that he walked out of the study leaving his wife to fume in that most wonderful way of hers.

On the other side of Llantwit Gwyneth Rees was in turmoil. The reality of Illtyd leaving home to venture into the big wide world without her there to protect him tore her apart. She knew that one day he would become a man and leave her, but did it have to be now? She struggled with the love for her child; yet should she allow this love to deprive her son of such a thrilling opportunity? Such a dramatic adventure? Because for John that is exactly what it would be: an adventure he might never again have the chance to enjoy. She had spoken with Rachel, but uncertainty still lingered. After some hours of soul-searching she finally made up her mind. Her love must prevail.

When Gwyneth told Owen about John singing with the Silver Songsters she received a somewhat surprising response. He hadn't exploded, hadn't quoted dire warnings from the War

Poets and hadn't immersed himself in ale. Instead he had smiled and said, "Well, I did have reservations when you first mentioned this musical enterprise, but after some careful thought I have changed my mind. It will do the boy good. Teach him to share things and think of others. He's been an only child for too long and he's been spoilt – as well you know, Gwyneth. As long as his education doesn't suffer, then good luck to him. Apart from anything else it will mean he can torment some other poor devils for a while. No, it will be a good thing providing of course that this Steffani chap is not one of Mussolini's fanatical henchmen. He isn't, is he Gwyneth?"

"Don't be silly, Owen. Actually he isn't Italian at all, so I've been told. He's from Suffolk apparently."

"Good, that's all right then." Owen couldn't help but smile at his wife as he said, "Illtyd John Rees, the Silver Songster – bloody hell! God help them!"

PART 2

CHAPTER 13

London. June 1937

Nine months had passed and neither John nor Issy had had time to miss home or their parents. The New Year had come and gone and so had their fifteenth birthdays. Their lives had become a helter skelter, a Ferris wheel and a waltzing passenger car all rolled into one. They travelled north, south, east and west, singing and singing as two of Steffani's 21 Silver Songsters.

They performed in most of the Moss Empire theatres and many, many more. Sometimes they topped the bill; at other times they had to give way to people like Ambrose and His Orchestra, Vera Lynn, Will Hay and Max Miller. The list was endless. Topping the bill was important for variety players, a fine dressing room depended on it. As there were so many boys in the Songsters they always joked that they would be 'Top of the stairs' at their next performance! John and Issy were making money too – one pound a week! Neither of them were spendthrifts, so most of their earnings went straight into their own Post Office accounts. Their parents never asked for a penny.

At first the two boys had experienced some underlying resentment from the other Songsters, who were all about the same age. Many had come from poor homes and industrialised wastelands, unlike John and Issy who had known open fields, fresh eggs hidden in haystacks and the stench of steaming cow pats. Their 'posh' accents didn't help either, albeit John's rose and fell with a sing-song cadence of lively rhythm.

One boy had been a real menace. Will Perkins from Manchester (or Gargoyle as he had been nicknamed on account of his huge mouth and the threatening rows of uneven teeth sharpened by neglect and decay) was both older than John and Issy, and bigger. He believed, mistakenly, that his age and size allowed him a certain seniority over the other boys, a seniority that entitled him to bully and terrify. One morning he had barged into their bedroom demanding some cigarettes. Gargoyle was a man now and always smoking when Steffani or Mr Sideway weren't looking. Steffani always insisted that the boys keep away from tobacco, since he didn't want their pristine voices damaged. Of course, his own voice was immune to any harmful effects from tobacco; he was an adult after all, so smoking actually improved his voice – or so he maintained.

"Come on boys, let's have your baccy," Gargoyle had demanded. John and Issy had looked at each other. They only shared the odd smoke now and again and were certainly not professional smokers, not like Gargoyle anyway. He snarled in his usual toothy way, but on this occasion neither John nor Issy were prepared to jump as expected. "I said, where's your baccy?" Gargoyle demanded again.

"Bugger off, Gargoyle," John replied as blunt as ever. "We don't have any, and even if we did we wouldn't share it with you, you ugly sod. Why don't you go and frighten somebody else with those bloody fangs of yours?"

For a moment there was total silence. Gargoyle had never been challenged like this before and it took a few seconds for his brain to register the outrage. When it did he pounced, evil spirits having to be warded off at all costs. He tried to attack John first. As Issy was slightly bigger he would leave him until last. He came at John, hands held out and teeth bared, just like the Gargoyle he was. John ducked, punched him on the chin and yelled, "Get in quick, Issy! Grab his arms!" While Gargoyle floundered around on the floor Issy took one of his arms and John took the other. "The toilet! Quick!" John ordered. The two boys dragged Gargoyle out of their room and down the corridor to the toilet. One look from John and Issy knew exactly what they were going to do. John kicked open the toilet door and nodded to Issy. Gargoyle was struggling but unable to release himself from the boy's hands. He was not the only one who had grown stronger. Next thing John shoved Gargoyle's head down the toilet pan while Issy gave the chain a firm tug. Water flushed, pipes rumbled and that was the last time Gargoyle ever demanded tobacco from either John or Issy. As the two boys walked away from their drenched and humiliated attacker John looked at his friend and laughed, "Let Gargoyle try lighting a fag now, eh? Oh, and thanks for the helping hand, Issy."

"Any time, John," Issy replied. "Any time."

Yet another strong link in their chain of friendship had been welded together.

One other boy, Nick Harding from the East End of London (nicknamed 'Trwyn', Welsh for 'nose', on account of his monstrous hooter, which was always blocked up or dripping dew drops) had also needed some taming, particularly when he had accused John and his family of having unnatural 'relations' with cows and sheep. At one point even an unsuspecting pig had been the victim of John's familial 'relations'! After a few more fights John and Issy were left alone, even respected. They always fought together and always tried to protect one another. All the Songsters knew that to annoy one meant annoying the other as well, so if one was bad enough, two was disaster and a bloody nose.

One Saturday morning at the Trocadero Theatre in London John was rehearsing with one of the older boys, Jim Stratten. Jim's testicles had finally given up any last remnants of innocence and dropped to the floor with a bang louder than anything the Songsters' drums could produce, according to Jim anyway. He was now employed as a pianist. Mornings were always a quiet time in a theatre so both boys, for want of nothing better to do, started fooling around with the piano. Jim launched into a rendition of 'When The Skeleton In The Cupboard Started To Dance', John started hitting the high notes at the opposite end of the scales to the pianist and generally abusing the song and his voice.

All of a sudden there was a loud shout from behind them and Steffani appeared. "What the hell do you think you are doing, boy?!" he bellowed. "Do you want to ruin your voice? Do you? Screeching like that? You bloody fool! Never let me hear you treating your voice like that again! Do you hear me?"

"Yes Steff, yes," John quickly answered. He had never seen Steff so angry. This was one occasion when backchat was out of the question.

"And you, Jim, should know better. I'll deal with you later. Now get back to your digs. Now! Both of you! And John, don't ever let me hear you messing about like that again. Do you hear me?!"

As John made a hasty retreat he called over his shoulder, "Yes, Steff! I hear you! I hear you!" When the two boys had gone Steffani sat down at the piano. He had been grooming young John for six months, perhaps now it was time to put his plan into action and fill up his bank account. Time for John to go solo. God knows time was at a premium where boy sopranos were concerned. Even he was impressed by the high notes John could hit. The boy had only been playing around when he had caught them earlier, but even then his range had been superb. The boy was a coloratura, no doubt about it. He could sing E above top C with ease. He was unique. Steffani had just the song in mind. A song that up until now had only ever been sung by female sopranos. The Theatre Royal, Norwich, would be the place. John would make his debut there – and hopefully plenty of money for Steffani. They were due to perform there in two weeks time. Some practise would be needed, but not much. John was ready now, as ready as he would ever be.

Perhaps now was the time for both John and Issy to go home and see their parents Steffani reflected. They hadn't been back home since the touring had started, and that had been nearly a year ago. John's voice could certainly use a rest before his debut. Yes, they could have a week off. Steffani would just have to rearrange a few things.

While Steffani was thinking about his meal ticket and how long it would be valid for, Issy was still trying to find John. John was the early riser, while Issy would stay in bed for as long as possible, or at least until Bertram Sideway dragged him out of bed. As he entered the stage door of the theatre a young girl bumped into him. Their faces almost touched as blond curls played with Issy's nose for a second or two.

"Oh! I'm so sorry—" Issy blurted out, his face going as red as the lipstick the girl was wearing. He had never been so close to a young girl before, his sister notwithstanding and she of course didn't count. As he apologised his eyes clashed with the girl's and in a split second he now knew what John had been going on about on the train all those months ago. All he wanted to do was kiss the girl there and then, French or otherwise. Jesus, did he want to kiss her! She was beautiful. His arm was still attached to hers, stuck permanently or so it seemed. "Er . . . oh, sorry again," he muttered as he removed his arm, "I . . . er . . . can be so – um – clumsy sometimes." The girl stood back from him and smiled. Deep green eyes and startling red lips caught him and wouldn't let go. Her blond curls seemed to trap him again as they fell around her shoulders.

"That's all right, my fault," the girl smiled again, "shouldn't be in so much of a hurry. Well, must be off. Bye, bye." With that the girl – or was she a woman? Issy couldn't be too sure – ran off up the road. Issy remained standing and a little lost. So was this what approaching manhood was all about? he thought. Girls who caught you with their eyes then threw you away?

The girl with the red lips and blond curls stayed with him for the rest of the morning until he finally caught up with John at their lodgings.

"Where have you been, Issy?" John was in one of his impatient moods again. "Our lessons start at twelve o'clock. It's nearly that now. You know what 'Sideways' is like. I've been in enough trouble this morning as it is."

"Where have *you* been, more like?" Issy replied calmly, quite used to his friend's outbursts. "I've been to the theatre looking for you. Anyway, what have you done now?" John was always in trouble about something.

"Oh, nothing much. Just playing around, but Steff gave me hell all the same. Worries about my voice; you know what he's like about his precious Songsters. Anyway never mind all that, it's geography this afternoon I think. It had better be, otherwise I will have done the wrong homework again and you know what that means. In the shit again, never seem to get out of the stuff, do I?"

"Don't worry. It's geography," Issy confirmed. "I wouldn't let you crib the wrong stuff now, would I?"

John smiled. Where would he be without his friend's brains? "No, I suppose not. It's all a bit unfair if you ask me. We're the only two boys who have to do lessons. The rest can hardly read and write, but they get away with it."

"That's parents for you, John. No point moaning about it. Besides, as you have said, you don't fancy working down the pits, do you? Or in a factory. An education will make sure we never go anywhere near either of them."

"Yes, you're right again Issy. As always. Been out on one of your walks, have you?"

"Something like that. I did go to the theatre as I said but you'd gone. I met a . . . oh nothing."

"You met who, Issy?" Issy was looking uncomfortable. Even embarrassed. "Come on Issy, you're not telling me something I can tell. Who did you meet?" John was genuinely curious now. His friend was quieter and more intense than he was, but they never kept secrets from one another. "Come on, Issy . . . I don't believe it! You're blushing! Must be a girl! Must be!" For once John was able to exercise a little perception, if not sheer guess-work. "Well, well. You met a girl you like. Did you kiss her then? A French kiss? Who is she? Is she pretty? What's she look like?" Issy looked at his friend and despaired. If he didn't tell John something he would never hear the end of it.

"Oh John, why don't you mind your own business? If you must know I just bumped into a girl . . . at least that's what I think she was, although she was wearing make-up and looked very grown up . . . I just couldn't tell. Must have been older than me though, she looked it anyway; probably a new act or something. I haven't seen her before."

"What do you mean 'You think she was a girl', Issy? Don't you know the difference? You have a sister after all."

"Of course I know what a girl looks like, you idiot. It's just that she looked more like a woman that's all. Not like Sheyna at all. You know there were lumps in the front of her dress. And her legs . . . well! I watched them as she walked away from the theatre, couldn't take my eyes off them I can tell you."

"Lumps, Issy? Titties you mean surely? Definitely a woman then. Only women have titties, girls don't." John looked at his stricken friend. "Too old for you Issy by the sounds of it, but dreams don't harm. One day we'll be old enough to go after women – real women. Come on now, we'd better go to our lessons. Old Sideways will be waiting for us in the dining room, and you know what a bugger he is if we're late."

Bertram Sideway was waiting for them as expected, his bald head shining and twinkling as he sat at a dining table covered by a floral tablecloth. Some maps of the world exaggerating the size of Great Britain, some exercise books and pencils lay in front of him. He was not in a good mood, but then he never was. One side of his thin lips was always turned down in a sideways slant of dejection, thus the corruption of his name into 'Sideways' instead of Sideway by his two tormentors. Laughter or even a modest smile rarely lifted his lips, such was the misery of his life. His morose demeanour was the result of an equally morose wife, a wife whose inexhaustible tongue, buck teeth and sour expression waited patiently at home for her husband to return. This was never going to happen. The stage had beckoned and Sideway had taken flight. Not a player by heart he had done the next best thing, namely management. Or at least management of the stars that Steffani, his employer, tried to nurture. Even this, however, had failed to remove the permanent scars left by a poisonous harridan with a mouth bigger than any stage. Demolished by disgrace as an academic over an innocent faux pas with one of his female students and desperate to hide from his wife, he had sought refuge in the fantasy world of the stage, even if he only ever stood in the wings. The travelling took him well away from the place he had once called home and the place where his biggest mistake of all lived. The disgrace and even the First World War trenches had been as nothing when compared to the woman he had been fool enough to marry.

Not far off sixty now Bertram Sideway was happy to look after his theatrical charges as long as they didn't give him too much trouble. The present double act however were constant trouble, although he had to admit that neither of them seemed to have a malicious bone in their bodies, which was more than could be said about some of the boys, those from less salubrious backgrounds that is.

When John and Issy were seated opposite the learned Sideway he pushed a map in front of them, tugged at his blue polka-dot bow tie, and asked them to memorise it. They would be tested later. He peered at them through spectacles that hung on the tip of his nose waiting to take flight just as he had done a few years before. The grey whiskers that covered his face and his identity – a Cambridge don guilty of some silly slap and tickle was a crime worse than murder, albeit that the real crime was being caught out, after all perversion and pederasty had been de rigueur at Cambridge for centuries, regrettably though it did not carry the death sentence – never moved when he spoke, rendered motionless by his abject misery. When thirty minutes had passed Sideway duly tested, marked and moaned at the boys' efforts, then coughed into a bright red handkerchief the size of one of the national flags he was always trying to make the boys memorise. His eyes glanced around the dining room which was typical of most lodging houses of that time: a massive mahogany table and nothing else, apart from the odd withering aspidistra and a few dejected pictures, usually of the landscape variety. Lodging houses with big tables were always an essential requirement; there were a lot of Songsters, not usually all in one place though.

"Now then, young fellows," Sideway muttered, pulling his blue polka-dot bow tie again with one hand while he tried to straighten out the lapel on his scruffy grey wool suit. "It is time you went home to see your parents. I have been instructed by Steffani to arrange your immediate departure. The nine o'clock train out of Paddington tomorrow morning returning exactly one week later. Your parents have been contacted, so they will meet you at the station. Here are your tickets." He rummaged around in his pocket, produced the tickets and handed them some cash. "Now off you go and don't get into any trouble. By the way, you have been writing regularly to your parents I trust?"

"Oh yes, Mr Sideway, every week," they answered as one.

"Good. I'll give you some homework to take back with you before you go. Some more arithmetic I think, Rees. You know how you wallow in the complexities of mathematical conundrums. A noble endeavour, young fellow. A noble endeavour indeed, even for your primitive intellect!" For a moment his lips seemed to move slightly, but this was impossible. Sideway never smiled; he always looked as if he had the skin of his arse stuck to his face. Most of the time John had no idea what the man was muttering about anyway. The two boys left the dining room and Mr Sideway, who looked as suicidal as ever. If John had taken the time to look he would have noticed that his friend's face was as forlorn and desolate as their ruined teacher's. If Issy didn't see the only girl on the planet again that night he would probably never see her again.

Variety people never stayed in one place for long.

CHAPTER 14

The long journey home to Llantwit Major finally ended up in their mothers' arms and a tug-of-war with embarrassment. Both John and Issy had changed. A year or so away from home had accelerated maturity and independence; their bodies too were tightening up and becoming more muscular. Still only fifteen they had come to rely on each other, not their parents.

The unique experience of singing in the 21 Silver Songsters choir had set them apart from other boys their own age. Travelling all over the country had broadened their minds and their perceptions. Although they were still only boys and to begin with had shed many a homesick tear, the singing and adventure had soon prevailed. Their youth was saying 'Good-bye', even though their voices refused to move on. Their homes and their parents remained firmly fixed at the backs of their minds, but both rarely came out from hiding.

Sheyna had come along with her mother to meet the boys at the station. She gave Issy a hug and a kiss, then stood back to let the mothers have their way. John managed to look at her again over his mother's shoulder. She had grown up too, even prettier than before. He couldn't tell if any titties had sprouted though, her long baggy blue dress hid anything lurking beneath. For a moment he wondered if she wore a brassiere – now that really was grown up. He had only ever seen one and that was on his mother, though what they held was still a bit of a mystery. Like John, Sheyna had grown taller too, but the black hair and huge blue eyes remained exactly the same. She had caught his eyes as his mother tried to suffocate him. Her look had been direct and brazen. She was lovely, really lovely. Her eyes quickly turned away, leaving John wondering what she had meant, what she was trying to say.

While Issy was having his own breath squeezed out of him he too was thinking about girls. More particularly the girl he had met at the stage door. He had not seen her again, and the disappointment had kept him awake the night before. She could be anywhere now, so he was never likely to have the chance to kiss her, even if that chance had seemed horribly remote.

Both John and Issy had no idea why their attitudes to girls had changed so dramatically. Before, girls had been such silly, daft creatures. To a certain extent they still were, the trouble being that now one look at female silliness could result in an immediate physical reaction, the size of which could cause red-faced embarrassment, particularly if singing on the stage – embarrassment that sometimes simply refused to go away. Short trousers didn't help either. No one had told the boys anything about all this. They had only heard crude schoolyard conjecture and stories about buns in ovens and swooping storks leaving babies under bushes. That is apparently how they had come into the world, and no one had told them anything to the contrary. The whole business of 'girls' confused and confounded both John and Issy, and neither was able to enlighten the other.

Owen Rees was waiting for John when he and his mother walked into the kitchen. Owen had missed his son and the opportunity to make up for lost time. Although he had almost encouraged the boy's departure, he now felt that perhaps in some ways it had deprived him of the chance to truly satisfy his guilt where his rejection of the boy was concerned. The way he had turned away from his son, had blamed the boy, still troubled his conscience. Although alcohol was no longer his saviour and he and Gwyneth had managed to find a kind of love again, or at least a more certain love, his son remained a part of his life that was unfinished. Unresolved. He was still unsure whether or not his son had fully understood his actions, his temporary neglect. The boy seemed a happy, well adjusted child. Could he do more damage by trying to explain? Could his guilt do more harm than good? He looked at John and

97

felt enormous pride as the boy walked through the door. The Songsters had changed his son: the maturity about his movements, a new confidence and directness, the boy was definitely growing up and would be a handsome man, no doubt about it. He also enjoyed a natural charm, but would he know how to use these gifts properly?

Owen stood up from his chair and looked at his son. "Illtyd John Rees. The Prodigal returns. How are you, my boy?" John stood in front of his father and held out his hand. Men didn't hug and kiss each other, John had learnt that much.

"Grand, pa, just grand," he replied. They shook hands warmly. "Firm grip now John, always a firm grip. Remember what I taught you. You don't want to shake hands like a woman now do you?"

"No, pa."

"Good. Now come and sit down and tell your mother and I all about your adventures. We have some things to tell you too."

John told his parents all and everything about the choir, where they had performed, whom they had performed with, Steff, Mr Sideway . . . His tales went on for well over two hours. When he had finally finished and worn out his tongue, Owen Rees managed to say, "Well now, John. Your mother and I have something to tell you as well." John looked at his father. He had one of those serious looks on his face. What had happened, he immediately thought? Was the churchyard being filled up with one of his relatives again. His father never put on that expression unless something was up. "Your mam is expecting a baby, John. Soon." Soon. But how soon was 'soon'? John wondered. There wasn't a big bulge in her stomach, so any baby must be years away. For a moment he considered the puzzle of buns and storks, and yet he had seen women with sticking-out bellies one minute then nothing the next, apart from some screaming baby that is. Confusion again.

"A baby! Another brother for me!" John exclaimed. "That's grand, pa. Really grand!"

"Hold on there now John, we don't know yet whether it will be a boy or a girl."

"Oh, I see," John muttered, not only confused but puzzled as well. He thought you just told the stork or baker what you fancied, boy or girl. Why didn't parents explain these things! "When will my new brother . . . or sister be arriving then?"

"Oh, in about seven month's time I should think." Oh well, at least his parents knew when the baby was arriving, that was something. So where babies were concerned 'soon' meant seven months. He was learning. He didn't bother to ask for any more details, he knew the answer. Buns and storks, shit they got around and how the hell could a 'bun' turn into a brother or sister anyway? Must be one hell of a baker and as for storks, well . . .

The following morning John was hauled out of bed by his father.

"Come on, lad. It's a beautiful day. We're going for a walk and a swim. It's been a long time since we've spent any time together. Come on, get dressed. I'll wait for you downstairs."

An hour later father and son were walking along a riverbank not far from their home. It was turning into a hot day, even though summer had yet to properly announce itself. Multi-coloured dragonflies jumped along the surface of the river, then disappeared into grassy clumps that gripped the river bank for dear life. Gnats hovered above the surface of the river tormenting wild trout, while pike lurked and lingered in sinister hiding places waiting to pounce. A sharp sunlight was on the side of the hunted as it crept through trees and bounced along the water trying to give them a fair chance.

John was immediately struck by the peace of the country-side. He had almost forgotten what it was like, even though he had lived in it all his life. In recent times all he had known was the hubbub of people crushed together trying to earn a living and many dying in the attempt. There was no applause here, no laughter or din of desperation. Rolling trams stuffed with glaring people, struggling motor vehicles with squeaking horns and pavements crushed by the footsteps of a thousand leather-clad feet belonged to another place, another time.

Father and son walked calmly side by side, each understanding the river and its desperate life in different ways. The man with his maturity and knowledge saw innocence fighting with tragedy, while the boy could only wallow in his own simple joy and ease as he searched for answers that he knew were simply not there. The man regretted that he knew some of the answers and immediately wished that he had never looked in the first place, while the boy just waited to find out in his own particular way. Then Owen breathed deeply before breaking the silence.

"John, there are some things I would like to explain to you. You are growing up now and perhaps you will be able to understand." Owen looked at his son and hoped he was doing the right thing. He had thought long enough about it. "John, there might have been times in the past – certainly after your brother died – when you may have felt that I . . . well, that I no longer cared about you as much as you have the right to expect . . . I know, particularly when I had drunk too much, that I didn't treat you as well I should have done. You might even think there were times when I was quite unkind – cruel even."

Owen sighed. "I remember that time you were playing football. I should never have hurt you the way I did. I was far too harsh – not that there were times when you didn't deserve a good clout, believe me." Owen allowed a smile to intrude upon his concerns; after all, he had been a proper handful when he was a child. No doubt that was where his son had got it from. "Anyway . . . it was wrong and I am not a man that believes in using his hands whenever he feels like it. As you know I have rarely disciplined you in this way. I am sorry, John, truly sorry. You must understand that both your mother and I were still grieving over Sam . . . and we still grieve, John. It will never go away. But this grief . . . this terrible loss made me do things that were not in my heart. Things that were not me. I . . . er . . . ."

Talking about 'love' with his son wasn't easy, and for once Owen blessed his love of poetry. "I love you dearly, lad. I always have and I always will. Can you understand that?" John looked at his father and saw the struggle in his eyes. The contrition. He didn't know about death, how could he? He didn't know its horror, its permanent blight. But he did know that his father was sorry. He was also aware that there had indeed been moments in the past when he had felt that his father no longer loved him. But these had only been moments that had gone as quickly as they had arrived. Pa's and mams loved their children, didn't they? What else were they supposed to do? Bit by bit John was beginning to understand things. Death again and mossed-up gravestones. Well, the graveyard had never hurt him, so what was there to worry about? Sam hadn't meant to hurt either, of that he was certain. They had loved each other.

John didn't know what to say to his father. He had never seen him like this before. It was a shock. Fathers didn't apologise to sons after all, let alone talk about love. Growing up was becoming more and more complicated. At last John managed to speak.

"Don't be sad, pa. I know you love me. I know . . ." John found it hard to talk about love too. Like most things in his young life, love was a thing that he could take for granted. He had never tried to work it out. What was the point? It was always there and that was that. He couldn't imagine hating his mam and pa. He didn't really hate anyone, not even Horace Horace. He didn't know how to.

"Good, then there's no more to be said. Now shall we have that swim? Let's look for somewhere that's been receiving all the sunlight. It will be warmer. Come on now!"

After about ten minutes they found a spot just waiting for flailing arms and legs. They stripped naked and jumped into the water. Owen and his son wrestled, swam and played. The laughter between them exorcised Sam's ghost once and for all and confirmed a love that had always been strong, even though it had sometimes been dashed on uneven ground. Wounded and bloody, it had healed and come through. For the man this had brought peace and harmony, for the boy a gratitude that had only ever been slightly shaken.

After they split up, John swam slowly away on his own and made for the bank as he didn't have his father's stamina or his strength. Owen noticed his son in the corner of his eye and decided to follow him. He too was getting tired. As he pushed with his leg his ankle was suddenly caught by some weeds on the riverbed. He struggled to free it with his hands but was unable to get a grip. Without warning an acute and terrible pain gripped his chest. The breath was knocked out of him as he tried to shout, "John! John!" It was useless; his voice, like his body, refused to react properly. The pain had taken over everthing that he was and should have been. Owen tried one last plea for help, but the subtle tunes of the river, the whispers of a breeze, Owen's own weakness and the explosion in his chest forced his head beneath the water. As he sank, he struggled for breath, his mind fighting the agony that woudn't stop. It wanted to kill. It wanted to hear the last gasps of human breath. Owen fought its ruthless purpose. He fought and fought. He tried to shout, to scream, but water kept churning up his voice. The river threw him up for one last glimpse of life, one last cruelty. As Owen's eyes filled up with water for one last time he saw his son pulling himself up and out of the river. The boy was safe, thank God he was safe.

The weeds gave one last tug and finally had their way.

The vicar stood next to a deep brown hole, another pile of earth reminding him that his congregation was being seriously depleted yet again. It was a sign of the times. Even Prohibition in America had not stopped the wicked ways of Sodom and Gomorrah. Painted women, brash music, when would it all end? His flock was no different. Most of them preferred the sin of the public house to his church, and Owen Rees had been no exception.

The man had succumbed to the evils of drink many times, but thankfully the Lord had finally intervened – although on this occasion even the God-fearing vicar felt that His intervention had been a trifle intemperate. Owen Rees had signed the pledge a good while back after all. He did not quite merit the journey to Heaven this soon.

The serious expression of religion on the vicar's face didn't twitch as his black and white cassock confirmed his allegiance to both birth and death. In spite of this contradiction he managed his pastoral duties well enough, Faith was extremely versatile, and God even more so. At least He wasn't too fussy about who went into His soil or who was dabbed with His holy water. The vicar knew the Book of Revelation off by heart, so he wasn't really looking at the Bible as he confirmed the fact that dust always went to dust and ashes likewise. It was God's will and that's all there was to it, and this included the dust and ashes.

The vicar looked at the mourners for a moment and wondered what his wife had prepared for supper. It was a pity the good Lord hadn't 'intervened' where her cooking skills were concerned, God knows he had prayed hard enough for her deliverance. Satan himself roamed around her kitchen and cursed her cooker on a daily basis he was sure. He looked at the widow, Mrs Rees. The poor woman had suffered enough, now this. Fine looking woman too, not like his wife anyway. The vicar was surprised that his wife's taut and bitter jowls hadn't scared the Hell out of Satan years ago. What he wouldn't have done to get his hands on Mrs Rees's . . . ah well, blessed are the meek! Neither she nor her husband had been regular visitors to his church in recent years; in fact Owen Rees hadn't been seen at all. The boy had been a regular if agitating member of the church choir, yet even that had come to an end since his parents had allowed him to go on the stage. The stage of all things, the vicar briefly thought as he mumbled away at God and the mourners, not always sure if either were actually listening.

Mind you, His ears had accepted young John's departure into a world of debauchery and sin, so maybe it was just the Lord working in one of His mysterious ways again. He did have a habit of doing that – so mysterious in fact that sometimes even the vicar had no bloody idea what He was up to.

The vicar's cassock rustled as he concluded the service and watched the mourners grab a fistful of earth and throw it on the coffin lid. John followed his mam, but had no idea why he was being forced to throw a clump of soil in his father's face. If he had done that when his father was alive he would have been hammered into the following week, and rightly so. His mam pulled him away from the gaping hole and his curiosity. He had never been to a funeral before, not even his brother's. He managed to see a silver nameplate, but didn't even have time to read his father's name. He couldn't read his mam's face either, covered as it was with black lace, or see the tears that fell from her eyes as love tried to catch them. Neither did he notice her hand as it strayed across her stomach and stayed there.

"Look John, Issy is over there," Gwyneth tried to smile as she pointed, "by the church gate. Go and see him, but make sure you are not too long. No longer than half an hour, all right?" Death, she knew, was no place for youth. John didn't argue with his mother; even he knew when there were times to shut up. Yet he was glad to see Issy, so off he went, even though he knew deep down that his mother needed him. She had to, he was the man of the house now and there was a baby on the way. He wouldn't be long.

"Hello, Issy. What are you doing here then?" John asked as he walked up to his friend. "Not much fun here I can tell you. And the vicar hasn't forgotten my peashooter either. He was giving me the evil eye, at my pa's funeral too!" John managed to push a smile into his lips. Tears were certainly out of the question, particularly with his best friend standing in front of him.

"Come on, John," Issy said gently as he took his friend's arm, his eyes as always saying far more than his tongue. "Let's go for a walk. Get away from here for a while." A few minutes later they were standing by some old stables at the back of the churchyard. Issy rolled up two cigarettes and handed one to his friend, John hadn't quite mastered the art yet. "How are you feeling, John?" Issy asked with a degree of uncertainty as they both puffed away thoughtfully. He didn't know whether to say he was sorry for his friend's loss or simply act as if nothing had happened. "Horrible things, funerals. I've been to two. My grandparents."

"Oh, I'm alright thanks Issy. I know what you mean though. Seeing my pa down there in the mud – well . . . it was just . . . just . . . Don't know what to say, really. Still can't work out how it happened. He was fine one minute – you know we were only playing around in the river – and the next he was gone, caught up in some weeds or something, so my mam tells me anyway. Maybe I could have saved him, Issy. You see I'd left him Issy . . . left him." And then it happened. The days of sudden manhood collapsed. The realisation that death was forever, finally dawned. John cried. The tears fell unhindered as boyhood and innocence returned to release and liberate.

Issy's arms wanted to hold and comfort, but he paused. Friends didn't do things like that. Hugging and fussing was for girls and mothers. His arms seemed stuck to his sides, even though he wanted to move them in John's direction. He stared down at the grass, shuffling from one foot to the other. Where could his eyes go? Where could his friend's tears go?

At last friendship took over and Issy put his hand on John's shoulder. He said nothing. He let John cry and cry until his own compassion couldn't take any more. His arms finally lifted and he placed them around John. He would hold him for as long as he had to. He felt John's pain and for a moment wished he could take some of it away for himself. John, the joker, the buccaneer, was growing up just like him and now only tears stood between them. Issy felt for his friend, grieved with him, and knew more than ever before that he would always be there for him.

When John arrived back home his mam greeted him with eyes that were resigned and yet strong. He had already wondered how she would stand up to this sudden death, this sudden wound. He had seen his mam knock her head against a wall when Sam had died. He had heard her wails and seen her destruction. And yet she had come back. Back to him. Back to his father.

"Ah, John you're back. Good, doing what you are told for once. Now then go and ask our guests if they need anything more to drink or eat. Off you go now. I have things to do." Gwyneth disappeared into the kitchen, leaving John still coming to terms with parental loss and tragedy. He grunted to himself, braced his shoulders and went into the living room. All sorts of people were there, from the local butcher to the family solicitor. Black ties pulled stiff starched collars even tighter and female blackness restricted itself to dresses and skirts that fell to the ankles. Men talked with men, mainly about Owen Rees's fine boozing reputation and the profound tragedy it had been when he had signed the pledge – a great loss indeed to the community, never mind his demise. Women gossiped by themselves as usual; they had nothing in common with their men, not even death. Oddly there didn't seem to be much grieving going on. At least the low murmurs and quiet voices that John had expected seemed to be absent. Funerals were supposed to be all about tears and sad faces, weren't they?

One old crone who must have been around in the time of the pyramids sat slumped in one of the armchairs dribbling sherry and asking for more while releasing a barrage of stinking farts right in the vicar's direction. "Pass the tea, vicar," she had cackled after releasing one particularly loud expulsion of wind. Those not in the immediate firing line had had to turn away laughing, while others kept straight faces and continued to struggle with the sanctity of death. To make matters worse another shrivelled ancient of indeterminate years sitting next to the old woman had remarked romantically as he clicked and clacked his false teeth, "Oh my, Doris, you make me quiver with love when you fart like that . . ." – the old boy had paused for a moment before adding with a delicious smirk – "Well, maybe not, you'd blow my bloody teeth out!" This time the whole room had exploded with laughter. This was a Welsh funeral after all and humour was never too far away from the surface, albeit that Death still hovered around the room.

John continued to do as he was told and went around all the mourners asking them if they needed any more to drink or eat. Most refused the food but accepted the drink. At the end of the day three people were carried out, the solicitor was found asleep in the toilet and two people couldn't get home at all. They stayed the night and were allowed to sleep off the drink with a degree of dignity. This was only right and proper after all. The choirmaster Evan Evans excelled himself yet again, but this time it was not in front of a choir or a big band; he had been caught by the vicar's missus rogering the solicitor's wife against one of the walls of the house. Apparently Evans had tried to run for it, but had forgotten to pull up his trousers and ended up nursing a broken nose and damning all women to hell, skirts up or not. His looks were more important, not that the vicar's wife gave a damn, the ugly hatchet-faced sow, from North Wales too. Bloody typical!

All in all Owen Rees had been given a fine send off to eternity, and no doubt he would have been proud of his wife's efforts in seeing him on his way. John remained more confused about death than ever before, but he did know that wherever his father was, heaven or hell, the man had loved his son with all his heart.

CHAPTER 15

"You must go back, John. You must and that's the end of it. Now, no more arguments." Two weeks had passed since Owen's death and John was already a week late going back to the Songsters. It was at times like this that Gwyneth missed her man. Owen had always had more authority with the children than she. Mothers nurtured and loved, fathers detached themselves and disciplined. This arrangement usually worked well enough, but what happened when one of the parents died? John, a wilful child at the best of times, had never dared to defy his father. With Gwyneth however there were no such limits. Apart from anything else she had spoilt the boy since Samuel's death – and now she was paying for it. John would exploit her love whenever he had the chance.

"I'm not going back mam!" John shouted. "I'm the man of the house now. Who is going to look after you and the baby. I will need to find a job, bring some money in."

"You most certainly will not, John! You will do no such thing. You will go back to Steffani and you will finish your education. You will also sing until your voice . . . Well, until Steffani no longer needs you. I will not be responsible for depriving you of all the travel, all the singing. The excitement. I wish I had been given such a chance. Your father would turn in his grave if he thought that you were going into some menial job at your age. Besides, your father has taken care of us and I have some money too, so we'll not want for anything."

"I'm *not* going back and *that's* final, mam!" John stood before his mother red in the face, fists clenched and almost stamping his feet. The cat had disappeared out of the kitchen in fear of its life.

"Don't you defy me, John Rees! If your father was alive now he'd have his belt to you!"

"No he wouldn't! He never used a belt! Anyway he's *not* alive, so there – and *I* decide what I'm going to do with my life, not you!" That was it, Gwyneth finally snapped. She had had enough. She had lost a son, lost his father, was pregnant and now her brat of a son was being belligerent and disrespectful.

"Right! That's enough!" she shouted and slapped John hard across the face. Next thing she pushed him towards the kitchen door smacking his backside every inch of the way. "Now, get up to your room and don't you dare come out until I tell you to. You do not speak to me like that again – *ever*! Do you understand? *Do you*?!" This time John did as he was told. He had to, he was in a state of shock. His mam had never clobbered him like that before. Shit, it had hurt. His face stung and his arse ached. He sat on his bed and didn't move. So much for being the man of the house!

Gwyneth made herself a cup of tea and sat down at the kitchen table. She hated herself. Her hand hurt from the impact with her only son's body. She had never hit him like that before. Why did John have to be so difficult? Why? Couldn't he see that she was forcing him back for his own good? Nothing would make her happier than to keep him at home with her, but that would have been so selfish. It would also have betrayed Owen. She knew that John was only thinking of her, and in some ways she wanted to love him all the more for it – not that this was at all possible – but even so, he had the whole world at his feet. His future was more important than hers: of that she had no doubt. She knew best, not a fifteen-year-old who was still throwing tantrums.

Her hands gripped the teacup as her eyes concentrated on one or two tea leaves floating around on the surface of the tea. After a minute or so she looked around the kitchen. It had always been Owen's favourite room. She remembered how he had often sat at the table marking exercise books until the early

109

hours. He was still at the table even now. At least death could never kill off memories. His deep green eyes were still looking at her, loving her. In spite of Samuel's death, in spite of the drink she knew he had always loved her. It had never wavered. She remembered how his black hair used to shine underneath the light, how his face would look so intense as he read aloud some poetry from the trenches. Gwyneth heard her husband's ghost reading Wilfred Owen again,

> 'What candles may be held to speed them all?
> Not in the hands of boys, but in their eyes
> Shall shine the holy glimmers of good-byes.
> The pallor of girls' brows shall be their pall;
> Their flowers the tenderness of patient minds,
> And each slow dusk a drawing down of blinds.'

She had not yet had time to say a proper 'Goodbye' to her husband. The chaos of death and marbled words had taken up so much time. The child growing in her womb and John had monopolised her love, her care. She had not given Owen all the tears he deserved. She had not given him her love. Now as she sat alone and watched tea leaves dance and play her grief finally arrived. Owen was gone, and whatever was she going to do without him? How could she carry on without his strength? How could she live without his touch upon her face? How? At last she gave way to her own special heart and allowed torrents of tears to drive away her grief.

CHAPTER 16

The railway station was quiet. A long journey lay ahead of the two boys. Issy had stayed at home to keep his friend company. Sensitive to John's young grief Issy's mother had insisted that this be the case and no one argued with Rachel Kaddar, least of all Steffani. He could go and sing – literally! The two boys were heading for the Palace Theatre in Manchester. Steffani had told the boys' mothers to book them First Class tickets for which they would be duly reimbursed. For most boys of their age travelling First Class would have been the chance of a lifetime, but not for John and Issy. Since joining the choir they had become quite accustomed to this mode of travel. Steffani always insisted that the Songsters had the best, particularly his up-and-coming star singer.

John and his mother sat on a bench exchanging the odd word or two. John grunted while Gwyneth sighed with maternal resignation. He was still sulking about his mam's violence and domination, but knew there was nothing he could do about it. His mam was right after all; his pa would have turned in his grave if John had refused to go back. Still, he didn't see why he had to go back gracefully. His mam could suffer a bit and he knew exactly how to make her miserable. He could play his mam better than his own voice!

Issy eventually turned up with his mother and sister. It was turning into a hot July day so the mothers were dressed in light cottons and floppy hats. Issy's sister was a sight, better even than two weeks before when she had met them at the station. Once again John realised how much Issy's sister had grown up. He remembered immediately that last look in her eyes when they had been at the station. Sheyna was wearing a simple white cotton dress reaching modestly below her knees. The dress was given a touch of colour by her deep olive skin and a bright blue bonnet with a navy-blue silk ribbon. Her black hair fell about her shoulders like teams of wild black horses running out of control. For a moment John wondered again what was beneath the cotton dress but gave up on the idea. The girl really was a lovely sight. As soon as she saw him her face beamed a modest smile, and he was certain that it was all for him. For a brief and wonderful moment, he and Sheyna's blue eyes were all that existed on the platform.

She walked up to him and said, "Hello John, I'm so sorry about your father, I really am." John snapped out of yet another of life's mysteries and mumbled, "Thank you . . . er . . . Sheyna. Yes . . . thank you very much." He wanted to say something else but was totally lost for words. Sheyna saved him. "You must be looking forward to going back. I wish I could come, all that fun and music. Never mind. Maybe one day."

"Er . . . yes, maybe one day," John managed to mumble again, staring at his feet as he did so and wishing to all the Gods that he was wearing long trousers instead of the short buggers of boyhood. Sheyna seemed so grown up, the way she carried herself, the way she spoke was all so – well – womanly, and yet John had to pinch himself that he was actually older than her, by a year or so anyway. At their age a year was a life-time. Before he could say anything else a train steamed into the station and drowned out any further conversation. John's mam pulled him to her and hugged him. Saying 'Goodbye' to her son, particularly at this time, was hard if not impossible. She had to be strong, at least for Owen's sake. John at last gave in to his mother's love; he could never really be unkind to her. He hugged her back but avoided any silly kisses. Apart from anything else Sheyna was watching, and he was older and thus more grown up than her. He had to be. Rachel Kaddar ushered his friend onto the train as John followed. Before long doors

112

clicked shut as blue-clad guards waved green flags and tried to avoid blasts of steam blowing them into infinity. As whistles shrilled and ignored parental tears the train began to pull away, and the slow tap-tap of steel against steel wandered around the station as John tried to take one last look at his mam. As always his stomach lurched as a tear or two welled up in his eyes, but this time his eyes also struggled to take one last look at Sheyna Kaddar too.

A middle-aged man wearing a navy-blue suit and soft brown felt hat had been standing a few feet away from the Reeses and the Kaddars. There was a certain nonchalance about his demeanour, and yet his face betrayed a scarred understanding of love and its stubborn memories. His eyes seemed to absorb everything around him while at the same time exploring every nook and cranny of human frailty and endeavour. As the boys had boarded the train and said their farewells the man was reminded of other younger times in his own life. Times that were gentler and more innocent. He had noticed the young girl and boy, the intensity. He saw more than the parents and feared for their future.

CHAPTER 17

Two weeks later it was a hot August Monday in Manchester where the Songsters had been singing at The Palace. Issy stood in front of the stumps and concentrated. Cricket was a serious business, even if the stumps and bails had been chalked onto the theatre wall and the ball was a soft tennis ball pinched from one of the jugglers. Issy held the cricket bat in a tight grip as beads of perspiration peppered his forehead.

"Get on with it Jawbone, will you? Start bowling!" John shouted as he bent down ready to catch his friend out. The boy lining up to bowl – whose real name was the more kindly but no less amusing Michael Crapper – had been blessed with the beast of a jawbone. It jutted out so much that his bottom row of teeth protruded way beyond the upper row. He could sing though for all that. "If you don't stop messing about, Jawbone," John shouted again, "I'll tell Sideways not to give you any more bananas!" John then lowered his arms and swayed them from side to side while using his precious voice to imitate a chimpanzee. As he pranced around, the other boys including Issy started to laugh.

"Sod off Rees!" Jawbone yelled in his Geordie accent. "Now shut up, or else!"

"Or else what, Jawbone? Going to beat me to death with your jawbone are you?!" There was more laughter, but no one took the banter seriously, least of all Jawbone. He ignored the insults and threw the tennis ball straight at Issy who managed to block it and whack it straight back.

For some unknown reason Jawbone suddenly decided to change the Marylebone Cricket Club rules, so instead of catching the ball – which he did with admirable dexterity – and keeping it in his hands, he dropped it to the ground and kicked it right back at Issy. Unfortunately for the unlucky Jawbone, one of his shoes shot off his foot and went straight through a window as the tennis ball smashed through another.

'Christ!' Jawbone shrieked, 'that's buggered it!' All the boys, including Jawbone, dived for cover knowing that retribution would not be far away, but before any of them managed to hide and prepare their stories a voice boomed out from the stage door, "All of you stay where you are!! Don't any of you move!" It was Sideway. As he walked up to the five miscreants who had invented this new style of 'cricket' they all looked at their feet and tried to work out who or what to blame. Sneaking wasn't an option, as it would incur a retribution far worse than anything Sideway was likely to dish out.

"And whom, pray tell, is the budding Stanley Matthews?" Sideway asked, his lips lurching more violently to the side of his chin than usual, "although I doubt that even *he* could manage two windows in one kick." Silence. Sideway eyed each of the boys up and down; it was impossible to avoid the certainty of their guilt. "Honour amongst thieves and villains, eh?" Silence again. "Very well. The wages due to *all of you* will be duly deducted for repairs and there will be no more 'cricket', or for that matter 'football', for the rest of the month. Now away with you all, apart from you Rees . . . Oh and Crapper, do try and retrieve your shoe and apologise to anyone who may have been knocked on the head, or worse – killed!"

"Killed?" Crapper wailed and ran off as fast as his shoeless foot could carry him.

"Now then, young fellow," Sideway looked at John, "a word if I may." Look out, what was coming here? John immediately thought. Whenever Sideways wanted 'a word' it usually meant trouble. "You are to be . . . er . . . promoted as it were. Indeed, you are to be billed as 'Britain's Greatest Boy Soprano' at the the new Theatre Royal in Norwich next Saturday. Top of the bill too I hasten to add. A great honour for one so young."

"Pardon?" John muttered, not certain about what he was hearing.

"Young fellow, do you not understand plain English? . . . Ah wait, you being from the wild and barbaric Welsh Marches may have something to do with your lack of comprehension perhaps. Be that as it may. I repeat: Steffani – and I am mindful of his misguided wisdom – has decided to make you the star of the show as it were. Your wages I am instructed are to be increased to the princely sum of five pounds a week from next Saturday. Now before you start getting above yourself, three pounds of that will be sent home to your mother and you will keep two pounds for pocket money."

For the briefest of moments Sideway's face altered ever so slightly, the wrinkles actually creased into a semblance of softness and understanding. As far as he was concerned Death merely proved the fact that Life was a thoroughly futile and puny exercise in nauseating self-indulgence. However, the death of one's father, he had to admit, could be a troubling time and so demanded at least a modicum of sympathy, even when the recipient of this restrained 'sympathy' was young John Rees. "It is possible . . ." Sideway continued, "indeed – at least I suspect – that the income will be well received in light of your mother's . . . er . . . recent loss. I am further instructed to advise you *not* to divulge these financial details to anybody else. No one at all. Is that clear, Rees?"

"Yes, sir."

"Good, because should your sudden commercial good fortune be known to all I have every confidence that sedition and rebellion will result, and that really wouldn't do at all. You may or may not be aware that your comrades rarely if ever earn more than one guinea a week. And that's the best of them, so do restrain that magnificent voice of yours where your wages are concerned." As usual John had trouble understanding what Sideways was going on about, but he got the gist. At least he thought he did – he never quite knew with Sideways.

"Yes, sir. I will," John finally replied.

"Capital. Now, Steffani will be doing more extra practise with you over the next week, so keep out of trouble. He has a particular song he wants you to learn. Remember your debut as 'Britain's Greatest Boy Soprano' is on Saturday night at the Theatre Royal. If for any reason – and I mean *any* reason – you are unable to perform, Steffani will be an extremely unhappy man. He has invested a great deal of time and money in you and you would do well not to forget it. Now off you go back to your digs. I will see you later. Oh and be careful, some of the other boys . . . well . . . might feel a little . . . er . . . jealous, although somehow I do not believe that such a turbulent and petty example of human angst will cause you any undue anxiety." Shit! John thought, what was the daft bugger going on about now? Why couldn't he speak plain English? John thought he saw the beginnings of a smile appear on the troubled face of Sideways, but whatever it was it didn't last for long. Funny man, Bertram Sideway; always looked as if he'd just followed through on a fart.

"I will, sir. I will," John answered as Sideway walked away leaving him in yet another state of flux and bemusement. So that's what all the practise with Steff had been about over the past week, and there was more to come. 'Britain's Greatest Boy Soprano'! And all he had ever done was sing in a church choir, annoyed the shit out of the vicar and Evan Evans and fought just about every daft bugger in Steffani's 21 Silver Songsters!

His pa would have been proud of him!

CHAPTER 18

Later that day it was early evening when John told his friend the news.

"How much?!" Issy gasped as he actually tore his eyes away from the book he was reading, a biography of Bismarck, the 'Iron Chancellor' and one of Hitler's predecessors. Issy always had his head stuck inside a book. Reading was all very well, John thought, and certainly kept Sideway happy, but what he personally lost in intellectual acumen he made up for with animal cunning. Some of the stuff Issy read was beyond him, but by no means was he stupid; lazy and bone idle where schoolwork was concerned maybe, but never stupid. Even his long-suffering teachers would have agreed with this, including Sideway.

"Five pounds a week," John confirmed. The boys were sitting down on their beds. The bedroom was more or less like every other bedroom in every other lodging house across the country: clean, simply furnished and comfortable, but not like home at all. Apparently their digs were always the best money could buy – according to Sideway anyway and the boys had no reason to argue, the grub was always good they had to admit – and sometimes they even stayed in posh hotels. The hotels were always much better though. More exciting, more people, more chances for mischief.

"You're not telling me fibs now John, are you?" Issy questioned. "You know what you're like."

"I'm telling you Issy, Steff's paying me five quid a week and I'm to be top of the bill next Saturday when we sing in Norwich. Doing a solo, but don't know what yet, Steff hasn't told me. Three quid to my mam mind, but that doesn't bother me, my mam could have the lot for all I care."

"Well, well. Good for you John, I mean it, I really do. 'Britain's Greatest Boy Soprano', eh? Britain's Greatest Bugger more like!" Both boys laughed. Issy didn't often use bad language, but when he did it was usually appropriate. "And top of the bill John, too. Whatever next?"

John looked at his friend. He knew he was under orders to keep his wages secret, but Issy was his best friend and secrets didn't count amongst best friends. Issy was genuinely happy for him. Sideway had mentioned 'Jealousy' but John had known that Issy would never be jealous and he had been right. The smile on Issy's face was sincere and hard to ignore.

"You know, Issy," John said quietly when their laughter had died down. "I wish we could both have been up there topping the bill; you and me, two of the greatest boy sopranos in the land. That would have been much better. I am sorry, Issy, that Steff has kept you in the chorus . . ."

"Now, John. Don't be silly, will you? You've got a better voice than me, always have had. Anyway, you're not good at everything. You're no good at cricket – or football for that matter. You're always losing your temper or annoying the other players!"

Issy was in no doubt that John's long face and sudden seriousness indicated his displeasure at being the only choice for a solo performance. John was rarely sullen, and if he was there was usually a good reason. "Come on, John. You deserve everything you get. You've got a wonderful voice, so stop being so miserable. Besides, what difference does it make? Neither of us will be singing soprano for the rest of our lives, so stop being so stupid. My voice will be the first to go too. I'm older than you by a few months, don't forget. Now, just get up on that stage and give them your best."

"Yes, you're right there," John replied more cheerfully. "Our voices will break sometime or another, so Steff keeps telling me anyway. Not sure what breaking voices are all about though, Issy."

"Something to do with becoming a man I think."

"Oh, is that right? So when do girls become women then? When they get titties I suppose."

"Could be, but I'm not sure exactly."

"Not sure, Issy? I don't believe it!" John was really starting to perk up now. He was never downcast for long. "There's actually something you don't know! Well, bugger me, I must put that in a letter to my mam!"

"Very funny, John. Now, how about some good old fish and chips? You can pay, you're rich now anyway!" As soon as fish and chips were mentioned John brightened up even more. They probably wouldn't be as good as Johnson's back home, but you couldn't have everything in one day, could you?

"Good idea, Issy. The landlady here's a bit mean with the chips and Sideways is out, so his evil eye isn't watching our every move."

"Come on then, let's go." Issy pulled John up from the bed, glad that his friend was back to his normal self. He didn't like it when John got all thoughtful and serious – he had enough of both for the pair of them!

CHAPTER 19

The following Saturday night the theatre was full to the brim. People of all shapes and sizes squeezed into red velvet seats and craned their necks to achieve the best view. Elevated boxes allowed the toffs to take their time and observe the lower orders at play. Everyone had made an effort with their dress. Men were covered in their Sunday Best suits and glistening with hair oil, while women purred and tempted with loud make-up and extravagant boas. Bright colours of all descriptions waiting to be amazed and entertained bobbed along the aisles past young, sequined and near naked women standing with trays in front of their waists piled high with matches, cigarettes, sweets and chocolates. Men leered and dribbled, pinched and prodded, but eventually sat back and waited for the fun to begin. Saturday night at the theatre was always a night to remember, particularly when the dancing girls leapt around the stage and bare legs reached up to the heavens and down again.

John and Issy were waiting in the wings. The Songsters were the closing act and John's solo the very last act of the evening. "Not long now, John. Are you nervous?" Issy asked as he stood next to his friend.

"I'm shitting myself, Issy."

"Don't be stupid."

"I'm telling you! I think I've shat myself – filled my pants. Have a look will you? Steff will go berserk." With that John bent down to allow Issy to give his white shorts a thorough examination.

"Oh, what next John?" Issy moaned as he peered at his friend's arse. "No. Sorry to disappoint. Not a brown stain in sight. Anyway, what's the matter with you? You're the last person I thought would be nervous. You love attention."

"Not the attention of hundreds of people I don't. Suppose I mess things up? Can you imagine it? Don't mind making a fool of myself in front of a few people, but have you seen the crowd out there, Issy? Jesu, they've already booed one daft bugger off the stage. That fire eater. Set his hair on fire – not that they cared out there. Jumped around like a bloody firecracker he did. The crowd thought it was all part of his act at first and started laughing, until they realised it was for real. I'm telling you, they're a mean lot tonight."

"No, missed that. Bet it was funny though. Is the man all right? I mean, can't be funny burning all your hair off, can it?"

"Don't ask me. Last I saw he was being taken out on a stretcher. I'll be next. Passed out from stage fright."

"You'll be great, John. Now stop worrying. Let's enjoy the other acts for a bit and take your mind off things."

Like all the other Songsters they were both wearing white sailor suits with blue piping, short white socks and black patent leather shoes. Their trousers only went as far as their knees, but Steff had refused to clothe the boys in the longer variety. They wouldn't be *boy* sopranos if he had allowed that, would they?

John's stomach continued to gurgle and leap as they watched magicians, tap dancers, illusionists, chorus girls and comedians all trying hard to earn a few paltry shillings. For the majority of performers variety was a hard place to be and a good supper not always certain. At long last it was turn of the the 21 Silver Songsters. They lined up on the stage and waited for Steffani to give them their cue. He was wearing evening dress and sat at a white grand piano. As usual his long nose sniffed and explored as it looked for any possible mistakes in the line up, any dull patent leather or any boy about to do something wrong – like the boy who stood behind the other boys picking his nose.

"Here you, Ceri Cant," (he couldn't either, not when he was picking his nose anyway and he was Welsh, as if one in the choir wasn't enough!) Steffani had hissed, "carry on picking your nose like that and your stupid *Taffy* head will cave in!" All the boys knew that when on stage Steffani was king and not to be trifled with. Any pranks were strictly off limits. Steffani looked at the boys when they were finally settled, nodded his head and began playing. The Songsters sang 'Tales From The Vienna Woods', 'The Blue Danube', Schubert's 'Serenade' and and Dvořák's 'Humoresque'.

When they had finished and the applause had died down Steffani stood up from the piano and walked over to the microphone that stood in front of the stage. His black tails gave his voice an elegant radiance as it echoed around the theatre. "Ladies and gentlemen, thank you for your kind applause. I would now like to introduce a boy with the most wonderful coloratura soprano voice that you are ever likely to hear in this lifetime, or indeed the next. Tonight is his debut, and I assure you that you will not be disappointed. Ladies and gentlemen, please sit back and welcome Illtyd John Rees from Llantwit Major in South Wales, who is I believe the greatest boy soprano now living in Great Britain!" Steffani stood back, held out his arm and ushered John up to the front of the stage. "Ladies and gentlemen, I give you, Master Illtyd John Rees . . .!"

Nerves spiked John's feet as he walked up to the front of the stage and hoped all that practise with Steff had not been wasted. This was the first time he had ever performed solo in front of such a huge audience. Steff had trained him in the song he was about to sing, but all the training in the world could not prepare him for this awesome spectacle – and he was the spectacle! When Steff had first tried to teach him the song he had complained bitterly, "I can't go that high, Steff. I can't!" All Steff had said was, "You can and you damn well will!" Eventually he could, but right now he was not so sure. His vocal chords were being demolished by stage fright. The stage lights cut out the audience, but they were out there – Jesu, they were out there. For a split second he wanted to cry and yell out for his mam. Where was her warm bosom in his hour of need! What if his voice refused to perform? What if it didn't answer the call. Oh shit, what had he done to allow himself to be tortured like this? Oh help me God!

There was a sudden silence in the theatre, irritable feet stopped shuffling, cigarettes were thrown on the floor and crushed by impatient shoes and all eyes concentrated on the small young sailor boy perched at the front of the stage. He was made even smaller by the waves of red satin drapes that hung from the ceiling behind him. John stood in front of the microphone and waited. His voice had to answer the call. It had to. Steffani played an introduction and then nodded at John who braced himself, breathed in as he had been taught and started to sing Bishop's 'Lo! Hear the Gentle Lark'. No boy soprano had ever sung this song before, since hitting E above top C was only ever achieved by female sopranos. John's prayers were answered as his voice cast its spells and touched the audience with fingers softer than the air itself. Spines tingled up and down and tears welled as the beauty in his voice weaved and spun, waltzed and pirouetted. There were those in the audience who were forced to remember past loves and recently broken hearts as fingers touched and eyes saw more than the young boy in front of the microphone. He enthralled and silenced the irritable and shuffling shoes and he subdued even the whispered gossip of hair-netted street-corner chatterers. People could only stare and swallow as their eyes refused to leave the boy whose voice floated, pounced and captured. It had been a long time since the audience had witnessed such innocent joy and purity, a long time since a Saturday night had felt so profound.

When he had had finished the *"Encores!"* and *"Bravos!"* nearly threw the roof of the theatre up into God's lap and later in the evening Gracie Fields came into the boys' dressing room with a cake and asking for "The boy with a beautiful voice."

John's voice had answered the call.

Later that night and after the trauma of singing solo Issy and John were enjoying the company of Ken 'Snakehips' Johnson and some members of his West Indian Orchestra

"Hey, man. That was one almighty piece o' song there!" Snakehips enthused." Where d'you learn to sing like that, eh?" Snakehips was always impressed by good music, whitey or nigger; mind you, nigger usually came out on top. Before John could answer – although he didn't think that singing in a church choir would go down too well with the sambos – Snakehips flashed his blinding white teeth and beamed, "A little celebration is called for, yes? You smoke? Of course you do, who doesn't?" Snakehips' six-foot four-inch frame towered above the boys and seemed to pour all over them. Every joint and bone in the man's body enjoyed a fluidity and flexibility of movement that would indeed have made even the most venomous of snakes slither away in shame.

Issy and John looked at each other. Where was Sideways? Or worse, Steff? Nowhere to be seen, so it would be all right for them to enjoy a bit of adult baccy. Snakehips took a pull on what appeared to be a cross between a cigar and a cigarette, at least in size anyway. "Here we are, brothers. Have a drag and hear the birds sing sweeter than any nightingale!" Snakehips passed the 'cigarette' to Issy who took a long pull and then passed it to John, coughing as he did so. "Phew, Snakehips, that's strong stuff! Wherever did you get it?" Snakehips threw a friendly arm around Issy's shoulders.

"From the good Lord above, brother. That's where. Comes right out o' paradise iself. Nectar brother, pure nectar." John passed the 'cigarette' back to Issy, who couldn't seem to get his hands on it fast enough. "Great tobacco this, John, don't you think? Not as strong as my father's. Smoother altogether."

"Yes, much smoother," John replied like the true professional he was and reaching for another turn on the 'nectar'.

Fifteen minutes later both boys were flat out on some stage props. Their legs had gone and so had their voices, apart from the occasional giggle that is. Sideway and some of the Songsters had eventually managed to carry them back to their digs without Steffani knowing, luckily for them and much to the amusement of Snakehips and his West Indian compatriots. They may have been able to play the odd tune, but they also sure as hell knew how to smoke!

CHAPTER 20

The following morning Issy and John woke up with what can only be described as their first real hangover. Heads crammed with the perforating echoes of jangling steel bands and dancing sambos with massive cigarettes hanging out of their mouths were the first recollections of the night before to thump into their brains. Issy for once was the first one out of bed.

"What happened, John? All I can remember is puffing on a big cigarette. If tobacco can make you feel like this, then what the hell can strong drink do? I feel terrible."

John just about managed to slowly raise his head from the pillow.

"I don't know, Issy. Must have been the fags . . . Never thought baccy could affect you like that though. How did we get home? I don't remember anything?"

"Neither do I and I feel so sick. What about you?"

"Me too . . . oh . . . oh!" John leapt out of bed and made a dash for the bedroom door. "Oh Jesu, I'm going to be sick!" he yelled as he ran into the corridor. One look at John and Issy, ever the natural harmoniser, shrieked, "Wait for me! – Oh God, my arse is about to explode!" He ran after his friend, gripping his backside for dear life as he did so. "Oh God! Oh God!" Issy shrieked again as a barrage of squelchy wind propelled him on his way. There was only one toilet on the corridor as the two boys soon found out and friendship flew out of the nearest window.

"I was first, Issy, now bugger off!" John managed to squeal just before wrenching open the toilet door and letting rip a torrent of last night's supper all over an unsuspecting Sideway who was sitting on the toilet at peace with the world and enjoying a nice quiet read of the *Sunday Times*.

"Good Heavens—!" Sideway shouted, leaping up with shock and in mid bowel movement. "Oh my word!" he blurted out, "What *are* you *doing*, you wretched boy, you . . .?! Look at me! *Look at me*! You villain! You brute!" Sideway was covered in puke from head to toe and his rear end was in an even worse state of disrepair. As teacher and pupil stared at each other speechless, Issy, his trousers at half mast, barged passed both of them, threw himself onto the toilet seat and promptly blasted hell out of the pan.

"Oh God . . . God!" Issy managed to whimper as his bowels whined and ricochetted him onto another planet.

Sundays were always quiet. God didn't like entertainment on Sundays, or any other time for that matter as far as the two boys were concerned. After their debacle with Sideways they hadn't been allowed out until lunchtime. In fact lunchtime was their limit for the next week, but so far Steff hadn't got wind of their misdemeanours; if that happened then God help them.

Sideways wasn't so bad really the boys decided as they walked into Norwich on their way to the Cathedral. He hadn't sneaked on them, but to be fair he never did. Going to the Cathedral to repent had seemed like a good idea earlier on. Besides, according to John, there was nothing else to do, he being an expert on all Cathedral cities of course. As they walked through what had once been an old Anglo-Saxon market place called Tombland and then into the medieval Cathedral precincts Issy told John how the Cathedral was about nine hundred years old and had possessed one of the tallest spires in England, second only to Salisbury Cathedral. Issy also told him that for some unknown reason the Cathedral didn't do a ring of bells.

"What! No bells, Issy! A church without bells! It can't be a proper church if it doesn't ring any bells. Don't be stupid. How do you know all this anyway? Got it out of one your books, did you?"

"No, actually I read the information plaque thing at the entrance while you were searching for another toilet – *again*!"

"Ah, shut up will you. You weren't much better this morning. How are your pants by the way? Clean and up to Sideway's standard are they?"

"Very funny . . ." Issy chuckled. "Well, more shit comes out of your mouth than my back passage, and that's a fact, John." When it came to a witty retort he was usually faster than John.

"Oh shut up, smarty pants – or should I say shitty pants," John replied, for once quicker than his friend. Issy always got the better of him when it came down to words; it was all those books again. Normally he would have laughed along with his friend, but his stomach was still bad in spite of the dubious concoctions Sideway had made them drink. "Anyway, good job Sideways didn't dump us in it, Issy, doesn't bear thinking about. Steff would have been so angry. You know what he's like about baccy and singing. Dread to think. Hellish stuff that baccy though, wouldn't mind some more given half a chance."

"More, John! Are you mad? More? My stomach is still rolling from last night, not to mention my head."

"Oh I know, but it didn't half make me feel good – at the time anyway. I felt bloody marvellous after that first puff. Grand!"

"Yes, you're right there," Issy had to admit, "made me feel all relaxed too. Still I don't want to feel like this again thank you, and neither do you."

"No, Issy. I suppose you're right, and imagine if Steff had found out? We'd both be packed off home to Wales in a trice. No, no more baccy for a while Issy, you're quite right."

"Good, glad to see you're seeing a bit of sense for once. Now then come on, let's go and explore a bit. I love history and old buildings."

"I don't, but there's nothing better to do I suppose. God seems to be all over the place, though I bet he's not too happy with us at the moment. It's all a bit creepy around here if you ask me. Can't we go and walk down by the river? I bet He's not down there."

"Oh don't be silly, John. Besides, God loves a sinner according to you Christians anyway, so stop moaning. Come on, let's go and learn something apart from boring songs." John followed his friend for the rest of the morning. Romanesque architecture, North Transepts, colourful roof bosses that looked too serious for their own good, flint, mortar, limestone brought from Caen, cloisters and ancient monasteries all meant nothing to John, but he could see the delight in his friend's eyes and didn't have the heart to spoil his day.

As they were walking out of one of the entrances and back into Tombland Issy stopped right in his tracks and pulled John's arm making him do the same.

"What? What's the matter with you?" John asked, a note of panic in his voice. "You look as if you've seen a ghost!"

"Look, John! . . . Look at her. She's so beautiful."

"What? Who? Where?"

"The girl walking towards us, that one in the red skirt and hat. Have you ever seen a girl look so pretty? Look at her face, her blond curls." John's eyes followed Issy's and eventually he saw what all the fuss was about. Two girls were walking towards them arm in arm, the girl with the blond curls dressed in a pleated red skirt and white blouse. She was giggling as a breeze tried to blow her red hat off. His mam wore pins to stop that kind of thing John thought for a moment, so why wasn't the girl doing the same? As the girls drew closer the one wearing the hat saw Issy and walked straight up to him. John had to agree she really was a picture.

"Well, well, if it isn't Mr Clumsy. What are you doing in Norwich? Are you following me or something?" She remembered Issy from London, even though as far as Issy was concerned it had been a lifetime ago. He had never thought he would see her again. Her eyes smashed into Issy's face making him look down at the ground as embarrassment demolished him. "Haven't you got a tongue then? Come on, don't be shy. I'm Charity Like, and this is my friend Cynthia. And you are . . .?" Issy at last

130

managed to pull his eyes away from his shoes, but he still couldn't manage to look this Venus in the eyes.

"Er . . . hello again . . . um, Charity. My name is Issy and this is my friend John." Charity stood back from the two boys and allowed her startling green eyes to examine them up and down. She concentrated on John for a moment, "Aren't you the boy who sang that lovely song last night?" John was not too happy about being called a 'boy', at least when girls were around and the expression on his face showed it.

"Yes, that's me," John replied. Like his friend he tried to avoid the intensity of Charity's green eyes, she really was a cracker. Her friend was pretty too, but she didn't seem to smile much. Everything about Charity smiled. Her whole face, her body, everything.

"You have a lovely voice, I must say," Charity continued while her friend looked this way and that as she ignored the boys. "Where are you both from then?" she asked. John was the first to speak, as usual.

"I'm from Llantwit Major and Issy here is from Berlin. Well, he was from Berlin, but now he now lives up the road from me in Llantwit."

"Where's Llantwit Major for heaven's sake?" Charity enquired with an amused expression on her face as she looked at John. "Not something to do with the army is it? You're Welsh too, aren't you? Must be with an accent like that. You must be from the valleys then. Is your dad a miner? Do you bathe in one of those tin bath things? You look quite clean to me." This time John was able to look the girl in the eyes – well, at the cheeks below them anyway.

"Well, you have a funny accent too and no, I'm not from the valleys and no we don't use a tin bath. And before you ask, I don't go to bed with sheep at night either." He still didn't know what this English obsession with sheep and Welshmen was all about, although it sounded funny for all that.

Charity laughed at John's joke, so maybe she knew more than he did although her friend continued to look bored and

131

disinterested. Issy listened to the conversation and continued to do a good scuffing job on the ends of his shoes. Charity's attention moved away from John and concentrated on Issy.

"You are a quiet one, aren't you? You don't say much at all. Are you a singer too?"

"Yes, I'm one of the Songsters. I sing in the choir." There was something about this boy from Berlin that caught Charity's interest.

"If you're from Berlin, how did you end up over here then? Not something to do with Mr Hitler, is it?" Issy finally plucked up the courage to look Charity Like directly in the eyes.

"Something like that."

Charity persisted. "'Something like that?' You can sing but you can't talk. How very odd."

"I can talk if you don't mind, but only if there is something worth saying."

Charity looked sharply at him. "Ooops – all right then . . . Issy." She paused for a moment. Her pretty good looks were not having much of an effect on this one. There was a superior air about him, although his face seemed to contradict this immediate impression, any severity was tempered by the humour and kindness around his lips and blue eyes. He also exuded a definite warmth that was really quite compelling – for a moment anyway. "How old are you, then . . . Issy?" Charity was not about to give up on this odd boy from Berlin. He was different somehow, not like the normal 'variety' type. "Funny name that too, 'Issy'."

"It's short for Israel—"

"Israel? You must be a Jew then?"

"Yes. I am Jewish. And if you stop interrupting me I'll tell you how old I am."

"Oops again . . . sorry. Aren't you the touchy one!" Charity smiled and Issy nearly fell over – again.

"I'm fifteen – well, sixteen in three months time. John here is three months younger." It was John's turn to interrupt as he stuck his head in between his friend and the girl. Issy seemed to be stealing the show and that wouldn't do at all.

"We're really the same age," John said as he looked at his friend. "Issy here always gets it wrong. Anyway, where are you from? And how old are you?"

"Too old for you boys," Charity giggled. She was about one year older than Issy, but at their age a year could span several lifetimes – more so if the older party was a girl. "Look at you," she continued to tease, "you're both still in short trousers and not a whisker in sight!" Before either of the boys could voice their objections the sourpuss friend finally said something.

"Come on Charity, we haven't come out to play with these two 'children'. Let's go." The cruel edge to the girl's words cut through both boys.

"All right, all right Cynthia, I'm coming." As Charity walked away she looked at Issy and John. Her eyes seemed to say, 'I'm sorry'. Before turning a corner and being lost forever she shouted, "By the way, I'm from Birmingham and I'm one of the chorus girls! We'll chat again when you've grown some whiskers!"

CHAPTER 21

While John and Issy were beginning to learn something about the capriciousness of young love, Rachel Kaddar sat on an old bench and listened while Debussy stretched across the village green and stirred her memories, pushing them backwards and forwards. For a while she lost herself in the music, her mind flowing along with a beauty that both distracted and provoked unhappy moments and feelings intertwined with regrets that could find no home. A distant tractor stopped growling, birds remained in their nests and dogs refused to bark as the pianist played. A distant church clock chimed the hour, but even this intrusion went unnoticed as the pianist seemed to dominate both machinery and nature itself. His fingertips caressed and loved; the music was everything that the pianist could ever hope for. He was happy in his own world, in his own way. No one could touch or hurt him.

Eventually the music stopped and Rachel's mind went back to where it had been before she sat down. Ezra had gone to London for a few days on business and taken Sheyna with him. Rachel actually had some time to herself for a change and she intended to take full advantage of the fact. It had been such a long time in more ways than one. Their daughter was growing up, and in Ezra's view she needed to be taught some culture and independence. The suffragettes had won their war and quite right too, but of course this didn't count where Rachel was concerned. Hers was still to love and obey, and who was she to disabuse him? Perish the thought! It was definitely a lawyer or a doctor for his daughter, but for his wife . . .? Well, cooking and kitchen sinks were the order of the day.

Naturally Rachel took little if any notice of her husband's delusions and continued to do exactly as she pleased. She humoured and pampered when required while keeping a firm hand on the reigns, even though Ezra still fooled himself that he was master of all he surveyed. Rachel had not been created to be the docile toy of any man. She knew how and when to plume her feathers and when to indulge her coquettish arts. She ran the family unit in her own way to ensure efficiency and calm in the household. She knew when to deceive and when to comply. Rachel was all woman, and even her own husband wouldn't contest this inalienable fact – though sometimes he was not quite sure what it actually meant.

Rachel continued sitting on the bench even though the music had stopped. She didn't want to go anywhere. She had arrived at her intended destination and for now that was enough. She had come to this small village in West Sussex only to look at a distance and hopefully to listen. Debussy had confirmed her hopes, but she had yet to actually see. She was forty-five now and her husband ten years older.

So much had happened in her life over the years. She hadn't married until her late twenties. For some, being unattached at such a mature milestone in life could only mean a future of empty, childless shelves, a bitter spinsterhood or 'unnatural' lesbian friendships. Her striking beauty and formidable personality had caused even greater confusion for the lies and distortions of 1930s propriety. Many a suitor had tried to win her hand, but her independence and absolute faith in a perfect love had restrained any easy surrender to a comfortable and secure substitute.

For Rachel love had to consume and overwhelm; anything less was unacceptable. Her stringent conditions on matters of the heart had finally paid off when the Visiting Professor of European History, Ezra Kaddar, had walked into her office at King's College, London. His erudite voice and refined aura had won her heart even before he had spoken one word to her. He

135

had asked her to type some papers he had been writing on one of the more esoteric controversies of Habsburg and Bourbon Europe. For the first time in her life she had fumbled with the papers he had handed to her and had even been a little lost for words. All she had been able to do was stare at his eyes and mumble. Embarrassment had collided with her normal diffidence on a grand scale. How dare he!

Ezra of course didn't notice a thing, being far too besotted with the Habsburgs and Bourbons. All this changed though as Rachel bullied, bossed and forced her victim to love her. As it turned out this hadn't been too difficult a task. Ezra had willingly finished his love affairs with Miss Habsburg and Miss Bourbon and complied with a love that was just too wonderful to ignore.

Rachel smiled as she remembered their courting, her conniving and her determination to have her way. That had been sixteen years ago now and they still loved each other just as much if not more so. There were times when Ezra had his own way, but sometimes – and these times were extremely rare she had to admit – she was none too sure who was doing the humouring. This thought was quickly banished from her mind as the piano started to play again.

It was a Chopin Nocturne. If Debussy had forced her to reflect in spite of the pain, Chopin brought a deep inconsolable sadness and regret. The composer gave life to an uncertain memory, to the reason why she was here. She wanted to knock on the cottage door that was home to the pianist, she wanted so desperately to look at him closely, but knew she must not. So many years, so much love. A simple knock could destroy so much. Tears began to fall from her eyes as she despaired and tried so hard to reconcile the unknown.

Suddenly the piano stopped playing Chopin and launched into a different piece of music. This piece was brutal, even vicious, and yet it was infused with a strange benevolent passion. Rachel had never heard it before. For a while she listened and tried to comprehend. Eventually she stood up and walked back to the railway station, unable to bear the beauty any longer. Her perfect love continued to overwhelm. And hurt so profoundly.

The pianist stopped playing when Rachel started to walk back to the station. On occasions Chopin and Debussy could be an indulgent diversion, but they rarely answered all the questions. He did not know why his fingers suddenly stopped moving – sometimes they really did seem to have a will of their own – and his eyelids fluttered with unease.

Then he sensed he was being watched. There was someone in the vicinity. Not in the room, he was sure of that, but close by. Although he had no idea who they might be, he knew they were there and that they meant him no harm.

He just knew

He stood up and walked towards the window. He needed to feel closer, he needed to sense. As he stood before the window he allowed his eyes to look out straight across the village green, urging his senses to feel and observe. They rarely let him down. Nothing again. He turned around and traced the top of a table with his fingertips. His steps were cautious as his fingers became his eyes. His feet moved slowly, as although he knew where everything was sometimes the char woman would inadvertently rearrange things. He sat back at the piano and decided that perhaps it was just his imagination. Sometimes he thought he heard or felt things that simply were not there.

He sat motionless for a few moments then started to play his own composition again. The darkness had been with him all his life, but the piano always brought him a bright and clear internal light. Loneliness – or was it just that he was alone? – never disturbed his dark world.

CHAPTER 22

While Rachel was looking back and trying to loosen her grip on the past, Ezra was sliding his arm around his daughter's waist. "Look Sheyna," he said quietly, "look at the colours – quite dazzling. See how exultant the painting is. Ulysses has won. You can hear the wails of Polyphemus, can't you? You can hear the taunting of Ulysses. Look at the sunrise to the right, the bright colours, the thickness of paint. The magic. You see Sheyna, art is the only thing that distinguishes us from the animals, although some men would corrupt and destroy even this."

Sheyna listened to her father as she always did. She recognised the sublime beauty before her eyes, and for a few moments even her father's words failed to impinge on the vision of perfect drama.

"Yes, daddy. I see. The painting is so . . . well, I can't take my eyes off it. It almost seems to touch me. It's so alive."

"Exactly, child. That's its genius." Ezra looked at his daughter. Her long black hair, clear unblemished skin and eyes that could have challenged even Turner made him fearful and sad. His little girl was turning into a woman. Never again could there be the dependence, the unquestioning love. The innocence. "Never forget that even in a cruel world, Sheyna, there are still some things that can rise above man's contempt for his own species. God willing, light will always prevail over darkness. We can only hope, Shenya. We must never lose that hope. Now, come. It's nearly time to meet your brother, and let's see if we can manage a little treat for my only daughter. You can have what you like now that your mother is out of the way. But don't tell her I've been spoiling you or she'll start beating me about the head!"

138

"Don't be silly, daddy," Sheyna laughed. "Issy is the only one she ever beats about the head, and even that has never hurt him. Mind you, he's getting a bit big now so she had better watch out."

"So are you, my daughter," Ezra said as her budding womanhood disturbed him once again. "So are you." They walked from the National Gallery to one of the Lyon's Tea Rooms at Piccadilly. The excitement and chaos of London's West End reminded Sheyna of Turner's picture. There really wasn't much difference between the blinding of the one-eyed Cyclops and the rush to be somewhere as soon as possible. People seemed to dash from place to place as quickly as the red-cloaked Ulysses began his retreat from certain death and revenge. Why were people in such a hurry? Sheyna wondered. Well, she would take her time over some tea and cake no matter what everyone else did.

When they were seated at a table all Sheyna could do was wonder yet again at all the activity. Cutlery and china scraped and scratched while waiters and waitresses avoided a tea-soaked disaster by crashing into one another. She had been used to Berlin, but living in a rural environment had made her accustomed to a more retiring lifestyle. She had adapted quickly to her new life in Wales. The young were never old enough to become too attached to one place, but there had still been times when she had yearned for the cosmopolitan activity of a big city. Now though she was not so sure she ever wanted to go back to it again. Cities seemed to boil with potential violence amidst the dirt and an unpredictable wasteland of human immorality. Loneliness and disillusion lurked on every street and in every torrid corner. Faces deceived, words denied and nothing was ever what it seemed. Cities frightened, their ugly mystery supreme.

A huge portion of melliferous *apfelstrudel* sat on a plate in front of Sheyna and made her tongue tingle. It was not the same as her mother's, whose pastry was so thin you could see right through it. All the same, the sweet apples, raisins and currants made her jaw ache. She was about to start eating when Ezra stood up from the table and said, "Ah! Your brother has arrived!"

Sheyna followed her father's eyes and saw Issy walking towards them. His friend John was walking behind him. For a moment she saw nothing of Issy as John's golden red hair caught the light which somehow seemed to lift him above the general melange. All of a sudden the apples and cinnamon didn't seem so appetising as her stomach jumped in all the wrong directions. Issy arrived at the table and shook his father's hand as he leaned over and kissed Sheya on the cheek.

"Hello, father. Sheyna. You don't mind if John joins us, do you?" Issy asked. Ezra immediately noticed how grown up his son was. The boy was more confident, certain of himself. The stage was teaching him more than any book, Ezra had to reluctantly admit.

"Of course not!" Ezra smiled.

"Couldn't leave him behind father, because he sulks if he's ever left out of anything."

"Not at all. Now come on the pair of you, sit down and have some tea. Would you like to order some cake?" John was the first to answer; he usually was when there was any cake on the menu.

"Oh, yes please." He grinned, having already noticed all the cakes and sweet things on offer as he had walked in. He hadn't noticed the terrifying redness that had suddenly erupted on Sheyna's cheeks though. No one had. In fact no one had taken much notice of her at all.

"Well boys, what have you been up to then? Aren't we fortunate, Sheyna, that the boys are singing in London this weekend? We will be going to see them tonight. A special treat. It's such a pity your mother can't be here." It wasn't at all. Ezra had conspired to meet Issy all on his own, but more than that he had wanted to spend some time alone with his only daughter. He loved her so much, and yet they rarely spent any time together alone. For once Rachel wasn't ordering everyone around; he didn't want to think of the fireball that would start rolling once his shiftiness was discovered. He smiled to himself. Rachel the Warrior will experience another of her apoplectic fits when she finds out. She didn't 'sulk' when she was left out of something, she exploded. Ezra couldn't help but smile to himself again at the thought. They would both enjoy sending themselves to sleep that night though, just as they always did after a bout of Rachel's intemperance.

The chatter at their table competed with all the other chatter that whinnied and winked around them. Sheyna stayed modestly silent, but her eyes never left the handsome face of the golden-haired Welshman. And in her eyes he was a 'man'. His face had changed in the year or so she had known him. Although these changes might not have been noticed by anyone else, the year had reduced John's puppy fat and callowness of childhood. The cut of jaw and chin were gradually becoming more pointed and distinct. His eyes were turning a deeper shade of green too, and seemed to hold more wisdom than they were prepared to divulge.

Sheyna had no idea why he had this effect on her. From the first time she had set eyes on him there had been something so demanding in his eyes. Even then she had been unable to withdraw from his casual glance. Secretly she imagined what kissing John would be like, touching him. Sheyna knew nothing about love and felt that no doubt John knew everything about it. The wisdom again. He had travelled, hadn't he? Lived away from home. He was so much more mature than she. Although he hadn't said much he seemed so confident and sure of himself. For an awful moment she wondered if he had kissed a girl or even touched her in a way that she had seen her mother and father touch. There had been the odd occasions when she had heard her mother moan softly after going to bed. She had never heard any sounds come from her father and had often wondered what these odd noises were all about. Did her mother have some painful illness that she was keeping secret from Issy and herself? After all, her mother never moaned in that way at any other time. It really was most odd. But then everything about her feelings toward John were 'odd' too.

The conversation was all about the Silver Songsters, although totally excluded, Sheyna still wished that she too could have been part of such a marvellous adventure. What bliss it would have been to sing alongside John! As she dreamed her fingers fiddled nervously with the red check tablecloth and her shy giggles tried to camouflage her self-conscious awkwardness. She always felt awkward when John Rees was around.

"So, John, you are the greatest boy soprano in the land," Ezra said, "and you Issy the greatest harmoniser! You must both be very proud." Up until now John had kept uncharacteristically quiet, apart from the odd sentence or two. It happened sometimes. If nothing else his parents had taught him to behave properly in company. He appreciated the welcome that Ezra and Sheyna had given him, but he still felt a little intrusive. It was a family occasion after all. "Come on now, John," Ezra persisted, "you have been extremely quiet, and this – according to my son – is an unusual event. You have been very modest about your achievements, young man, and as commendable as this is, a little more of your opinion would be appreciated. I think Issy has been reading too many books. An admirable pastime in its own way, but intellect can be tiresome when exploited. Now, tell us what it's like up there on the stage all on your own?"

John coughed into his hand before speaking. He might not have noticed Sheyna blushing, but he had certainly noticed everything else about her. There were definitely a couple of 'lumps' on her chest as Issy would have put it, although he couldn't be certain whether these were made of flesh or the crinkling of her dress. He was no expert after all. He briefly wondered if he ever would be. He remembered how pretty she had looked at the station, the white dress and blue bonnet, the smile that had nearly knocked him off his feet. She was looking at him now and once again he felt that her intense blue eyes were only for him. For a moment Charity Like sprang into his mind. The dark and the fair. He had liked her too. Charity was different, but no less pretty than Sheyna. Where Charity was confident and sure of herself Sheyna seemed reserved and shy. John knew that Sheyna could be bold when she wanted to be, even bossy; the threat to sneak on he and his friend's smoking habits immediately came to mind, but there was still a lovely calmness about her, a softness in her eyes and smile that seemed to demand care and gentleness. She wore no make-up, so her face was more natural than Charity's; even so, he could still have kissed the pair of them until their lips dropped off! Right now he felt as if he was in front of another audience. He had become used to the attention, but Sheyna was actually giving him another dose of stage fright. He found himself wanting to please her – not to impress, just please. In spite of all the people in the tea shop, once again Sheyna became the only person that mattered. He tried not to look at her, but each time he tried his eyes would wander back to her pretty face. It was his turn to blush now as Sheyna's eyes looked directly at him and waited.

He coughed again into his hand, "Well . . . it's . . . it's wonderful really. Mind you, you can't see anyone. The stage lights blank out everyone's faces. This helps. I remember my first solo. Jes—oh sorry, I mean, well . . . it was frightening, but you get used to it. I don't mind singing solo now, at least I don't get so nervous. I love singing I suppose, so it's not hard. Issy has the hardest job, 'cos singing in a choir can be difficult. You know, all that harmonising and the other boys playing up. Jawbone and Gargoyle are always playing pranks. They don't mean any real harm though. At least Gargoyle isn't a nuisance anymore."

"Gargoyle, John, Jawbone? Who are these Gargoyles and Jawbones?" Ezra asked. Issy quickly interrupted John before he could say anything.

"Oh they're just friends, father. Nicknames of other Songsters." Issy wasn't about to go into detail about the exact nature of their 'friendships'. Flushing peoples' heads down toilets would definitely not have impressed his father. Neither would smashed windows, unusual cigarettes and a constantly irate Sideways.

The conversation continued along less perilous subjects such as home and hearth until it came time for Ezra and Sheyna to go back to their hotel. When they were standing outside on the pavement Ezra shook John's hand and so did Sheyna. As her hand lightly touched John's she said quietly, "I'm so proud of you, John Rees. Good luck for tonight." Her eyes stayed attached to his for a few moments before she disappeared into the ebb and flow of a monstrous crowd. He didn't want her to go. Jesus, he really didn't want her to go! Was this love? he dared to ask himself. No it couldn't be, he was far too young.

Later that night John's voice removed worries about the future and the past. His voice took people to other, more exotic lands and places, tempting them to up sticks and move on – in their minds at least. The impossible radiance and shine of his voice soothed hard times, everyday concerns and petty nuisances as it reached into the hearts of those who would listen and forced a deluge of unhindered emotion. Men hid their tears while women dabbed at eyes unable to hold back. For a few minutes some couples even held hands and started to remember why they had fallen in love all those years ago. At bedtime that night, soppy 'Goodnight' kisses and clumsy ardour floundered with starched-up nightwear and the crunch of creaky floorboards, but lust and sometimes even love got there in the end. If only John knew what his voice could do!

Sheyna Kaddar thought of none of these things as she watched and listened, how could she? All she saw and heard was a golden boy soprano who made her heart leap and her spine tremble all the way back to Wales.

CHAPTER 23

The pianist listened intently to the tap of his white stick on the pavement – one tap in the wrong direction could mean life or death – while at the same time his nostrils confirmed the fact that he had just walked past a woman. He could always tell the difference between male and female. There was a different aroma about a woman – more delicate than a man's, more subtle and less primitive. Sometimes though it could be unnatural and undeserving of the female kind. Perfumes and eau de cologne corrupted their natural smell and didn't always confirm their cleanliness.

The pianist's image of beauty relied wholly upon his imagination and touch. Music brought light and colour to his life, but he could never be absolutely certain that his touch told him the truth. Even an innocent fingertip could sometimes betray. The only certainty where his touch was concerned were the keys of a piano, which could never betray or lie. His blindness had never been an impediment where his work was concerned, his acute aural capacity and phenomenal memory easily compensating for his lack of sight.

The lingering smell of femininity stayed with him for a moment and reminded him of his childhood: his mother's bosom, her hair touching his face. Her smell had been clean and pure. It had never changed. He remembered the deep voice of his father, always strong, always present and the rugged masculine smell that somehow complimented his mother. He remembered their laughter, all the sounds of happiness. Sound and smell. He didn't miss his sight, how could he? He had never seen. Apart from anything else he had learnt a long time ago that eyes never saw what the brain didn't know.

He tapped his way into a Post Office, bought some postage stamps and then made his way to a small grocer shop. His fingers examined and his nose smelt. They were more able to detect freshness than the grocer himself. Whenever Mr Jacks saw or usually heard the pianist about to enter his shop his eyes would immediately scan all the fruit and vegetables to make sure they were all fresh and in perfect condition. The tapping would also set off a nervous tick in Mr Jack's right eye. The whole village depended on the pianist's nose, and if it turned upwards in despair then his whole stock would go to the local pig farmer. The pianist wasn't a man to be trifled with and neither was his nose. Blind he may have been, but the villagers rarely noticed anything untoward. His nose and fingertip more than made up for the eyes that looked yet couldn't actually see.

The pianist finished his shopping for the day and returned home. There was a composition that urgently required his attention. The men in London were getting impatient just as they always did. People in Europe were also waiting. So many people wanted the blind man's genius and yet he could never see the awe and wonder in their eyes and on their faces. This never bothered him; for although he had no ego and didn't even know what he truly looked like, he did know that his music was more important to him than the thoughts and reactions of others. As he put his finger on the keyhole and eased the door key into the lock, he knew his piano would be waiting. It had become his only true friend and family.

PART 3

CHAPTER 24

The Songsters were singing at The Empire in York. Although a year had passed since John's first solo performance he was still top of the bill, while Issy remained in the choir. John's mother had given birth to a baby sister. At first John hadn't been too happy about a girl, yet when he had seen the small bundle of noise his views had changed. Thinking of Sheyna had been enough to soften his immediate objections. He had wanted another brother, but life had already taught him that you can't have everything you want; the baker and stork weren't that daft. His mam seemed happy enough with their decision any-way, so who was John to complain? He didn't know exactly why, but his own mind concluded that maybe another Sam wasn't such a good idea after all.

That had been the last time he and Issy had gone home, and it seemed a lifetime away. On a Saturday afternoon both boys were twiddling their thumbs wondering what to do. Afternoons were always the worse time for the Songsters. Sideway and rehearsals were usually finished by one o'clock, leaving all the boys to their own devices for the rest of the day until they started performing in the evening. Tonight was their last per-formance in York. They were sitting down in the lounge of a small hotel overlooking the River Ouse. The hotel, despite its size, was crammed to the brim with Georgian history, much to the delight of Issy who immediately waxed on about the splendid Georgian style of the building. As usual John grunted with appreciation and humoured his history-obsessed friend. Their boredom was relieved when a man walked in and asked them where he might find Steffani.

"You may find him in his room," Issy had replied politely.

"Yeh, I've tried that. No answer. A pity. And who are you then? A pair of Steff's Songsters?" The man had one of those vulgar American accents that seemed to drawl and assume absolute authority. He was dressed in a green and yellow striped blazer, a yellow open-necked shirt and white cotton trousers. He carried a cream flat cap and a pair of chamois leather gloves in his hand. Why the man was carrying a pair of gloves was a mystery to both boys; it wasn't cold after all. Judging by his clothes and suave manner, the man had money and was also extremely sure of himself the boys quickly concluded. A thin moustache crossed his upper lip with a swish as his green eyes darted around the room. The man was tall and athletic, almost seeming to bounce around the floor as he spoke.

"Yes," Issy replied to the man's question, "John sings solo and I sing in the choir."

"Gee, is that so? So Steff ain't here at the moment, huh?" the man said as he pushed a hand through a mop of wavy blond hair. He was up there with the stars of the silver screen all right, Issy thought to himself.

"No. At least we haven't seen him, apart from this morning at rehearsals that is. He is staying here, we know that," Issy confirmed.

"Shucks, never mind, I'll try again later. You see I'm over here doing some publicity for Slazengers. I use their rackets. Best there is, boys. Steff is an old friend of mine. Thought I'd look him up." The man looked down at John and Issy. He was tall all right and looked just like a film star, even if he apparently was not one.

"Look . . . er . . . you two boys seem a bit bored. Do you fancy an ice cream or somethin' to eat? Keep me company until Steff turns up. Bet there's better food around here than in this place. My name is Hank by the way, Hank Marshal. I'm a champion tennis player, you may have heard of me. Wha' d'ya say?"

150

John and Issy looked at each other. Ice creams and expensive grub were never to be sniffed at. This man looked as if he could afford the best that York had to offer. He was a star after all, wasn't he? A sports star maybe, but still a star – or at least famous, not that either of the boys had ever heard of him. Tennis was a rich man's sport after all.

"Well, we—" John was about accept the offer when he remembered the last time someone had offered to buy him an ice cream and suddenly the offer didn't seem so attractive. "Er . . . how about some fish and chips instead?"

Hank laughed.

"Fish and chips? Yeh, I guess I've heard of 'em. Fish wrapped up in newspaper ain't it? I know you Limeys love the stuff. Don't suppose there's anywhere around here where you can get a burger is there?"

"A what?" John asked with a puzzled expression on his face.

"Never mind." Hank was not about to explain the origins of the great American hamburger. Not that he knew anyway. Like most Americans, history wasn't one of his strong points. Besides he had more important things on his mind. "Come on then buddies, let's go find some real ol' fashioned English fish and chips. By the way, what are your names?" The two boys told him as they followed him out of the hotel. Their stomachs were already starting to rumble in anticipation.

After an hour trying to find a suitable fish and chip shop, success arrived in a grubby establishment half way down an alleyway leading to nowhere. Neither of the boys noticed that these days their chins no longer rested on the stainless steel counter of the chip shop and neither did they have to lift up their arms to roll coins along its surface. They had both passed their sixteenth birthdays, but Issy was the taller of the two and broader. John objected to this slight advantage but was convinced that he would soon catch up. Issy was only a few months older after all, so by John's reasoning he would be just as tall in three months time. He was not so sure about the broader shoulders though, that might take a bit longer. The wisps of hair around John's private parts were another matter. Issy was definitely ahead of John in this quarter. His friend was accumulating a huge black bush of wiry curls around his winkie, whereas all John could manage was a modest smattering of reddish nonsense. Issy's armpits had also started to sprout, and this really was disconcerting. Nature played some daft tricks, and most of them seemed to be played on John. Even Issy's chin was starting to fluff and darken up! John was convinced that Issy's hairy advantage had something to do with his Jewish background, and he often wondered if there was any way he could become a Jew too.

When the two boys had ordered they left Hank at the counter and went to sit down. The table was all tea stains, salt and vinegar. The dirtier the chip shop the better as far as they were concerned.

"Hi, mam. Say, can I have a coffee?" Hank asked the worn-out girl behind the counter. The girl, whose off-blond hair was as greasy as the fat cooking the fish and chips, looked at him as if he had just escaped from the local lunatic asylum.

"Say that again?" the girl asked with a bemused expression on her face.

"Coffee, mam. Aw shucks, I forgot. You Limeys don't drink coffee, do you? How about some tea?"

"If you can call it that," the girl confirmed, "more like cats piss if you ask me." It was Hank's turn to look bemused.

"Cats—?" he started to enquire. "Gee, never mind. A glass of water then." Hank received his water and paid for the food.

As he sat down at the table he said, "Damn, boys. You Limeys sure know all about service huh?" The boys ignored the sarcasm and tried to hide their giggles. If Hank thought he could get coffee in England, imagine what would have happened if he had asked for it in Wales! Jesus! They had met plenty of Yanks while singing in the Songsters and none of them had impressed. Loud, brash and thought they owned the world.

Sideways had told them that America was a nation of 'bounders' and 'cads', and they had seen nothing yet to alter this view. Hank Marshal was certainly no exception. Both boys had noticed something else about him too, but neither of them could quite identify it. There was something that wasn't quite right.

While they were eating Hank boasted about all the tennis tournaments he had won. He was the best tennis player in the world, no doubt about it. As far as John and Issy were concerned the fish and chips were far more interesting. When they had eaten their food which was nearly as good as Johnson's back in Llantwit they returned to the hotel. For some unknown reason, upon their return Hank didn't seem so keen to see Steff after all, and seemed more interested in keeping the boys company.

"Hey, buddies. You wanna smoke?" he asked as he sat down on a chair in the hotel lounge. "Come on, keep me company until Steff shows. He shouldn't be too long now. You're on the stage in a couple of hours, aren't you?"

"Yes we are," Issy replied still standing up. Neither he nor John had warmed to the man, even if he had given them a treat. All they wanted to do was to return to their room and maybe catch a little sleep before tonight's performance.

"Hey, what are your rooms like? Comfortable? Never stayed here myself. Wouldn't mind seeing what they're like. Can you show me?" By this time John had sat next to Hank and was enjoying a smoke. He was a true professional now, unlike Issy, who had finally decided that it didn't do his health much good – or his voice. He smoked now and again, but avoided excess. For Issy to begin with it had been fun to show off, but that was all. As Hank finished his sentence his hand fell on John's knee and stayed there. As John wondered what to do about Hank's hand – it didn't seem right somehow – Sideway walked into the room. Their tutor and guardian took in the scene in seconds.

"Oh, looking for Steffani are you, Mr Marshal?" Sideway said, without waiting for an answer. "Well, you won't find him

153

scurrying around somewhere in the nether regions of young John's kneecap – and I emphasise the word 'young'. Now, be so good as to remove your dishonourable intentions to another part of York, or better still to another country altogether – a country where your perversions may be exploited with impunity. America, perhaps? A scurrilous colony riven with vagabonds and villains, would you not agree? Now off with you sir, and make sure I do not see you molesting my boys again, otherwise our ancient and astute press might learn about your depraved inclinations!"

Hank Marshal didn't argue and left the hotel as fast as his feet could carry him.

When the tennis player had gone Sideway explained in as polite a way as possible what Hank Marshal's 'depraved inclinations' were all about. "So young fellows, please be a little more circumspect about the people you choose to share your time with. I cannot protect you all the time. You are now informed about some of the less admirable qualities of our great species, so heed what I say and do not let yourselves be fooled by the likes of Hank Marshal again, champion tennis player or not. He will do you no good. Now, up to your room and start getting ready for tonight. Go on. Away with you now!"

When Issy and John returned to their bedroom they were both in a state of shock.

"Did you hear all that, Issy," John nearly whispered. "I mean, winkies up the . . .!? You don't think old Sideways is having us on, do you? I mean winkies up the bum?! I can't believe it! I mean how . . . *how*?"

"Don't ask me, John. I've read a few things that made me wonder, but that's all. I had no idea that some men actually like doing that kind of thing. I mean how could they? Doesn't make sense to me. No sense at all."

"Well, what Sideways has told us does make a bit of sense when you think about it. You know we have seen some strange men on the stage, haven't we? What about those men who seem

154

to act more like women than men? You know, the ones who talk like our mams and fuss like them. I've often wondered about them. Isn't normal, is it? And as for having a winkie up my arse, well doesn't that just take the biscuit! What about all the shit?! Mind you, that Hank seemed quite normal; at least he didn't prance about the place like our mams or some of the men on stage. How can you tell then? That's what I'd like to know! Hank did seem a bit odd for some reason, but he wasn't like our mams, was he?"

"Oh, shut up now, John. The thought is making my back passage twitch!" This time shock turned into humour.

"Better not do up your shoelaces in public again then, ay Issy? Never know who's going to pounce on you with his winkie ready and cocked!" Both boys were laughing now.

"Well," Issy said, "at least we know what 'Queers' are now."

"Don't we just," John agreed. "Good thing too, bet it's bloody painful an' all! Come on then, we'd better get dressed as we're on stage soon. Last performance in York and you know what Steff's like . . . Hey, you don't think he's a—"

"Don't be stupid John, besides he likes women too much. He's always got a woman on his arm and you know it."

"Well, Sideways told us that some men like men and women. Can't work that one out at all."

"Oh, shut up. And John, I think I'll sleep with my back against the wall tonight and a pillow up tight against my backside. Don't want to put temptation in your way, do I?"

"Bugger off, Issy."

Waiting to perform was always a nerve-racking time. Issy sympathised with his friend and appreciated that his own part in the choir was less demanding. That time when they had met his father and sister in London Issy knew that John was just being kind. He always was. At least when Issy sang he had nineteen other boys to hide behind, and any mistakes could be blamed on someone else.

155

To try and occupy John's nerves until they went on stage – in spite of his bravado he was always jumpy before a performance – Issy suggested that they go and talk with some of the other performers. There were always interesting people to talk to who had all kinds of stories to tell. He dragged John to one of the dressing rooms and walked in without knocking.

The young Songsters were usually shown more tolerance for their bad manners than other performers. They were young and expected to make mistakes, although Steff didn't always toe this indulgent line. When the two boys barged into the dressing room they were met by a sight that would stay with them for the rest of their lives, a sight that at their age they could never possibly hope to see. No book or picture could have prepared them for the vision of rampant loveliness that nearly pulled their eyes out. About six young nubile girls confronted them and all were naked or semi naked, apart from the odd sequin here and there. Issy and John stood in the doorway and gaped. Anything else would have been unthinkable.

"Oh, hello boys," a dark-haired girl said, "come in for a preview, have you?!" She made no attempt to cover up her swaying breasts that both boys were sure had just arrived from Heaven. For a few moments neither of them could breathe. There were 'lumps' everywhere of all shapes and sizes. Some drooped, some stuck out and some were so big that that the two boys had to step backwards. Nipples fit to burst strutted around the room pointing in all directions. Some were small and brown but full of cheek, while others were like plump red cherries, ripe, juicy and full of pique. Perfect round buttocks, paler and smoother than vanilla ice cream, rubbed together as the girls clamoured for space in the small dressing room. "Well, now look at you both," the dark haired girl laughed, "haven't you ever seen a girl naked before?!"

"N – n – no . . . urm . . . no, we haven't," John managed to murmur through lips about to explode. He couldn't take his eyes off the black patch at the top of the girl's legs. Some of the other girls had patches of a different colour and some didn't have any patches at all!

"Well, make the most of it the pair of you. Now bugger off, you've had your fun!" With that the door slammed firmly in their faces. Issy and John remained where they were.

"Did . . . did you . . . just see what I just saw, Issy?"

"I did, John," Issy replied from some faraway place that certainly wasn't York.

"Did you see those titties, Issy. Those legs, right up to . . . they went. I mean I know we've seen them on stage, but . . . but . . . *naked*?"

"I did."

"And those bums? And the hair? Did you *see* the hair?! All the colours of the rainbow that hair was. Bloody lovely!"

"I did."

"Does Sheyna have hair like that, Issy?" John mumbled not quite knowing why he had asked the question.

"Don't know. Must have I suppose." Issy managed to answer, still in a state of shock.

"I've never seen the like. And those titties! Did you see those titties?! Jesu, Issy!"

"I did, I did." Issy had gone extremely quiet, more so than usual. His face was expressionless. Not even an eyebrow moved.

"What's the matter, Issy? You've gone all white. They're only titties and bums you know. They can't hurt . . . at least I don't think they can. Mind you, my winkie is hurting a bit at the moment I can tell you. It's throbbing like buggery. Is yours? How can I go on the stage like this?! Steff will go mad and these short trousers don't help! I'm telling you Issy I've got a problem here. What's your winkie like?"

"The same." Issy just about managed to say as his hand reached into his trousers and tried to rearrange things.

"Look, what's the matter with you, Issy? Why aren't you saying anything?"

"Ch . . . Charity. Charity Like was in there, at the back of the room. You didn't see her?"

"Charity . . . Charity Like? Was she the one with the big titties then?"

Suddenly Issy's voice changed. There was a hint of anger in his tone.

"Don't talk like that, John! She wasn't naked either – well at least not everything was showing. She was wearing one of those chorus girl outfits, part of it anyway."

"Oh, pardon me," John demurred. Issy rarely expressed any anger about anything. It was always John who was the hothead. There was silence between the two boys for a moment, then Issy said,

"I'm sorry, John. It's just that she's a nice girl, that's all. Don't you remember? She was the girl we met in Norwich; you know, the one with the spiteful friend."

"Oh yes . . . I think I remember that one. The spiteful one. Charity, she was the pretty blond one, wasn't she? Told us she'd only talk to us when we had grown up or something. Mind you, at least she was nice about it, not like the other one. Didn't see her in the dressing room though. All I could see was titties and lovely round bums. Ooops, sorry again! Got a soft spot for her have you, Issy? That's all right. I think your sister is nice too."

John had no idea why Sheyna's name had slipped off his tongue again. He hadn't told his friend how much he liked his sister as he hadn't fancied the ribbing, but Sheyna was often in his thoughts. He had been disappointed at not seeing her the last time they had gone home, but hadn't said anything to Issy. Seeing all those naked girls tonight had just reminded him of Sheyna. He couldn't help wondering what she looked like naked, and Issy hadn't even been able to tell him whether she had hair or not! She must have some hair and titties by now, even if she was a bit younger than him. He had hair after all, but none of it seemed to be appearing on his chin; although he looked every morning there was never anything to see. Issy was growing an excuse for a beard, but not enough for a razor.

158

Just as well too, since the thought of Issy being a man before John was just too mortifying to think about.

That night John sang 'The Way You Look Tonight' and all he could do was think about the way the chorus girls looked and which way his winkie was pointing. As the choir sang the popular 'William Tell' song followed by Handel's 'Largo', Issy's voice refused to attack the higher notes. His vocal chords were allowing nature to take its course regardless of what Issy thought. He started to panic as notes cracked and croaked, but there was nothing he could do about it. He couldn't help what was happening in spite of Steff's fearful nose and angry eyes. It must have been the sight of Charity Like's sequined body. It must have been.

That night, as John was finally falling asleep and starting to dream of naked angels trying to bend his livid winkie back into place, he heard some unusual tapping come from the headboard of Issy's bed.

"What are you doing, Issy? I'm trying to sleep here," he managed to mutter, annoyed that his angels were being disturbed.

"Oh nothing," Issy managed to gasp through clenched teeth. "Mind your own business."

Some naked angels had obviously decided to help Issy out too.

CHAPTER 25

The following morning Issy was beside himself. He couldn't eat any breakfast and he had been asked to see Steff at ten o'clock. He didn't know what was worse. Seeing Charity again or being sent home by Steff. It was clear that his voice was 'breaking', so would he be any more use to Steff? Last night he just hadn't been able to reach the high notes; every time he tried his voice would turn into sandpaper. He was sure of one thing though. He was becoming a man, and hadn't Charity Like insisted that before she spoke to him again he would have to be a man, or at least have grown some whiskers? Well, wasn't he a 'man' now? His winkie was doing strange things, his voice was turning into a man's and he was starting to grow some whiskers – not as good as his father's he had to admit, but maybe if he started using a razor the growth would improve. That's what he been told anyway. One of the comedians had also told him to rub black boot polish into his face at night, but Issy wasn't that much of a fool, although he had a feeling that John would give it a go. His friend was desperate for a hairy face and would try anything. Ever since they had seen those chorus girls all John had gone on about was shaving; the first thing that morning he had even gone out to buy them both a razor and shaving brush. Neither of them had quite known what to do with the items until Sideway had come into the bedroom and observed.

"Young shavers, eh? You, young Issy, may require the services of a razor, while you, young John, are better off as you are. Do you really want to bother with the tiresome business of having to shave every day? Delay the inconvenience my boy, delay the inconvenience for as long as you can. God knows, your beards will continue to grow even when you are dead."

John ignored the advice just as he always did. Anyway, he was having enough trouble trying to grow a beard while he was alive, let alone dead!

"Do you think some black boot polish will do the trick, Mr Sideway?" John asked. "We've been told that it's just grand for young shavers like me and Issy. Be like a couple of apes in no time we've been told." Sometimes, and these occasions were extremely rare if not nonexistent, Sideway could consider a humorous jape. He rubbed his chin thoughtfully for a moment and said,

"Well now. That might just do the trick. Yes, I have heard that black boot polish can be admirably effective where the promotion of hair growth is concerned. Yes indeed. Rub it into your chin before going to bed. I'll leave some in your room later on – a special concoction that only I know about."

Issy looked at Sideway then at John. Well, if Sideway had some magic potion to produce an instant beard then his cock was a kipper – and not the sort that Jews wore on their heads either! By now the two boys had replaced the word 'winkie' with 'cock' like all the other boys, since 'winkie' was far too childish and still used by their mothers for heaven's sake! Anyway, if Sideway's potion was so effective then why was his head, to use one of John's expressions, as bald as a badger's arse?

John could have a go, but Issy was having none of it. They had been given the tip by a comedian, so what good was that? What on earth was Sideways up to? Issy wondered. Mind you, he was never one for a joke, so maybe . . .

CHAPTER 26

It was Sunday morning and they were off to Newcastle the following day. Today was the last chance that Issy had of seeing Charity again. And he was desperate to see her, really desperate. In all the months that had gone by she had always been at the back of his mind. It would have been impossible for him to have spoken to her last night; too much chaos and too many people around.

As it was still not yet eight o'clock Issy decided to see if he could find Charity. It was a forlorn hope he knew, but he had to do something. He took his time getting dressed that morning and for the first time in his life used a razor on his face. He was surprised at how smoothly the razor cut across his skin without making him bleed to death. John was still trying to work out how to use his, although as far as Issy could see there was nothing to use the razor on. He humoured his friend all the same.

While John fussed about in front of a mirror Issy told him he was going out for a walk. He did not elaborate any further as John was quite used to his 'walking' escapades. However, he did need to explain where he had managed to find a pair of long black trousers. Issy hadn't forgotten the words of Charity the last time they had met.

"Long trousers, Issy!" John didn't miss much at the best of times, and these certainly wouldn't go unnoticed. Issy had tried to creep out of their room surreptitiously, but John had been too quick. "Where *did* you find them?" John had exclaimed. "I haven't got a pair! You sly bugger!"

"Oh be quiet, John. I bought them in London ages ago."

"You didn't tell me. And it couldn't have been *that* long ago. We're growing too fast according to my mam anyway. You could have told me; I would have bought a pair too. Right, that's it! I'm going to buy myself a pair as soon as we get to Newcastle, and bugger Steff!"

"You do that, John. Mind you, you might look a bit silly wearing long grown-up trousers and no beard to match!" With that Issy had dashed out of the door leaving John to fume and swear on his own.

Issy had decided to try the theatre first. Normally there wouldn't be anyone around at this time, particularly on a Sunday morning, but sometimes performers would do a little extra rehearsing while it was quiet. Issy hoped so anyway.

When he arrived at the theatre the place had an almost eerie quality to it. He stood at the back of the auditorium for a few minutes, sensing the echoes of rowdy applause that still seemed to crash into the air. Then the noise died down, just as it always did, and the whole place fell silent and moribund. Issy suddenly felt alone, even fearful. The empty hollow vastness of red and gold seemed to be threatening him, but he couldn't understand why. Murmurs of dead variety players crawled out from wherever they were hiding and told him not to go on.

Issy breathed in deeply. What was the matter with him? Why was he listening to the empty air? He braced himself and muttered, "Don't be so stupid! There's no such thing as ghosts and phantoms!" He turned his back on the darkness and echoes of momentary euphoria and made his way to the dressing rooms, his footsteps failing to allay a feeling of trepidation.

He searched and knocked, but there was no one to be found. There had to be someone in the theatre, otherwise how had he been able to get in through one of the stage doors? Eventually he bumped into a decrepit cleaner who looked like one of the old witches out of Macbeth. She wore red threadbare slippers and an overcoat that was so big it disguised who she really was. Her white head bobbed up and down as she hummed to the melody of some ancient song and mopped along a floor that, like her own life, had never had a beginning or an end.

163

"Er . . . hello. You couldn't tell me if you have seen a Miss Charity Like anywhere could you?" Issy asked, even though he knew the hopelessness of his question, but he was prepared to try anything. He was getting more like his friend every day. The old woman raised her bent head and leaned against the filthy wet mop.

"Charity Like, you say?" the woman said quietly not wishing to outrage the mop by any sudden noise. She knew what her only companion was like. "I've heard of her. Chorus girl."

The woman didn't say anymore; she was just a poor skivvy in a lowly world infested by the poverty-stricken and foolhardy. She bent down and carried on mopping. She had seen the look in Issy's eyes so many times before: the hope, the belief in youth – and love. Her own eyes had been like that once. She had been a singer then with a fine voice. The theatre had had its way, and now she just mopped up bitter memories and pretended that she still lived.

"Look . . . please," Issy persisted, not believing his luck that the old woman had actually heard of Charity. "Do you know her? Do you know where she is – please." His voice was almost a whisper now, unable to reach even a note of panic. The woman's head tilted upwards again and looked at the handsome young boy trying to be a man. Her lips moved, but they didn't smile. She saw again a kind of love. A memory.

"No," the old woman replied, "I don't know anything."

"But . . . but you just said you knew her." Issy could not give up.

"Did I?" the woman said as her eyes returned to the floor.

"Yes you did. Please tell me if you know where she is. Please." The woman looked up again and saw only tears waiting to fall. She knew all about tears and men, even young men. She sniffed silently. There had been plenty of those too. Now her mop and bucket had become her life and her disaster, but even so something about this young man moved her.

"Try the Hotel Mirimar up the road. That's all I know. Now leave me be."

"Thank you." Issy tried to smile his gratitude, yet somehow he knew the old woman wouldn't appreciate it. "Thank you so much." The old woman watched Issy walk off in pursuit of love and almost called him back. Instead she gripped the handle of her mop more tightly and muttered to herself, "So be it."

Issy found the hotel, but walked straight passed it. He didn't know what to do. What if Charity wasn't there? After all, the old woman didn't exactly inspire confidence; in fact Issy wasn't at all sure whether the woman was even sane or not. Those eyes of hers had almost chopped him to pieces. They had sparked and threatened for a moment and then returned to some place that only she knew about. She had made him shiver for a few moments too, just like the empty auditorium.

He stood on the pavement a few yards way from the Hotel Mirimar and rolled himself a cigarette, courtesy of John, while he decided what to do next. He had been on edge all morning. He rarely smoked these days but sometimes he couldn't resist and this was one of those times. His fingers were trembling as he tried to roll the tobacco into the thin cigarette paper. Some passers-by noticed his indecisive vagrancy but said nothing. He stood still as his nerves betrayed and tortured. Lungs full of smoke didn't help his desire to discover and find out. Would Charity talk to him? What was he going to say? Would he use the right words? She must have had plenty of suitors; after all she was so pretty. Why should such a lovely girl be interested in him? He was only just out of short trousers for heaven's sake, and was going to make a complete fool of himself! Yet after three cigarettes he finally walked up the steps to the hotel door.

The hotel was not one of the grand ones that he and John had often stayed in. This one was more of a boarding house, although he had known plenty of these places too. It was still early for a Sunday morning and quiet. He stood in front of the door and raised his fingers to a brass knocker that defied him to

165

knock. His fingers paused and then withdrew. Indecision again. He tried once more, but this time his stomach turned in a somersault and jumped out of his backside. "Oh God! What are you doing to me?" Issy wailed to himself as his stomach propelled him back down the street.

When his stomach had finally calmed down he rolled another cigarette and hid in a doorway for another few minutes as he braced himself for another try at the doorknocker. His whole life now depended on it. He had never paid much attention to all the doorknockers he had thumped throughout his young life, yet now this solitary piece of brass had become the centre of his universe. Madness, bloody madness! Throwing the cigarette to the ground and gritting his teeth he finally walked back up to the hotel door, inhaled deeply and knocked. It seemed like ten lifetimes before someone finally opened the door.

"What do you want, young man?" A bespectacled woman, thinner than one of his mother's bean poles and with a face sharper than any hatchet, stood before him and examined him from head to toe. What coven had she just appeared from? was Issy's first thought. This was just not going to be his day. Two hideous witches in one morning! The thin woman's grey hair was scraped back into the severest bun he had ever seen. She wore a black dress underneath a floral pinafore. She must have been in mourning Issy immediately concluded too, given her face was as black as the dress she was wearing. For a moment Issy wondered why all women seemed to wear floral pinafores. He could never imagine Charity wearing such an outrage. An evil scowl remained on the woman's face as she waited for an answer from Issy.

"Good morning, madam," Issy finally replied. "I'm, er . . . looking for my friend, Miss Charity Like. Is she staying here, please?"

"Do you know what time it is, young man? Not yet nine o'clock and my guests have not finished their breakfast. Now, call back at a more convenient time please and be off with

166

you!" The destroyer of romantic endeavour was about to slam the door in Issy's face when at last his inherent boldness leapt out at her. He had learnt a long time ago how to handle bullies, and this one was no different.

"Madam, I have asked a polite question and believe I am entitled to a polite answer." The woman was taken aback by this boyish defiance; perhaps he wasn't so much of a boy after all. He was wearing long trousers and an expensive jacket, the wool appearing to be of the finest quality. He also spoke with some authority and his accent had an upper-class ring to it. The woman knew class when she heard it and was not one to presume above her station. Besides, who knew who the father was? She had learnt a few things about bullying herself along the way.

"Charity Like, you say. Yes, she is one of my guests . . ." She paused for a moment while she looked Issy up and down again. "I'll go and see if I can find her. You wait there. Gentleman callers are not allowed into this establishment. I run a respectable business – and don't you forget it, young man. Whom shall I say is calling?"

"Oh, Issy. Issy Kaddar."

The woman left Issy to worry and fret as she closed the door, but at least she hadn't slammed it shut, unlike the chorus girl last night.

Well, he had done it now. And there was no John to fall back on. Right now he could have used some of his friend's cheek. Would Charity be annoyed at being disturbed at such an early hour? Issy hadn't thought of this. Theatre people aften slept late, including himself. He would rather have faced a hundred old hags than an annoyed Charity. Still, he had found her and at the moment that was all that mattered.

She had probably forgotten his name, but she might come to the door anyway, if only out of curiosity. For a minute or two he wondered if this had been such a good idea; maybe he would have been better off trying to catch her at the theatre, but then how could he? There was no show tonight and he was off to Newcastle tomorrow. A few more minutes passed and then the door finally opened.

Charity Like stood before him, fully dressed this time. She was wearing a plain brown pleated skirt and cream blouse. Her waist was so narrow that Issy's fingers would have touched had he placed his hands around it; he had forgotten how petite she was. Her hair looked as if it had just been sprinkled with nectar from the Gods and her green eyes made Issy's stomach gurgle again. This is what too much reading did for you, Issy immediately thought. His father was right. This time she wasn't wearing any stage make-up, but this just seemed to make her even more beautiful.

"And who might you—?" Charity started to say. "No, wait a minute . . . you're that Songster boy, aren't you? I've met you before . . . Was it Norwich? You were singing in the theatre last night and your Welshy friend was singing solo again." Charity smiled, and relief made Issy's stomach turn again. At least she wasn't dismissing him out of hand, even if she did seem more interested in John.

"Yes, I'm Issy. Issy Kaddar."

"Yes, I remember . . . Now, let's see, have you started shaving yet?" She rubbed his chin with her fingers. "Hmm, very smooth, I must say. Although you've missed a bit at the side and your neck, it's all red too." She then stood up on tip toes and sniffed his face, "Don't you put any cologne on your face afterwards, tut tut?" Charity giggled. "Long trouser's too! Well, well, quite the young man about town, aren't we?"

"I . . . er . . . er . . ." Issy just couldn't speak. All the words he had prepared ran away with Charity's smile and touch. He had never been touched like that before, not by a strange pretty girl anyway. He couldn't be certain whether Charity was mocking him or just being playful. He hoped with all his heart that it was the latter.

"Still don't say much do you, Issy?" She was as forthright as he remembered, but this time she was looking at him more intently. Her spanking green eyes didn't reveal much, but her interest was certainly not as casual as it had been the last time they had met. She was used to young men chasing her, but she remembered how she had seen something different about this Issy that time in Norwich. His dark looks, the defiance in his eyes. There was something about him that was so serious and yet amusing. That time in Norwich his friend had been the forward one, or certainly the most talkative and cheeky of the two. He had been handsome as well in his own childish way. But neither of them had been old enough. It was surprising what a year or so could do to a boy.

"Well, I . . ." Issy tried to explain.

"It took some courage coming here." Charity tried to give Issy's shyness a helping hand. "How ever did you find me? Been reading about Sherlock Holmes have you?" Charity giggled again, but couldn't help being impressed by Issy's resourcefulness. "Come on, how did you find me?"

"The cleaner at the theatre told me you might be here. I just thought I'd try . . . well . . . to see you." At long last some confidence was beginning to return to Issy's voice. He hadn't been turned away out of hand, and at least Charity was smiling.

"Ah yes, that old cleaner knows everything. So, why did you want to find me?" Charity was teasing and testing now.

"Well, I . . . er, saw you last night in one of the dressing rooms at the theatre . . ."

'Ah, so you were one of those boys who caught us all naked were you? What a nerve! You didn't see much of me though, did you? Well only my—"

"No . . . er . . . not at all." Issy started to blush at the thought of all those naked girls. He went even redder at the thought of how his cock had reacted.

"You're blushing, Issy! How sweet!" Charity teased again. Never mind about being 'sweet', Issy could have died right there and then on the doorstep.

"I just wanted to see you. That's all. You said we could talk again once I started shaving and was wearing long trousers. So

169

here I am – shaving and in long trousers." This time Charity laughed; one minute Issy was looking down at his shoes the next he was challenging her.

"Your voice is deeper too, Issy. A bit crackly but definitely deeper. You haven't mentioned that yet."

"No I haven't, have I?" Manhood could still be a little embarrassing. "Actually it might mean me having to leave the Songsters soon." Charity saw the disappointment in Issy's eyes, but she also saw strength and that unique warmth that she had encountered in Norwich.

"Oh, never mind," Charity replied softly and with under-standing. She knew all about the tragedy of the stage. "I expect you'll find something else. You don't look the sort of chap who can be kept down for long somehow."

"Don't I? What do you—"

Before Issy could ask what Charity had meant, she said: "Look, I've got nothing much to do for the rest of the day. How do you fancy going for a walk? Maybe we can find somewhere to eat later on. What do you think?" Charity was being her ususal bold self, it came naturally. She had learnt a long time ago that being bold was the only way to survive. She didn't know this Issy at all and going out with strange boys wasn't her usual habit, but there was definitely something different about him and she wanted to find out more. "By the way, how old are you?"

"Seventeen next birthday."

"What month?"

"February."

"What date?"

"Look," Issy was getting annoyed now, "does it really matter?"

"Yes, yes it does. To me anyway. Girls are never older than boys. I might look stupid."

Maybe Miss Like was not so grown up after all, Issy thought as he said, "February 2nd. Happy now?"

"That's all right then – just. I was seventeen two weeks ago. So I'm only five months or so older than you. It will have to do

170

I suppose. Mind you, you do look older than you actually are, I'll say that."

"Good, I'm glad you think so. Now, about that walk." Issy couldn't believe his luck, but he also noticed that he was beginning to take charge of things. The tables were being turned and he was enjoying every minute of it. Charity wasn't so formidable after all, and he even began to wonder what he had been so worried about. Anyway she was only a girl who was not that much older than his own sister, and since when had Sheyna ever frightened him?

"Come back at eleven o'clock sharp. I don't like being kept waiting . . . although somehow I don't think that would bother you."

"Eleven o'clock then. I'll be here," Issy replied firmly. "Oh and you're not bringing that friend of yours are you?"

"Who . . .?"

"That miserable girl you were with in Norwich."

"Oh, Cynthia you mean." Charity smiled. "Yes, she was a bit of a moaning minnie I'll grant you that. No, don't worry, she won't be coming along. I haven't seen her for a long time. I don't think she likes boys anyway – prefers girls if you know what I mean." Issy didn't know what she meant but nodded sagely. "I might just bring the landlady as a chaperone though."

And with that Charity closed the door slowly, smiling as she did so. For a moment their eyes met and both knew that something had happened.

They just knew.

CHAPTER 27

John was still in their hotel room when Issy returned.

"And where have you been then, Issy?" he asked as he browsed through some Variety newspaper.

"Mind your own business, John. And can't you find something better to read for once? Something that might teach you something!"

"Look now, Issy. You stick to your history. Anyway, I do read books now and again."

"Do you now? Like the books I gave you over a year ago. You haven't finished colouring those in yet!"

"Ha. Ha. Very funny. Now, come on, where have you been? Long trousers, shaving. You look like the cat who's just got the cream. Look at you, your face hasn't stopped grinning since you walked in through the door. What's going on . . .? I know, it's that Charity girl isn't it? Come on Issy. Own up!" Issy knew that if he didn't tell his friend something he would never hear the end of it.

"Oh, all right. I went out to see if I could find Charity."

"The girl we met in Norwich? The one you saw again last night?"

"Yes."

"Well, you must have found her. You can't stop smirking. How did you manage it? York is a big place."

"A cleaner at the theatre told me. Strange woman, but she knew where Charity was staying anyway. I went to the hotel and just asked if Charity was staying there. She came to the door and I'm seeing her later on. Eleven o'clock in fact."

"What! Bugger, Issy you move fast I'll say that for you! How did you get up the nerve? I'd have been filling my pants!"

"I was, don't worry. Anyway, Charity was very nice. We're going out for a walk later."

"Well, good for you is all I can say. Well done. Not right though, is it Issy? You've been the first to shave, first to wear long pants and now you're the first to take a girl out. I've noticed that your voice goes a bit strange every now and again too. That can only mean one thing." John thumped his friend on the arm, but the usual bravado couldn't hide his disappointment. There was no spite in his words, no jealousy, but he simply felt that he was being left behind. Never mind the girl; the fact that Issy's voice was breaking before his didn't help either. The thought of his own voice breaking in the middle of a song terrified him and sometimes kept him awake at night. At least Issy enjoyed the camouflage provided by the other boys in the choir.

John had yet to make up his mind what was worse: his voice breaking and no longer being Britain's Greatest Boy Soprano, or never being a man and able to chase the girls properly. The latter seemed to be the greater of the two evils; after all, what was a life without pretty girls? In any case there was nothing he could do about becoming a man, voice or no voice. Issy noticed his friend's change of mood just as he always did.

"Come on now, John. There's plenty of girls out there. Plenty. All waiting just for a smile from the best boy soprano ever heard this side of the Danube. And when your voice finally breaks you'll have a beard before you know it – and then you can sing bass. You'll be the best bass singer in Britain."

"You think so, Issy?"

"Of course."

"What happens if Steff sends you home, Issy? You're seeing him in a few minutes." Whenever John looked down at the floor and suddenly went silent it usually meant he was upset about something. Neither trait came easily to his friend. Issy knew John; they had shared so much together, experienced so much. There was a sort of love between them, a growing

173

masculine love that didn't poison and pervert in the sense that Sideways had told them about. He and John were brothers in everything but blood, they loved each other and yet no words of explanation or confirmation were ever demanded. It was a simpler love, less volatile or emotional than their feelings for girls. It was a love that required respect and hidden recognition, a love that both boys treasured and guarded jealously. When they had first met this love was young, even juvenile, but manhood was adding bricks and mortar, substance and strength. They had fought for each other, protected and taken the bruises and bloody noses. Neither had ever deserted the other in times of need, even when one had been wrong, for theirs was a friendship that could guide, criticise and even induce anger, but it didn't judge, it didn't run away when things got rough, and it didn't betray.

Both boys took and both boys gave, but their love and their friendship always endured. Issy looked at his friend and saw the sadness. More than anything else Issy knew that John was worried about Issy leaving him.

"Look, John," Issy said quietly, putting his arm around his friend's shoulder, "whatever Steff decides to do about me, you're not going to be alone, are you? There are plenty of other boys you can have fun with. Not to mention the girls. And anyway how long do you think your voice is going to keep on hitting the high notes? We both know Steff. Once the voice cracks he no longer makes any money out of us, so it's 'Goodbye and thank you very much'. If he sends me on my way then you won't be far behind, I'm sure of that."

"What will you do if Steff sends you home?" John asked, not sure if he wanted a reply. Since seeing Charity that morning the thought of having to leave the Songsters made Issy break out into a sweat. How would he ever see her again if he was sent back to Wales? Issy had no idea how to talk to John about his feelings for Charity. They both intimidated and confused him. One moment he felt on top of the world, the next scared out of his wits. John would probably burst out laughing if he tried to explain the turmoil that was going on in his mind. He tried to hide this emotional trauma from John as he said casually, "Oh, I don't know. Maybe carry on with my education. I'd like to go to university to study history like my father. But who knows?"

Who knows indeed? Issy wondered. He was a reader, both of newspapers and history. He had also experienced the hatred of Hitler's Germany and the dictator's ambitions. Issy didn't want to worry John, but he feared for the future just as his parents and many of the performers backstage did. Issy had heard the hidden words. The whispers.

The Songsters had been largely protected from the threats of imminent war, the theatre both cosseting those in it and shunning the unthinkable. Issy was becoming a serious student of history, and everything he had learned warned against the appeasement that the British government seemed determined to pursue. He wanted the gentler world of academia and books, but doubted that this would arrive without bloodshed. Suddenly he feared for Charity too.

"Yes, Issy." John interrupted Issy's fears. "That would be just the thing for you. Your head is never out of a book! I hope Steff doesn't send you home though, Issy. I really do. You're my best friend after all. None of the other boys would be the same."

"Now, come on John. It's not like you to be miserable and . . . well . . ." – Issy paused for a moment, knowing his friend didn't like anything too soppy – "we'll still be friends whatever happens. We'll always be friends, John. Always. Now I'd best go and see what Steff has in store for me."

"Come back to the room as soon as you know, Issy. Don't go chasing after Charity."

"I will. I won't be long – and don't go smoking in here. You know what Sideways is like."

"Oh bugger off and bugger Sideways too. I'm fed up with everyone telling us what to do all the time."

"Doesn't take long to get back to your old self, does it John?" Issy laughed as he walked out of their room.

Steffani was waiting for Issy in the hotel lounge. As usual he was immaculately dressed in a brown wool suit, crisp white shirt and brown paisley tie. He was sitting down in an armchair smoking a cigarette and sniffing the air with his long nose. Trouble, Issy immediately thought as he walked slowly up to a chair next to Steffani and sat down. He couldn't help feeling like some condemned man about to view eternity from the end of a rope. He fiddled with his fingers nervously as he waited for the drop.

"Good morning, Issy. Now then, you're no good as a boy soprano any more and that's all there is to it," Steff stated without ceremony. He was never one to mince his words or his pocket. He sniffed the air for a moment or two while Issy despaired at the prospect of a future without Charity. At this point even the hangman's noose frittered away to the back of his mind. "You can still be in the choir though for a while anyway, until I get a replacement. Your voice hasn't gone completely. You can still harmonise I trust?"

"Oh yes, Steff. I won't have any trouble with that."

"Good. Very well then. You can carry on for a while if that's all right with you. A few weeks, maybe a month or two. At the moment I just don't know exactly how long it will be; these things are not an exact science I'm afraid. Either way it won't take *that* long to find someone, so you can tell your family you will be home soon."

"Oh, that's fine. Great, Steff," Issy replied trying not to show his excitement. He had been given a reprieve! The scaffold would have to wait a bit. Issy couldn't believe his good fortune for the second time that morning. The fact that Steff had been curt and abrupt flew straight past his thoughts of Charity. He had always known that the Songsters couldn't go on forever. Everyone had to grow up, even young boys. Peter Pan really was just for the fairies. Even so, he was still grateful for having

176

been able to enjoy such a thrilling musical adventure. Not many boys of his age were so lucky.

"Good. We're off to Newcastle in the morning to perform there for a week, so see Mr Sideway about the arrangements. Oh, and keep that young John in line and make sure he doesn't smoke, will you? He'll be sorry if I catch him – and you can tell him that!" That was a good one, Issy thought, and there's Steff puffing away like there's no tomorrow. What a hypocrite!

Being kept on was 'great' with Issy all right, and even greater when he thought about Charity. Going home would have meant certain death where she was concerned but this reprieve gave him a better chance of chasing after her no matter where she was. And chasing her all over the country, even the world, if he had to, it made no difference. He was utterly besotted and infatuated with her. He just hoped he could make her feel the same way.

She had to.

CHAPTER 28

When Issy arrived at the Hotel Mirimar his nerves were about to snap and he stank of tobacco. The baccy smell didn't bother him; everyone smoked and everyone stank of it, so he wouldn't stand out in any way. But the nerves? Now that was a different matter. They seemed to crawl all over him and devour everything they touched.

He was early by fifteen minutes so he marched up and down the pavement, girding this and that, smoking his lungs out and daring to recall the sight of Charity's titties. 'Jesu' to quote John, they had been made by Jehovah Himself! Not spongy monsters like his mother's, but big enough. They didn't seem to need one of those huge brassiere things either; the one his mother wore could have sailed the Seven Seas and back! They simply stood where they were and pointed. He remembered the nipples, as he had never seen anything like them. Bright red and sticking out like hat pegs. What he wouldn't have done to give them a squeeze! The very thought made him light up another cigarette.

Eleven o'clock was about to strike so he walked up to the hotel door and knocked. In a few moments Charity opened the door and walked out. The way she moved, the flowing red skirt, her delicate ankles, the nipples that tried to hide, everything about her almost made Issy stop and stare. He had seen loads of pretty girls since being in the Songsters, but none had affected him like Charity. She had something more, something unique and indescribable. She seemed to tip him upside down and back again. This inexplicable attraction, this dire need was too much for Issy. He didn't know what to do about it or how he should react. It was there and he couldn't shift it, no matter how hard he tried.

"On time then," Charity said with a smile. "Good. Right, where are you taking me?" She took Issy's arm without asking and led him through the gate and onto the pavement. Issy didn't know what to do. He was none too sure about the arm-holding either. His mother and father were always doing that, and right now he didn't feel much like a parent.

"Well . . . how about the Roman Wall?" Issy finally suggested when he had got over the sight of Charity.

"The Roman Wall?"

"Yes, there's bits of it all over York. Don't you like history?" John and Cathedrals suddenly entered his mind. What if Charity felt the same way as John about history? York Minster was definitely out of the question then, ditto the Mansion House and Castle Howard. Anyway, Issy was reluctant to spoil his time with Charity who was far more important than any lumps of stone and fine architecture. He wanted her all to himself. History could go and sing for the day!

"Well, can't say I've ever really thought about it that much. As for 'Roman' walls, well I suppose I can give it a try."

"Good. Come on then. Let's walk." It didn't take Issy long to be in control again. As they walked the warmth of her arm was sending all kinds of sensations through his body and mind. How could a girl's arm be so captivating? he wondered.

"You're from Berlin, Issy, if I remember correctly. That's right isn't it? How did you end up over here then?"

"It's a long story, believe me. I'm still not sure myself, I don't think my parents are either. Herr Hitler doesn't like Jews much right now, so Germany is not a safe place to be. Very few places are safe for Jews at the moment I can tell you."

"But why?" Charity asked innocently. "You seem very nice to me." Charity was obviously unaware of the voracious blood-thirsty Jews depicted by Hitler's propaganda machine. Issy looked down at Charity; she was only about five foot three inches and he was nearing six foot and still growing. There was a sincerity in her voice this time. Her usual casual banter seemed

179

to be lacking. "You don't seem to have much of a German accent either, not like the ones I've heard on the radio or seen in the pictures anyway. Not much of any accent, come to think of it. Well, a bit posh maybe, but there's nothing wrong with that."

"No, my mother is English. Born in London. She met my father there. He was from Berlin, and that's where they ended up until we came over to Wales about two years ago. My father is a professor . . . Oh, and I have a little sister. Well, actually she's not so little now."

"Professor! See what I mean. Definitely posh!" Charity couldn't resist baiting Issy, his studious seriousness demanded it.

"Anyway, Charity, you're from Birmingham aren't you? I quite like that accent of yours. And you're not far off 'posh' yourself."

"Do you? That's unusual. Most people hate the Black Country accent. As for being 'posh' you should hear my mother. Lady Muck if ever there was. Still thinks she's on the stage most of the time." Charity laughed and Issy laughed with her. Charity hadn't thought Issy was the laughing type but she soon realised her mistake. When he laughed all that darkness of his disappeared too.

As they walked around the outskirts of the city, Rome's might was only referred to in sketchy detail so absorbed were they with one another. Charity told Issy how she had come to be on the stage. She had enjoyed a happy childhood spent mostly in Birmingham, which had been her parents' base in between bouts of stage and variety. This had all come to an abrupt end when her father – a loving and generous man, although she admitted his generosity was fitful – had accidentally given himself a tonsillectomy while swallowing a sword and died. In spite of her father dying somewhat unexpectedly and his swords with him, her mother had carried on dancing until her body had started to ache and finally tighten up. Following the onset of this physical demise, it seemed that the only thing left

180

for her mother to do was to pass on the sequins of the variety business to her daughter.

Charity had grown up quickly and had few illusions where the human race was concerned. Self-reliance was her motto and independence her Bible. At the moment though both were being a trifle undermined. Charity was not the only one feeling as if a bomb had just been dropped on her head, German or otherwise. This Issy boy was doing things to her that no other boy had managed before.

Eventually they bought themselves some tea at a small refreshment stall that overlooked the Ouse. An occasional old boat chugged up the river unsure of whether to keep going or remain still and see what happened. Even the boats seemed to notice the unsure young couple sitting on the grass and trying to be part of one another.

"Aren't you hungry, Charity?" Issy asked in that considerate way of his. "I mean I thought you wanted something to eat."

"Oh, don't worry about food. Besides we'd be hard pressed to find something even half decent on a Sunday. Now, tell me more about yourself, about Germany. I love hearing about other countries. One day I would like to see the world, you know. One day." The more Charity spoke the more Issy was unable to help himself. She was starting to feel the same way about Issy, but being a young woman she was hardly likely to reveal the fact. As the two young people sipped and explored, watched and learnt, neither was aware of the true import of young love, its destruction and joy, its untouchable innocence and brittleness. In a moment of perfect union when their eyes touched over a cup of tea Issy and Charity fell into a state of the most perfect of all loves.

The love of unblemished enthusiasm, the love of the unique, the love of something entirely new, but most of all the first impossible love of untried youth.

Later that day the footsteps of both Issy and Charity were slower and more considered. Issy kept looking at his watch as if willing the minute hand to pause and reflect if only for a short while. When they eventually arrived at the Hotel Mirimar Charity withdrew her arm and turned to face Issy.

"Well, Issy. I've had a lovely day. I've even learnt some history too. The Rise and Fall of the Roman Empire no less. Aren't you clever!"

"No, not really," Issy replied not knowing what else to say. What else to do. Instead he just pleaded to all the Gods ever created that the Hotel Mirimar would simply disappear. "I would really like . . ." He started to say but his tongue stopped as the Mirimar loomed and threatened. It looked as if it wanted to devour Charity in one awful gulp. He coughed into his hand, shyness prevailing again. "I would really like . . ." he repeated, but still the words wouldn't come out. Trying really hard to ask the hitherto most important question of his young life, his tongue refused to obey. Then Charity came to the rescue yet again, each of them a curious mix of submission and domination that they almost seemed to assume in turns.

"Can we see each other again then, Issy?" Charity asked, her forward manner not disturbing him this time. He was getting used to it. How could he resist anyway?

"Of course, Charity. But the trouble is I'm off to Newcastle tomorrow. I was hoping, I mean really hoping that somehow we could meet up there. I know that sounds stupid but well . . . I was hoping anyway." The serious expression on Issy's face had returned. He was in turmoil again. Recently he never seemed to be in anything else.

"Well, isn't that a coincidence!" Charity nearly shouted, her own relief quickly appearing in her smile. Neither of them had given any serious thought as to how exactly they were supposed to see each other again. They both assumed that this would just happen somehow. Time and place meant nothing to their hearts, any more than did distance or travelling. They just wanted to see each other again, no matter what. Complications were for old people. "I'm in Newcastle next week too!" Charity beamed. "For two weeks I think. And then it's back home to stay with my mother for a while. I've earned enough money now to see us through for the next few months."

"That's wonderful, Charity! Wonderful!" Issy said excitedly. "But . . . how . . . how will I reach you? I don't know what theatre I'm singing in yet."

"Oh, don't worry about that. I'm not too sure where I am yet either. The manager hasn't told us yet, me or the other girls. Anyway not to worry, it won't be hard finding out where the Silver Songsters are. You're famous now you know. How is that Welsh friend of yours by the way . . .?"

"Oh, he's fine when he's not annoying me." Issy managed an edgy grin, still not wanting the Mirimar to swallow up Charity.

"You're very fond of him, aren't you? I can see it in the way you smile when you talk about him."

"Yes, I suppose so. Not all the time though, believe me."

"Nonsense. Now, I must go. I really must." They stood facing one another and for a few moments the whole world became a place that neither of them knew anything about. Issy wanted to reach out and touch Charity's face with his fingers, he wanted to feel her skin, he wanted to be close to her and feel her senses. Her smile had become all and everything. "I'll find you in Newcastle, Issy," Charity said quietly, "I promise." She looked up at Issy's face and touched his lips with a fingertip. She looked from side to side to make sure no one was looking then stood on tip toe again and kissed his cheek. It was quick and fast. A rapid declaration of something he wasn't entirely sure about. No passer-by would ever have noticed. Charity was a modest girl, even though her dancing on a stage plagued by impropriety may have insinuated otherwise.

She disappeared into the Mirimar and left Issy touching the first kiss of romance he had ever known.

CHAPTER 29

Charity had tossed and turned Issy's attempts at sleep and had also ensured that he had no appetite for the bacon and eggs that were staring up at him from the dining table. As usual he was the last one to get up and the dining room was deserted. He had fiddled about with the bacon before deciding that his stomach would erupt if he swallowed any of it; this had nothing in particular to do with his religion, but still, sometimes where God was concerned, it was probably best to play safe. There was Charity to think about after all.

Although the egg yolk made him want to run and puke, good manners insisted that he eat something, or at least show that he had made an effort. He didn't know what was wrong with him as his stomach didn't hurt or anything, it was just that he had no appetite. He managed a sip or two of tea and the odd slither or two of greasy egg white before giving up on the whole sorry business and making his way to the station. The sooner the better as far as he was concerned. Charity would be on her way to Newcastle sometime today and he couldn't wait to see her again. In fact his whole life – and his stomach – depended on it, not to mention his sleeping habits too.

John was supposed to be waiting for him at York railway station. The night before he had wanted to know everything about Issy's walk with Charity. Had he kissed her? Had it been a French kiss? Where had they been? What had they done? Did Issy have a squeeze of her titties? What were they like? Issy had told him as little as possible, determined not to go into detail about the way Charity made him feel. Normally there were no secrets between he and John, but girls and Charity in particular? Well, that was another matter: he couldn't get the

184

girl out of his sight or his mind. She was everywhere he looked and in everything he thought. How could he explain these extraordinary mysteries to his friend? He wouldn't know where to start.

They had both been instructed to meet Sideway at the station for the journey to Newcastle. At first Issy had difficulty spotting his friend as John was nowhere to be seen. He wasn't in the waiting room and neither was he milling around on one of the platforms. Eventually Issy found him hiding behind a newspaper stand by the ticket office.

"What are you doing, John? I've been looking all over for you. And why are you wearing a scarf around your chin? It's summer you know. Look, the sun is shining!" John grunted in reply. "What's the matter with you?" Issy persisted. "You look stupid with a scarf around your chops in the middle of summer. Why aren't you talking properly? Have you got a cold or something?"

Eventually John lowered the scarf and Issy burst out laughing. "Oh, John! Oh dear me! Your chin is as black as 'Snakehips' Johnson's arse! You turned sambo or something? Oh bugger, John! You do look a sight!" John had been expecting all this, but he wasn't about to be let off the hook yet. Sideway appeared at the side of Issy. He had taken to sucking a pipe and wearing a deer stalker these days. Neither of the boys had any idea why. Perhaps it had something to do with his always trying to be one step ahead of the Songsters.

"Ah, there you are, boys," Sideway said. "What's all this . . . commotion?" One look at John's face was enough. "Oh goodness, young fellow! Goodness me! Is that the black shadow of unshaved masculine stubble I observe or is it my 'special concoction'?" Even Sideway was having trouble controlling himself. It was payback time as far as he was concerned. John had become the tormented instead of the tormentor for once. For a moment Sideway actually smiled. A yelp of laughter had tried to get out, but once again Mrs Sideway jumped up into his throat to stop it.

"What . . . what am I going to do, Mr Sideway?" John pleaded. "What *am* I going to do? I can't go on stage like this! Steff will go mad, I'm telling you. I've tried all sorts. Every type of soap I could lay my hands on but nothing works. What am I going to do, Mr Sideway?" Issy was still laughing. "Oh, shut up Issy, will you! This is serious!"

"Can't help it, John! You look such a sight!" Issy couldn't stop laughing. "Perhaps you ought to plaster black boot polish over the whole of your face. Go the whole hog, you'd be a proper sambo then!"

"I'm telling you, Issy, shut up will you?!" John was starting to square up to Issy who was nearly falling over with uncontrollable mirth.

"Now, now boys. Let's not have any fisticuffs," Sideway interjected, "Issy, my boy, now control yourself." This time Sideway couldn't help putting a hand over his mouth to restrain himself, Mrs Sideway or not. "No need to worry about the stage, young fellow. There has been a change in the arrangements. We are going to London for a few days, Newcastle has been cancelled. And you can stop fretting about your chin. I have another 'special concoction' that will remove your 'stubble' in an instant. Perhaps now my boy you will not be so keen on shaving your chin until its time has arrived, eh?"

John Rees might well have been more irritating than any 'concoction' but Sideway knew when a joke had gone far enough. He would never admit it, but he actually had quite a soft spot for the boy. Sometimes he even wished he had been more like him in his younger days. Perhaps he would have been a different man now if this had been the case. The odious Mrs Sideway would never have blighted his life, of that he was certain.

"Pardon?" Issy couldn't believe what he was hearing. His whole world was being blasted to smithereens. How could Newcastle be cancelled? No, it couldn't be! It couldn't be. What about Charity? "You can't do that!" Issy almost shouted. "You can't!"

"Whatever is the matter, young fellow?" Sideway asked, slightly shocked by young Issy's panic-stricken reaction. "Why should it bother you where you sing?" Issy had always been the quieter of his charges. The most self-controlled. This outburst was totally out of character, not like Issy at all.

"Well . . . um . . . we just can't, that's all, Mr Sideway," Issy replied more quietly as he tried to keep control of himself.

"That's no answer is it, young fellow? No answer at all. London it is, my boy, whether you like it or not. Steffani has been offered a recording contract with Decca Records no less that is far too lucrative to ignore, the second largest record label in the world I may add. They have recorded people like Bing Crosby and Al Johnson. So what do you think of that? And you, John, will be singing two solos all to yourself! Your favourites.

"We will be in London until Friday. After that you two boys can go home to see your parents for the weekend, and then a week today we will be going to Newcastle, as previously arranged. Don't you want to see your family, Issy? It's been quite a while after all." Issy didn't know what to say. He remembered that Charity was in Newcastle for two weeks, so he might just make it. He had to. Right now she was far more important than any 'family'.

"I suppose so," said Issy, grudgingly, Decca Records or not. He knew there was nothing he could do about it. Steffani's word was law, and Sideways wasn't far behind.

CHAPTER 30

Steffani had earned his money, so all was well with his bank and his pocket. John had recorded solo his favourites as promised, Henry Bishop's 'Lo! Hear the Gentle Lark' and Rudolf Friml's 'Smilin' Through'. The Songsters sang a medley of popular hits too including 'Never Break a Promise', 'All Ashore' and 'Penny Serenade'.

During all the recording sessions it never occurred to John that he was some kind of star, like all those fantasy people he had seen in the pictures. He had been told to sing into a microphone and that's what he had done. The fact that his individual voice was known throughout the land meant little if anything to him. Both he and Issy remained disarmingly unspoilt by their status and good fortune; in fact it was Steffani who seemed more concerned about their voices than they did. Neither of them quite understood why. Their charming naivety would one day astonish them.

All the boys had done their jobs and it was off to Newcastle on Monday morning. It was now Friday afternoon and John and Issy were sitting on a train on their way back to Wales. Issy, who loved his sleep, was trying to doze, while John was thinking about Sheyna and Charity Like. All this business with Charity was starting to annoy him. All week Issy, normally a quiet and self-contained individual, had been irritable and distracted, wandering around in some strange place of his own. Even John had found it hard getting through. The odd thing was that his friend didn't seem to be miserable as such. Despite laughing every now and again in his usual boisterous way somehow it sounded different, as if in his head he was really somewhere else. It had to be this Charity girl. His friend was in love, whatever that meant, as all 'Love' had done for John so far was bewilder and confuse. Was Issy feeling the same way as John had felt the last time he had seen Sheyna? Jesu, all this 'Love' thing was beyond him. Perhaps he ought to stop trying to understand it. Apart from this he felt left out of things. Charity was older than both of them, and for Issy to get as far as he had was quite an achievement. Issy wasn't saying much about his afternoon out with Charity, but John was sure that Issy had kissed her if nothing else. As for going further, well that just didn't bear thinking about.

John tightened his jaw, now back to its normal colour if still a little livid from all the scrubbing, and decided that he must kiss a girl and soon. He had to catch up with Issy no matter what. The trouble was who? Although girls were constantly flowing in and out of his life, there were none whom he could seriously consider kissing – or more to the point who would let him kiss them. It was, after all, a pretty personal business and most of the girls he encountered were older and had men anyway.

His voice and the short trousers didn't help. Mind you, at least the latter had been remedied – off stage anyway. The chaotic recording session in London had seen to that. Issy had helped him choose two pairs of proper trousers from a tailor's in Saville Row, one for the summer and one for the winter. He was wearing the summer pair now, a blue cavalry twill. He felt like the Cock of the Walk, but without the ability either to crow in a manly way or attract hundreds of dribbling girls going out of their minds trying to kiss him. The only immediate prospect that came to mind was Sheyna. Would she let him kiss her though, that was the thing? After all, this kissing business could be a frightening affair. How did you do it for a start? The real kissing, the way they did it in the picture house. Sometimes these kisses seemed to go on forever. He used to get bored with all that soppy stuff, but his views had changed and so had the antics of his cock. Issy wouldn't tell him how exactly you were supposed to kiss, the sod.

The thought of kissing Sheyna suddenly made John sit up. The last time he had seen her had been over a year ago. He hadn't forgotten how he had felt standing on that pavement outside the tea rooms. He remembered Sheyna's words again, 'I'm so proud of you, John. Good luck for tonight'. She had held him with her beautiful stark blue eyes and touched his hand. He could have kissed her all over there and then, even if he hadn't known how. Nature would have found a way, he was sure of it. It had always found a way with his pets all those centuries ago, hadn't it?

For the rest of the journey John thought about Sheyna and Issy tried to dream about seeing his lovely Charity again.

CHAPTER 31

After allowing his mother to fuss and spoil him all day Saturday and Sunday morning John decided he had had enough. His new little sister, Winnie, had become more objectionable than he remembered. His mam still refused to go into any detail about his sister's arrival. The baker and the stork were all very well, but both he and Issy had learnt a thing or two since being in the Songsters. When the pair of them had finally discovered the true nature of human reproduction they had been amazed, if not a little disconcerted. Jesu, if their cocks were capable of making babies then what else might they do? As for Winnie, well, the odd bit of howling had been tolerable, but now the little bugger was running around hell for leather trying to make everyone's life a misery. So John, fed up of having his ears poked and his face dribbled over, decided to go and see Issy to get away from it all. He had wanted to do this earlier, but his mother had insisted he stay at home. Sheyna's beckoning lips were far more urgent than anything going on in the house, but he could hardly tell his mam that, could he? Eventually he had managed to creep out of the back door with a, "Won't be long, mam; just going to see Issy for a bit. Sort out the trains for tomorrow." He was gone before any objections could be raised by his mam or Winnie, who for some unknown reason had taken a bit of a shine to her only brother.

When Issy opened the front door to his house John was standing there, long trousers, oiled hair and a great big fatuous grin on his face. He had obviously taken time getting dressed before coming over. Not like John at all, not when it was only Issy around anyway. "Come on Issy, let's go for a smoke," John suggested looking over Issy's shoulder to see if there was any sign of Sheyna. The hallway to Issy's house was empty and seemed far too peaceful. This was worrying.

"What happened to you then, John?" Issy asked. "I was expecting you sooner."

"Pardon?" John was too busy trying to catch Sheyna to listen to anything Issy had to say. "Oh, um . . . my mam and Winnie." He continued to peer over Issy's shoulder as he added distractedly, "They wouldn't let me out. You know what it's like."

"Do I? Not really. Never mind. Come on then, let's go to the summerhouse." Apart from that time waiting for Charity Issy still didn't smoke much, but the odd one now and again was all right if it kept his friend happy. "Looking for Sheyna are you, John?" Issy smiled knowingly, far too smart to have let his friend's affections for his sister go unnoticed. He had seen it all: the station 'Goodbyes', the tea shop in London. The eyes. John had even talked about Sheyna in his sleep.

"What? Sheyna? Don't be stupid, how is she anyway?" John's nonchalance was not at all convincing; besides Issy knew him too well. They had eaten together, slept next to each other, fought and laughed together and looked after one another for such a long time now. The only secrets either had concerned girls. And even these had arisen more from self-conscious embarrassment than anything else.

"She's fine, John. She's around here somewhere. Would you like me to call her? I expect she'd like to see you."

"What? Oh no. No. No need for that."

"Are you sure now?" Issy repeated, enjoying the awkward movement of John's feet, not to mention the eyes that avoided Issy's at all costs.

"Of course I am. Come on, Issy. I'm gasping!"

The look on John's face was a picture. He was always hopeless at trying to hide things. That's why he was always being caught out. There were times when it was impossible not to tease his friend, but Issy wasn't cruel either. He also understood what girls could do to a boy. Look at the state he had been in over the past week. However, he was just better at hiding it than his friend.

"Let's go and have that smoke then. I expect Sheyna will come and say 'Hello' later on anyway. She knows you're here. Seemed pleased to know you would probably call over some time or another. She likes a smoke herself so she tells me. Oh and John, try not to set yourself on fire this time, please."

"I won't. Trust you to remind me. Bloody Issy!"

The two of them walked to the hidden summerhouse at the bottom of the garden. Any onlooker would have seen two confident young men who seemed to know where they were going. Issy was just over six foot now, taller than John by a couple of inches. Where Issy was broad and muscular, John was lean and lithe. Both boys – or were they men? Neither could be too sure – were developing into handsome specimens. Issy's looks had become darker and more phlegmatic, particularly his deep blue eyes which like his sister's could demand and entrap, while John's looks had become stronger and more sharply defined. His head had evicted the last remnants of reddish outrage and replaced it with more gold. When the sun was right his hair alone could transfix and make the girls sigh with envy, not that he was ever aware of it.

This time the boys' cigarettes came from a packet, and there was no concern about being caught smoking. What could their parents do now? Even the way they smoked had matured and acquired a degree of sophistication. In many respects both boys were far ahead of their peers, some of whom were still playing with scruffy footballs in the back streets of Llantwit Major. They had been away for more than two years now and during this time they had seen and done things that most boys of their age could only dream about. Neither John nor Issy felt any smugness about their success or even talked about it much. They had both known from the start that the Songsters would come to end one day or another, and this in itself tempered any feelings of hubris or ego.

As they smoked John asked, "Issy, how much longer do you think you have with the Songsters? You've told me Steff is looking for someone, but that can mean anything." There was that concern in John's voice again, the concern at being left alone.

"I don't know, John. I really don't," Issy replied gently. "All I hear from Steff is 'I haven't found a replacement yet.' It's a bit annoying really. I can't settle. Still I don't suppose I'll be around for much longer. If I know Steff he'll find another boy soprano quickly enough. Then it's home and university . . . I hope." Suddenly this prospect didn't seem like such a good idea, not without Charity anyway. His feelings had yet to recognise the more practical implications of love such as money, a roof and food on the table.

"What about Charity? I know you hope to see her next week, but what will happen when Steff throws you out? And me probably not long after."

"Oh, let's not think about that now John. As for Charity . . . well, who knows, eh?" Issy tried to make light of things, but the prospect of having to say 'goodbye' to Charity filled him with dread and left him in a cold panic. "You finish your fag for a minute while I go back and get us something to drink. Bottle of beer all right?"

"Fine," John replied. These days, like the cigarettes, even drinking beer had lost some of its fun. There was no longer the fear of being caught out – those unannounced footsteps, the danger – when Steff wasn't around, which was most of the time.

Some minutes later as John was about to stub out his cigarette Sheyna arrived from nowhere, taking him completely by surprise.

"Hello, John." She grinned as she stood before him. "Issy said I would find you down here. He's talking with daddy at the moment. About his future I think. He says he won't be too long."

Sheyna Kaddar stood in front of him, utterly captivating just as she always was. Her long black hair tumbled and ran around

194

her face trying to find somewhere to settle, while her blue eyes looked straight at him. "May I have a cigarette too?" she asked as her eyes challenged him and her delicate fingers moved some wild strands of hair out of her eyes. It was a simple gesture, deliberate and refined, whilst at the same time contradicting the passionate fire that leapt from her pupils. She was so utterly feminine and yet the boldness of John's memories still stood before him.

"Er . . . yes, of course. Here we are." John fumbled with the packet and passed her a cigarette. He lit it with a match just as he had seen the film stars do. Sheyna's fingers handled the cigarette expertly. She inhaled the smoke like a real trooper. When was he going to stop being impressed? John wondered momentarily.

"How are you then?" she asked. "I haven't seen you since that time in London. You were wonderful on the stage that night. Your voice, well . . . I just don't know what to say. You're taller as well and your hair isn't so red." So far Sheyna had been doing all the talking; she wasn't like her brother at all.

"Good, I'm . . . er . . . glad you liked the performance," John replied with a hint of hesitancy in his voice – or was it shyness? This girl was managing to do things to him that even his own mother was incapable of. "Um . . . how have you been anyway? You seem a bit taller yourself." Sheyna was still only about five foot three inches and unlikely to grow much taller, which suited John just fine. He didn't like big girls or girls that were taller than him anyway.

"Do I? Well, I am fifteen now. Nearly sixteen, so I suppose it's bound to happen. Bit like you really. School is boring but I'll be leaving soon. Probably be a secretary like my mother or something."

"Well . . . er . . . you should enjoy that."

"I don't think so somehow. I'd rather do something more exciting. You know, like parachuting out of aircrafts or something."

"Pardon?" John couldn't believe what he was hearing. Sheyna looked as if she meant it too.

"Why not for heaven's sake?" she replied. "There might be a war soon, so my father says anyway. Why should men have all the fun?" The prospect of war had never entered John's mind and it didn't now.

"There won't be any war, Sheyna. Mr Chamberlain says so."

"Don't count on it, John. Lots of people are worried you know. Anyway, let's not talk about war. It's horrible. People getting killed and everything. It terrifies daddy."

"Were . . . um . . . you really serious about jumping out of aircrafts, then?" John asked. He had to know. Sheyna giggled and smirked at the same time.

"Of course not, silly. I'm not that stupid."

"Glad to hear it, Sheyna." John liked her name and enjoyed saying it. It was so easy and soft. He lit up another cigarette; this was worse than his first night as a solo artist.

"Come on, let's go and sit on the step. Enjoy the sun," Sheyna ordered and took John's hand without asking. When they were seated on the step to the summerhouse she didn't let go of his hand. John didn't know what the hell to do. "You're all nervous, John. Whatever is the matter with you? Don't you like holding my hand?" Didn't he like it? Jesu, he was nearly in a swoon!

"Yes . . . um . . . yes, it's nice," he managed to mumble. Her hand was so small. So precious.

"Good. I've wanted to hold your hand ever since I first met you." Sheyna's voice was quieter now as her eyes seemed to examine the ends of her shoes. "I hope you don't mind."

"No. I don't mind at all, Sheyna. It's nice, it really is."

"I'm glad you like it," Sheyna whispered, enjoying the feel of his hand in hers.

For a few minutes the two young people said nothing as sunlight and a gentle breeze tried to bring some order to their thoughts. Each wanted to desperately hold the other and to touch until darkness hid their hands. Holding hands was wonderful to be sure, yet somehow it didn't seem to be enough, although there was something so intimate, so overwhelming about this simple gesture that both wanted more, more of whatever it was their confused minds were feeling.

John finally gathered up enough courage to touch Sheyna's cheek with his finger and say, "You know . . . I've missed you. I really have. I've often thought about you. Wondered what you were doing, where you were." Sheyna turned around to face him. Neither of them knew what to say or do next. The lovely tension ravaged them both. Dare he? Dare she?

"Me too, John," Sheyna finally managed to reply, "every day."

She moved John's hand and held it to her chest. She looked down at their locked hands for a moment and then at John. His green, sometimes brown eyes looked back at her. In that moment she saw the same uncertainty, the same mysterious pause, as she herself was experiencing. She released John's hand and placed her own on his cheek.

"Oh John, I have missed you so much." She lifted her face to John's as her lips parted slightly. "Kiss me, John," she pleaded. "Oh, please kiss me."

As their lips joined Nature arrived, just as it always did, to make this first, profoundly innocent and untainted kiss the most memorable and uniquely exquisite experience that they would ever again encounter or forget. They kissed and they kissed, nothing else mattered as their lips, mouths and hearts became one.

The *kinema* had a lot to answer for.

When they heard Issy approaching the summer house they both quickly undid their hands and lips.

"Are you still here then, Sheyna? Been enjoying John's company have you?" Issy smiled in that knowing way of his, not that his knowledge or imagination for that matter needed much prompting. John and Sheyna stood up awkwardly trying to look as if nothing had happened. Their flushed cheeks and laboured breath tended to give the game away though. "Mother

197

wants you, Sheyna, to help with the supper or something, so off you go now."

"Don't order me around Issy, otherwise you'll be sorry!" Sheyna was not a girl to be ordered around easily, least of all by her brother who wasn't much older than her anyway.

"Disturbed something have I?" Issy teased.

"Oh, go to hell, Issy."

"Now, now, no need to be like that! I was only joking, so calm down."

Sheyna raised her eyes upward, shook her head and then looked straight at John. Time and Nature had run out on them. She went up to him and whispered in his ear, "Write to me, John, every day."

"Hey, what's going on?" Issy demanded.

"Mind your own business, Issy!" Sheyna retorted angrily.

With that she walked off with her skirts and hair flying behind her and her blouse slightly ruffled. As she walked away John felt an excruciating sense of loss. It was worse than the death of his father; at least when that had happened he had been old enough to know that no parent lived forever, the grave-yard had told him that. This though was something entirely different. Now he really did know what Issy's odd grinning and distant behaviour had been all about. And as for kissing Sheyna, well he could never have believed anything could be so wonderful. It had been better than the singing, the beer and cigarettes all rolled into one! He didn't dare to imagine what touching the rest of her would be like and she had titties too! Jesu! Big 'uns at that – not that he had actually felt them, but his hands had felt the bulges through her blouse and that was all he needed to know. For a moment he wondered if they resembled any of the bosoms that had ambushed him that night when they had mistakenly walked into the chorus girls' dressing room. What a thought!

"What are you staring at then, Issy?" John demanded. "And why have you got that stupid Cheshire cat expression on your face again, eh?"

198

"What? Me? Nothing, John. Nothing at all."

"Is that so? Well, what happened to those bottles of beer anyway?"

"Ah those. Yes, I'm sorry . . . er, I forgot. Father wanted to talk with me." When Issy's eyes started to look up, down and from side to side John knew something was up. They knew each other equally well, and neither was particularly adept at lying. He decided not to push the point as he now knew for certain that Issy had contrived the whole thing with Sheyna. No doubt she was as innocent as he, not that it mattered either way.

At last John smiled at his friend, "Thank you, Issy. You sly bugger."

"All in a day's work, John. Now perhaps you'll stop nagging me about Charity. We're equal now, right?" Issy wasn't too sure about this, but he held his tongue. He didn't think he had got as close to Charity as John obviously had with his sister. The two of them had also had the advantage of being left alone in a secluded summerhouse. Bloody hell!

"Right," John confirmed, satisfied that he had now evened the score on the kissing front anyway, although Issy still hadn't told him much about the outing with Charity. He had hinted at kissing, but that was all.

Later that day as John walked home, he finally began to understand something about love: its calm and its chaos, its generosity and its cruel obsession.

But most of all he had felt its fearsome grip and was overcome with gratitude.

CHAPTER 32

On the Monday afternoon '*Streaks*', as it had been fondly nick-named by locomotive men, was waiting for the boys in London's King's Cross Station. John and Issy stood back from the peacock blue *Mallard*, staring in wonder at its streamlined luxury and futuristic design as it sat on the tracks and gloried in its new-found fame as the fastest steam locomotive ever built. It had beaten the Germans by reaching a speed of 126 mph on the 3rd July 1938 to hold the world record. The Third Reich record for steam locomotive speed had been 124.5 mph back in 1935. *Mallard* had become a symbol of national self-respect; Hitler hadn't had it all his own way.

The boys were met by the deer-stalkered Sideway who immediately ushered them onto the train and into their seats.

"This is the finest train in the British Empire, young fellows. It's beaten the Germans in both speed and style, so enjoy this privilege while you can. You are blessed both of you, and don't you forget it. How many other young fellows in this scepter'd isle, this earth of majesty, this other Eden, this precious stone set in the silver sea – ah, it has been such a long time, I digress . . ." John looked at Issy and whispered.

"What is the old fool on about now?"

"Shakespeare, 'Richard II'," Issy whispered back.

"And who the hell is he when he's at home, eh?"

"You know damned well you ass head, coxcomb and knave. Now shut up."

"What's a—?"

"Did you say something, young Rees?" Sideway interrupted, quite used to the furtive and no doubt derisory remarks of young Rees. The boy was a buffoon, if a likeable one. "Could it be a

200

contribution perhaps to the unparalleled beauty of Shakespeare's poetry?" Unlike Issy's father Sideway felt no compunction in 'exploiting his intellect' where young Rees was concerned.

"Er, no . . . Mr Sideway. Just saying to Issy here what a grand train this is. Oh, and you can tickle your arse with a feather while we're at it."

"I beg your pardon, young fellow. What did you say?"

"Particularly nasty weather we're having today, Mr Sideway. Oh yes, particularly nasty weather." Issy had to turn his face from Sideway. John was such a wicked devil. Always funny, but always wicked too. Sideway looked at John with one of his perplexed expressions and continued,

"Yes, indeed. Now, as I was saying . . . how many other young coves would sell their own mothers to experience this unique mode of travel? How many I ask? Remember this country is still feeling the dastardly effects of abject poverty. Industry has been devastated, the young walk on bare feet, unemployment is rampant. Do not forget the Jarrow Hunger March less than two years ago."

"The Jarrow what?" John was being bamboozled yet again. Even he knew something about Shakespeare – how could he not? His father had always been quoting him but 'Jarrow'? That really was pushing it.

"Oh dear. Oh dear, young Rees," Sideway responded with a look of utter despair in his eyes. "Have you learnt nothing from our lessons? Nothing at all?"

"Well, I remember the Jarrow whatever-it's-called," John lied.

"That's something then, and so you should. Has it not occurred to you how calculating and prescient the London and North Eastern Railway has been? This luxury service may have prompted envy – nay rebellion – amongst the great unwashed, but has this transpired? No, indeed not. And why? Learn young Rees, learn. Now, I shall endeavour to enlighten that gnat's intellect of yours. You see the LNER judged the mood of the nation with admirable expertise. It organised a special train to take the Jarrow Marchers back home to Jarrow in the north of England free of charge after they had walked three hundred miles to London in protest at their impecunious misery. The masses have been behind this world-breaking speed record from the outset, and why? Prestige, my boy, prestige. And propaganda. Britannia must still be seen to rule the waves even if, at this present moment in time, it is a moot point. The good Mr Goebbels must not be seen to have things all his own way after all." Sideway looked at the blank expression on John's face and sighed. He had tried, at least he had tried. "I shall be sitting in the next compartment young Rees, so do refrain from partaking in any of your objectionable antics . . . at least until we arrive at Newcastle. Do I make myself clear?"

"Oh yes, Mr Sideway. Very clear indeed."

"Capitol. Steffani will be meeting us at the theatre for rehearsals tomorrow morning. The hotel is all arranged, so it will be an early night for both of you. No arguments."

"Very good, Mr Sideway," both boys answered in unison.

When Sideway had finally disappeared the boys sighed with relief.

"Phew! Sideways doesn't half go on sometimes, Issy. Shakespeare one minute, Jarrow whatever they are called the next. He wears me out, I'm telling you."

"He means well, John. So humour him. That's what I do. He does know an awful lot though. I've learnt a great deal from him anyway. The trouble with you John is that you're lazy. Bone idle."

"What do you mean? Just because I don't bury my head in a book most of the time like you doesn't mean I'm lazy."

"True, but you could try harder with the lessons. You're not daft after all. Just lazy, as I say."

"Well, thank you for that – mind you, I suppose you're right. Don't want to be walking around without any shoes on my feet, do I? Come to think of it, I do remember something about those Jarrow people. I do read the papers sometimes . . . when you're not looking! How poor they were. Suppose we don't know much about that kind of thing really, do we? I mean, have you ever gone hungry, Issy?"

"No. I haven't. Can't imagine what that's like."

"Neither can I. It must be terrible." This time it was John's turn to stare out of the compartment window deep in thought. He didn't 'think' very often, but when he did he usually came to the right conclusions. "You know, Issy, we have been lucky. Very lucky."

"Yes we have, John. Let's hope that neither of us ever forgets it."

"We won't, Issy. I don't think so anyway."

Issy started to read one of his history books while John watched all the people getting on the train. Both boys were having difficulty concentrating. John was still getting over Sheyna and her kiss, while Issy could not get the prospect of seeing Charity again out of his mind. He was on tenterhooks and had been all week. At least John had been spared all that waiting and disappointment at being sent off to London and Wales without warning. Issy was still smarting at having been deprived of a week with Charity, not to mention the fact that she may have gone somewhere else upon discovering that the Songsters were performing a week late. The only thing that had kept him going was that she had said that she was going back to her mother in Birmingham for a while, so she would not be in any rush to leave Newcastle. Why had he not asked for her address? At least he could have written to her to tell her what had happened. Sometimes he was more of a dolt than his friend! Would she still wait for him, that was the thing? She had said she was dancing in Newcastle for two weeks, so they might even find themselves at the same theatre, but even so they had only really spoken with one another once. She might have forgotten about him already. Oh God, these fears of his were driving him mad! One minute she would be trying to find him at the theatre, the next minute she would be rushing off back to her mother.

Finally Issy picked his book up again and tried to read, saying to himself as he did so, 'Calm down Issy, calm down. She's only a girl after all – mind you, some girl!'

As the train started to move off and John and Issy contemplated the more poignant and in John's case prurient aspects of first love, three men entered the compartment and sat down. One of the men, a handsome, striking middle-aged man, sat down first and seemed to ignore his companions. He walked with a limp and yet this did not seem to detract in any way from his natural air of authority. His elegant navy blue narrow pinstripe suit was in sharp contrast to the black paramilitary uniforms of his companions.

The well-dressed man peered at the two boys briefly, his eyes seeming to pass straight through them before he suddenly barked at his two companions: "I told you both *not* to wear those clothes! Why did you not heed me?" The man was angry. There was an aristocratic upper-class clip to his voice, a voice that demanded attention and obedience. Without waiting for an explanation the man added, "I will not tolerate unnecessary provocation. Go to the lavatory and change. Now! Both of you. We are on a train for pity's sake, not a march!"

The two men stood up, they were muscular and broad. Both looked as if they knew all about street fighting or worse. One was shorter than the other, but no less threatening. They were wearing Sam Browne belts, black military-style shirts, ties and trousers.

"Sorry, Sir Oswald . . . It's just that as we are in London, and after that business at Cable Street . . . and well . . . er, other incidents . . ."

"Never mind Cable Street," the elegant man interrupted, "that was nearly two years ago, man. The Jewish residents got above their station, that was all. Now go and change before you find yourselves breaking the law even before we arrive in New-

204

castle. Do I have to remind you both of the insidious Public Order Act? Political uniforms and even, God forbid, so-called 'quasi-military style organizations' are banned. Now off you go before your stupidity exhausts me yet again."

The two men did as they were told and left the compartment.

John hadn't heard one word of the altercation that had taken place in the compartment. Love, kisses and Sheya had seen to that, whereas Issy had seen and heard everything. The man ordering his minions around had to be Sir Oswald Mosley. Issy had seen photographs of him and read about him in the newspapers. Mosley's British Union of Fascists was renowned for its violent confrontations with Communist and Jewish groups. The two thugs with him were obviously a pair of notorious 'Blackshirts'. All of a sudden Issy felt extremely uncomfortable and for the first time in years feared for his safety. He was a Jew and nothing could ever change the fact. He had heard the rumours of what was happening to Jews in Germany: the mass arrests, the labour camps. So far nothing of this nature had happened in England, let alone Wales, and at least he had never been a victim of any overt persecution. Sly remarks and the odd childish insult were a Jew's lot. He had grown up with it and Wales was no exception, but out-and-out violent prejudice and hatred – well, that was another matter.

Issy had experienced the fatal poison of Jew hating in Germany. He had seen the loaded guns in the eyes of the perpetrators, the knives in their hearts ready to butcher and mutilate. He looked at the refined aristocrat sitting opposite him and knew with absolute certainty that the clothes, the fine education, the breeding meant nothing. The elite, the well educated had become the Devil's own regiment in Germany. They were striving to be the planners and alchemists of mass destruction and genocide, as learning traded knowledge and civilised values for racial hatred and extermination.

The two ruffians returned and sat without speaking either side of Mosley while he read *The Times*. Issy caught one of them staring directly at him. He turned his eyes away immediately. Neither of the boys had exchanged any of the usual pleasantries with their travelling companions, which was unusual in itself. The silence started to make Issy feel awkward, although he was not sure exactly why; he had overcome his initial discomfort and momentary fears, and what on earth could anybody do to them on a train – and *Mallard* at that – in the middle of London? Still, the man who had stared at him made him edgy. Was he being too self-conscious? he wondered. Too sensitive? Being a Jew could do that sometimes. Demons hid around every corner and hedge. He looked at John, still staring out the window and no doubt thinking about Sheyna's 'titties'. His friend was impossible. He nudged John. For once the silence was too much and he couldn't concentrate on his book, a history of the Knights Templars.

"What's the matter, Issy?!" John almost shouted, as he had been just about ready to squeeze Sheyna's left nipple.

"No need to shout, John," Issy whispered as he looked at their travelling companions.

"Sorry, Issy. I was miles away. Are you bored or something? Not like you. History given up on you or something?"

Issy squeezed John's arm. It hurt.

"Ouch! What did you do that for? I only said you were bored. What's the matter with you?!"

"Stop calling me Issy, will you?" he attempted to say quietly into his friend's ear.

"What? What are you on about, Issy? And why are you whispering?"

Issy looked at John right in the eye. It was a warning look. At last the penny dropped. John didn't quite know why the penny had dropped, but his friend didn't look at him like that for nothing. Before he could say another word, Mosley lowered his newspaper and glanced at Issy.

"Ahh, young man. 'Issy'," Mosley said gently. "I believe that is a shortened version of 'Israel' is it not?" Issy looked

206

back at Mosley defiantly. Why should he have to hide his name? For a moment he felt ashamed of himself, his cowardice.

"Yes, it is. Why? What's it got to do with you?" Issy answered, his voice firm and challenging. Mosley was slightly shocked by such an aggressive response from one so young. His eyebrows shot up as he continued to look at Issy.

"A spirited Jew, it seems. How impressive. Your ilk are not renowned for their spirit, are they? Unsavoury commercial exploitation perhaps, but spirit, courage? I think not." John's instincts were now on full alert. The two men with the posh one were a lively pair of buggers, no doubt about it. They were big too, but then neither he nor Issy were small anymore either. Now they were both much stronger as well. Issy looked directly at Mosley and said, "You're in England now, Mr Mosley." He emphasised the word 'Mr'. "And your Jew-hating antics are not tolerated. So why don't you and your two monkeys go to hell?"

'Oh Jesu,' John thought, 'here we go'. Issy was usually the passive one, but once he was roused, look out! One of Mosley's thugs leapt up from his seat, fists clenched.

"You filthy little Jewboy runt!" the other shouted. "Do you know who you are talking to?"

"Yes I do, actually," Issy repied calmly. "Sir Oswald Mosley no less – King of the Fascists."

The man who had stood up made a lunge for Issy. "You Jewish bastard you! I'll give you—!" Before the man was able to land a punch Issy managed to kick him smack in the groin despite being seated. Even John was impressed. The man howled in agony as he fell to the floor while the other thug jumped up to join in the fray.

"You little Jewboy shit, you!" the other man yelled. By this time John had stood up, fists at the ready; as usual size meant nothing to him. The man was about to dive in when a raised voice bawled.

"That's enough! That's enough! Now sit down, all of you!" Mosley had not stirred from his seat, but his voice was enough.

That was the aristocracy for you, Issy had to admit: order out of chaos with just a few words. This time Issy didn't argue. Instead he stared at Mosley who was looking at him with a modest degree of admiration in his eyes. He actually smiled as he said: "You know young man, I am not another Herr Hitler, in spite of what you may or may not have been told. I may admire some of his political reforms, but I am not a fool either. You fought well I must say and with courage. You are to be commended. Now, I think it best that both I and my . . . er . . . friends remove ourselves to another compartment. We do not want another untidy fracas now, do we? Oh, and I apologise profusely for any . . . er . . . inconvenience they may have caused you. I will deal with them in due course. Now, good day to you and your companion."

With that Mosley stood up and turned to the 'friend' still bobbing about on the balls of his feet waiting to throw a punch. "Out! Now!" he barked as he looked down contemptuously on the man on the carriage floor still moaning and holding onto his manhood for dear life. "And bring that imbecile with you!"

When the two boys were finally left alone John looked at Issy and grinned.

"Well, Issy, I'd better not call you a Jewboy then, had I? You might try some of that handiwork on me!"

"Hell, John. Those men could have killed us . . . if Mosley hadn't stepped in, well—" Issy suddenly stopped talking in mid sentence.

"What's the matter now, Issy?"

"Er, I think it's me who's filled his pants this time!"

CHAPTER 33

It was late afternoon when *Mallard* finally pulled in to Newcastle station. The prospect of seeing Charity again both lifted and dropped Issy's spirits. The doubts retuned again. Had she gone home? Had she forgotten about him? These anxieties just wouldn't go away. Sideway led the way through a throng of busy people until they reached the exit gate. Tickets were punched and faces ignored as the three of them made their way out of the station and on to the hotel where they would meet up with some of the other Songsters. As they were waiting for a taxi there was a shout of "Issy!" and heads turned. Issy looked to his left and saw a running Charity charging in his direction. He couldn't believe his eyes.

"Issy! Issy! There you are! Where have you been?" Charity gushed as she ran up to him and took his hands in hers. "I have missed you and thought you were gone forever!"

"But how . . . how . . . did you know I was at the station?" Issy managed to say, beside himself with excitement at seeing Charity again.

"Oh, your Mr Steffani told me," Charity replied, unable to stop her grins and smiles. "He was very nice."

"I'm sorry about not being here when I said, I really am," Issy spluttered, "but some recording things came up and there was nothing I could do about it. I'm really sorry, I mean I did't have any way of getting in touch with you . . . I . . ." Issy tried to explain further, but Charity quickly interrupted.

"Oh, don't be silly now. You're here and that's all that matters. I knew you would turn up sooner or later. So stop apologising!" She stood in front of him, not letting go of his hands. She was so beautiful, so new. Her green eyes held him and wouldn't let go as her brown hat tilted awkwardly in an attempt to keep all the blond curls at bay.

Sideway had stood aside to watch this sudden meeting of two young hearts. He had been like that once he remembered, not with his wife though. Such eyes and touch would have been impossible with her. Even at the altar. He watched this remarkably pretty girl and handsome young man as they both tried desperately to restrain themselves. They were in a public place after all and kisses and hugs were out of the question, particularly at their age.

Sideway saw the innocence and the need in the two. He also saw a part of himself that life had long ago set adrift. He looked at the solid youth, the enthusiasm. For a moment he regretted and allowed his memory to be disturbed by a girl that time had immortalised. She had been pretty too and clever. He remembered days of cloistered love and punts that never went very far. He remembered reading poetry together, the kissing in between stanzas and the hands that would not let go. She had been his life then. All of it, until war and the Red Cross had ruined her life and his. The two had conspired to blow away her prettiness and their love. He had looked at her grave once and that had been enough. Love would never return again. He had never wanted it too.

"Er – excuse me," Sideway interrupted. "Young Issy, we do need to get on. And you, young lady . . . are?"

"Oh, I'm Charity. Charity Like. How do you do." Charity held out her hand and Sideway took it.

"How do you do, Miss Charity. A pleasure. Now you must excuse us. We are late already. Come along young fellows, The Empire beckons."

"You go on, Mr Sideway," Issy said. "I'll follow you." Issy was not about to let Charity out of his sight in a hurry. He had been beside himself for over a week.

"Well now, Issy," Sideway replied with that superior edge of his. "You might just find that a little difficult being as you don't know the name of the hotel."

"Oh . . . oh yes, I see what you mean." Issy was actually replying to Charity. They still hadn't untangled hands or taken their eyes off each other.

"The Grand," Sideway sighed. "*The Grand*, Issy – did you hear me? It's a mile or so up the road. Not far."

"Pardon . . . Mr Sideway? Oh yes, The Grand. Good. I'll see you later, then." Sideway grunted and gave up. Dear Lord, he had been like that once. Not a disagreeable condition he smiled to himself, in spite of the risks.

"Very well. And don't be long. You're performing later on, don't forget."

"I won't." Issy nearly added, 'Now bugger off, Sideways,' but thought better of it.

John had been watching all this along with Sideway and like Sideway was reminded of the past. Or at least in John's case the day before, if you could count that as the 'past'. Yearnings of kissing Sheyna again ran amok, let alone anything else! Charity was not the only one doing the 'missing'. As soon as John was in his hotel room he would start writing – and to hell with the performance later on! Not that he ever really needed to prepare much. Singing was singing; it didn't take that much effort. You either could or you couldn't.

When Issy finally turned up he had that 'all teeth and gum' grin all over his chops again.

"Nice-looking girl that, Issy. Got to hand it to you," John remarked as Issy started to get dressed for the evening performance.

"What do you mean?" Issy replied, a tetchy note of suspicion in his voice.

"What do you mean, 'What do I mean'?" John replied quickly, noting the angry whisper in his friend's voice. "I just said that Charity is nice. Bit of a cracker. That's all."

"Yes she is. Don't you start fancying her now, John as I won't have it!"

"Pardon? What on earth's the matter with you?!" John hadn't expected this touchy response from his friend since Issy was rarely touchy about anything. "I only said that Charity is a nice-looking girl. I've told you before. Whatever is wrong with you, Issy?"

"Oh, sorry. Nothing. It's just me. You know I haven't seen her and I was all worried. You know what with Steff making us go to London and all that. I missed one week with her and I'm still angry about it. Sorry, John. Don't take any notice."

"That's all right," John mumbled. "I think I know how you feel. I'm . . . um . . . missing Sheyna too." John was still none too sure how Issy would react if he really knew how deeply he felt about Sheyna; after all she was his sister.

Issy stopped dressing for a moment and sat down on his bed. He looked at his friend with those penetrating blue eyes of his.

"Look, John, I know you like Sheyna." 'Like' was putting it mildly, but John kept quiet. Issy was reading his mind again, he was always at it. He had no idea what was coming. When Issy got all serious it was best to shut up. "And I know she's my sister and all that, but you don't have to worry about my feelings. You really don't. I can see you're wondering whether I approve or not. Well, don't. It's nothing to do with me and Sheyna is a big girl now" – Issy smiled – "at least she likes to think she is." He punched John's arm. "Mind you, lay off her titties! I've caught a glimpse and she's not in short supply in that area I can tell you!" Both boys laughed. The mind reading had been accurate – again!

"I don't think Charity is either, come to think of it, Issy."

"No, isn't that a fact. We both caught more of a 'glimpse' that night in the dressing room." The two boys remained silent for a few moments. Then Issy said, "I still remember all those naked bodies, John. Do you?"

"Don't I just. How could I forget, Issy?"

"Do you want to touch Sheyna? You know, her skin. Her body? Because when I'm with Charity all I want to do is . . . well, touch her. Do you understand?"

"Oh I do, Issy. I do."

At this point John didn't want to go into much detail where Sheyna was concerned. Issy might be all right so far, but if John blurted out what he really wanted to do with Sheyna his friend would probably have a fit. Mind you, what exactly these 'doings' were all about remained a bit of a mystery. No doubt Issy was in the same boat. He had kissed Sheyna, but whether it had been a real 'French' job or not, who knows? At first John had thought Sheyna was trying to eat him alive, but he had soon got into the swing of things. It had been a bit sloppy, but nice for all that.

"What was kissing Charity like, then Issy?" John asked. "You still haven't told me. What's the big secret anyway? You know about me and Sheyna. Did you give her a 'French' kiss?" So far he hadn't pushed Issy about this, having assumed that Issy had kissed Charity. After all, yesterday Issy had said that they were both now 'equal'.

Before answering Issy went into one of his intense head-scratching moods. He often did this when he was reading.

"Well, now John," Issy scratched, "I haven't exactly . . . um . . . er . . . *kissed* Charity yet. Not in the way that you and Sheyna have done anyway. You know, lips together like in the pictures. She kissed my cheek that was all."

"What?!"

"You heard."

"You mean you didn't stick your tongue in her mouth? I've beaten you to it! Well, bugger me! I'm first at the post with the fillies then. Great! See Issy, you might have the brains but you're not so sharp with the girls. Bloody great. So much for history!" Issy had been expecting all this and as usual took it all in good spirits.

"Oh shut up, John. What's this about tongues anyway, sounds disgusting?"

"Well now, you can discover that for yourself, Issy. I think – but I'm not sure – that the tongue bit is what French kissing is all about. I asked Sideways."

"Sideways!"

"Why not? He knows just about everything."

"Yes, you could be right there. Well I'll just have to find out for myself then, won't I? Now come on, let's finish dressing, otherwise we'll have old Sideways after us."

"Bloody short trousers again," John moaned, "that will give Charity a laugh. When are you seeing her again anyway? Is she performing at the same theatre as us?"

"Yes."

"Great. We can watch her dance then."

"Yes . . . yes we can," Issy agreed. John missed the note of uncertainty in Issy's voice. The wariness. The ridiculous short trousers were not helping either; for once his friend was right about something.

Later that evening Issy, John and some of the other boys stood in the wings and enjoyed the entertainment. Stéphane Grappelli and Flanagan and Allen all delighted the audience with their music and humour, while Jawbone and Gargoyle remained as ugly as ever, no matter how much make-up was splattered on them.

It wasn't long before Charity appeared on the stage. A black top-hat tilted slightly on top of her shining curls as she expertly twirled a white baton around her body. A red bow-tie and tight red silk shirt covered in silver sequins only just concealed the upper part of her torso as a tiny pair of black shorts seemed to push her legs right up to the ceiling and beyond.

"Cor, will you look at them legs!" Jawbone gasped. "And the tits! What I wouldn't do to get my 'ands on 'em!"

Issy turned around and nearly thumped him.

"Don't you talk about her like that, Jawbone," Issy threatened, "otherwise I'll punch you into next week!! Do you hear me?!" No one messed with Issy, so Jawbone kept quiet as ordered. John had had enough sense to keep his mouth shut too – he already knew how sensitive Issy could be where Charity

214

was concerned – even though it was impossible to ignore her body, particularly as he now had some idea of what was beneath the silk and sequins. For a brief moment even Sheyna was banished from his mind as he watched and dribbled. She moved with a grace and speed that was utterly astonishing. Her legs seemed to have a will of their own as they danced and made all the men in the audience wonder where they had gone wrong. The other girls behind her were no match for the legs that swayed, tapped, jumped, somersaulted and forced the women in the theatre to push their skirts down even further. It was a bloody disgrace! When she did the splits every man in the house wanted to take her home and find out for themselves whether female legs could actually do that kind of thing or whether it was some kind of theatrical trick. Imagine the possibilities if it was genuine!

Eventually Charity left the stage and as she passed the boys she gave Issy a quick peck on the cheek.

"I'll meet you outside later," she whispered. "Wait for me." Jawbone and Gargoyle couldn't believe their eyes .

"What?" Jawbone stammered, "What was all that about, Issy? Fuck, she kissed you! She kissed you!" Gargoyle couldn't believe what he had just seen either. His lips parted in an extra special rictus as he stood still and gawped.

"Have I just shat a miracle or what?" he managed to say.

John looked at his friend and felt Issy's discomfort. His anger. Love wasn't supposed to be like this, was it? They had all seen plenty of dancing girls before and he and Issy had even seen them naked, but there was something different about Charity, the way she danced, the way she seemed to tease so blatantly. John hadn't been the only one to notice. He remembered his own dirty thoughts as he had watched her. No doubt the other boys had been thinking the same things. He wouldn't have wanted anyone else to think like that about Sheyna either. It was all right for him of course, but anyone else? Well, that wouldn't do at all. The very thought made his stomach turn.

As the evening went on, the sense of growing anticipation in the audience could almost be touched. All the tickets had been sold in advance, and those who had not been able to obtain one stood at the back of the auditorium shuffling and whispering at the prospect of listening to Britain's Greatest Boy Soprano, Master John Illtyd Rees. Most people were in the theatre just to hear this famous boy about whom they had heard so much. John had become a professional now, he knew the vocal ropes and had reached the top. His stomach still jumped with nerves, but being the old campaigner that he now undoubtedly was he knew that once the singing started they would soon disappear. There were few things capable of diminishing pure beauty.

As he walked up to the microphone and stage lights obscured all other living things the audience, John's audience, for they were now truly his, stirred for a moment as their eyes respected and wished. Chests stopped heaving from the demands of earlier humour and ribald music as hands stayed still to gather strength for the urgent clapping that they knew must come. The coloratura boy soprano's reputation always went before him.

John stood in front of the microphone, arms at his side, and waited for Steffani's cue. The theatre had become an eerie mausoleum, a tomb of total silence. Nothing moved, not even the air. John looked out at the blackness and felt the admiration, the anticipation. The love. In these few moments Sam, his father, his mam, Sheyna and even Winnie all became one delightful and cherished thought. The catharsis of his voice always healed and always remembered. He started to sing what had become his most famous calling card, Bishop's 'Lo! Hear The Gentle Lark'. Thousands of people had bought his records, but nothing could beat seeing and hearing this handsome young boy in the flesh. John's voice hoarded and treasured, it made the audience seek places they had never been to before. It made them wonder and forced them to reflect. Wherever John went they went with him, they could not help themselves. Suddenly halfway through the song as John began to hit

'E' above top 'C' his greatest fear pounced from nowhere. It ambushed and ruined. His voice refused to answer the call. It bolted and ran and there was nothing he could do about it. The hopeless beauty of his voice was finally succumbing to the inevitable. Age was taking no prisoners. John stood in front of the microphone arms raised in supplication as the voice that had brought him fame and fortune surrendered to Nature and her impossible demands. The piano stopped and mourned while Steffan's eyes lashed and whipped John's young body with fury and disappointment. The finest boy coloratura soprano he had ever heard was moving on to the darker and more dangerous world of manhood. Steffani could have wept, not for the shocked disappointment that silenced the audience or the grim hiatus of a tragic 'Goodbye', but for the desecration of an unblemished purity. John's voice was snapping, breaking into a million pieces, his vocal chords were losing their magnificent innocence and his testicles were dropping towards the floor with a determination that not even Steffani could prevent. John's days in the Songsters were now numbered along with Issy's, whose voice was already sitting in a condemned cell waiting for the final drop.

As John suffered the most devastating humiliation his young life had ever known Issy waited outside the theatre and paced. He was oblivious to the tragedy taking place within.

Why did he always feel so tense at the prospect of seeing Charity? She was not out to hurt him after all. Earlier that day they had walked around the shops of Newcastle, eventually stopping at a tea shop to enjoy more intimately each other's words and gestures. As each sentence passed between them the love deepened and became more urgent. They talked and listened, laughed and joked. There was no one else in the tea room apart from themselves, no other conversation or laughter apart from their own. Their eyes refused to wander and their hearts refused to let go as each became the other's whole world and all and everything that could ever matter.

At last Charity came through the stage door and ran up to Issy.

"Hello!" She beamed, her smile as usual making Issy more nervous than ever. Charity was so natural, her emotions so free and easy. Not like him at all. He smiled back unable to do anything else. All he ever seemed to do when Charity was around was smile. He couldn't help it. Before he could say anything Charity took his arm and said, "Come on, let's go for a walk. It's getting late so we had better keep to the main thoroughfares. There's nowhere we can go at this time of night, at least I don't think so. I don't fancy a public house – those places are always so rough, don't you think?"

"Well, I've never really spent much time in them, but I know they don't have a good reputation. Maybe we could try my hotel. It's very posh and it has a quiet lounge there. We both look old enough to go unnoticed. We could have some tea or something." Thank God the theatre was only a stone's throw away from the hotel where he and John were staying. He had been able to dash back and change into long trousers before meeting Charity.

"Aren't you the lucky one, posh hotels, fine service. How do you manage it? It's cheap doss-houses for me. Lowest of the low we chorus girls, you see." Issy stopped Charity in her tracks and pulled her around to face him.

"Don't say that, Charity! You're not the 'lowest of the low'. Nor will you ever be. I saw you dance earlier on and you were wonderful, you really were and don't you ever forget it. Besides, I'm only there because of John. He's the star you know, not me. The other Songsters are always put in cheaper hotels. Steff daren't upset John by splitting us up, that's all."

Charity immediately saw the intensity, the care in Issy's blue eyes and knew without doubt that he meant every word. She was touched too by his protective instinct toward her. They stayed looking into each other's eyes. At this moment neither one wanted to move away. Charity wanted Issy to kiss her there and then, to hold her in his arms and kiss her until she swooned. It was late and the road was quiet, no-one would notice a lover's kiss would they? She continued to look into Issy's eyes, to urge, to demand. He stared back, uncertainty again. Tension. He held her hands in his. The moment had arrived. The moment that kept holding on to his dreams and wouldn't let go. It had to be now. It had to be.

"I . . . I . . ." Issy managed to mumble as his head dropped to stare at the pavement. "Oh . . . I, er . . . look, let's go and have that tea, shall we?" The kiss ran away faster than a frightened rabbit; it had hovered between them long enough, so to hell with the pair of them! Charity could have kicked Issy there and then, but instead she let out a long sigh and dragged him off down the road. From now on she decided, she would have to take the initiative. She was older than Issy after all and far more sophisticated in more ways than one.

As they walked to Issy's hotel Charity said, "You know just before I came to meet you the theatre suddenly went silent. It was odd really, not the usual silence when someone is singing or something – it was just, well . . . oh, I don't know. Come to think of it there wasn't any applause either. Most odd. Maybe somebody's act just died on them. Funny lot, audiences." The notion of John's voice being demolished by manhood never entered Issy's head. Why should it?

"Yes, they are," Issy replied. "I've seen a few performers die, and yet some of them come back for more. That's variety for you, I suppose. For some people it's worse than drink." Suddenly the prospect of having to leave the Songsters made Issy go cold. It wasn't leaving the stage that bothered him, it was the thought of losing Charity. "You know, Charity, I don't think I've got much more time left on the stage. Steff hasn't found a replacement yet, but he tells me that he does have someone in mind. It's up to the parents apparently. I have a feeling it won't be long. He as good as told me that this morning."

219

"Leaving the stage, Issy?" Charity looked shocked. "But you can't! . . . I mean . . . Oh, sorry . . . but what will you do?" Now it was Charity's turn to go all cold. This was one thought that had never occurred to her. Young love again. It was supposed to be immortal, it couldn't possibly die. "You can't leave the stage, Issy. You simply can't! I mean what will happen to . . .?"

"What will happen to what, Charity?" Issy insisted. It was his turn to take the lead now. He needed to know. "What will happen to what, Charity?" he repeated.

"Well . . . um . . . you and me, Issy. I couldn't stand the thought of not seeing you. I mean we've become . . . er . . . well close, haven't we?" Suddenly Issy started to feel all warm and stupid. Even his stomach did a few somersaults.Charity had answered all his questions, all his uncertainties, in those few simple words.

"Yes . . . yes we have," Issy replied, unable to stop himself smiling. "I want to go to university to study history though."

"Do you? To be a professor like your father?"

"Maybe. Who knows?"

"Perhaps I can study with you, Issy. Then we won't need to be apart!" Charity giggled.

There was a difficult silence for a few moments as both of them quickly decided that the future was best left well alone. For now anyway. It would only spoil their precious time together. And apart from anything else it was far too frightening to think about.

"What a lovely thought!" Issy smiled again in that enigmatic way of his. "Now come on, we're nearly there."

Before they walked into the hotel foyer Issy stopped Charity and held one of her hands in his. He touched her cheek and pushed one of her blond curls out of her eyes with his fingers. "You know, Charity, I don't think we will ever be apart. I really don't. I won't let that happen anyway, believe me." He lowered his head and for the first time kissed her on the lips – a long and gentle kiss, a kiss of love, nothing more nothing less. Some

220

people walking past noticed and remembered. There was no anger, no moral outrage.They just wished and carried on walking.

When their lips finally parted Charity whispered, "Your friend won't be back for a while Issy, so will you show me your room? I really would like to see it."

Later that evening Issy finally mastered the art of French kissing – with Charity's help – and it wasn't disgusting at all! He mastered a lot of other 'arts' too.

John would have been proud of him!

CHAPTER 34

A quiet sobbing woke Issy up in the early hours of the morning. He could still smell Charity; she was on his skin, the bedsheets, everywhere. He looked across at John's bed. What was the matter with his friend? He was crying. John rarely cried, if ever. The last time Issy had seen any tears come from John's eyes had been at Owen Rees's funeral. He got out of bed.

"What's the matter, John?" Issy asked gently as he switched on a light. He knew about his friend's pride, its strength and its weakness.

"Nothing, Issy. Go away," John replied from beneath a bundle of white sheets. Issy hadn't heard John come in. Nothing unusual there; lately it had been his friend's habit to stay on after the show and enjoy some fun with the other performers – particularly if they were black and had some of those gigantic ciggies.

"Come on, John. What's the matter?" Issy persisted. "Don't try brushing me off and don't be so stubborn. Something's wrong, now what is it? Come on."

Eventually John raised his head from beneath the sheets. He didn't overdo it though. "Shit, Issy," he snivelled, "My voice . . . my voice cracked right in the middle of the 'Gentle Lark'. I'm buggered."

"What do you mean?"

"It was terrible, Issy. Oh Christ, I could have died."

"But . . . but . . ." Issy didn't know what to say.

"No 'buts' Issy. That's it. Bloody voice!" John almost shouted. "Couldn't break slowly, could it? You know, prepare me bit by bit like you. Had to start breaking right when I'm on stage, didn't it. The bastard! Tried to hit the high notes and all that came out was a bloody croak! Can you imagine it? Sounded like one of my stupid toads after my mam's been at them, I'm telling you. The crowd went all silent. You could have heard a pin drop. It would have been better if they had booed and shouted at me to get off. But all they did was sit there like a bunch of lemons. You should have seen Steff's face. I just ran off the stage, didn't know what else to do. I thought he was going to explode. Well, Britain's Greatest Boy Soprano just died a thousand sodding deaths, make no mistake. I will never go back on the stage again, that's for certain – and to hell with Steff and his bank balance!"

"Oh . . . oh . . . Well . . ." was all Issy could manage to say. So John must have been the cause of the 'odd silence' that Charity had talked about. For a moment Issy realised that John could have walked into their room much earlier than expected, the thought forcing him to take in a deep breath.

"Why didn't you come straight back here then?" Issy asked, at the same time relieved that his friend hadn't as he would never have been allowed to live it down. "You knew I was here. I am your best friend after all."

"Oh, I just walked around the streets for a while," John said quietly. "I didn't want to talk to anyone." Sheyna would have fitted the bill just dandy, but that wasn't to be. He could have talked to her all night long. "You know Issy, it's not the fact that my voice is breaking – I'm glad it's happened in some ways, I might even start shaving properly now– but it was the humiliation. You know, in front of all those people. I let them down, Issy. And you know over the past couple of years people have come to expect a bloody good boy soprano . . . Now those days are well and truly over and that's a fact." John wiped his eyes. The tears had stopped falling and Issy was beside him just as he always was in times of need.

"Well, John," Issy said. He knew how much John loved entertaining an audience. "You know it had to happen sooner or later."

"Yes, I know, Issy. I know. Doesn't make it any easier though . . . Oh well, looks like we'll both be going back to Wales together then after all." At last John managed a smile. As usual, being down in the dumps didn't last long where John was concerned. His pride was damaged, but he would soon recover. He always did.

"Yes, I suppose so, John." The lacklustre response from Issy didn't go unnoticed.

"Is something wrong, Issy?" It was John's turn now to be the understanding friend and confidante.

"Well, Steff told me this morning that there's a possible replacement for me."

"Oh, did he? I see . . ." John thought for a moment and then said kindly, "Well . . . I mean you can get on with your studies now, can't you? It's what you've always wanted."

"Yes, I know John but even so—"

"Ah, don't tell me. Charity."

"Yes. Charity."

"Now that could be a bit difficult, but as my mam always says, 'Where there's a will there's a way'. So just find a way to keep seeing each other. Who knows, she might be dancing in Wales or you could even study somewhere in England. There are plenty of universities after all. Come on, Issy. Cheer up and anyway I'm the one who's in the shit right now so don't you start!" Although John hated the idea of his friend possibly taking off with Charity he couldn't blame him. The girl was a real gem after all.

"Yes, John." Issy at last grinned. "For once you're right. We'll find a way. We'll sort something out I expect. Now can we go back to sleep? You know what I'm like if I don't get enough sleep."

"Don't I just."

"Oh and John."

"Yes."

"My father has always said that if you can go through life and count at least one loyal and true friend on your fingers then

224

you are a fortunate and blessed man. I believe him, John. And you and I will always be friends – and don't you ever forget it, you stupid devil!"

"I know, Issy. I know. Now come on, let's go to sleep. I'll have to face Steff in the morning and tell him I'm off."

"He'll be all right, John. Don't worry. Probably be glad to see the back of us, I mean we haven't made his life all that easy, have we? What with the drink, that funny tobacco and all the fights with the other boys. No, don't you worry about Steff. And as for Sideways, well, he will probably have the bunting out and the Sally Army to sing us on our way! Now, goodnight."

"You can say that again," John smirked underneath the bed-clothes. "The miserable old bastard!"

CHAPTER 35

"You can't just 'Go home' when you feel like it, John. Wherever did you get that nonsense from!" Steffani was angry; he didn't like his boys having ideas of their own. Theirs was to sing and his was to conduct. They were sitting down in the lounge of the hotel. "I decide," Steffani continued, "when you leave and no one else. Your voice hasn't fully broken yet, so at least you can still harmonise in the choir. Solo is out of the question of course. I've already lost your friend, but fortunately I do now have a replacement. The new boy's parents have finally agreed. The money did the trick, just as it always does with people who are poor. We are performing tonight and how do you think I can find someone to replace you that quickly? How? It's bad enough that the Songsters no longer have a solo soprano – at least someone who is up to your standard. And there's the tickets that have already been sold. I could lose a fortune."

"Well, not much I can do about that," John replied a little too carelessly. "You've always known, Steff, that my voice would break sooner or later. The gravy train couldn't go on forever, could it?" John's maturity was taking Steffani by surprise. He was quickly realising that he couldn't treat John like a boy anymore. "You know, Steff," John said firmly, "all you ever think about is the money. Well, I've made you plenty. A lot more of the bloody stuff than I've got in the bank anyway—"

"That's enough!" Stephani interrupted furiously. "How *dare* you swear at me!" Steffani was really getting mad now. John's voice had been paying for his luxurious lifestyle for quite a while. It was bad enough that the boy's voice was breaking (and with it Steffani's bank account) without having to put up with his impertinence. Steffani had always known that John's voice could not go on indefinitely. He was right about that, but even so the suddenness of it had left him unprepared. John stood his ground and looked defiantly at Steffani.

"Look, Steff. You can't do a thing. I don't have any contract with you and do you think I don't know why? If I'd had a personal manager you'd have lost out and you know it. My mam knew it, but she's too much of a lady to argue with the likes of you. Now I'm off whether you like it or not. Stuff your Songsters, in fact you can shove them right up your arse! Cheerio." John stood up and walked off.

Steffani, on the verge of an apoplectic fit, shouted after him, "Damn you, John Rees! Damn you!"

"Come on, Issy. We're off," John ordered a few minutes later as he barged into their bedroom. Issy had been waiting in their room for John to finish with Steffani. He had tried all morning to dissuade his friend from taking such drastic action, but he also knew that once John had made up his mind then that was that. Where John would push his heels through concrete rather that budge an inch Issy would compromise and reason with the cement. Issy had seen Steffani earlier that morning, only to be told that he could go back home as he was no longer needed. He had been given some cash, a 'Thank you' and a kick up the arse.

"Off where, John?" Issy demanded. They were a long way from home and there was Charity to think about. Issy hadn't said a word about the previous evening with Charity and was not about to now, as John was in enough of a lather at the moment. Apart from anything else the thought of having to satisfy John's crude curiosity just didn't bear thinking about. As for the things he and Charity had done, well, he couldn't stop thinking about it. Mind you, the look on John's face would be worth it. The temptation quickly dissolved at the memory of Charity's touch. She had led and he had followed. He hadn't known what else to do. To begin with there had been the childish

227

fear of nakedness with all its vulnerability and hidden places. Then there had been the overwhelming mystery of a journey into the unknown as emotion and desire had crept around them quietly before moving in to turn them both inside out. It had all gone on and on – one minute together, the next nowhere at all. Touch and kiss, on and on. No, these things were definitely for he and Charity alone and not to be shared, not even with his best friend.

"Well now," John replied as he scratched his chin. These days he was always scratching his chin, scratching in anticipation, unlike Issy who always scratched his head when he was in deep thought. "I haven't really thought that one out. Can't stay here now, can we? I've just told Steff to shove his Songsters right up his arse."

"You *what*?!" Issy almost shrieked.

"You heard," John said calmly, "or do I need to shout?"

"You told Steff *that*?! God help us!"

"Don't be stupid now, Issy. There's nothing he can do about it. The Songsters are over for us, so it's back home for me" – John nearly added 'and back to Sheyna' but thought better of it – "and off to university for you . . . wherever that will be."

"Just you hold on there now, John. I'm not going to just drop everything and take the first train back home. There's . . . well, there's Charity to think about."

"Oh, is there now? You surprise me." John looked at Issy innocently.

"Well, you know we like each other."

"'Like'? 'Like?'" John was starting to laugh. "Can't say you're in love, can you, Issy! You just can't, you daft sod! Come on Issy, admit it. You're in love!" John then started to jump up and down yelling, "Issy's in love! Issy's in love!" Issy looked at the spectacle. It was so typical of his friend to start making fun of him.

"Shut up, John! Just shut up!"

"Issy's in love! Issy's in love!" John continued to tease.

"Right, that's it! I'm off!" Issy shouted as he grabbed his case and made for one of the cupboards. "To hell with you. Make your own way home. Anyway, at least I know about a girl's body! And a lot more than that too!" Issy immediately regretted his last few words. The cat was out of the bag, so much for keeping things secret. John would never stop now.

"What! What! What do you mean? 'About a girl's body' and 'A lot more?'" John immediately stopped playing the fool, this was serious. "You didn't have a squeeze of her titties, did you Issy? Jesu!"

"Much more than that, John. *Much* more." It was Issy's turn to tease and annoy now so he might as well make the most of it. "We . . . well, you know."

"'We' what? Issy! Come on, tell me!"

"Well, you know. We did 'it'."

"Did what for Christ's sake?!" John couldn't believe what he was hearing. "You didn't . . . I mean, well . . . you didn't . . . *did* you, Issy?"

"I did and it was well . . . marvellous. I mean really marvellous." Issy was enjoying this, the look on John's face was something to behold.

"'Marvellous?!'" John shouted. "Jesu, Issy! 'Marvellous'?! You actually did 'it!'" John was beside himself with envy and jealousy. Issy had managed 'it' first and he was still only sixteen but still, it must be some kind of record. John stood in front of his friend open-mouthed, and for once unable to say a word.

"Are you trying to catch some flies or something, John. You look as if you've just farted in the middle of one of your solos." After a few more seconds of silence John finally managed to squeak.

"You did 'it'? I mean you actually, well er . . .? Bugger me, Issy, bugger me . . . Now you're not lying now, are you, Issy?" This 'it' thing was still a bit of a grey area where John was concerned in spite of his backstage antics.

229

"Yes, I did, John. Now can we talk about something else, please?" John was not going to be put off this easily. He wanted to know everything.

"What was it like, Issy? Come on, what was it like? Did you squeeze her nipples? Your sister taught me how to squeeze them—"

"She *what*, John?!" Sometimes John did get the better of his friend. Not often, but sometimes. Now it was Issy's turn to look shocked. "Sheyna showed you how . . . how, well, to . . . I don't believe you! Where could she have learnt to do that?" The thought of his little sister knowing how to have her nipples squeezed was just beyond the pale.

"Don't ask me, but she sure as hell knew her business. Like you say, 'Marvellous' it was."

"You didn't do anything else now, did you John?" Issy was really getting worried now. Sheyna was his little sister after all, and not allowed to get up to the things that he and Charity had got up to.

"Might have done," John replied cryptically, enjoying the demolished look on Issy's face. "If you won't tell me anything, why should I tell you?"

"Now look, John."

"Never mind, 'Now look, John'. I'm not telling you anything, so go and read a book or something." The hell of it was that there wasn't much to tell. He and Sheyna had kissed and that was all. Mind you, in some ways that had been enough. God, he couldn't wait until Sheyna tried to swallow him whole again. Given half a chance he would have done a lot more, but it was not to be. At the time his cock had ached and throbbed like a good 'un for all the good it had done him. Issy was still staring at him with that hopeless, imploring expression he always used when he wanted to play the martyr, and as usual John was unable to resist, so he decided to exercise some tact for a change. "Oh, all right, don't get yourself all worked up now, Issy. Nothing happened between me and Sheyna. Nothing more than a kiss anyway. I would have liked" – John just about managed to stop himself in time – "er . . . some more kissing but you turned up. Bugger!" John grinned, saw the relief in his friend's face and quickly changed the subject, a gesture with which Issy was only too happy. "Now then, enough of all this dirty stuff, Issy. What are we going to do? At least we're not short of money, that's something I suppose." Issy quickly decided that John was telling the truth. He had done nothing more than kiss his sister; if he had managed anything else then no doubt Issy would have known. John might have fooled him for a few moments, but he would never have been able to keep it up. John was a hopeless liar at the best of times. He let the matter drop and accepted the truce.

"Find somewhere to stay first, John. Steff isn't going to pay for us here, is he? We need a bit of time to work things out. And I must see Charity, I really must." Issy looked directly at John. For the first time in their friendship John saw a different intensity in the blueness of his friend's eyes. It was an intensity that he had only come to understand since kissing Sheyna. The love for a young woman: fretful, enormous, wanton and brave. "I don't know about you, John," Issy added quietly, "but I'm not rushing home. Like I say, there's Charity." John looked at his friend.

"I understand, Issy. I think I know how you feel. Sheyna makes me feel the same way."

"Well, then, you had better get off home, hadn't you?"

"I can't do that, Issy. I'm not leaving you up here on your own."

"Don't be daft. I'll be fine."

"No you won't. Four fists are better than two. It's a big city, lots of opportunity for trouble. I'm staying with you . . . Oh, and don't worry, you can kiss Charity and . . . well, you know . . . as much as you like. I'll keep out of the way. But I'm not leaving you up here on your own until we work out where we're going or what you're going to do. Anyway, I suppose

I'm quite simple really. I'll go home and find a job or something. So for once, Issy, don't argue!"

Issy didn't argue. Instead both boys enjoyed a few minutes of silence and reflection. Their seventeenth birthdays were not far away. Their lives were changing with a drama far greater than anything they had hitherto experienced on the stage. Deep voices, tentative lessons in sex, stubborn beards that in John's case always seemed to be promising but never delivering, as well as a future fraught with uncertainty, made both boys sit still and think. There were no adults around to guide them now, no higher authority. No one to explain. For a long time they had been taken care of, even pampered. Their lives had been full of adventure and fun. Everyday had been different, new. Responsibility was an unknown concept, a strange commodity that both intimidated and titillated. Manhood had most certainly arrived, and with it the mastering of their own destinies. There were no longer any grown-up restraints or any ironclad fists of discipline and control. They were on their own. To climb and fall, to go and to return. But most of all, as they both sat thinking, their young minds tried to satisfy and placate the towering and inept demands of young love – its pristine hope, its naïve appetite, but more than anything else its tumescent and reckless obsession.

A knock on the door disturbed their anxieties.

"Come in!" John shouted. If it was Steff then he would be in for some more of the same. It was bad enough that his voice was going, along with all the fun – not to mention the other stuff.

Sideway walked in.

"Well, young Rees. You have certainly excelled yourself this time I must say."

"Now look—" John was about to begin another belligerent tirade but Sideway stopped him.

"Enough of your spleen, young fellow," Sideway said calmly. "I really think there's been enough of that for one morning."

This time John kept quiet. He might have made fun of Sideway on occasions, but there had also been a healthy respect for the man too. Boring old codger the man might be, but he had always been kind to the boys and tolerant. The calming influence of Bertram Sideway had an immediate effect on John's defiant angst and disappointment.

"Yes. I'm sorry, Mr Sideway. Sorry for my rudeness to Steff too." John could exercise humility when he wanted to. Besides, Steff might have been a money-grabbing old devil, but he had never done any harm to either himself, Issy, or any of the other boys for that matter. This was John all over. Fire and brimstone one minute, all calm and charm the next. The redness of his hair might have been less fearsome, but the same could not be said for his temper.

"No apology required, young man."

"I beg your pardon, Mr Sideway."

"There is no need to apologise. Not to my good self nor indeed to Mr Steffani. We both understand how you must feel, particularly after last night. It must have come as quite a shock, yes indeed. Now then I have just spoken to Mr Steffani and he has asked you to forgive his . . . er . . . reactions to your . . . um . . . last confabulation as it were. He would like you to stay on if at all possible, at least for the rest of the week. Two weeks would be even better if it's not too inconvenient. We are performing in Cardiff next week so . . . Well, you will almost be home if we're there. You can still sing in the choir and it will allow Mr Steffani time to find a replacement. He does understand that it may well be your preference to return home immediately, but would appreciate just two more weeks of your fine voice. He is also happy for young Issy to remain with you even if he no longer sings in the choir. Commissions and all expenses paid of course."

Issy looked at John, his eyes urging him to accept the olive branch. What was two weeks after all and it would save them some money and give him time to sort something out with

Charity. John's immediate reaction was to say 'Yes', but being the awkward little sod that he usually was he made Sideway sweat.

"Well, I don't know, Mr Sideway," John replied. "After all, being in the choir isn't like being the star of the show after all." Sideway looked at him, suspicion almost hounding John out of the room. Typical. He knew his charges. Once again, he wanted to smile, he just couldn't help it. Illtyd John Rees was such an utter rascal.

"Well, young Rees, Mr Steffani is more than happy to pay your usual fee as it were, together with a generous bonus if it will help your decision."

"All right then," John replied, not even pausing for some polite thought. "Two weeks it is."

"Jolly good, young fellow . . . Oh, and no more tantrums I trust."

"Not me, Mr Sideway."

"I take it that's a 'no', young Rees?"

"Oh, indubitably, Mr Sideway," John grinned. "Indubitably."

Sideway grunted and left the room. There were times when even his fingers twitched where Master Illtyd John Rees was concerned.

CHAPTER 36

The pianist sat down on the tartan rug that he always brought with him to the Downs. It had been his mother's and still retained some of her scent. He came to the Downs at the same time each day in the summer anyway, and when his music allowed. Habit was everything, it ensured familiarity. Certainty.

It was lunchtime so, as always, he started to eat some beef sandwiches and drink from a bottle of beer. His father had enjoyed his beer too, but never too much and never on a Sunday. The pianist ate and drank with the delicacy that his profession demanded. As he chewed on the beef he tried to look across the Downs, since there were times when he felt he could almost see or at least feel. A passer-by would not have immediately recognised his lack of sight or anything untoward. His eyes were a rich blue and looked quite normal.

The maturity of his late twenties had blessed him with fine looks and a slim, muscular build. His dark, dimpled chin defied any weakness, likewise the sturdy lines of jaw and cheek. His jet-black hair was long for those times, falling about his neck in a disorder that would never have been tolerated where his music was concerned. As he tried to see, the sun pounded his open-necked collarless white shirt. He hated stiff collars and ties almost as much as he hated the formality of performing to an audience.

The pianist enjoyed these hours spent out in the open. He could feel the air, the space. There were times when he wondered if eyesight was such a wonderful gift after all. There were so many ugly things in the world. His mind could see obscenity and horror as well as beauty. As he ate his eyes roamed around the Downs making an effort even when they knew it was hopeless. The pianist was unaware of their exertions; he was happy in his peaceful haven, content with the warm air.

"Hello again!" A female greeting came from somewhere above him. The pianist turned to the familiar voice and heard the rustle of a skirt as the woman sat down. "How are you, Tristram? I haven't seen you for a while. Been off on one of your concert tours, have you?" Tristram's expertise with sound and smell had already told him all he needed to know about his companion. She was a young woman aged about twenty-four or thereabouts. He was certainly older. Her voice, her perfume and her body were all unmistakeable. He also felt her smile and her warmth. They had met on numerous occasions, the woman always seeming to take her walk at the same time as Tristram took his.

"Hello, Clarissa. Yes, I've been away for a month or so. On tour."

"May I have a sip of your beer, Tristram? It's so hot, more so up here on the Downs."

"Yes of course. Do help yourself. There's plenty left . . . I have already been drinking from it though." Tristram's voice was masculine without being obvious; there were no deep tones, but neither was it effeminate. It resembled some of his compositions, light and seeming to grapple with the air.

"Oh, I don't mind as long as you don't. I don't think I'm carrying any deadly disease anyway – at least I hope not!" Clarissa giggled and placed the bottle to her lips. "Golly! Very unladylike, this. Swigging from a bottle. My father, the dear colonel would be mortified. He's only just getting used to the fact that I drive, and if there's a war, well look out! I'll be in there in the thick of it, don't you worry." She lit a cigarette and blew out the match with a puff of smoke.

"Do you think there will be another war, Clarissa?" Tristram asked. He was always interested in what this young woman had to say. She was always so . . . well, so vivacious and self-opinionated.

"I hope so! Daddy seems to think it's inevitable and so does just about everybody else, apart from that twit Mr Chamberlain." The odd plum slipped into Clarissa's mouth when she spoke, but these occasions were usually tempered by a common sense and practical approach to life. The upper class twangs in her voice were really quite attractive, particularly when she blasphemed – which wasn't often. "Frightful business I know, but what an adventure for we young women. The government is bound to need us. Not to do any fighting of course, but then again who knows? I wouldn't mind shooting some Germans. Look at the way they're carrying on; scoundrels and swine the lot of them!" Tristram smiled; there was nothing like a public school education. Any war would be won in a sportsmanlike manner and with equal aplomb. It would all be one great and amusing *Boy's Own* adventure with some Biggles and Manfred von Richthofen thrown in for good measure.

"I suppose you're right," Tristram conceded. "But do you really want a repetition of the last war, Clarissa? All those dead men. All the wounded and maimed. Do you?" Clarissa thought for a moment as her face fell into a gorgeous pout. Had Tristram been able to see he would have fallen in love with her pout, if nothing else. It had been made to devestate any man, blind or otherwise. Clarissa was red haired, pale and so beautiful that in truth she should never be allowed to go near any war. She also longed for a time when Tristram could see. Maybe not with his eyes, but his touch and his heart would be more than enough.

"No, maybe not," Clarissa replied carefully. She was sitting next to a genius after all. She blew out a puff of smoke, her emancipation having begun a long time before any threats of war. "Not when you put it like that anyway . . . Now, let's talk about something else. Where have you been on your tour? Somewhere interesting no doubt. What a life you lead, Tristram. It must be so exciting. Come on, tell all!" Her enthusiasm was infectious, it lifted and forced a feeling of optimism. Although Clarissa thought he could not see her love she was gravely mistaken. Tristram knew and despaired. He wanted so much to love, so much to touch. He felt her smile, knew its charming attraction. He was desperate to return her gifts, but how could he? His blindness would only inflict and wound beyond repair. For a moment he wanted to cast Clarissa away. To be rid of her. Any light in his darkness could cause trouble. Instead he turned his face toward her. He knew what her eyes were seeing, what they were looking for. He heard her breathe out smoke, then join her fingers together in her lap and imagined her flowing red hair fall around her shoulders in bundles of pure delight. Tristram knew that he was sitting next to a masterpiece of womanhood who also happened to have fallen hopelessly in love with him, and who adored him beyond words.

CHAPTER 37

"I have to go back on Sunday, Issy." Charity held Issy's hand as she spoke. They were sitting in the lounge at Issy's hotel. "My mother is expecting me. She always looks forward to me coming home. You know what mothers are like."

"Yes, yes. I know, Charity. I'm supposed to be off to Cardiff on Sunday too. Not singing, those days are over, just keeping John company. I'm going home really. My parents only live a few miles away. It's Tuesday now, so we don't have long." The thought of being parted was too much for both of them.

"Oh, Issy. What are we going to do?"

"Well . . . er . . . Birmingham does have a university, so there's an excuse to visit there. *'Per ardua ad alta'*."

"Pardon?" said Charity, not having the faintest idea what Issy was talking about.

"Oh, the university's motto," Issy smiled. " 'Through hard work, great things are achieved'." Latin. I did a little research."

"Really." Charity giggled, not quite grasping what Issy meant. "Latin as well. Whatever next?"

"You know, I . . . er . . . don't have to go to Cardiff, Charity. Steff's got a replacement for me now. I'd only be keeping John company . . ." The thought of leaving his friend suddenly made Issy feel miserable. How would John react? Would he be upset? They had always done everything together. Issy was beginning to understand how love sometimes demanded sacrifice and hurt. Charity noticed Issy's thoughtful silence. She was beginning to recognise them in an instant. Sometimes he would appear distracted, even with her. She knew that he didn't mean to offend, she also knew that it was just his way. He was a thinker.

"What's the matter, Issy?"

"Oh, nothing much. Just wondering how John will react if I tell him I'm not going to Cardiff with him . . . if I . . . well . . . go home or something."

Charity took Issy's other hand in hers. She still didn't grasp what Issy was hinting at as she said gently, "He'll be fine, Issy. He's a tough young man that one, make no mistake. He'll get along just fine without you for week or so, so don't you worry. You're not his father after all."

"Anyway, if you're going back to Birmingham, Charity . . . well . . ." By now Issy had had enough. He had tried hinting, but Charity was simply not going to be bold enough, since on this occasion she was letting him take the lead. "Look, Charity, I, um . . . well, I was thinking that maybe I could stay up in Birmingham for a week or so instead of going to Cardiff. You know, while you stay with your mother. I've got plenty of money. I could look over the university campus and so on. I can't stay with you though, that wouldn't do at all." Charity laughed. She had known all along what Issy was hinting at, but being female making life easy was not in her lexicon, and not where young men were concerned anyway.

"You can say that again! My mother would go in to one of her vapour fits! She's always having the vapours, my mum! There's plenty of guest-houses and hotels though. Oh, please Issy, come and stay if only for a few days. Please."

"Right then. So it's decided. We'll both go to Birmingham. I'll stay there for a week then go back home, as by then even my parents will be wondering what's happening. I'm not going to tell them much though. I'll just say I went to have a look at the university. Mind you, if I know my father, when it comes to my education it will be Cambridge or Oxford. Still, we'll see."

"Talking of John," Charity said with a concerned tone in her voice, "How is he? That must have been terrible for him the other night. It makes me shiver just thinking about it?"

"Oh, he's back to his normal self now. Full of hell as usual. He's gone out somewhere. Probably buying some new clothes."

"Is he now?" Charity said quietly as she moved closer to Issy, her voice losing some of its normal feminine pitch. Issy also noticed that her cheeks had started to turn slightly red and it wasn't from coyness either. They were sitting on a settee so there was little room to escape. "Does that mean then," she whispered, "that we can have the room to ourselves for a while, Issy?" Issy looked into Charity's green eyes and gave up. One look was enough to set his trousers ablaze. Issy didn't reply. Instead he took her hand and led her to the hotel elevator. It was his turn to explore and conquer.

For both Issy and Charity the future was still best left alone. All that mattered at that moment was their youth, their spirit and the depth of the feelings that had grown between them. All they wanted was to be together. No words of love had been spoken yet; to speak of such things was far too threatening, for neither knew where such words would take them. They were young and untried, oblivious to the cruel world that hovered above them waiting for an opportunity to strike.

As Charity and Issy enjoyed the post-coital harmony of body and soul, John was standing in a fish market trying to decide whether to buy the cockles or the mussels. He hadn't eaten either for a long time and that was one thing he missed about Wales, particularly the cockles. His mother used to fry them with Welsh bacon and laverbread. The fat on the bacon would give a unique taste to the cockles and pulped, black seaweed that usually made most Englishmen sick.

He was losing himself in the stall of gaping mouths, greasy eyes and a foul stench when some breaded crab balls caught his eyes.

He hadn't seen these before, and the first thing that crossed his mind was the size of them. Jesu, must have been one hell of a sized crab to have balls like that! They were even bigger than his! He smirked at his own crude humour and decided he would leave the crab balls to their own devices. The cockles would have to do. Pity his mam wasn't around to fry them, and they wouldn't be the same without the bacon and laverbread, but never mind, he would be back home soon and back to his mam's cooking. He ordered a bag of cockles, plastered them with pepper and vinegar and sat down on an old wooden bench. He ate a handful and quickly decided that they were not as good as the ones in Wales. For a few moments he realised that he was missing home. He had been away for more than two years now, a long time for a boy his age. He toyed with the word 'boy' for a while and knew that it no longer fitted somehow. His voice had broken, his body had developed muscles in all the right places – hadn't it just? – and his chin was darkening up nicely. Well, 'darkening' was probably the wrong word, it was growing a reddish fur which was better than nothing. He thought of Sheyna, his mam and Winnie. All three were as important as each other right now. He had written to Sheyna as promised and always received a reply almost by return. She had demanded that he write every day, but that had just been too much. Her handwriting was always neat and easy to read, not like his at all. He hadn't forgotten their kisses either; in fact he had finally managed to work out what his friend got up to every night before they went to sleep. Well, if you can't beat 'em, join 'em, ay! And bloody great it was too!

John finished his cockles and started to walk back to the hotel. As he walked he realised he may have been missing home, but that he would also miss singing on the stage. The excitement, the constant activity. The crowds that always applauded, their yells of 'Bravo!' and 'Encore!' He would miss the sambos with their funny tobacco, the girls who flaunted and laughed, and the comedians who never stopped joking even when they had been booed off the stage He would even miss the stage fright that always hung around the theatre and his stomach. As people passed him he began to fully realise how good his life had been in the Songsters and how grateful he was. He and Issy had often discussed their good fortune, but somehow it now seemed more certain, more tangible. He quickly concluded that there was more to breaking voices and wispy chins than met the eye.

Suddenly as people pushed into him on the narrow pavement, manhood didn't seem to be so attractive after all. It had a rough, untamed side, a side that he had seen all too often in other performers on the stage. Spite, selfishness, ego, greed and vanity consumed the stage and the players who trod on it. Beneath the glamour, was a place where lives had been broken and chopped up by the addiction to self and the delusions of clapped out approbation. Even he had sometimes allowed vanity to curl up his heart. Look how he had felt when the inevitable had happened. But really the only things that had been hurt had been his pride and smugness. He hadn't been mortally wounded, had he? And yet he had cried like a baby. For a moment he was ashamed of himself. How could he behave in such a way? Issy was never like that; all he cared about was Charity and his books.

Eventually he came to the hotel entrance and paused for a few minutes. No, perhaps saying goodbye wasn't so bad after all. The theatre, he decided, was not the place to be a man. Not a good man anyway, and certainly not a man who wanted to be true to himself. It could never, never truly compete with Sheyna's kiss and honesty either.

When John arrived at their room and tried the door handle it wouldn't open. He tried it again, it still wouldn't open. What was going on?

"Issy! Issy!" he shouted as he knocked the door while simultaneously trying not to disturb any of the other guests. "Are you in there? Why have you locked the door? Answer me!" There was no reply. Perhaps Issy had accidentally locked them out. He had done it before. John knocked the door again, still no reply. He was about to call one of the porters to let him in when the door opened slowly. Issy was standing there wrapped up in a bed sheet.

"What?! What . . . Issy, what are you doing? Haven't you had enough sleep? It's four o'clock in the afternoon!"

"Er – yes. Well . . . I wasn't exactly . . . er, well . . . sleeping . . ."

"Well, are you going to let me in or not?" Before Issy could reply, John barged straight past him.

"Oh hello, Charity." John grinned. "Fancy seeing you here. Been helping Issy out with his history lessons, have you?" He looked Issy up and down. "Been trying to be a Roman senator has he by the looks of it?" Charity remained utterly composed as she sat on a chair over by one of the windows. She was fully dressed and seemed to be in total control of all her faculties, unlike Issy who seemed to be dying with embarrassment.

"Something like that," Charity replied calmly. "Actually, Issy was having a bath. Anyway, how are you John? I was sorry to hear about what happened the other night."

"I'm fine thank you, Charity. Had to happen sooner or later, so no point in making a carry-on about it. Not so sure about Issy here though. He seems to be taking the Roman Empire a bit too far if you ask me. Shit, Issy. Go and get dressed, and stop looking as if you've just filled your pants will you? I'll keep Charity company while you're at it." Issy grunted and disappeared into the bathroom.

John sat down opposite Charity. As he looked at her more closely he noticed that her lipstick and eye shadow were all smudged and askew. Right now, Charity Like didn't look quite so beautiful after all. Her face no longer seemed to shine and captivate and there was a raw, unforgiving sharpness to her eyes as she looked at him. For a moment he shifted uneasily on his chair and wondered if Issy had seen the difference too. Probably not, he was in love after all. Thank God Sheyna didn't wear any make-up, John thought; at least with her there would never be any nasty surprises between day and night. Without the make-up Charity just didn't look like Charity. It was all a bit creepy as far as John was concerned. Still, his friend loved

244

her and that was all that mattered. In her present state though, she sure as hell wasn't for John.

The two chatted for a while before Issy came out of the bathroom. John had never known him to dress so quickly.

"Right, John," Issy said. "I'm just going to walk Charity back to her lodgings. I won't be long. And don't say anything to anybody. Sideways nearly caught us coming up in the elevator. All perfectly innocent too. We only came up here to have a private talk, you know away from everybody. I was just having a bath when you knocked."

"Is that so, Issy?" John replied in that mischievous way of his. "Sorry to disturb then. Can't understand why you had a sheet around you though. I've seen it all before after all." At any other time he wouldn't have minded seeing Charity in just a bed sheet, preferably around her ankles of course, but he still couldn't get that look in her eyes out of his mind. As she followed Issy out of the door she seemed to push her body right into John's face, who then wondered if the eyes and make-up weren't so bad after all.

"I won't be long, John," Issy said over his shoulder. "Don't forget you're in the choir tonight, even if I'm not. I'll see you later." With that Issy closed the door and disappeared into his very own loving world.

An hour later Issy returned as John was cursing the short trousers that Steff still made them all wear. Issy was never out of long trousers now, John raved to himself. Bloody hell, and to think that leaving the Songsters had seemed like some kind of disaster! Imagine how embarrassed he would have been if he had walked in on Issy and Charity wearing short trousers?! Or worse, if he had caught them in the middle of some 'slap and tickle' as some of the performers called it. 'Private talk'! What did they take him for?

"Hello," Issy mumbled as he sat down and picked up a book.

"And hello to you, Issy." John could see by his friend's face that good humour was definitely not going to be the order of the day. "What's the matter with you?"

"Nothing," Issy replied not taking his eyes away from the book. His face was blacker than usual. More intense. John knew all the signs.

"Come on now, Issy. What's the matter? Look, I'm sorry if I disturbed you and Charity, but how was I to know? You should have warned me."

"Forget it. Now leave me be. Besides I saw the way you looked at her and I didn't like it. Isn't Sheyna enough for you?"

"Sheyna? What has Sheyna got to do with anything?" John was taken aback by the anger in his friend's eyes. The hostility in his voice. He had never seen Issy like this before. Not with him anyway.

"And you had better keep your filthy hands off her too!" Issy threw the book on the floor and leapt up. "Do you hear me, John!" Issy shouted. "Don't you ever look at her like that again! Ever! Do you hear me! I mean it!" Issy was almost spitting with temper. John took a few steps back. What was wrong with Issy? He had totally lost control, not like Issy at all. He had murder in his eyes. John tried to stay calm.

"I don't know what you're talking about, Issy," John said calmly. "Charity? Sheyna? Why are you being like this? Why? I haven't done anything. What's the matter with you?"

"You, that's what! I knew what you were thinking when you saw Charity walking out of the room! Well, she's my girl, right? And you keep away! I've seen you looking at her before. Looking and thinking what you could do to her. Well, I'll kill you if you go anywhere near her, do you hear me?"

"Have you gone quite mad or something, Issy?!" John was starting to shout now. "Don't be a fool. What makes you think she's so special anyway? Jesu, she didn't waste her time dropping her knickers for you, did she? For God's sake, she must have been fucked from Lands End to John o'Groats and back again!!" John didn't not know why he had said this, his bloody temper again. It was so cruel. So brutal. And yet . . . perhaps he was only trying to protect his friend in the only way he knew how. Charity's eyes again.

For a moment total hatred filled the room. Nothing moved and nothing stirred. The two friends stared at each other, neither daring to speak. Issy broke the deadlock with a fist that sent John flying. He hit the floor but quickly recovered, stood up and squeezed his nose back and fore. Issy started to dance on the balls of his feet as he raised his fists ready for the attack that he knew must come. John had never taken a punch without throwing one back, it simply wasn't in his nature to stay down even though he knew that Issy was bigger and stronger. Silence again. Nothing moved. John stood and raised his fists. Issy waited. Both boys clenched and unclenched their hands. They stared at each other, neither one moving. At last John used his sleeve to wipe the blood from his nose and smiled.

"Well, that's buggered this shirt. Steff won't be too happy, I can tell you. I think you've broken my nose too, you Jewboy bastard. Spoilt my good looks."

Issy slowly relaxed and dug into his pocket for a handkerchief. He handed it to John.

"Wipe the blood up with this will you . . . I'm, er, sorry," Issy said gently, his eyes looking down at the floor in shame. "I don't know what came over me. I really am sorry, John."

"Ah, never mind, eh. The bust up nose will give me character. Good punch that, Issy. Nearly kept me down. I'm . . . well . . . sorry too, Issy. No need to say the things I did. Sorry." John held out his hand and Issy took it. They both knew that it would take more than a chorus girl or a sister to ruin their friendship. They had also been given their first lesson on the sometimes dangerous and unpredictable demands of love.

CHAPTER 38

With only two days to go before the boys were supposed to be going to Cardiff, Issy hadn't told John yet that he wouldn't be going with him. Their fight had been forgotten, apart from John showing off his broken nose. Sideway had fussed and forced him into a hospital, but there was nothing that could be done. It wasn't that bad a break apparently. At least John didn't look as if he had spent most of his young life in a boxing ring. His nose wasn't squashed, it was just a little bent which was fine with John. Character again. He looked like a man of the world, weatherbeaten and rugged just like the stars at the picture houses.

Issy and Charity were sitting in a tea shop in the middle of Newcastle.

"I'm glad we are going to go to Birmingham together on Sunday," Charity said. "My mother can't wait to meet you, Issy. Oh, I've told her you're eighteen by the way and you're a friend, if that's all right. You're seventeen in two weeks time anyway and she'll never know the difference. You look a lot older than you actually are, you know. It's all those dark shadows on your chin." Charity leaned forward and stroked Issy's chin. He had a lovely chin, strong and masculine. There were other things she couldn't keep her hands off too, but at the moment she had to exercise restraint.

"Yes, that should be all right, Charity. I'll book some train tickets tomorrow." Whenever Issy sat facing Charity he couldn't take his eyes off her. He was happy to sit and look. His eyes absorbed every line of her face, every hair on her head and every movement of her facial muscles. Each time she smiled every part of him would smile with her, he just couldn't help it. He felt a complete fool, but since when had love ever been wise? he wondered. He had read enough to know that love knew no limits. Look at the recent abdication of the King, look at Helen of Troy or Cleopatra. Love was pure insanity and that's all there was to it. Worse than religion and war put together.

"I'm really looking forward to being with you for a whole week," Charity grinned. "Just you and me. It will be wonderful, it really will." She took Issy's hand, it had become such a natural gesture now. So normal.

"I'm looking forward to it too, Charity," Issy replied enthusiastically. "Really looking forward to it. We can have a day out on the Malvern Hills. I've got plenty of books to take with me too. There's loads of reading I need to catch up on. Sit and enjoy—"

"Books!" Charity snapped as she withdrew her hand. "Books! Issy, what are you talking about? You're not going to spend our whole time together reading are you?!"

"Well, I . . . I—"

"Now, you listen to me. I don't want to see any books on that train, Issy. There's plenty of time for you to read when we're apart. I don't understand how you can even think of such a thing. Books indeed!"

"I was only—"

"'I was only' nothing, Issy. When you're with me Issy, nothing else matters. Do you understand me. Nothing! I am the only one that matters Issy, and nobody and nothing else. Do you hear me? No books Issy or it's no me!" Issy was forced to sit back in his chair. Charity's outburst had shocked him and taken him completely by surprise. It had shocked some of the other people in the tea shop too. What was the matter with her? He had only mentioned taking some books with him. As he looked at her he saw a sudden change in her eyes, her face. The charm disappeared as her love seemed to retreat and bolt. He had seen her determination, her will, before. But this was different. There was spite and an almost unbearable hatred. Where had this outburst come from? Why? How could she be so vicious? He didn't understand. Suddenly there was a seething ugliness to her anger, an unpredictability that was both cruel and ruthless. Charity needed taming. He might have been in love and a fool, but even foolery had its boundaries.

"Is that so, Charity?" Issy said quietly, although she had caused enough of a scene already. Public displays of anger were both crude and undignified; after all he had been brought up to be a gentleman. "Well then, it will have to be the books, won't it? At least they do as they are told and don't answer back." With that he stood up and left the tea house.

Charity sat still, rigid. So still it was frightening. Her eyes remained fixed on the teapot as she calculated and schemed. At last she said to herself, 'Right then Mr Kaddar, no one walks out on me. No one. Unless they want to live to regret it.' A few moments later she picked up her handbag and made for the door. She had already worked out what to do.

John was shaving and praying at the same time when he heard the door being knocked. Shaving was a serious business and not to be rushed. He looked down into the sink. As usual there were lashings of shaving soap, but bugger all in the way of genuine manly stubble. He sighed at the mirror, but his disappointment didn't last long as he knew that one day soon his prayers would be answered. Hadn't he sung enough bloody hyms in his time? Even the Good Lord couldn't be that deaf! He took a towel from the rail and at last wondered who could be knocking. It couldn't be Issy as he was out with Charity. It must be old Sideways, fussing like a demented old woman again. He didn't bother to make himself look decent as he opened the door in just his underpants.

"Oh no! Charity!" he exclaimed as he saw who had been knocking. "Wait there!" He slammed the door shut and ran back into the room to put on a pair of trousers and a shirt. What could she want? he thought quickly. She was supposed to be with Issy. He went back to the door and opened it again.

"Please, come in Charity. I'm so sorry you – er – caught me at an inconvenient moment."

"Did I, John? I'm so sorry," Charity said casually as if nothing had happened. "Wait a minute," Charity remarked as she was about to walk passed him. She examined John's chin with her fingers. "Dear me. You've cut yourself shaving. More practise is needed I think." She touched his skin and John didn't know what to do. What was going on? First the girl had caught him virtually stark naked, now she was fondling his chin. This really was too much. She was scaring the hell out of him.

"Er, Issy isn't here," John mumbled. "I thought he was with you."

"No . . . he's gone to the library. Taking some books back or something. Do you mind if I sit down, John? My feet are hurting, we've done so much walking. He said he'd see me back here." Charity removed her shoes and started to rub her feet. "Ooooh, that's better," she groaned. "Much better." John was still standing by the door looking slightly lost. He really didn't fancy another bout of fisticuffs with Issy; neither did his nose come to that – a slight bend was one thing, an ugly break quite another.

"Why are you still standing by the door, John? I don't bite, you know. Come and sit down and stop being so shy." Charity was aware of John's nervousness, having often had this effect on boys and men. She sat back in her chair and shook her head. Her blond curls fell into her eyes and she pushed them back with her hands, a gesture she knew that was both attractive and enticing. Charity knew how to use her body, she was an expert. The stage had taught her how to manipulate and tantalise, the end was always the same. John still hadn't moved. "Come on, John," she insisted. "Come and sit down and talk to me."

"Well, just for a minute. I was on my way out actually. How long will Issy be?"

"Oh, a good hour I should think. You know what he's like when there are books around!" Charity giggled and the sound forced John to sit down. The girl was suddenly irresistible again. His previous misgivings jumped out of his brain as a rush of blood poured into his nether regions. As for Charity's green eyes, well, John was only a strapping sixteen-year-old after all.

As he sat down he couldn't help but wonder what lay beneath her dress. She had hitched up the hem to her knees in the process of massaging her feet and he couldn't stop his eyes from attaching themselves to her calves. Every time he tried to look elsewhere back they would go. He couldn't help it. If they were not looking at her legs then they would stare at her bosom, a bosom which heaved and pushed right into his face. Oh Jesu, what was he going to do? He had to get out. The only time he had been in such an intimate position with a girl had been that time with Sheyna. Then he had been in control, up to a point anyway. This was not the case now though. Somehow he felt that Charity was calculating his reactions, playing with him. He wasn't sure, but he knew something was wrong. His instincts were warning him and yet he was finding it impossible to resist.

"How is Issy's sister, John? Sheyna isn't it? I hear you are both quite fond of each other. Is that right?"

"Oh, she's just a friend that's all. She's very nice though." John didn't know why he had said this. Why he had been so offhand about Sheyna. A sudden sense of betrayal added to his feelings of guilt.

"That's not what Issy tells me," Charity said slyly, unleashing a brazen smile on John's awkward shyness and clumsy manhood. "He says that she's much more than a friend. He even caught you both kissing." The pretty green eyes teased again as John fidgeted in every direction apart from Charity's. He didn't know what else to do. He wanted to run out of the room, but her eyes wouldn't let him. He knew he shouldn't be

252

talking to Charity like this; although the conversation itself was innocent enough, there was an irresistible threat, even danger, inhabiting the air between them. His friendship with Issy was having boiling hot lava poured onto it, and there was nothing he could do about it. He hadn't forgotten the incident with Issy when they had come to blows. Nothing more had been said about it, but even so he still remembered his restraint, how he had kept his fists under control for the first time in his life even when he had received a sound thumping. All in the name of friendship. Now though, the girl sitting opposite him had more power than all the armies of Europe put together. He couldn't fight back. He didn't want to fight back.

"Yes, we . . . er . . . kissed, but that's all, Charity."

"I love kissing, John," Charity purred quietly. "Did you enjoy it? I could kiss all day long. I love touching too. Do you?" Oh Christ! John thought as his trousers nearly exploded and her eyes continued to demolish his sense of decency. He tried again to look away from her, but it was impossible. Her bloody eyes. They just wouldn't go away. They reached into him and strangled what was left of any honourable intent.

Charity stood up and took John's hand, "Would you like to kiss me, John? Touch me, like Issy does?" John was still sitting down with his other hand in his lap, trying to hide the rampant enthusiasm that was about to rip his underpants to shreds.

"I . . . um . . . well . . . I . . ." was all John could mutter as Charity pulled him up with her hands and said softly,

"We have plenty of time, John. Plenty."

Charity Like, was not only an accomplished artist with her impressive legs, she was also a consummate adept in the art of seduction. Had William Congreve been watching he would have clapped his hands with delight, yet again:

> 'Heaven has no rage like love to hatred turned,
> Nor hell a fury like a woman scorned'.

CHAPTER 39

When Issy returned to the hotel John was nowhere to seen. In fact Issy had gone to the library, if only to think things through. He always thought better when there were books around. He had discovered a side to Charity that he didn't like. Her wilful nature he could live with having been brought up with wilful women, but in the tea shop there had been something else that he hadn't seen before: vindictiveness and contempt. He couldn't get how she had looked at him out of his mind, and this had shaken him. Perhaps it was his imagination. Love did strange things; after all he had learnt that much. He knew he was no expert on the trying shinanigens of love, indeed he was an out-and-out novice, but even so he was a quick learner, and like his friend he trusted his instincts. He sat down in the hotel room and tried again to collect his thoughts, or at least bring some balance to them.

Was Charity's attitude enough to make him stop loving her? The answer must be a firm 'no'. How could he stop loving the only girl who had ever truly mattered to him, not counting Sheyna of course? He had read about insane infatuations, where men and woman became so obsessed with love they would kill and even take their own lives. He didn't believe he was that far gone, but then again look how he had punched John in a moment of 'insane' jealousy. He shivered for a moment as the implications of what he was thinking sank in. Hell – this love business needed some sorting out! At least with a book you knew where you were – most of the time anyway!

Some time later Issy finally concluded that he wasn't 'infatuated' after all. Young he may be and apparently prone to such aberrations, but he was more mature than most boys of his age.

He even looked older than his years. In one way this was an advantage, yet in another way maybe it wasn't. Perhaps he and John had sacrificed more than they realised. No longer innocent and no longer naïve, waking up in the morning had become much more complicated for them.

Issy sighed and stood up. What was he to do about Charity? The thought of never seeing her again sliced through him and made his stomach turn. He remembered her smile, her kiss. Could there ever be anything else? Anything else worth fighting for? He knew there was a bad side to the girl, but like him she was young. Maybe in time? And what about his faults? There were plenty of those, as John was always pointing out. He could be moody and arrogant, and even mean and spiteful. Well, maybe not so much of the last two. No, falling out over a few books was silly. Childish even. That was it really; both he and Charity were behaving like children and this was plain ridiculous. They were adults now after all, or supposed to be anyway.

Issy looked out of the window and decided that he must put things right. Charity was a lovely girl, he knew it, she was just human like him. Nothing serious. Maybe she was just having the usual monthly vapours like his mother. All women had these, according to John anyway. Yes, they would go to Birmingham as planned, everything would be fine.

A few minutes later John arrived back at their room. Before Issy could say anything he quickly remembered that he hadn't told his friend about not going to Cardiff with him. Women! Or in his case girls, although he was none too sure which category Charity actually fell into.

"Oh, hello Issy. I, er . . . thought you were out with Charity," John mumbled, looking at Issy's feet as he spoke, "having tea or something."

"What's the matter with you, John? You look a bit down. Nothing has happened has it? You haven't fallen out with Steff again, have you?"

"Er no. No. I'm not down at all. Bit tired though. Been doing lots of walking."

"Well, don't be too tired. You're on stage tonight and tomorrow night. Then it's back home. Are you looking forward to seeing that sister of mine?"

John had sat down on the bed, still trying to avoid looking Issy straight in the eyes. An awful thing, conscience.

"What?" John replied distractedly.

"Sheyna. Are you looking forward to seeing her? The pair of you have been writing enough letters."

"Yes. Yes we have." John still wasn't prepared to be particularly talkative.

"Look," Issy demanded, "what's the matter with you, John. You come in here all miserable and you won't even talk properly. Have I done something to upset you or what?"

"No, Issy. Of course not. Like I said I'm just a bit tired. I am looking forward to seeing Sheyna though. I know it's only been a couple of weeks but well . . . well, I've missed her. I'm very fond of your sister you know, Issy. Very fond indeed." John wanted to add, 'now more so than ever' but resisted the temptation. He felt utterly wretched. Sick. Looking at the trusting eyes of his friend made him feel even worse. He wanted to repent, to purge himself. He wanted to admit his guilt and take the thrashing. He wouldn't have raised a hand to defend himself. He deserved every punch. Not only had he betrayed the most loyal and dependable friend he had ever known, but he had also poisoned his feelings for Sheyna.

Up until Charity had walked into their room life had been simple and easy to understand. There had been no shadows or a need for hiding places. He had been able to keep his head up high. For so long he had begged and badgered the Good Lord to sacrifice his virginity, to make him a whole man once and for all. The performance of his life had come and gone, but it had left him with nothing but a vivid sense of loss and craven morality. How could he have been such a fool? How could he have allowed Charity to have her way with him? He knew the answer lay in his pants, but did it have to be so destructive? The thought of Issy finding out made him shiver. Charity had made him promise that he say nothing, as if he needed to promise! But why had she done it in the first place? Why had she come to his room? That look on her face when she and Issy had been caught out returned with a vengeance. The 'Why's' wouldn't stop tormenting him as he looked at Issy and wanted to run. All that time spent thinking about 'it', all the frustration in trying to achieve 'it' and what for? A momentary splash of lust followed by an intimate deluge of guilt and remorse. 'It' could go to hell and back again.

"Well, John, I'm very glad to hear about your feelings for Sheyna," Issy responded crisply. Then he paused, before adding quietly, "Actually there is something I need to talk to you about."

At last John was finally able to look directly at his friend. "Is there? Must be serious then. You've got that Sideways look on your face. All doom and 'the world's about to end' look."

"You can talk, John. Your face looks worse than a Catholic priest's with a red hot poker stuck up his bum." Crudity usually made John laugh, except this time it didn't seem to be having much of an effect.

"Very funny. Now, what do you want to tell me that's so important."

"I'm not going back to Cardiff with you." With John it didn't pay to beat around the bush. "I'm going to Birmingham with Charity for a holiday and to meet her mother." Issy waited for the annoyed response, but none came. They had always done everything together, and he had expected at least some moans of discontent from his friend.

"That's all right. I'll be fine in Cardiff," John replied genially. "I was planning on seeing Sheyna anyway. Just as well you'll be out of the way. I won't have to put up with any of your bloody teasing!" This time John actually smiled.

"Good. I thought you might have been a bit annoyed that we weren't going to be together for our last week in the Songsters."

"Ah well, Issy. All good things and all that. It's time for the big wide world now, I think. For both of us. Promise me one thing though, Issy. Swear to me."

"What?" Issy had already realised that his friend was troubled by something. He knew John so well he rarely missed anything. The only thing he didn't understand was why his friend was keeping his troubles to himself. It wasn't like John at all. He himself could be introverted and self-absorbed, but not John. It wasn't in his friend's nature. The only thing Issy could think of was that the days of the Songsters were over and that John was more unhappy about it all than he was letting on. John allowed a few moments to pass before saying anything, apparently struggling to find the right words.

"Look, Issy. Will you promise me . . . I mean really promise, cross your heart and hope to die . . . that you won't allow any girl to ever come between us . . . I mean what with Sheyna and Charity. I would hate – well, I really *would* hate – our friendship to end. I mean it, Issy. I really do. We've been through such a lot together, you and me. And well I . . . er, well, I like you, if you see what I mean." Issy looked at his friend and saw his struggle, his trial. John had never been one for fancy words, always leaving those for Issy to work out.

Issy sat down on the bed next to his friend. "John Illtyd Rees," he said kindly and with feeling, "I will never let any girl ruin our friendship or come between us. Never, I promise you. Cross my heart and hope to die." Issy smiled. "Besides, who else will I ever find to watch my back so well or use his fists in my defence? I'm Jewish, John, don't forget it. I know how people can be. How they can hurt. But you . . . well, that has never meant anything. From the first day we met in that church you offered me your friendship and it has never wavered. Now, whatever it is that is worrying you – and I know that's there's something – forget it. There's a whole new future out there for both of us. There will be plenty more Songsters after us who will come and go. I'm here and I always will be. To fight for you as you have always fought for me."

John turned and looked at his friend as he said, "Good. Let's shake hands on it then – and don't you forget, Issy." The two boys shook hands with a solemnity that would have done two Rabbis proud. "Now then," John grinned, "I'd better start getting dressed. That old bastard Steff is always going on at me for being late. I won't miss his nagging, and that's a fact, Issy. Worse than my bloody mam he is!"

CHAPTER 40

It was Saturday morning. John was off to Cardiff the following day and Issy was supposed to be going to Birmingham with Charity. Although he had previously decided to make things up with her, the night had brought doubt and uncertainty. The black hours always changed things, always maddened and exaggerated. One minute Issy had known what to do, the next a dull sleep would change his mind as fury fought with love and love fought with reason. When daylight finally arrived Issy had decided that there was no turning back. There couldn't be. Charity had seen to that. He couldn't fight her even when fitful sleep and unrequited desire had forced him to open his eyes and see. She had pushed him to a perilous brink, but he had clung and held on. What else could he have done?

Issy dressed and decided to go and find Charity. He had given her most of a day and all night to see some sense. Even so he was none too sure who was supposed to apologise, if indeed an apology was in order. He had convinced himself that they had both been wrong, so this issue would no doubt be addressed when he saw her. He left John in a deep sleep. His friend had been talking more than usual in his sleep that night, so he didn't try to wake him. Before closing the door Issy briefly wondered again what was wrong with John. Sleeping late, talking in his sleep. His friend really was upset about leaving the Songsters after all, for all his bravado and cheek. Oh well, he'd get over it, as he did most things.

As Issy walked to Charity's lodgings he knew that he had made the right decision. The very thought of holding her in his arms and kissing her lips again convinced him. All that worry during the night had been for nothing. Demons only ever came out at night to ply their mischief and deceive; well, they hadn't beaten him, they hadn't made him surrender. He knew Charity would feel the same way now that she had had time to calm down. He shouldn't have walked off, not like that anyway. Mind you, she shouldn't have been so quick with her tongue either. As he walked up to the door of her lodgings he started to grin. What a stupid pair they both were, arguing over nothing. He knocked on the door and waited. Before long a comedian he had met a few times answered the door. The man was bald and smoking a cigarette. His shirt collar was undone and his braces were struggling to keep his belly up.

"Hello, there. What can I do for you?" the man asked as he peered at Issy and smiled. For a moment the man's tongue stuck out of his mouth and moved from side to side. A joke was hanging on the end of it Issy was sure. The comedian's eye's lit up for a moment as he prepared to deliver one of his best, before remembering that he was not on stage after all but standing in a reality that he had long ago shunned. A sullen silence occupied the space between them before the comedian's face dropped back into the sadness of normality, and Issy once again felt relieved at his own departure from a world of artifice and transience.

"Is Charity Like in, please? I'm a friend of hers."

"Are you? Well, I know who you are talking about but she left early this morning. Going home, so she said at breakfast – wherever that is." The look on Issy's face told the comedian to stay where he was. On a doorstep in reality.

"But it's only just gone nine o'clock now," Issy managed to splutter. "Are you sure?"

"I'm sure all right. Helped put her suitcase in the taxi. Pretty girl that one, wouldn't mind some of it myself," the comedian leered. "What's she like, eh?"

Issy stared at the comedian. In a brief moment Issy's eye's brought together all the 'boos', 'get offs' and 'fuck offs' that the comedian had ever encountered during all his years on the stage. The blatant contempt in Issy's eyes forced the comedian to take a step or two backwards. The lad facing him was a big bugger and not about to be amused by his repartee, as worn out as it was. "Er . . . look . . . I didn't mean that," the comedian said, his expression softening, "only joking, habit of mine I'm afraid. I'm sorry, but Charity did leave this morning. Going to the station she said . . . but wait a minute . . . yes, she did say that she was going to drop her case at the station and then do some shopping. Something for her mother I think. You know you might just catch her before she gets on the train. I don't know what time her train goes but—" Before the comedian could finish his sentence Issy was gone. He remained standing for a few more moments and remembered. He then dropped his cigarette on the floor and went back inside. There was nothing really funny about life or love after all he thought, as he closed the door, returned to his own lonely world and waited for the next laugh.

Issy looked at his watch. It was nine thirty. He had just seen the departure time for the Birmingham train. Nine thirty. Oh God, no! he pleaded as he ran for the platform. Please, no. Please, no. The train for Birmingham was spitting steam and noise as it prepared to depart. He heard a guard shout and a shrill scream from a whistle. A bright green flag waved at him from the corner of his eye. He saw people turn their heads and wonder. He kept running. Compartment windows laced with steam tried to hide their occupants. Another blast from a whistle added to his panic and desperation. Oh God, this was unbearable! No, please not this – not now! The train started to pull away. His lungs were bursting. Where was she? *Where*? He ran alongside the huge metal beast and tried to look in, but all he saw were blank faces who didn't want to know. He tried a moving door handle but it refused to turn. He was locked out. Young and old, men and women, saw his need but turned away. He continued to run down the platform. Searching. Trying. Not giving up. The train was gathering speed. He couldn't keep up for much longer. Please God, no! I beg of you, please no! He tried another door. The handle defied his urgency. Then he saw her. Her face stared. Her eyes didn't move. Her lips didn't move. Charity saw him running and remained seated. Issy ran alongside her carriage as he hammered on her window and shouted. "Get off, Charity! Please! Get off! Please! I'll – I'll . . . Stop the train! Please someone stop the train!" He kept shouting for the train to stop but he knew it was hopeless. There was nothing else he could do. The platform came to an end and Issy stopped running. "Please, Charity," he managed to say in one last resigned gasp. There was nowhere else to go. As Charity pulled away, Issy saw her lips move into a smile, or at least something like one. "No, no!" Issy pleaded as the lips that had forced him to love disappeared on a journey to a place he knew nothing at all about. He stood still and lowered his arms. His lungs heaved and his heart struggled. His mind sought refuge from a pain that he had never before encountered, a pain that was more destructive and precise than any surgeon's scalpel. He leaned against a pillar and stared at the empty track, as a savage sense of loss forced his eyes to spew a flow of tears that ran down his cheeks and fell onto a cold concrete floor.

As the railway tracks echoed a final farewell to first love Issy vowed he would never stop looking for Charity.

Ever.

When Issy returned to the hotel later that morning John was waiting for him. He had walked the streets for a while, trying not to be sick, trying to make sense of things, trying to compose himself. He wasn't at all sure he had achieved any of them.

"Where have you been, Issy? Not like you to get up so early. Been sniffing around Charity again, have you?"

"No. No John, I haven't." Issy lay down on his bed and said nothing more. John took one look at Issy's face and new that something bad had happened.

"What's the matter, Issy? Your eyes are all red. You've been crying."

"Nothing, John. Now leave me alone." John stood up from his chair.

"No Issy, not this time. I won't leave you alone. What's happened? Tell me?" Charity hadn't let on, had she? Oh God!

"Look John. Just mind your own business, will you?"

"No, I won't, Issy!" John replied firmly. "I'm not leaving here until you tell me what's the matter. Now come on, spill the beans! You're all upset about something. Doesn't do to keep things all bottled up. You're a bugger for doing that, Issy. Now come on, stop being so stubborn. Don't start my antics; take it from me they never help, only make things worse. It's Charity, isn't it?" Issy looked at John. Perhaps his friend wasn't so thick skinned after all.

"Oh, all right . . . if you must know, yes," Issy said slowly. His heart and eyes were still raw. "Charity and I had a tiff yesterday. Silly really. Over nothing. At least that's what I thought. Well, she must have taken things to heart. Anyway, she took off this morning back to Birmingham. I ran to the station to try and catch her, but the train was already moving off. She saw me though, John. She saw me. All she did was smile as I tried to stop her – if you could call it a smile. I'm sure she was gloating or even mocking me, that's what it seemed like anyway." Issy turned away from his friend. Proper men didn't cry or show their hurt.

John went and sat down on Issy's bed. So that's what her visit to their room had been all about. She had used him to get at Issy. The wicked hussy had caught the pair of them! Worse still, John had seen it coming. Her face without make-up, that look in her eyes. John placed his hand on Issy's shoulder. He had to stay calm. Issy was in a bad enough state now, so imagine what it would be like if Issy knew the real truth about he and Charity.

"Look Issy, I don't know what to say, but I'm here anyway. Makes a change, doesn't it? When it comes to the tears I'm the

one usually using your shoulder. I'm here, Issy. You know that."
John tugged at his friend's arm. "Come on, let's go out and get
drunk. Bugger Steff and his precious audience. He can do without me for once. Doesn't need me that much anyway." He
pulled Issy again. "Come on, Issy. Howling all night on your
own isn't going to help. Let's see if we can find some other
chorus girls to have some fun with. There are plenty of them."
Issy finally stopped looking at the wall and turned round.

"Yes, John. Why not?"

CHAPTER 41

The following Saturday night John was standing in the chorus line of Steffani's 21 Silver Songsters singing 'Sweet and Low'. The New Theatre in Cardiff was not quite as full as John had come to expect, but then he was no longer Britain's Greatest Boy Soprano so it was hardly surprising. John stood behind the other boys and made a desultory effort to join in and keep in tune. He noticed the immaturity around him: the silly white uniforms with their black buttons and black cravats, the shiny black patent shoes, the fluffy white socks and of course the supreme insult to his manhood – the white short trousers. God forbid if Sheyna were to see him now. Briefly he recalled how he used to sing solo the first sixteen bars of 'The Way You Look Tonight'. How he wished he could sing that now, just for Sheyna.

This was his last night with the Songsters. In some ways it was also the last night of his youth and the dream he had been living for more than two years. It was an ending, a shutting down of something unique and extraordinary. Being in the chorus was a final act of attrition that humiliated and condemned, yet also uplifted and fortified. The gradual and painful metamorphoses from boy to man, from the veneer of juvenile irrelevance to the sturdy fibre of sentient awareness, from infatuation to untested love all played a part in John's mind as he tried to come terms with his last performance. His last short-trouser'd spectacle.

Issy was waiting for John in the wings when the Songsters finally finished. John had bullied Issy into keeping him company for the last week, the misery of Charity Like notwithstanding. There was to be a leaving party. John had been unsure about this, but Issy had insisted. If singing to a vast wave of admiring faces was one thing, standing in a group of people with glasses raised was another. Strangely John hated any fuss, off stage anyway.

"Well, John," Issy said. There was still a dull remoteness, even a desperate echo in his friend's voice. John knew that there was only a small part of Issy in the theatre. Where the rest of him was only the fairies knew. "That's your last performance. How do you feel?" For the first time in a week Issy managed to raise a smile – Issy rarely smiled gratuitously at the best of times – and shook John's hand. "Come on, there are some people waiting to see you." Issy pushed John along a corridor and through the usual motley chaos of performers waiting to die or jump for joy. They stopped outside a door and Issy started to open it.

"Wait, Issy! Wait, will you?"

"What's the matter, John?"

"Nerves. Bloody nerves."

"Don't be stupid. Now get in there will you!" Issy ignored John's 'nerves' and shoved him through the door.

A group of about ten people were all crushed together in a small dressing room. There was Steffani, Mr Sideway, and some of the Songsters. The chattering stopped as Steffani tapped a spoon on a large glass vase.

"Gentleman, our star has arrived. Silence, if you please." Steffani's long nose shifted around the dressing room; he never stopped trying to sniff out trouble, even at a farewell party. "Fill your glasses gentlemen, please. A toast is in order." Some corks popped and whizzed around the air as they tried to find somewhere to land. Space was precious after all. Bottles gurgled and complained as glasses were filled and Steffani held the floor. One boy who had never even seen a bottle of champagne before, let alone taste what was in it, started to gulp it down as if his birthday and Christmas had arrived at the same time.

"Young Speeks, you pleb, control yourself!" Mr Sideway admonished. "There's plenty of time to enjoy the grapes of Bacchus. Behave yourself!"

Steffani coughed into his hand.

"Gentlemen, now if you please. We are here tonight to say 'Goodbye' and 'Farewell'. We are also here tonight to express our sincere thanks. Illtyd John Rees is leaving us. Nature has cast her spell and sadly we are powerless to prevent her mischievous ways. Tonight we lose the finest jewel in the Songster crown we have ever possessed. My long career has never witnessed a coloratura soprano voice so beautiful or so fine, and I doubt that it will ever do so again. We thank you, John Rees, for allowing us all – the Songsters, myself and of course the great British public – the privilege of hearing you and enjoying your incomparable talent. Our thanks must also go to your faithful companion, Issy Kaddar . . ." Steffani stopped for a moment and grinned at the two boys. "Where would we have been without his good sense and easy spirit I ask? His steadying influence and of course . . . his calmer ways.

"So, Gentlemen, sadly we must now say 'Goodbye' or perhaps *au revoir*, for who knows in the world of theatre and variety? We wish you both the best of futures, the best of happiness and the best of good fortune. Gentlemen, please raise your glasses. I give you Britain's Greatest Boy Soprano, Master Illtyd John Rees!"

Later that night when all the excitement had died down there was a knock on their door. It was Bertram Sideway. 'Oh no', was John's first thought as he switched on a light and opened the door. 'What have I done now? Jesu, I'm off home tomorrow!' Sideway was standing in the doorway.

"Now young Rees, I know it's late but I would appreciate a word. Do you mind if I come in?"

"Um no – of course not, Mr Sideway. Please." Sideway walked in and sat down on a chair.

"I've . . . er, well I've, um . . . come to say my own 'Good-bye' as it were, young Rees."

"Oh, have you, Mr Sideway? Well, that's very good of you I must say." John had no idea why Sideway had turned up as all the 'Goodbyes' had already been said. Issy was still fast asleep. Nothing ever woke him up, apart from Charity that is. Sideway moved back and fore on his chair then dug into one of his pockets. He pulled out a posh-looking package. It was bright yellow and had a blue ribbon holding it together.

"I, um . . . well, I've brought you a going-away gift," said Sideway as he handed John the package. "I will miss you, young Rees. Not perhaps your miscreant ways – although I may even miss those—" Sideway continued, with a smile that nearly knocked John off his chair, "but I will miss you, young fellow, and that's a fact. Anyway, I have come here to give you my own personal farewell and to wish you a wonderful future. Now then, it's late and you will be going home tomorrow. Good luck young Rees and may God be with you." Sideway stood up, shook John's hand and walked toward the door, but not before turning around and adding with another smile, "Although I suspect you will try even Him, young Rees. Use my gift well and with wisdom. Adieu, my friend."

When Sideway had gone John opened the present. It was a solid gold fountain pen. Bertram Sideway had been given it by his father on the day of his graduation.

CHAPTER 42

The wet and hungry cold of winter had arrived. It was the beginning of October as Tristram sat alone listening to the news on his radio. The Munich conference had confirmed Chamberlain's 'peace in our time' and imminent war had been avoided. The only member of the Cabinet to resign had been Duff Cooper, who had felt that Chamberlain's ill-judged statement could only serve to decelerate the much-needed push for rearmament.

Tristram was not convinced. There wasn't a day that went by when he didn't feel the threat of war. It was in the shops and in his walks on the Downs. Although he had never personally experienced the horrors of war his music reflected it. His sensitivities had responded to the cauldron of hatred and violence and the pointless death of millions. For a moment his black world ignored the lack of light.

He had heard Clarissa's naïve enthusiasm and been mildly amused. He hadn't seriously attempted to make her understand. Her comic-book views had been best left well alone. He had also refrained from revealing his own frustrations. Tristram was no pacifist. He had been too young to fight in the last war, and too blind. The coming war, for he was convinced that war was inevitable, would be no different, apart from the fact that his age would not preclude him from fighting. His lack of sight, however, most certainly would. Nothing much had changed. He knew he would volunteer if he could see, even though he was fundamentally against the unholy prospect of mass slaughter. But how else was one supposed to stop it? As he switched off his radio he sighed at his impotence. He was about to return to his piano when a knock on the door prevented him from doing so.

"Hello, Tristram." A voice announced when he opened the door. "May I come in?" There was no doubt as to whom the voice belonged.

"Clarissa, yes of course. Please come in." Clarissa had never been to his house before. He was not even sure how she had managed to find out where he lived. He hadn't told her, but then it was a small village in which everybody knew everybody else's business, so it couldn't have been particularly difficult. When he had heard her voice he wasn't sure whether to be pleased or annoyed. His home was his sanctuary, a place of peace and creative 'aloneness'. It had been years since any female presence had sat down in the sitting room. She was wearing a long fawn coat and a brown tweed hat as she brushed passed him in that determined way of hers. And there was that usual aroma about her, always unmistakeable, always Clarissa.

"It really is the most awful weather out there you know, Tristram, most inclement. May I take my coat off and sit down." He heard her shake her coat and felt some raindrops tickle his face. "Ooops! Sorry, didn't mean to soak you too!" Clarissa was her usual presuming self. It could both irritate and charm. Tristram was still trying to discover which one he preferred. Even her irritating ways had an attractive lure about them.

"Yes, do," Tristram replied pleasantly. "Let me take your coat for you – and your hat."

"How do you know I'm wearing a hat, Tristram?" Clarissa asked as she passed him her hat and coat. "You can't see, for heaven's sake!" Tristram smiled at the honest way she referred to his handicap. He loathed pity and sympathy in equal measure. People never seemed to understand that one cannot miss what one has never had.

"Oh you'd be surprised what I can see, Clarissa. Now, would you like some tea? Then perhaps you can tell me what this visit is all about."

"Well, that would be just lovely, Tristram. Thank you. Milk and one lump of sugar, please."

"Right, well, make yourself comfortable. I won't be long."

As Tristram was making the tea he felt the same apprehension he always did when Clarissa was near him. One moment he wanted to reject, the next to receive. He could smell her body, it was all over him. It both excited and subdued. Her voice too – so disarming, even beautiful. She reminded him of some of his own compositions. As he poured the hot water into the teapot he suddenly realised that he could compose something about her. It would bring her closer to him without the need for physical touch and disappointment.

A few minutes later as he poured the tea Clarissa said, "What a lovely cottage you have here, Tristram. It's so warm and cosy." He had never seen the lacey chintz, floral curtains and dark oak furniture. His head sometimes struck the low oak beams, but not often. Having grown up with them he usually knew when they were about to attack. His memory could describe the house in detail. His mother had always been his young eyes.

"Yes. I've always lived here. It was my parents'."

"You were an only child, weren't you?" Clarissa's inquisitiveness never stopped to take breath.

"Yes, no brothers or sisters."

"Well, aren't you the lucky one. I've got two of each. I'm in the middle."

There was a pause in the conversation as Clarissa sipped her tea. Her eyes looked at Tristram and tried to work out what to do next. The man was impossible. His eyes may well have been blind, but that didn't mean he was blind to a pretty girl's advances, did it? Men could be so dim sometimes. She didn't give a damn about his lack of sight. He had poured the tea without as much as a 'by your leave' and had brewed it without any request for help too. He was completely self-sufficient and certainly no cripple. He was so handsome too, and clever. What was the matter with him?! Oh God.

"Now then, Tristram. You're probably wondering why I'm here."

"The thought had crossed my mind," he replied, as a slight smile crossed his lips and left Clarissa wondering who was actually running the show here.

"Well, my parents are having an anniversary party up at the manor house, and I would like you to come, or rather daddy would like you to come. Sorry, slip of the tongue. He fancies having a famous composer as a guest; you know, impress his army chums, boring lot that they are. Well, will you come?" Tristram sat back in his chair and put his fingers together. He thought for a moment.

"I'm not sure, Clarissa. I'm never terribly comfortable at parties. And I don't dance either. I have tried, but I tend to bump into people so . . ."

"Oh, never mind the dancing!" Clarissa implored. "I'll look after you, I promise. And I've told daddy that he mustn't ask you to play anything. He can be such a rogue, and I know how you don't like public performances near to your home."

"I really am not very good at parties, Clarissa," Tristram insisted. "I'm sorry, but whilst I appreciate your kind gesture the answer must be 'no'." Clarissa was not a young woman to be so easily fobbed off. While she enjoyed all those cardinal virtues of womanhood – namely beauty, wit and docility when required, together with a smouldering passion that could shake the will of any man – she also pursued an emancipated awareness of self and determined capability.

"Now look here, Tristram," Clarissa said firmly. "We are friends, correct?"

"I suppose so, yes. But we don't know each other that well. I mean admittedly we've spoken plenty of times on the Downs but I mean . . ."

"Oh, what nonsense Tristram!" Clarissa interrupted. "We're good friends and have been for quite a while, so what's the matter with you? Just say 'yes' will you? For me. Just say 'yes', please." Clarissa almost wanted to shake some sense into the silly man; why oh why did he insist on being so stubborn? It was only a party for heaven's sake!

Tristram's eyes looked directly at Clarissa. There were times when she was almost convinced that he could see. But if that really was the case, why then was he being so contrary? If only he could see what was in her eyes he would know. Just one look would have been enough. She was an open young woman, and not one to hide her feelings. The silence of indecision made Tristram fight his need to love. What use was he to a beautiful young woman who only wanted to run with life and not stop until they both reached the finishing line? He wanted to say 'yes', but he knew that this would be a beginning, the start of something that his body and mind may not be able to control. He had always wanted a woman's love; he was a man after all in every sense of the word, but sight always came before any such romantic notions.

"Tristram, what are you so frightened of?" Clarissa finally asked gently. "Please tell me as I really would like to know, I might even understand as well. I'm not as flighty as you may think – or stupid for that matter."

"I am not 'frightened' of anything Clarissa, I assure you," Tristram smiled. "It's just that I find large social gatherings somewhat tedious. People can be kind but intrusive without realising it. They want to know everything about me, every-thing about my music. It gets very tiring, believe me. Oh, and I certainly don't think you're 'flighty'. A bit like a butterfly who is always on the wing perhaps, but definitely not flighty." Tristram grinned. "And you're not stupid either; persistent yes, but not stupid."

"All right, I can understand all that," Clarissa said as she let out a breath of exasperation. "But I would like one evening with you, Tristram . . . just one evening. Is that too much to ask?" Clarissa placed her hand on his. He felt her urgency and her love. There had been other women who had tried, other women who had been remorseless in their attempts to cherish and to hold. He had always managed to hide both himself and his desires in his blindness, but somehow Clarissa was forcing him to see things he had always resisted. He felt her skin against his, he heard the softness and honesty in her voice and for once his stone walls started to crumble and fall apart. He couldn't help it, but his hand moved across hers, he needed to touch too.

"Very well, Clarissa. For you and only for you. But—"

"No buts, Tristram," Clarissa interrupted again as she tried to hide her excitement. 'I'll pick you up next Saturday evening at seven o'clock sharp. Will you be all right to do up your bow tie? I mean they can be terribly difficult. I'm always having to do up daddy's."

"I, er . . . Well, I suppose they do cause me some consternation now you come to mention it. My manager usually does mine before I play anyway."

"That's settled then. I'll call a bit earlier to help you dress. I'll enjoy that. You see we all need someone sometimes, Tristram. All of us. And it's no shame to ask for help either."

"No, of course," Tristram replied.

Clarissa paused for a moment. "Oh yes, I know. There *is* something I need to mention. You're not nervous about fast cars, are you? I mean I've got a spanking new red MG motor car outside. Goes like a rocket. And I do tend to put my foot down. Daddy bought it for me, he gave in, in the end. Still shouts at me all the time, but he's a real sweetie really."

"No, I don't mind, Clarissa. As long as we arrive in one piece."

"Oh, we will. Have no fear. I won't let anything happen to you dear Tristram, believe me."

PART 4

CHAPTER 43

Llantwit Major. March 1939

The 21 Silver Songsters were now a figment, a now-and-again thought, of both past and present. For John his singing would always be a part of his future too; not on the stage exactly, but in his personality and character. People throughout the world would wonder and listen to his anecdotes and reminiscences of his days as Britain's Greatest Boy Soprano. He would never forget, and neither would they!

Both boys adopted a different approach to their adventures with the Songsters. Issy was philosophical and resigned; for him it was an interlude, an exciting break from the intensity of academic endeavour. He had learnt other things however: things about people, about life and pain, things that he could never have known had he not joined the Songsters. John was still a star though, if only on a more local scale. He missed the stage far more than his friend, who remained ambivalent and unsure. The chaos and drug of applause, the ecstatic activity that never seemed to stop, the girls and characters were all part of a life that John had revelled in and loved. It took some months for his feet to finally arrive on terra firma, but when they did he shed no tears, no fanciful delusions about a past that to most boys would have been beyond their wildest dreams. Ever practical, John moved on and back into a world that was perhaps more normal, even if familiar and tedious. He now worked in a munitions factory in Bridgend making bombs. Occasionally one would blow up and break the boredom, although this was one hell of a way to be entertained, nothing like the Songsters. He had even started to play the piano again. Love songs to Sheyna had been the inspiration, but every time he tried to play them to her he would start to blush and give up.

One evening as John and Sheyna were out walking John suddenly stopped and looked up at the branches of an ancient oak tree. A cock pheasant was perched on a branch cleaning itself. "How do you fancy pheasant for supper then, Sheyna?" he asked.

Sheyna looked at him before replying, she never quite knew when he was being serious or just playing the fool. They had been courting now for six months, but there were still times when John could be unpredictable – amusing with it, but still unpredictable.

"No thank you, John. I don't really like game." Sheyna humoured.

"I mean it. One twist of his neck and it's in the pot. My mam is great with pheasant. The farmer won't mind – not that he'll know anyway."

"Are you serious, John?"

"Yes, of course I am. Used to poach all the time. My father used to play hell about it, but he never objected to the taste of roasted pheasant or tickled salmon."

"Oh, John. You're such a scoundrel. Don't tell my mother whatever you do. She's already calling you 'that John' as it is."

"All right then, I'll leave the pheasant for some other lucky devil's plate."

"Good. Now come on, it's getting late and I'm getting cold. You can walk me home, and this time come in to the house to say 'Hello' to my mother. She is always asking after you."

"Well, that surprises me. Your pa is all right, but your mam is always giving me the evil eye. Scares me to death she does."

"That's what mothers are for, John. I am her only daughter after all."

"Even so . . ." John looked at Sheyna and her wild loveliness that never seemed to diminish. As always he was unable to resist. "Oh, I'll come in and say 'Hello' then if it will make you happy. Anything for my Sheyna."

They were walking along a muddy path that ran through some woods leading back to Llantwit. John was seventeen now. His voice had finally settled at an acceptable level of depth and his chin required genuine daily attention. He had become a man and was content to behave like one – at least most of the time. As the two young people walked they held hands and kissed occasionally. Sometimes when they were alone they even explored each other's bodies, but never going too far or being too intimate. John knew things that Sheyna didn't, and it was best left that way. Sheyna was too good to be used and far too special. Wedding bells would bring decency and respect one day, and that's just the way it should be. They were young, there was plenty of time.They loved each other, wanted without condition and that was enough.

"How is Issy, Sheyna? I haven't seen him for a few days."

"He's fine, I think. I know my mother is worried though. He hasn't been the same since he came back from Cardiff. At first we all just thought it was leaving the Songsters that had made him all miserable, but my mother seems to think it's something else. He seems so unhappy all the time. He won't talk to anyone and just locks himself away in his bedroom. All he seems to do is study. He goes to the university at Cardiff each day, comes home and then shuts himself away. Every so often he goes off on his own for a few days. He doesn't tell anyone where he's going. He just disappears."

"I'll talk to him if you like, Sheyna. Maybe I can get some sense into his head. He has been moping around a bit lately I grant you. There's not much he can hide from me, so don't you worry now."

"Will you, John? It might help. He's closer to you than anybody else, even our father."

"Leave it with me. Now let's get you home and back to that dragon of a mother of yours."

John knew exactly what was wrong with his friend and he also knew where he 'disappeared' to: Birmingham. John knew

281

that Issy hadn't told his family anything about Charity, so who was he to interfere? In spite of Charity's cruelty Issy hadn't given up. More than six months had gone by, but Issy still searched for her, still loved and there was nothing John could do about it. Issy's heart had been broken, his love abused and cast aside, but he still kept hoping and believing. John had seen the tears and broken future in Issy's eyes. He had seen the agonising sense of loss. He had tried to console his friend, but to no avail. To begin with he had blamed himself, but he soon saw how daft this was in spite of the guilt he felt. Charity had come to him, not the other way around. And he knew why – to get at his friend. To punish him. Issy was better off without the likes of Charity, if only he could see it. If Charity had seduced him so easily, how many others had there been? So thank Christ Sheyna wasn't like that! Mind you, it was a good thing that Charity *was* out of the way; at least his part in the whole sorry affair would remain a secret, as the thought of being found out still made his bowels tremble.

CHAPTER 44

For once Rachel Kaddar was unconcerned about the romantic spooning that was going on between her daughter and 'that' John Rees. A letter sitting on the kitchen table was demanding all her attention. She sat down and picked up the letter. The address had been written by a female hand and not a particularly well educated one at that. Rachel knew the difference. She also knew the difference between male and female handwriting, as she had typed enough scholarly papers for both men and women to know. She sat back in her chair and knew as only a mother can that the letter had something to do with her son's unhappiness. Every time she tried to explore what was troubling him he would evade and prevaricate, being too much like his father in this respect. Understanding abstruse intellectual esoterica was fine, but understanding themselves? Well now, that really was beyond the pale! The letter was addressed to Issy. It was his property, his business and nothing to do with her, or so she tried to convince herself anyway. She placed the letter back down on the table and stared again at the handwriting on the envelope. Where had this female hand come from? The only letters Issy ever received were from the university.

Her curiosity continued to demand as her mother's love continued to excuse and justify. She knew that if she opened the letter Issy would never forgive her, particularly if the letter was of a personal nature, which if her instincts were anything to go by it most certainly was. Rachel knew all about love and had known all along that a girl had been behind her son's misery and self-imposed isolation. Love was never that hard to identify. Issy was a young man now with his own life, and she knew that she could no longer exercise her maternal will. But she also knew that a mother's love was far more powerful than any remote sense of propriety or even the imagined certainty of right and wrong. She picked up the letter again and ran it through her fingers. It could be Issy's undoing or his saviour. She placed the letter back down. God help her, its contents may be something she would prefer not to know about, although it could also of course be perfectly innocent. Issy had met a lot of young girls during his time in the Songsters, and boys will be boys after all. The letter continued to stare back at her and tempt while the handwriting condemned and refused to leave her motherhood alone. At last she picked up the letter, opened it and read. A few minutes later she sat back in her chair and despaired. "Oh, dear God, no," she said quietly to herself. "Dear God, no."

Rachel remained where she was for another hour while she tried to decide what to do. Her mind travelled back in time as she remembered, hated and forgave. Should Issy know the contents of the letter? Would this do more harm than good? Did she have the right to decide? She remembered her own past again. How it had also become her future and her torture. Could she inflict this upon an innocent young man or could she help him to avoid her own mistakes? She remained seated for another hour until at last she decided what to do. She had heard Issy come in and go straight to his room. There was no one else in the house, Ezra was away for the night in London and Sheyna had come in and gone out again to see some of her friends. John Rees had said a quick 'Hello' then disappeared, the look on her face having probably frightened him off. For a moment tears sat in her eyes, but she wiped them away as she called to her son. There was no reply. She called again, although these days her son had developed the annoying habit of ignoring her. His 'manhood' was infuriating. At long last Issy walked into the kitchen and grunted at his mother.

"Hello, mother. You did call, didn't you?"

"Yes. Yes, I did Issy. Please sit down, I need to talk to you."

"You look very serious, mother. Nothing's wrong is it?"

"Well, that depends on you."

"What do you mean?" Issy began to feel uncomfortable. He knew his mother wasn't one to make a drama out of things. He could also see that she had been crying. A bad sign as his mother had never been the weepy sort.

"A letter arrived for you earlier today, Issy. I opened it and read its contents."

"You opened a letter that was addressed to me without asking me first?" Issy remained seated but kept his voice under control. "I am not a child anymore, mother. Why did you do such a thing?"

"For your sake, Issy. Believe me."

"But mother, you had no right! None at all!" Issy was starting to raise his voice now. Rachel had been expecting this; she knew her son.

"Now, just you listen to me, Issy. You sit there and you be quiet while I try to explain. This is not easy for me. Now just be quiet and do as you're told for once." Rachel had not raised her voice which as far as Issy was concerned was far more deadly. For a few moments neither mother nor son spoke.

"Well, mother. May I have *my* letter?"

"In a minute. Now, Issy . . . there is something I have to tell you. Something that not even your father knows. You must promise me with all your heart that you will never repeat to a living soul what I am about to tell you. Whatever I say must never go beyond these four walls. Do you hear me, Issy?" This really was serious. He had never seen his mother so perplexed and troubled.

"Of course, mother."

"Give me your word, Issy. I mean it."

"I promise, mother. You have my word."

"Good. Now, many years ago . . . before I had even met your father or given birth to you and your sister . . . I had a child. A boy. The father was not much older than me. Neither of us really knew what we were doing. I was only sixteen and supposedly incapable of being a proper mother, although I didn't feel that at the time or since. My parents were terrified of scandal and how people might treat me – and them. As soon as the baby was born he was taken away from me, and I never saw him again. I never even had time to hold him in my arms or kiss him. To cherish and love him if only for a day . . . You see Issy, my parents knew best. As did society . . ."

Rachel felt her tears and tried to hold them back. It had been so long. This was the first time she had ever told anyone about her first born. Issy sat and looked at his mother. He didn't know what to do. He had never seen her so distraught, so vulnerable. She had always been the strong one in the family, the one that herded and corralled. Sometimes she would whip and tether, at other times love and heal. "Tristram – that's his name – was brought up by some distant relatives of my mother's. I was never told where he was or who was bringing him up. As far as my parents were concerned the whole thing had never happened. I was sent to another part of the country to have my baby. No one knew anything . . ." Rachel paused again as she tried to control her emotions. "I knew nothing about my child's life until three years ago. A letter arrived out of the blue from the woman who had bought Tristram up. My mother's niece. She was dying, so I suppose she felt for whatever reason that I had a right to know . . ." – Rachel paused for a few moments as she remembered the shock, the ancient rejection and anger – "I went to see your, er, brother, who lives in West Sussex. He's a famous composer now . . . I . . . I . . . didn't speak to him, didn't reveal myself." Tears were now starting to fall, and there was nothing Rachel could do about it as the years of frustration and disgust at herself for not fighting harder searched for escape and absolution.

"Tristram . . . Mother?" Issy said slowly trying to hide his shock. "It must be Tristram Cotterell. The blind genius. We have his records here. You're always listening to him. Oh mother, mother . . . Oh God, I just don't know what to say . . ."

"Yes, Issy. Yes, that brilliant composer and pianist is your brother." Suddenly all thoughts of the opened letter flew out of Issy's mind as he went to his mother and put his arms around her. "I'm so sorry, mother. So sorry."

"Don't be. He's a fine man and handsome too, like you. You are very much alike you know." Rachel held her son's head in her arms and sighed. Issy was his mother's child. There had not been one word of resentment, jealousy or judgement. Issy went back to his chair, his face deep in thought.

"Mother, he really knows nothing about you, about us? Nothing at all?

"No. Nothing. And I want it kept that way. Imagine the hurt this could cause your father. Your sister. My deceit. You must understand, Issy, and say nothing. I can still love Tristram at a distance, love him through his music. He must never know the truth, Issy. Never."

"But why? Why?"

"His life is settled, Issy. Happy. He creates and loves the world he lives in. A pure world. He would have loved his parents, I know they were always kind to him and looked after him selflessly. I cannot spoil his memories, I will not. He is secure in his parenthood and I want it left that way. You must respect my wishes, Issy."

"If that's what you want, then of course, mother. But why are you telling me all this? Why?"

Rachel lifted her handkerchief to her face and dried her tears.

"You will understand when you have read the contents of your own letter and why I decided to show it to you, notwithstanding that it is addressed to you. I am your mother, and whether you like it or not I will always protect you from harm. This is my duty. I'm still not sure whether I am doing the right thing, but so be it. Now then, this letter of yours, Issy. Will you listen please?" His mother was gathering her strength, preparing herself. Her son's heart was going to be hurt more than he could possibly imagine. She placed the letter which until now had been kept firmly in her pocket on the table,

Issy looked at the letter. It was still in its envelope. His name and address had been written by hand, the simple almost childish style of handwriting unmistakeable. He immediately remembered the scribbled sweet nothings from Charity that stage hands used to pass on to him.

"Go on, mother." For a moment he was tempted to reach across the table, grab the letter and run. In the same moment he almost wished it had never arrived in the first place.

"It was written by a Miss Charity . . . There wasn't any surnane," Rachel said slowly. Issy stirred and looked intently at his mother. First, a hitherto unknown musical genius of a brother, now Charity. What harm was his mother protecting him from? "You were . . . er, courting her, I believe. While you were away."

"Yes, we grew very close."

"Indeed you did, Issy. You've never spoken about her."

"No. She, er . . . well, she ran off I suppose. She didn't say 'Goodbye' or anything. I haven't seen her since that last time in Newcastle over six months ago. Why? I mean is it really any of your business?" The surly tone was back.

"Well, it's your letter so you had better read it." Rachel handed Issy the letter and watched while he read. She hoped with all her heart that she was doing the right thing. Begged. As Issy read his face started to drop. His eyes opened and closed as he paused and read on. It wasn't a long letter. It was short and to the point. Charity was pregnant with his child and she wanted money to support it. A doctor's certificate confirming her pregnancy was attached to the letter. Issy placed the letter back on the table and looked at his mother. That's all he could do. His tongue was incapable of expressing any opinion. No wonder his mother had told him about Tristram. She understood his predicament. Rachel looked at her son. She had been sixteen, her son was not much older. He may have been more worldly-wise than most boys his age, but in her eyes he was still a boy. For a moment Rachel nearly understood her own parents, but then they had allowed moral turpitude and the

288

venom of social outrage to interfere. Love and the welfare of their daughter's spirit had never come into it. She knew that Issy was far too young to bear the responsibility and burden of fatherhood. It could destroy his life. She knew this, but even so she wouldn't interfere. Couldn't. She would be there for him, to help if needed, but it must be his decision.

"Issy, I'm sorry for opening your letter, I truly am. But you haven't been yourself since you returned home and you know it. I have had my suspicions, as has your father. It seems we were both right. You fell in love with this girl and she rejected you. I feel for you, Issy. I really do. Can you understand now why I told you about Tristram? I didn't want to inflict those insidious 'what if's', those 'what might have beens' on you. The guilt, the desertion. I was given no choice, Issy. No choice at all. I can't do the same to you. Please understand."

Issy had never felt so confused in all his young life. He didn't know what to say or do. He needed time. He must have time. Rachel forced herself to recognise, partly at least, that her son was now a man. "You're a man now, Issy," Rachel said firmly as she tried to hide her sorrow. "It must be your decision and yours alone." Issy stood up.

"I must go to my room, mother. I must. I need time to think."

"Issy, before you go, and I'm sorry for asking you this, but is it possible that someone else is the father?"

"No. Certainly not. The doctor's certificate leaves no doubt. The number of weeks make sense. They tally with the last time we . . . er, well, you know. Apart from that there were no other boyfriends."

"And what about the money, Issy? I'm sorry, but I must ask. It is a modest amount. The girl must be working class. Your father can . . ."

"No, mother, I won't hear of it. I still have the money from my time in the Songsters. I saved most of it, but thank you."

Issy left the kitchen, but not before he had picked up the letter that had ripped him to pieces.

CHAPTER 45

"Stay still, Tristram, will you!" Clarissa was standing in front of him, her nose almost touching his. Her fingers were trying to do a bow in his black tie, if only he would keep still. "Oh, do stop twitching about, can't you, Tristram? These things are awkward enough at the best of times!" Tristram couldn't help it. The twitching. He had only been this close to Clarissa once before and that had been bad enough. Since then he had kept his distance. Being so close to her in such an intimate way again was unnerving him. He kept trying to pull his head back. Trying to avoid her breath, her smell. Both were sweet and so wonderfully compelling. His hands had reached up to hers once or twice, although he wasn't entirely sure why. Although it seemed quite natural, his mind would resist and so would his body, thus the twitching every time they touched.

"Oh, do stop jumping about, Tristram! I'm not going to strangle you, you know!" Clarissa was taking her time with the tie on purpose, but she wasn't about to tell Tristram that. Being so close to him was sheer heaven. An absolute delight. His lips were so close, so available. Oh golly! She spent as much time with the bow as possible before grudgingly standing back and saying, "There, Tristram. A finer bow you'll not find this side of the Atlantic!" She left her hands resting on Tristram's shoulders as she stared into his deep blue eyes. Oh God, those eyes! They couldn't see her own she knew and yet . . . She could have stayed like this all night, for the rest of her life even. She just couldn't help it. For a moment she thought she saw a hint of love shine back at her. She hoped so anyway.

At last Tristram's twitching suddenly stopped. His dimpled chin stayed still too. Oh, to hell with it! Clarissa couldn't help herself. If she didn't do something now, then she knew that

Tristram never would. She had been trying to make him kiss her for more than six months. She had hinted at her feelings for him, had almost punched him in the face with them, but still he resolutely refused to acknowledge her advances. She had even given him fruit cakes made with her own fair hand – well not quite, the cook had helped out. Clarissa's own cooking was usually a pyrotechnic disaster, and even the doting colonel refused to go anywhere near anything she made, sensible man!

She had taken Tristram out for drives in the country and even taken him swimming. His blindness had definitely been a handicap on the latter occasion! She had tried everything short of jumping on him and demanding that he give her his body unconditionally. The man was intolerable! If she didn't give a damn about his stupid blindness – which she didn't – then why should he? Dear God, his mind was better than a thousand army officers put together, one of whom was just the sorry type her father was always trying to match her up with! The Rubicon just had to be crossed, there was no other way. It was Monte Carlo or bust. This was a heaven-sent opportunity, and she wasn't about to let it slip from her grasp. They were so close, almost touching. She let her arms slide around Tristram's back, stood on tip toe and pulled him toward her. Then she kissed him. Tristram didn't have a chance. She held onto him and opened her mouth slightly allowing her tongue to touch his lips and then exploring further.

At last something deep inside Tristram snapped. He finally responded, what else could he do? His fears, his resolve had been demolished by a few fingertips and a pair of lips, magnificent though they were. He had kept Clarissa at bay for more than six months, but now even he had had enough. The woman was irresistible. He had fallen in love with her a long time ago, but his blindness had inhibited him. Now as her lips kissed his he held her tightly, never wanting to let go. They stayed like this for a few minutes. Kissing and holding. Eventually Clarissa pulled her lips away.

"Golly, Tristram. Whatever would daddy say?" Clarissa giggled and purred at the same time as she held his head in her hands and kissed his cheek. "That was amazing, it really was." She nudged her head underneath his chin. Oh, she could have licked him from head to toe. Tristram couldn't see how flushed her cheeks were or how crumpled her evening dress.

She looked at her wristwatch. "Oh no! The time! Come on, Tristram, quick. We must go. They will all be wondering what's going on. Can hardly tell them now, can we?" Clarissa was still laughing as she dragged Tristram by the arm and led him out of the house. He would have preferred to stay where he was and to hell with the party, but he knew how much it meant to Clarissa so he had at least to show willing. The poor girl had been trying to capture his heart for months. As he thought about this he suddenly realised how selfish he had become. This would have to change . . . and quickly.

The red MG raced around the country roads, hitting bends and sharp corners with a speed and determination that would have made even captain Malcolm Campbell blush. Clarissa's tongue and fingertips may have been light and angelic, but her right foot certainly wasn't. The canvass roof of the sports car was down even though it was March, and the air still had a brutal bite to it. As usual Clarissa drove with total abandon and only a whimsical awareness of speed and danger. They were not far from the party when Clarissa shrieked with delight as a particularly sharp bend tested her driving skills to the limit. The tractor driver coming in the opposite direction never heard her excitement, nor indeed did he see the sports car coming straight at him. It had all been too fast. In a split second Clarissa screamed and swerved. The car shot over a bank and tried to struggle with infinity before giving up halfway through its flight through the cold night air. Its racing red colour traced the moonlight as it twisted and turned like an irate firework on Guy Fawkes night before crashing down in an angry gush of steam and the screech of outraged metal.

CHAPTER 46

At the moment when Clarissa lost control of her car John was sitting in Issy's bedroom trying to believe what he had just heard.

"Pardon me, Issy?"

"Charity. She's pregnant."

"Oh . . . I mean, er . . . well . . ." John muttered. "God, I don't know what to say, Issy. But how – well I mean, how do you know it's you?" he finally managed to splutter.

"It's me all right. She sent me a doctor's certificate," Issy replied with total conviction in his voice.

"But even so, Issy. I mean . . . you haven't seen her for months. So how . . .?"

"The certificate says how many weeks pregnant she is. It fits. We . . . er, the last time we did it fits almost to the day. I checked my diary. Anyway, Charity wasn't a girl to have . . . well, you know, with anybody. I was the only one, I'm sure of it. Sure."

'Oh shit!' was all John could think. If Issy believed he was the only one, John knew otherwise, didn't he just! What if he was the father? Quite possible, Issy was right about the timing in more ways than one. Issy's bloody diary! He had always been scribbling away at it when they had been on the stage. Every night. Once or twice John had been tempted to have a sly peak, but the trust between them had been far more important than a quick glance at what Issy had done during the day. Trust. Bloody trust! Why did it have to drain and demand so much? John didn't want to dwell on this particular word for too long as he tried to keep a grip on his nerves. Those bloody nerves again, and he wasn't even about to sing solo either! Charity had left a day after showing him the ropes as it were, and Issy must have . . . Oh, no! Hold on. Issy must have managed it more times with Charity than he. Must have. Oh buggering hell!

"What are you going to do, Issy?" John asked.

"I'm going up to Birmingham. She wants some money to look after the baby. And maybe . . . What else can I do, John? I can't desert her, can I?" Issy said nothing about the conversation he had had with his mother. She had sworn him to secrecy and that was the way it was going to stay.

"But what about your studies, Issy? You can't throw all that away. You're a clever devil, so don't be a fool."

"Look, John, what else am I supposed to do? Would you leave Sheyna if she was in trouble? Would you?" John kept quiet. He knew that he could never desert Sheyna, no matter what. John looked at his friend. Oh, what a mess.

"Yes, all right Issy. I see what you mean. But are you going to pay her and come home or what? Like I say, there is your studying. Your books, Issy. You'd be lost without them."

"Well, there is Birmingham University. I've been thinking that perhaps I could study there, if . . . well, oh, I don't know."

"But Issy, what are you going to both live on? What about money? What about a proper job? And there's a baby! You're not thinking straight. I'm telling you as your best friend. Go up there, pay her off. Otherwise she will ruin your life. I know it Issy, and believe me she's not worth it!"

"What do you mean, John?" Issy demanded. "Not worth it?" Watch it, John thought quickly, he knew only too well how touchy Issy could be where Charity was concerned.

"Oh, hell, I don't know, Issy. But think about it. Is Charity the sort to give up the stage after she's had the baby? You know, become a happy housewife while you get on with your studying." John was getting frustrated now and annoyed at his friend's lack of common sense. Issy might have been the brain of Wales, but when it came to the simple things he could be as thick as cow shit. "Issy, look how she treated you. She ran off without saying a word. What type of girl is that? Look, I'm sorry, Issy, but Charity Like just isn't worth it. And she certainly doesn't deserve you. You're too good for her. Baby or no baby. Forget her, Issy. She's a bad lot. Forget her."

Issy listened. He knew that for once his friend was right. He remembered Charity's bitter smile as she had seen him run towards her at the station. He remembered the pleasure in her eyes as he had thumped on the carriage windows. But how could he visit her sins upon a child? His child. Worse still, he loved her. Dear God, did he love her. Not a day had gone by without her kiss, without her laughter. Issy knew that he shouldn't go anywhere near her. He knew. But his life had been a self-indulgent journey of maudlin excess these past six months, and he knew this too. The pages of his books had become an endurance test and an examination of his love. He had grieved and berated. Loved and hated, but each time his mind had finally gone back and his heart had given in.

"John, I must go to her," Issy said as he looked at his friend. "I must. I don't know what will happen when I get there but at least I must try. I love her you see John, and there's nothing I can do about it. Please understand." John saw the desperation in his friend's eyes. He knew there could be no more persuasion. No more common sense. He knew Issy and these days he also knew something about love.

"Right. I'll come with you, then. You shouldn't go alone, Issy. You'll get all upset again if something goes wrong, and I don't want that. You can be such an idiot, you know."

"No, John. I'm going alone and that's final." There was that unconscious intensity in Issy's eyes which John knew would brook no argument. For a moment he almost blurted out what he had got up to with Charity, since perhaps that would have done the trick. On second thoughts though that would certainly have made things worse, and no doubt he would lose Issy as his best friend into the bargain. This was unthinkable. As for who was the father of Charity's baby . . . well, he would cross that bridge when and if he came to it. Right now he hoped to God it wasn't him.

CHAPTER 47

"Where's that idiot of a daughter of mine? She's not in her bed! Shocking business this. As if crashing cars isn't enough, the bloody fool was talking about joining the Medical Corps the other day!"

The doctor sighed patiently. He knew the colonel and his wife, who at this moment was almost crouching behind her husband waiting for the next shell to explode. The colonel eyed the doctor up and down, his solid tweed suit and polished brown brogues leaving no one in any doubt that he was in the habit of giving orders. And yet the doctor saw something else in the deep green eyes. Compassion? An apology for having seen too much death and still being alive? His wife, a pretty lady in her time, had the resigned look of a woman who remained married and suffered for the sake of the children, but once again the doctor noticed something else. A tolerant but devoted love perhaps?

"I think you'll find her sitting next to Mr Cotterell's bed, colonel," the doctor replied.

"The composer? Pair of them should have been at a party, not here damn it!" The colonel stood ramrod straight. His voice quickly softened. "Walking wounded is she? Should have stuck to horses. What about the motor car?"

"Well, colonel," said the doctor, before taking a deep breath, "I gather it won't be doing any more driving. So the police tell me anyway."

"Ruined, is it? Damned girl! Cost me a bloody fortune!"

"Yes, colonel. I'm sorry. Now would you like to know the nature of your daughter's injuries? She had a miraculous escape I have to say."

"You've just told me she's walking around, damn it man. Can't be much wrong with her. Hasn't been shot, has she?"

"Shot? Er . . . no, colonel."

"Good! We'll have her back in the saddle in a trice."

"Colonel—" The doctor tried to speak, but waas interrupted.

"Yes. What is it man? Get on with it. My daughter's injuries."

"Yes, quite. She has some cuts and bruises and will need a few days' rest. Other than that she will make a quick recovery. She was extremely lucky. The car threw her clear of the impact and she landed in a bush apparently. This would have cushioned her fall. Prevented more serious harm. Your daughter is a strong young woman, colonel. And . . . er . . . very independent, if I can put it that way. She should not be walking around, but I'm afraid no one could stop her. She insisted on seeing Mr Cotterell. As I say, she's with him now.

"This Cotterell chap, the composer, how is he? My daughter's a bit soft on the man, thinks I don't know. Not dead is he? Don't want that daughter of mine unduly upset even if she is a complete fool."

"No, colonel, but he has received some serious injuries. Like your daughter he was lucky. He too was thrown from the car, but unfortunately he didn't have as soft a landing as your daughter did. He has a few broken bones, his tibia and fibula in his right leg, two ribs and a fractured skull. It's too early to give a certain prognosis on the head injuries, but they do not appear so far to be too serious. He has been conscious – not for long – but this is encouraging. He managed to speak a few words. In time we hope he will make a full recovery."

"Splendid, doctor. Don't want Clarissa moping around the house like a lovesick puppy do we? Cynthia, come along, don't dawdle. Let's see what that numbskull of a daughter of mine has to say for herself!" The colonel stomped off down the ward with his wife in tow, but not before she had looked at the doctor and raised her eyebrows.

When the colonel and his wife finally caught up with their daughter they found her in a small side room off the main ward. The colonel stopped in the doorway and held his wife back. Clarissa was facing the door. She was sitting on a chair next to Tristram's bed holding his hand and staring at his face as tears refused to stop trickling down her cheeks.

The colonel said to his wife quietly, "Wait, Cynthia. Wait. Now is not the time. We will come back later." He turned and marched his wife out of the ward. The colonel had seen his daughter's look so many times before on the battlefield. The despair, the helplessness and the passion. He loved his daughter, she was the special one, always had been. He had never really understood why this was so, as all his children were precious, but he also knew that Clarissa would have another brand new red MG as soon as she got out of hospital.

Clarissa sat next to Tristram and damned herself to hell. How could she have been so selfish? So careless? The man she had come to love so deeply was lying next to her, bandaged and hurt, all because of her. God, she could have killed him. What then? The policeman had given her a ferocious ticking off, but none of this compared with the guilt she now felt as she looked at Tristram. His face was bruised and cut and his bones broken, all because she couldn't keep her foot off the pedal. She had come close to killing him and the doctor hadn't spared her. She gripped Tristram's hand tightly. "'Oh, dearest Tristram," she whispered. "Please forgive me, please." Her heart was falling apart as she saw his pain and his strength. "Please forgive me, my love," she pleaded again. "Please." Suddenly Tristram's eye lid's opened. His deep blue eyes looked the same as they stared at her for a moment, then quickly shut.

"Clarissa? Is that you?" he managed to ask through a morphine-induced calm.

"Yes, yes my darling. I'm here, I'll always be here." Tristram sighed and fell silent again. After a few more moments he opened his eyelids again and tried to speak.

"Clarissa . . . I – I . . ."

"Hush, Tristram. Hush," Clarissa soothed. "I'm here." Tristram's face tensed as light crashed into his brain. What was happening? He closed his eyelids quickly. His imagination again. It must be. It had to be. There had been shapes. A blurred face looking over him. It couldn't be. He remembered the car, screeching tyres. Cold air and then nothing. Was he dead or alive? He recognised Clarissa's voice. Felt her hand. No, it couldn't be. Dare he open his eyes again?

"Clarissa?"

"Yes, my darling."

"It . . . it *is* you!"

"Yes, of course. Try not to speak, Tristram. You are very weak." Tristram collected all the strength he had left as he willed his eyelids to open. Fear and apprehension attacked him as he gritted his teeth. Yet he knew what he had to do, for in truth there was no other way. He opened his eyes. He saw the outline of a face, nothing else. Sight or no sight, he didn't need to see anything more as he gripped Clarissa's hand and threw his previous misgivings to hell and an early grave. He had grappled with death, had felt its rancid breath on his cheek, but now life was all that mattered – and love.

"Clarissa." Tristram pushed her name from his tongue as gushes of pain and euphoria flowed in and out of his body. "Will . . . will . . . will you marry me?"

CHAPTER 48

It had been such a long time, or at least it seemed that way. Issy had yet to learn that time developed a shorter measure as life progressed. He sat back in his seat and looked out of the compartment window. A few sullen cows were lying down, a sure sign of rain according to John. Life was so simple for a cow, Issy thought. Rather like childhood. Eating, sleeping, your parents doing everything for you, or in the cow's case the farmer doing everything. The rhythm of steam and speed rocked the train back and forth as Issy turned away from the cows and tried to unravel the business with Charity. She was probably expecting him to post some money unconditionally. Well, she had obviously forgotten that he was a Jew. No Jew parted with money unconditionally, a fact which currently was causing Herr Hitler considerable consternation. For a moment Issy actually smirked at the irony and the myth.

His stomach still lurched once or twice along with the train as he wondered what Charity would be like when she saw him. She had sent him her address, so he wouldn't have any difficulty finding her. He wished she had done this before since it could have saved him a great deal of heartache. Issy knew that he should be treating her request for money with contempt. He had an obligation to look after his own child, of course he did, but her calculating venality left a bitter taste in his mouth. Her letter had been curt, demanding. There had been no feeling, no care. In some ways it should not have surprised him, but it did. He had learnt that love was like that. It misled, it used, it tricked and it never gave up on all three. John had been right and Issy knew it. He should have paid off Charity and ran, but there was still the child. There was still his conscience and his inbuilt sense of common decency. There was also his love, and this more than anything else stopped him from running away.

As the train drew in to Birmingham, Issy still had no idea what would be facing him: a reconciliation, a torrid confrontation or simply the cold handing over of a banker's draft paying out most of the money he had earned with the Songsters. It all depended on Charity.

As he walked through the station Issy stopped at a poster that was already a month out of date. It was starting to curl away from the wall, but the name written in bold black ink was unmistakeable. Tristram Cotterell, his brother. Half brother was too difficult to say, although Issy didn't quite know why. For a moment he wondered if he would have gone to see him, tried to talk with him even. Yet if defiance where his mother was concerned didn't come easily, breaking his word was a different matter altogether. He paused briefly, then walked on. Maybe one day.

He found Charity's address in a rundown part of Birmingham. He had sung in Birmingham in other more simple days when he had been protected from the lashes of industry and its celebration of poverty. He hadn't noticed the black pall of smoke that hung over the city waiting to annihilate ambition and choke the life out of young lungs. He waited outside a large Victorian house for a minute or two. So this was where she lived. It was a far cry from the neat and proud exteriors of lodging houses that Charity normally stayed in. The banker's draft in his pocket suddenly ceased to be important. He lit a cigarette and sat on a wall. He remembered other times when the excitement of seeing Charity had forced him to smoke. He still indulged now and again, albeit reluctantly, some things at least remaining constant.

When he had gathered enough strength he threw down the cigarette and walked along the path to the front door. Weeds and neglected rose bushes enjoying their freedom added to his sense of dejection. The front door was slightly ajar, so he walked through the doorway and tried to distinguish where Charity actually lived. There were a number of doors with numbers written on their front panels. He walked down a long dark passage and finally found his destination. A dull and monotonous voice passed through the door announcing that Parliament was in recess. Issy stood motionless outside it. For a moment he wanted to slip the draft under the door and run. Perhaps this would be less painful – cowardly, no doubt, but less painful. Loving thoughts tried to strengthen his will while meagre memories tried to deter it. At last he raised his hand while recalling other, happier days. Then it stopped abruptly in midair, until finally Issy gave in and knocked.

"Who's there?" a gruff male voice shouted out.

"Issy Kaddar! I'm looking for Charity Like!" Issy shouted back. There was a quick exchange of mumbled voices behind the door as the radio suddenly stopped transmitting. A chair scraped across a bare floor. The noise cut right through Issy and almost made him jump. The door opened. A tall, broad-shouldered man stood in the doorway. There was a faint expression of something on his lips, something indefinable. A smile? Issy couldn't be too sure.

"You got the money?" the man asked, seeming to know the answer before it was even given. He appeared to be in his late twenties, but again Issy couldn't be sure. There was nothing intelligent about his face, but he still managed make Issy feel uneasy. His green shirt was spotless and ironed to perfection. Braces stretched across a muscled chest, holding up green army fatigues. His shirtsleeves had been rolled up to reveal tattoos of voluptuous, naked girls dancing along his tight forearms. An infantryman's jacket hung on the back of a polished leather chair.

Issy didn't reply directly to the man's question. "May I see Charity, please?" he asked politely. "Is she here?"

"None of your business, mate. Now 'and over the money and fuck off." There was an indifferent violence to the man's voice. Issy didn't move. He had encountered too many uncouth louts in his time to lose his nerve so easily.

"Not until I've seen Charity," he replied. The soldier noticed the remarkably cold blue eyes, eyes that were sharper than his bayonet. There was something else too: a simmering aggression. The lad was a fighter. They were the same height, but the soldier had weight and muscle on his side. Even so, the dark blue eyes that challenged as they stared back at him made him pause.

"Charity! Your sissy singer friend wants a word." The man breathed American bourbon over him. Issy knew the sweet smell from days gone by. "Be quick about it before I kick 'is sissy arse back to Wales!"

Issy waited, his heart thumped. Charity came from behind the door. She had been in the room all along. How could she have let him be treated like this? How could she have just stood by?

"Give him the money, Issy," Charity said matter of factly. He could have been the landlord calling for his rent. "It is the amount I wanted, isn't it?"

"Two hundred pounds, yes," Issy replied, unable to hide the sadness in his eyes, the humiliation. Charity's blond curls and face still shone with theatre and applause and yet there was something missing. It was all there in her green eyes. A moving blankness tinged only with greed and self-interest. She stared back at him and for the first time Issy saw the real Charity. He looked and tried to understand. Why? How? And yet he still wanted to love, to hold. One of her hands was struggling to keep her back straight and stop it sagging into a huge bulge that looked as if it was about to burst.

"Come on mate, 'and it over!" the soldier persisted as if it was his money "We're busy Charity and me. Got some unfinished business to attend to like." The soldier smirked at Charity while he squeezed one of her breasts. Issy looked and despaired. What was she doing with this man? What life would his child

303

have? Issy stood his ground. He wasn't going to hand over two hundred pounds to this animal.

"Charity. Charity, what's happened to you?" Issy asked gently. "You, you were always so . . ." Issy didn't have time to finish his sentence before Charity interrupted.

"Just hand over the money and go will you, Issy? There's nothing here for you. Nothing at all. Now do as I say, *please*." For a moment Issy thought he saw some compassion in Charity's eyes, even regret.

"Now for the last time, sissy singer," the soldier said impatiently, "do as the lady says: 'and over the coin and fuck off! I'm not tellin' you again!"

Issy could contend with the insults, he was used to them, but he could not contend with the way Charity was being treated. He sized up the ruffian standing in front of him and then turned around as if to start making his way out of the house. He didn't turn far, then feigned to his right and punched the soldier right on the chin. Most men would have been knocked unconscious by the weight of Issy's fist, but not this time. The man was a fighter too. The force of the blow knocked him back a few paces, but he soon recovered and came charging at Issy who had lost the advantage. A fist knocked him to the floor. He tried to get up but instead he was picked up and dragged into the room. Another fist landed in his face. There were screams and a foul stench of alcohol and human sweat as Issy started to lose consciousness. Before another blow could finish him off he heard a voice shout, "You bastard!" It was John. The soldier's fists were distracted for a moment as he let Issy fall to the floor. As Issy gradually came to his senses all he could see was John and the soldier grappling with each other as each of them tried to land a punch. John managed to land one on the soldier's nose, there was a crunch and a scream of pain as the man suddenly stopped moving and made a dash for his jacket. When he reached it he pulled out a gun from one of its pockets. He quickly cocked the revolver and waved it at Issy and John. By this time Issy had managed to get back up on his feet and move toward his friend. "Oh Jesus Christ, Issy boy, we're for it now," John managed to mumble as he moved closer to Issy. The soldier stared at them both, his breath was laboured and hard as hatred and fury almost tore them to shreds.

"Right, you pair of bastards, 'and over the money before I blow both your fuckin' brains out. I've got nothin' to lose. I've already got the army after me for murder, so a couple more won't make much difference. Might as well dance on the gallows for three as one, eh?" No one moved as the gun swung from side to side. Issy's hands remained still. "The money, you fucker, 'and it over. Now!"

Issy still didn't move.

"Give him the money Issy, will you . . .?" John shouted, "I'll pay you the bloody interest if that's what you're worried about, you Jewish sod!" Still Issy refused to budge. John's life was passing in front of him faster than *Mallard*! The barrel of the revolver was steady and determined. As the man had said, what difference would another two murders make? At last Issy moved a hand.

"Slowly now, nice and slow," the soldier ordered. "Any funny business and I'll blow you into next fuckin' week, got it?!" Issy retrieved the banker's draft and held it out. "What's this?" The soldier spat as he snatched the draft from Issy's hand. "It's a piece of fuckin' paper? Are you having a joke or what. You are, aren't you! You little . . ." He raised the gun and aimed it at Issy. John started to move forward to try and grab it. The soldier quickly turned the gun towards John and started to squeeze the trigger, but not before Issy pushed his friend out of the line of fire and leapt at the soldier. There was a loud bang as the gun discharged a bullet. It grazed Issy's arm but fury and temper pushed him on. He managed to tear the gun out of the soldier's hand and throw it across the room, by which time John was back in the fray and battering the soldier with every-thing he had. A few judicious kicks from Issy finally did the

305

trick. A few minutes later they were charging up the road toward the railway station and home, but not before Issy had pushed the banker's draft for two hundred pounds into Charity's hand.

As the train steamed out of Birmingham and away from both danger and love Issy was at last able to collect his thoughts and reflect. The banker's draft had been made out to Charity, so God willing the soldier would eventually be arrested and Issy's child given a chance. Charity would look after their baby he was sure. She was a woman, wasn't she? She might not have loved him, and it would take some time yet for him to come to terms with this cruel fact, but he knew she would love their child. He just knew. After all there was some good in everyone's heart, and this belief was all he had left. The only thing he could cling to and his only hope. Whatever else, Issy knew that he would always provide for the baby somehow, come what may.

"How is your arm, Issy?" John asked, interrupting Issy's reflections.

"A little blood. I was lucky. The bullet just scratched me. It doesn't hurt. My shirt is ruined though. I don't know how I'm going to explain it to my mother."

"Don't," John ordered. "Change sharpish as soon as you get home and throw it away. Bugger me, Issy, sometimes . . . " Issy looked at his friend who was sitting opposite him.

"Your nose is a bit swollen, John. Slightly bent too."

"Is it? Haven't had a chance to look what with all the excitement. Never mind. Character, Issy." John grinned. "Character."

For the first time in months Issy grinned back. It didn't take long though for him to return to his natural state, all serious and thoughtful. After a few moments of silence he asked, "John, how did you find me?"

"Your mam. Reckoned you might need a helping hand. Not wrong was she. Nearly got me killed, you did. Stupid sod. I was behind you all the way, Issy, not that you ever saw me."

"John?"

"Yes."

"Thank you."

"Any time, Issy. That's what friends are for isn't it? And you're my friend aren't you? Anyway, are you going to forget Charity Like now?" John hoped so. As far as he was concerned both he and Issy had had a lucky escape. Fatherhood at their age? Jesu!

"Forget . . . John? I don't think so. I will never forget, how can I? I can forgive though . . . and I can love again too. One day." John didn't mention the baby, why complicate things. He changed the subject to more important things.

"Issy, there is something I must say . . . something, um, well . . . far more important than Charity."

"Oh, what's that?"

"You saved my life back there, Issy." John's eyes would not leave his friend's face. "You saved my life. You took that bullet for me and I know it could have killed you. You were prepared to sacrifice your life for me, Issy. I . . . I don't know what to say." For once John was lost for words.

"Illtyd John Rees, I told you a long time ago that I would never forget the time you risked your own safety for me. Remember that time outside school? We hadn't known each other long. The Jew baiting. I told you then that I would never forget . . . and I haven't, nor will I ever . . . As you say John, 'What are friends for?' . . ."

Five months later, on 1st September 1939 at 4.45 a.m. Western Poland was propelled into despair as three thousand German tanks obliterated its borders and the world went berserk.

EPILOGUE

John continued to play Bishop's 'Lo! Hear The Gentle Lark'. As his fingers moved with memory Issy sat in another part of the room and remembered too. The red velvet chairs and the gold woodwork in the private room of the hotel reminded them both of other days, days of magicians and big bands. Of humour and chaos. Of love.

John had finally retired as a Registrar of Births, Marriages and Deaths, but Issy still lectured from time to time. He had been appointed a professor of Ancient History at Tel Aviv University and students still demanded his serious attention, although only when his arthritis permitted. The war had been kind to both men. They had served and fought together, but both had managed to avoid serious injury or an early grave. They had watched each other's backs as was their wont and survived. Like so many others it had been their friendship and not the cowardly 'Hurrahs!' of deluded patriotism that had won them their war.

They had both reached their eighty-fifth year, so it was a time to celebrate. All the offspring were there. The two men – for now their manhood could be in no doubt, even though John still persisted in scratching his chin to make sure a beard was ready to grow if required – met every year on John's birthday without fail. True friendship never recognised absence or distance. John had married his Sheyna. She was sitting next to Issy now, still beautiful and regal as she tolerated and indulged the great grandchildren who swarmed around their feet and demanded. Charity Like had not survived the war. A Luftwaffe bomb had destroyed the house in which she had been lodging during a dancing tour. As John had predicted she had continued dancing and had left her baby girl with her mother to be brought up in Birmingham. Issy had provided for the child, and at an early age she had come to him following the demise of her grandmother. He had never married, preferring the safer and more certain world of academia. His books and his daughter who was sitting next to Sheyna were all the love he had ever needed.

Issy had never tried to meet his brother. He had honoured his mother's wishes. Tristram had lived to a grand old age, surrounded by loving children and a devoted wife. His ability to see had brought a new insight to his music, a new genius. Issy had been to see him play on numerous occasions and often, like his mother, listened to his masterpieces at home in Israel. Issy's eyes had never been far away from his only brother.

As John finally came to the end of his famous song Issy walked up to him with his daughter and put his hand on John's shoulder. John had never met Rebecca before. The time was right. Over the years the two had always met in London and always away from their own homes and families. Ever since the war Issy had lived in Israel and John in his precious Wales. John turned around and looked at his friend.

"John, this is my daughter, Rebecca," Issy said. "You have never met her."

"Issy, you should be sitting down, you old fool!" John began to remonstrate as he stood up. "You shouldn't be . . . ." Then in an instant John saw Rebecca's green brown eyes and golden red hair, the impertinent set of her jaw, the wilful expression on her face. His chest tightened for a moment as his breath laboured. He couldn't speak.

There could be no mistake. Rebecca was John's daughter.

The two old men searched each other's eyes as each recognised that sometimes friendship could be both profoundly benevolent and supremely selfish, and like love could also demand the most agonising sacrifice. In a moment of clarity both men truly under-stood that those who believe there is love in the world are always the first to be hurt. Issy had known for years that his friend had betrayed him, but he had forgiven, even understood. He had loved Rebecca as his own. What else could he have done? How could he have given up his child in everything but blood? Also there had been the letters from John. His words of stability and of a loving family. Of Sheyna and his devoted love for her. How could he have risked destroying all that? His mother's words had never been forgotten.

John raised his arms and gently hugged Rebecca. The beauty of her middle-aged maturity stunned and shamed as she smiled.

"Hello, Rebecca," John said quietly as he tried to catch his breath. "How beautiful you are." He looked into her eyes and saw himself. Then he looked at Issy and it all became clear. He had been deprived of a daughter, but he had also given his friend a love that would have been impossible to replace. He instantly forgave as he knew Issy had forgiven him. Both men had taken and both men had received, but most of all the strength and love of their friendship had endured.

Like his mother before him, Issy had made a choice. As Issy held out his arms he smiled and said, "Happy Birthday, John. You old rascal." He knew it had been the right choice. John went to his oldest and dearest friend and as they held each other he whispered, "You're a bit of a rascal yourself, you shifty old yid."

Issy had made a promise to his friend all those years ago to never let a girl come between them and he had kept to it.

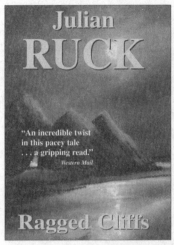

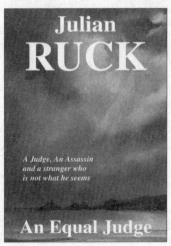

ABOUT THE AUTHOR

Julian is the author of the *Ragged Cliffs Trilogy* and legal thriller *The Bent Brief*.

He trained as a lawyer in London, has been a law lecturer and manager of LSC (Legal Aid) contracts for CAB'x in some of the most deprived areas of the country.

He is a columnist, journalist and weekly guest 'Letter from Wales' contributor to the influential Westminster Labour Uncut, guest public speaker and also makes contributions to both Welsh and national broadcasting and media.